The Secret of Sunrise Mountain

By

JOHN RICHARD MARSH

With

CAROL MALONE

COPYRIGHT

Printed in the United States of America

First Printing, 2018

ISBN: 978-1-7322904-3-3

Publisher: *JRM Productions*

John Richard Marsh Productions

1496 Gardenia Avenue
Camarillo, CA 93010
Facebook: author page: fb.me/JRMO4
www.JRM-Productions.com
Creative Consultant/Ghostwriter: Carol Malone
Cover and Interior Designer: Carol Malone
Editors: Jane O'Brien, Chuck Stevenson, Judith Mathison

FOREWORD

I've been a storyteller all my life. Telling stories is what helped me get through the unhappy experiences I had to endure. I was happier in my stories.

When I retired, my wife, Jane, encouraged me to accomplish something I had not ever attempted before. I began to jot down all the stories I'd told over the years on paper—literally on paper. Unlike other authors, I'm not the computer whiz.

Through living and experiencing the lives of Joe, Sam, Robbie, Jessica, Ricardo, Sal, Mike, and all the rest, I've found a career I can be passionate about, and tell stories all day long.

I hope you will enjoy reading my story. It is very near and dear to my heart, one I thought up years ago. Thank you for letting me communicate my new-found passion with you, and for allowing me to share compelling stories!

ACKNOWLEDGEMENTS

To my wife, Jane, who allows me the time I need to spend thinking up stories for my books.

To Rod Brown, without whom I would not have been able to follow my dream of writing books.

To Carol Malone, who takes my story ideas and turns them into manuscripts.

To Judith Mathison for her unique editing skills and her willingness to read my book over and over and over.

To my friends and family, who put hours of their precious time and efforts into helping me create my book:

John Alamillo, Paul Arbon, Greg Gose, Doug Hunt, Janet Kent, Todd Mains, Ron Speakman, Chuck Stevenson, and Larry Troxel

TABLE OF CONTENTS

CAST OF CHARACTERS IN ORDER OF APPEARANCE

Joe Mack – Cattle rancher, Vietnam vet, inherits Sunrise Ranch, widower of Cindy Johnsen

Cindy Johnsen Mack – Daughter of former ranch owner, Bert Johnsen

Grandpa Elmer Johnsen – Bert Johnsen's father won Sunrise Ranch in poker game

Checkers – Joe's favorite horse, buckskin

Chaco – Ricardo's pinto

Spike and Shep – Joe's faithful ranch German Shepherd dogs

Ricardo Sanchez – Joe's friend and ranch foreman

Salvador "Sal" Sanchez – Ricardo's oldest son and horse expert

Miguel "Mike" Sanchez – Ricardo's second son and horticulture specialist

Major Charles Donald – Government security for drone spy plane—the Peter Pan Project

Dr. Paul Basua – Indian Aerospace engineer from England

Sheriff Cody Warner – Local county sheriff, hates Joe Mack

Robbie Meyers – Joe & Cindy Mack's almost-adopted boy, IT student at CSU Chico, loves Jessica Stone

Jessica Stone – Samantha's daughter, vet student at CSU Chico, loves Robbie Meyers

Dr. Samantha Stone – Shadow Pines' only veterinarian, Joe's new lady love

Deputy Sheriff Pat Sayer – Sheriff Warner's deputy

Deputy Sheriff Pete Vargas – Sheriff Warner's deputy

Ruby Green – Owner of Red Ruby's Steakhouse and Saloon with husband, Bill

Bill Green – Husband to Ruby and co-owner of Steakhouse and Saloon

Marine Sergeant Aleksander "Chip" Kowalski – Military Police at SRM Facilities

Lettie Sanchez – wife of Ricardo

Ana "Penskie" Penn – FBI agent

Reed Jin-Ho Penn – Ana's husband, also FBI agent

Hawke – Mercenary assassin hired by Major Donald

Jim Ports – Double agent for the FBI and Major Donald, Ana Penn's handler

Locke – Mercenary hired by Major Donald

Butch Henry – Sharp-shooting mercenary sniper, friend of Major Donald

Mules – Harry Truman and Dwight D. Eisenhower

MAP OF SUNRISE RANCH COMPOUND

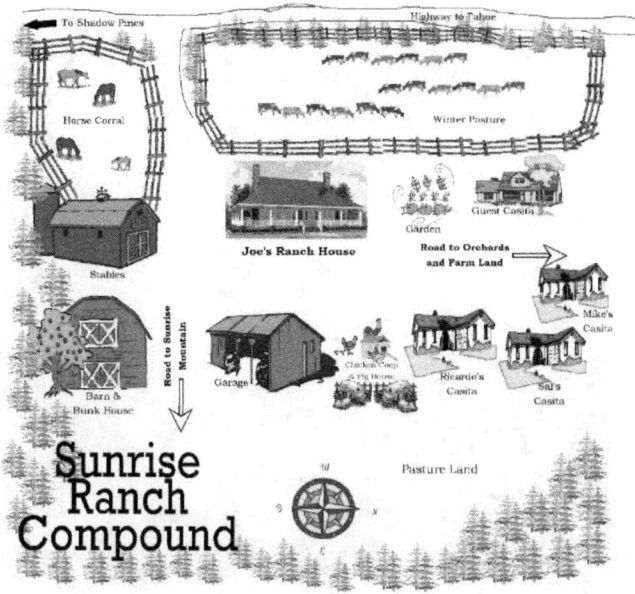

MAP OF SUNRISE MOUNTAIN RANCH AREA

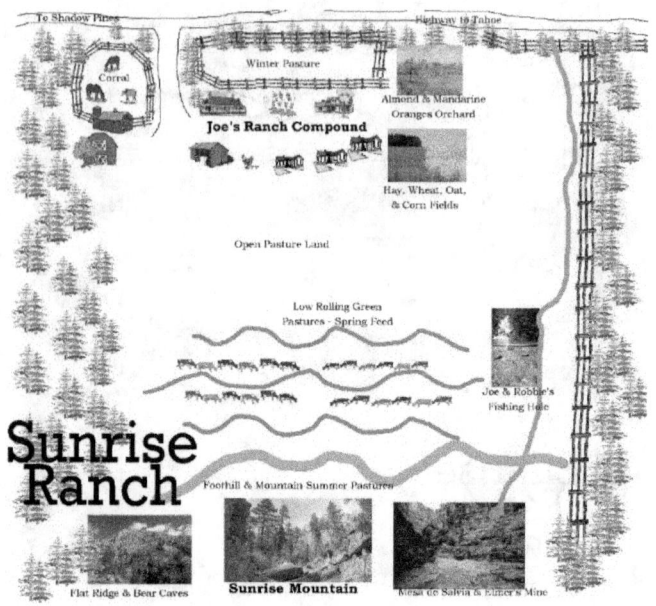

CHAPTER ONE
"Demonio plateado"—The Flying Silver Demon

March 17, 1998—Tuesday—**Sunrise Ranch in the mountains southwest of Lake Tahoe**

T**HE BOOM OF ROLLING THUNDER** and the horrifying movement of earth vibrated beneath Joe Mack's bedroll and jolted him from a sound sleep. "What the—" he hollered. Was this another earthquake like the Loma Prieta? In the muted light of pre-dawn, he fought the sleep-blanketed fog in his brain.

The frightened bellowing of cattle and the screaming neigh of a horse shook him to his socks.

His buckskin, Checkers, was in trouble.

Joe scrambled from under Lettie's homemade quilt in time to see his herd thundering down on him from the top of a grassy ridge. Dust from their stampeding hooves flew up behind them in the still air.

He sprinted for Checkers in his stocking feet and scanned the darkness for his ranch foreman, Ricardo Sanchez.

"Ricardo!" he shouted.

When he glanced over his shoulder, he noticed Ricardo's bedroll lay empty and Ricardo's pinto, Chaco, was gone.

Why hadn't Ricardo warned him?

Joe calculated his escape. Could he untie his horse and swing up to mount before the frenzied herd trampled him to death?

Only one chance to cut the lead rope and hurtle onto the horse bareback before the hooves of three hundred head trampled both him and the fear-stricken horse. Whipping out his pocketknife as he ran, he got ready to act. Near as he could figure, he had about a fifty-foot jump ahead of the herd.

1

John Richard Marsh

Checkers yanked against the tethered lead rope. His eyes were wild with fear. He stamped his hooves and neighed.

With his heart thundering as loud as the cattle hooves, Joe readied to cut the lead rope and leap.

"Whoa, Checkers. Whoa. Three ... Two ... Go."

With a trembling but quick hand, he sliced through the lead rope, gripped it, and swung up on Checkers' back. He clutched the black mane and nudged the horse. Checkers didn't need any motivation. He jumped two bull-lengths in front of the charging cattle.

Leaning low over his horse's back, Joe attempted to turn the cattle away from the tree line, but they were running too fast. If only he had his saddle and rifle.

Where were the dogs? Where was Ricardo?

He headed Checkers in a westerly direction away from the trees. Plunging into the forest in the semi-dark was suicide for a horse and rider. The low hanging branches weren't called "widow-makers" for no reason.

Although, he had no bride to make a widow.

Tugging Checkers' shortened rope to slow the horse was nearly as impossible as shifting the stampeding herd. Joe hung on for dear life and prayed he wouldn't fall off and get crushed to death, or worse, live as a broken man unable to work his ranch, like Cindy's father because of his injury.

Only sheer grit kept him clutched to Checkers' back.

The first rays of the morning lit up the east over Sunrise Mountain, enough to see how damned close the racing herd was to the tree line. Joe's knees ached from gripping the horse's sweat-slicked sides and from his own sweating hands slipping through Checkers' mane.

Go out in a blaze of glory. All good things must end.

Didn't Kenny Rogers sing those words? Joe hoped it wasn't his time just yet.

Out of the corner of his eye, he saw two black, brown, and tan bullets shoot past him. The German Shepherds, Shep and Spike. They barked and nipped at the lead bull's hooves.

Damned dogs. Hell, if they weren't gonna get themselves killed.

Joe's teeth were gonna rattle loose from the jostling bareback ride. He had to stop, or he would need back surgery.

Something charged up alongside the herd.

Ricardo.

The fool rode bareback like him, running the pinto as though the devil chased him. Before Chaco, Ricardo's pinto, plunged into the woods, Ricardo reined him in. He raised his shotgun and pulled the trigger. The boom of the gun sounded like cannon fire in the crisp morning air. The cattle heard it over the bellowing and the horses' screams.

The whole herd spun in the direction of open pastureland. Soon, they dropped out of stampede and scattered. At least they didn't plunge into the trees leaving him with dead cattle to deal with.

Finally, Joe pulled hard enough on the bit of lead rope for his horse to slow. Head bobbing in wild jerks and stops. Checkers wouldn't calm no matter how soothingly Joe whispered in his ear. When Shep stopped in front of the horse and whined, the horse ceased thrashing about.

Shaking and weak, Joe slipped from Checkers' sweaty back, his legs nearly buckled.

"What the … hell just … happened?" Joe sucked in air as he doubled over. His quaking hands rested on his trembling, aching knees.

Ricardo nudged the pinto and trotted over to Joe. "Is what I say yesterday to you. *Demonio plateado.*"

"Your *demonio* damn near killed me."

Ricardo pointed from the southeast corner to the north. "It fly from Flat Ridge to Mesa de Salvia just like yesterday morning." *Mesa* in Spanish meant *table*, and the tops of the two mesas on his property were elevated, and table-top flat. Mesa de Salvia stood at the north end of his property.

Still breathless, Joe let his gaze follow Ricardo's pointing finger.

Barely above the tree line of the mesa, a shiny silver object glided back and forth not more than one hundred feet above the ground. The sunlight caught the demonio making it shimmer against the cloudless blue of the dawn.

3

At first glance, Joe figured an eagle was flying low in the sky scouting for its breakfast over the lake beyond the mesa. Good fishing there. But it wasn't an eagle, not if the tinny engine whine was any indication.

Flying silver demon indeed.

"I'll be damned."

Ricardo shook his head. "Sí. I told you."

"Yeah, you did." Joe shook dust from his hair and clothing.

Just yesterday afternoon, a very frightened Ricardo had stormed into the barn where Joe was working on repairing the side rails of a stall. Ricardo had been out riding fences and keeping a close eye on the cattle. He ranted in broken English that he'd seen a shiny object in the sky, called it a *demonio plateado*.

"The *demonio* spooked the cattle," Ricardo told him, "making them stampede into the stand of pines. Took hours to round up and settle down."

For a long time, Joe couldn't figure out what a *"Demonio plateado"* was until Ricardo calmed down enough to speak clearly. Close as Joe could reckon with his Spanish/English dictionary, Ricardo had seen a "flying silver demon."

As Joe's ranch foreman, Ricardo Sanchez, a decade older than Joe's fifty years, was a sensible man with his feet grounded. He wasn't prone to flights of fancy or hallucinations.

His friend's black hawk-eyes didn't miss much. Under heavy brows, he mostly kept his comments to himself.

After the stampede, Ricardo had ridden hell-bent for the ranch compound to report his sighting. He had insisted Joe come back with him to the deep arroyos where the cattle grazed to see this demon.

When Ricardo finished his story, Joe had saddled up Checkers with his bedroll and followed Ricardo back to his campsite.

Right now, Ricardo circled the herd singing a Mexican lullaby in low, gentle tones. His stock horses continued to nervously stamp around, at least until Ricardo passed by them.

Joe was grateful for the older man's experience and gentle ways with the animals.

4

Though Ricardo's long-fingered hands showed mild arthritis and he walked more slowly each morning, he could be depended on to make sure the ranch functioned efficiently. Perhaps one of these days, he would step aside and let one of his capable sons take over the reins as foreman. But Joe doubted Ricardo would do that—too cussed ornery to retire.

Joe considered Ricardo more of a brother than a friend. Cut from the same cloth—they were hardworking men of action who loved the land, though they couldn't look more dissimilar. Joe, at six two, was rawboned, lanky, and sun-bronzed where the sunlight hit exposed pale skin.

Ricardo, naturally tanned, barely topped out at five-foot-ten and loved his frijoles and tortillas. His wife, Leticia, or Lettie as everyone called her, fed him well.

Ricardo's midnight black hair which he wore rather long was now shot through with gray. So was his dark beard. Joe kept his honey brown hair cut short—military style. He didn't like having a beard, mainly because it made him look like a grizzled prospector. He went clean shaven when he had the chance. Although working on the ranch sometimes found them away from a razor for days.

After rounding the herd once more, Ricardo walked Chaco over to where Joe was standing. The cattle dropped their heads and munched on ankle-deep grass. Joe pondered the flying nuisance.

"It's man-made," Joe said after Ricardo dismounted.

"*Qué? No Demonio?*"

"Government." Joe knew one word would describe it plenty. Where had the plane initially taken off from?

The U.S. government owned a lot of acreage on the east side of Sunrise Mountain right up to his property line. They experimented with God knows what. He'd heard strange things about SRM—Sunrise Mountain Facility—since he'd hired on to work as a ranch hand at Sunrise Ranch years ago. If the government was testing some type of secret spy aircraft over the land he now owned and were spooking his cattle, there'd be hell to pay.

No one messed with him, his ranch, or his animals.

He'd made a promise.

Back in 1910, Elmer Johnsen, son of Norwegian immigrants traveled all the way from Minnesota to make his fortune. While in Sacramento courting his soon-to-be-wife, Olina, Elmer won Sunrise Ranch in a poker game making him the second owner. The first owner hadn't had the fortitude to hold onto a ranch or make a go of one this size. Elmer knew farming and ranching.

Elmer's son, Bert, hindered by a severely injured left arm, the results of a fall off a horse during a cattle stampede, took over the ranch from Elmer.

Bert wasn't a great rancher mostly because of his impairment. Only months from losing the ranch, Bert hired Joe barely home from four tours of duty in Vietnam. Lost and shell-shocked, Joe passed through Placer County on his way to anywhere when someone told him about the owner of Sunrise Ranch hiring ranch hands. Because Joe had been raised on a working ranch back in Texas before escaping an abusive family situation to become a soldier, he took to working with Bert on the ranch and efficiently helped restore it to a profit-producing cattle ranch.

The ranch should've gone to Bert's only child, a daughter, Cindy. Before Bert passed in 1989, Cindy and Joe married—much to her father's frustration. When he died, he left the ranch in both Cindy and Joe's names. One of the stipulations of inheriting the ranch, Joe had to pledge he would never sell the property no matter what happened. Of course, then the unthinkable happened.

Cindy left him.

However, nothing or no one would force him off this land.

Joe glanced at his foreman. "We need to see where this demon flies off to after it's finished spying on my land, scaring my cattle and horses."

Ricardo removed his battered straw hat and beat it against his thigh. "Do we ride for the mesa?"

Checkers continued stamping his hooves and tossing his head.

"There now, boy. It's all right." Joe soothed the horse with gentle strokes to his long neck. "I don't think that'd do any good."

"What we do?" Ricardo asked.

Joe didn't answer. What could he do?

After ten minutes of watching the menace—the silver object—it disappeared over Pine Ridge Mesa, flying due north, not east. Ricardo's demon had to be a small plane and if so, wouldn't it have flown due east? The "secret" SRM military base in the Eldorado Mountains was tucked in behind Shadow Mountain to the east. Who else would be violating his property?

He yawned and stretched his aching back. Time to pick up the pieces. At Joe's back, Sunrise Mountain rose like a titan, the eternal guardian of his peaceful land. Beyond that, the morning sun blazed down on them.

If only Cindy were here to enjoy it with him.

For the last three years, sadness was his constant companion.

"If the *demonio* returns, the cattle will run their spring fat off." Ricardo blew out a breath. "*No es bueno para el Ganado*—no cattle sale at the end of summer."

"Damn." Joe kicked at a rock sending it skittering along the ground. Only one thing to do. "I've gotta tell the sheriff."

CHAPTER TWO
In the Wake of El Demonio

J OE WOULD RATHER FACE A PIT of rattlers than tangle with Sheriff Cody Warner. But this demon flying across his land was an invasion of his privacy and could destroy his property. It must stop. If the sheriff refused to help, Joe would take matters into his own hands.

"We'd better check out our campsite, see if there's anything left," Joe said to Ricardo.

He and Ricardo, tugging their horses behind, climbed to the top of a small rise and came upon what remained of their campsite. Their camping gear lay strewn over a wide area, and nothing much was left intact or recognizable.

Joe smacked his thigh and swore.

"Not much *bueno*." Ricardo booted what was left of the coffee pot, sending it banging down an embankment. "Ay, yi, yi."

Joe picked up his bedroll and the handmade quilt Ricardo's wife, Lettie, made for him. Only a few strips of cloth remained stitched together.

Realization struck hard, rocking him back on his heels. He glanced heavenward. If he hadn't awakened, he could've ended up in tatters.

Joe gazed at Shep and Spike, his two dogs at his feet. Their eyes darted in all directions, and they whined. They must've sensed Checkers' agitation because they stayed close. Rather than stake the horse again, Joe dropped the rope and commanded the dogs to "stay." The two sat on their haunches and glanced between him and the horse as if they understood.

Beside him, his favorite broken-in cowboy hat was a smashed and ripped mess. Damn. He'd taken years to break it in.

He located Checkers' bridle and reins. They'd managed to survive the stampede.

However, his saddle wasn't as fortunate. The horn and both stirrups were torn from his saddle, and the cantle—the upright portion of the seat or backrest—was broken in half. Luckily, the cinch strap remained intact. But hoof marks imprinted his beautiful hand-tooled leather fender—the part hanging down from the sides of the saddle where the stirrups attached. Hundreds of dollars of leather mashed or broken. At least his horse blanket remained in one piece.

Because no one did leather repair locally, he'd have to take a trip to the saddlery shop in Auburn, the next largest town to Shadow Pines.

He couldn't remember the last time he replaced his hat. The General Store should have one. He didn't relish riding bareback back to the ranch house from their destroyed campsite.

"I'll drive into Shadow Pines and see Warner," Joe said.

"Sheriff Warner, he no *amigo*."

"Could've fooled me." Joe huffed. "Cindy made us promise not to kill each other."

"Señora Cindy would no marry that, how you say, 'womanizing scum'."

Joe chuckled. "She called him that, didn't she?"

"Take my saddle, Señor Joe. Look better than yours."

"*Gracias, amigo*." Joe bent over to retrieve his saddlebag.

Ricardo picked up his bullwhip, snapped it overhead and grinned. "Whip is *bueno*."

Joe straightened, saddlebag in hand. "Keep the dogs. Have them help you round up the cattle. I'll send back the boys to help. Move them closer to the house in the lower pasture so they're out of earshot of that flying menace."

"Me and the boys we move them pronto."

Spike and Shep lifted their heads at the word "boys." Their tongues lolling. They loved round-up and responded well to Ricardo's commands even if half the words were Spanish.

Ricardo shook his head and dragged Joe's battered saddle over to Checkers. The horse side-stepped away from him when Ricardo tossed his own saddle on the horse and tugged on the cinch strap. He tied Joe's saddle to the back so Joe could take it to the ranch house.

Joe fastened Checkers' bridle on and gripped the reins. "I'll be back as soon as I can."

Ricardo nodded and whistled for the dogs.

Still prancing, Checkers kept shying away from him. However, Joe managed to swing up into the saddle and nudged the horse forward. He took a huge breath, filled his lungs with the chilly mountain air.

Riding the few miles back of narrow, high-country trails back to the ranch gave him too much time to think. Right before the excitement of the stampede, he'd been dreaming of Cindy.

In this dream, even though the incident took place fifteen years ago, the past mixed up with the present. Joe didn't care—he welcomed Cindy's supernatural visits.

The afternoon sky had been clear as a mountain stream. The shaded porch on the old ranch house Elmer Johnsen built for his lady love, Olina, wrapped cleanly around the whole place.

Joe and Cindy's favorite spot was the west side outside their bedroom long about sundown.

Cindy sat in her favorite chair, a white painted Adirondack he'd built himself and given to her when she was pregnant with their first baby.

Her belly slightly rounded, she smiled up at him. She would begin bleeding before the night was over and would lose the baby by morning. This was Cindy's fourth pregnancy and her last.

"Don't look so forlorn, my love," Cindy said.

He hooked one leg on the porch railing to gaze down at her. Her long, curly blonde hair had been caught in a bun tonight. He loved it loose and flowing to her waist.

"We both know what's going to happen in the morning." He closed his eyes, pictured her pinched face, all that blood, and his feelings of impotence at not being able to do a damned thing to help her.

"It was our lot." The fading light of the orange sun lit her smile, her dimples widening, making her cornflower blue eyes dance. "We had twenty wonderful years together, you and I, didn't we? I couldn't have asked for anything more."

He smacked his fist into the palm of the other hand. Everything was mixed up in his mind—past, present. He didn't know anymore. "It wasn't supposed to turn out this way. We should have had children. You should have lived."

"I'm not sad. Please, don't be angry anymore. That's not the way the Lord deemed our lives."

He wished he could swear, or curse, or shake his fist at the heavens, but his God-fearing bride would have none of that. So, he held his tongue. Most days he bit his tongue.

"Come." She held out her arms. "Sit by me and hold my hand. I miss you."

Cindy took his hand. With the other, she had cradled the partially-formed baby under her heart.

The dream came to an explosive end when a mosquito buzzed around his head. He batted at it, but it kept coming. Louder and louder still until he awakened to the cattle stampeding, bearing down on him. Damned mosquito turned out to be the demon.

Had Cindy's strange, confusing visit been an omen? Was she coming to get him or save him?

Who'd take care of the ranch if he died?

When Joe arrived back at the ranch compound, he trotted Checkers toward the corral beyond the stables. Ricardo's thirty-eight-year-old son, Salvador, Sal—the spitting image of his father—ambled out of the stables leading a feisty fawn-colored quarter horse gelding—one of Joe's newest acquisitions.

Sal, with a bachelor's degree in animal husbandry from the California State University at Chico, helped Ricardo and Joe around the ranch with the animals. As a master horse trainer, he currently put his effort into gentling the quarter horse to make him saddle ready.

With the horse on a lead rope, Sal approached the gate of the corral and glanced at Joe. "From the looks of you and Checkers, I'd say you've had trouble."

"Not much trouble." Joe huffed.

Joe lifted his sore leg over Checkers' back and slid to the ground. He stood for a moment and stretched out his back. For

11

the love of Pete, he needed a good night's rest on his specially made bed.

"Is that Pop's saddle?"

"Mine might need a repair or two." Joe untied the sad remains of his favorite hand-tooled saddle and let is slip off the back of Checkers.

"Looks like it got scrambled." Sal chuckled and yanked open the corral gate. He pulled the halter over the quarter horse's ears. "Yah," he said and smacked the horse on the rump.

The horse shot into the pasture with the other horses already there for their free time play.

"What happened?" Sal asked.

Briefly, Joe recapped the evening, the stampede, and the destroyed campsite. "I'm heading into town now to talk to the sheriff."

"You think the sheriff will help?"

Joe shook his head. "I have to report this."

"I'll rub Checkers down and see that he's settled with a good amount of hay and grain, and maybe a few carrots for his trauma before I saddle up and ride out to help Papa."

"Take Mike and the hands with you." Joe grinned and headed for the house and a much-anticipated shower.

After Joe showered in the river rock shower Cindy had him construct, he pulled on a clean pair of jeans and warm plaid flannel shirt. He polished up his going-to-town boots and stuffed his feet into them. Without a hat, Joe felt naked. "Can't be helped," he said and picked up the keys to his rig on the way out the door.

He paused before the photo of Cindy hanging by the front door. She was so lovely, all rosy-cheeked with shining eyes as she sat in her favorite chair on the western porch. He kissed two fingers and placed them over her smiling mouth.

"Sending my love, sweetheart. Thanks for the warning."

He jumped into the ranch truck, a 1993 fully loaded white Ford F350. Damn thing nearly cost as much as his prize bull, but worth every penny.

The rig kicked up dust as he drove down the gravel road through the pines to the main highway.

"Well, here goes nothing," he said to himself.

Compared to confronting Sheriff Warner about his flying menace, Joe preferred rattlesnake wrangling. The man was impossible to deal with, a real pain in the ass. And it wasn't just because he'd accused Joe of stealing Cindy away from him. Cody Warner wasn't a warm, cuddly human being.

What type of reception would they get when they approached SRM Facility about the silver flying menace? He prayed he wouldn't get his head blown off by some rogue military security type.

CHAPTER THREE

SRM—Sunrise Mountain Facility—Major Charles Donald (originally Dunajski)

THE HEAVY THUMPING BEAT of the rapper's grating diatribe squawked over the radio and threatened to make Major Charles Donald's ears bleed. "Corporal, if I have to listen to that song one more time, I'm gonna shove the radio up your a—"

"Yes, sir." The corporal interrupted before Charles launched into his long list of profanity. "I'll turn it off." He pushed the button on the Jeep's dashboard.

"Get Jiggy With It" ceased its deafening attack on Charles' ears.

He glared at his aide driving the black Jeep. He'd been listening to the thumping hip-hop crap all the way from Tahoe. Why did he put up with the corporal's music?

At a lodge near the south shore, he'd met with his NSA contact, the two senators from the Senate Armed Services Committee, and the defense contractor rep from Texas. None of them seemed pleased with his lack of progress. They held him personally responsible for the project to be completed on the target date of June 30.

Charles could shove all four irritating men out a moving car with a smile, a wave, and a cheery "see ya in hell." Nobody prevented him from getting what he set his mind to. Not some weak-minded senators, defense contractor, and especially not his spineless, desk-riding contact with the NSA. This was his baby and it would be till the end.

Charles fingered his ears. "Give me The Boss and 'Born to Run.' Now that's music."

"'Get Jiggy' sure made Will Smith a rich man," his aide muttered.

Charles slapped the rolled-up Sacramento Bee's daily racing form against his thigh. "Don't give a rat's ass. Get us to SRM before noon."

The corporal glanced sideways at him. "Has the silver mine mission changed?"

"Need to know basis, and you don't need to know."

The corporal shrugged a shoulder. "I heard talk."

Steam built up in Charles' chest. "I hate loose lips. You'd better keep it buttoned up, or you'll find yourself doing guard duty in Antarctica."

The SUV bumped over a cattle guard crossing, and the road narrowed to a dirt cow path. The government's way of trying to mask their research facility as some backwoods camping ground. It wasn't cutting it.

"Beautiful land here," the corporal said looking at Charles to comment.

Damned chatty guy. Why didn't they assign him a guy who wouldn't talk?

Charles glanced out the window. "Trees. No big deal."

He glanced back down at his crumpled racing form. Santa Anita in the third had a sweet little filly named Major Decision. Fate was with him. At fifteen to one, he could be a rich man by day's end. Anything to make a buck.

Top dog in his specialty of military and non-military security, Charles could be many things for many people—at the right price. This duty sure beat the hell out of mercenary work in the jungles of Brazil or Columbia. However, he missed the beaches and the half-naked women lucky enough to catch his eye and maneuver into his bed.

Right now, he was sub-contracting as a military security agent and in charge of this covert research into spy technology. His work with the aerospace division and the new spy plane turned out to be a pretty good assignment for a career military man. So what if he was wrongfully discharged. Those same candy-assed top brass needed him now to do their dirty work. Charles didn't care if they paid him. They didn't need to know he was using their expensive little toy to locate more shafts of silver for exploitation. Win-win for him.

The weak shocks of the lumbering vehicle jostled him around as they bumped over a thickly furrowed section of dirt road. He fumbled in his pocket for his mobile phone, held it up. Hell. No signal. Must call his bookie from Basua's office.

Why had his NSA contact demanded he work with Dr. Paul Basua, a namby-pamby, lightweight? Purported to be a world-class aerospace engineer, the guy would like to study rocks instead. Said his mum was a geologist from England and his pop was a noble-born prince or something from India. Who cared? Charles didn't. Civilian science contractor, bah. At least he had NSA clearance.

His aide drove the Jeep around the last curve on the miserably uneven road, and they approached the guard shack. Jutting out from an outcropping of rocks, a big sign read: SRM—Sunrise Mountain Forestry Service. Another bright idea of the government—as if people didn't know SRM conducted secret tests.

When his aide rolled down the window and announced, "Major Donald," the Marine sergeant on guard duty leaned in to confirm Charles was in the car. He saluted.

With an apathetic return salute, Charles said, "Sergeant."

"Yes, sir. Good day, sir."

The gate slowly rose allowing them to drive through. A bunch of cabin-like structures stood throughout a grove of giant Ponderosa, Sugar Pines, and some White and Douglas Fir. Charles particularly liked the Quaking Aspen surrounding his small guest cabin at the north end of the facility campus. Their new green leaves danced and shimmered in the sun and wind. Even though he fancied botany, he wasn't here for the scenery.

He had a mission, and it was critical this undertaking be successful—even if the plans had changed.

A low-lying building at the end of another bumpy dirt road housed Basua's office and lab. Resembling a run-down forest ranger shack at the east foot of Sunrise Mountain, no way to tell it was a secret high-tech lab for government and private party experiments that went several stories under the ground.

His aide found an open parking spot and killed the engine. "Safe and sound," he announced.

Charles narrowed his eyes. "Bout time."

The corporal quick-stepped around and opened the Jeep's door for Charles. Before he reached the outer door of the building, the corporal dashed to his side and opened that as well. Being a major had its perks, even if he wasn't an official major anymore. These people didn't need to know that, so he continued to wear the uniform.

"Go to the mine and make sure the cargo is packed properly and ready for shipment tomorrow. You're dismissed when you complete that task." He saluted the corporal.

"Thank you, sir." The corporal saluted and left Charles at the elevator immediately inside the building.

The defense contract company from Texas paying for the ore shipments and the experiments in Artificial Intelligent Reconnaissance—AIR, rented the bottom floor of the vast underground facility that had been dug out deep into the granite mountainside. Charles didn't mind going to the bottom level, which meant more privacy for him to alter the tenor of the experiments.

Dr. Paul Basua, the so-called accomplished aerospace engineer, leaned over a table where their prototype sat in the back of the large lab room. He wore his white doctor's lab coat over black trousers and black button-down linen shirt—his uniform.

The prototype—AIDA—Artificial Intelligent Device Airplane was a small aircraft or drone Basua had built. Like a model airplane in appearance, AIDA cost hundreds of thousands of dollars. The small plane was five feet long with equally long wings and stood nearly thirty inches high. With a search range of sixty-eight miles, it could stay up for six hours with a ceiling of fifteen thousand feet. The propeller, however, was not in the front. It was attached to the body of the plane to give a clear view of the swiveling camera attachment underneath. Charles needed the plane to skim much closer to the ground and granite walls of the sheer canyons.

When they conducted the first tests of the plane, Basua discovered an abandoned silver mine on SRM's side of the mountain. A rich vein of pure silver ore ran nearly through the mountain to the rancher's side. Several vast masses of silver veins several feet thick could be removed by shovel. The top brass at

SRM didn't know anything about Charles' operation to remove all the silver ore for his off-the-books employers. He'd keep it that way. Unfortunately, Basua knew too much about the silver extraction.

With a screwdriver, Dr. Basua tweaked something on the plane. He jerked when the door slammed behind Charles.

Basua, a giant of a man, looked like he enjoyed way too much curry and naan with hummus. His sizable hands were fleshy like the rest of his body. It was a hoot to hear him attempting to hide his Indian/English accent. He sounded like a British John Wayne when he spoke. Used too many British words for Charles' comfort. He was more of a big kid with a big heart who should be playing in the backyard with all the rocks he'd collected. Instead, he was the country's top engineer of this type of AI.

Charles needed him, so he sucked it up.

A colossal crocodile smile rippled across Basua's puffy face. "Major. It is good to have you back. I trust everything went swimmingly with the meeting?"

Charles grunted. Pulling out a desk chair in front of his workstation, he dropped into and swiveled around to face Basua. "We need to talk."

The back of the room where two AIDAs sat on industrial tables was wide and tall enough to house a life-sized Cessna. It resembled a damned crypt. Charles had to focus his breathing to keep from hyperventilating every time he walked inside this concrete tomb.

Counters with shelves housing airplane parts, equipment and tools dominated the walls, and computers on desks filled the center area. Highly polished cement floors made the tomb as icy as a night in Siberia. Charles knew from personal experience how cold that could be.

"Where're the techs?"

Basua used two young men as technicians. College kids on break from MIT Charles didn't care about their names.

They are taking lunch at present." Basua strode over to the tools on the counters and placed his screwdriver in a red toolbox in a specific spot.

He turned around. "You sound very serious."

"Big Man needs us to step up our search—get deeper into the canyons on the rancher's side of Sunrise Mountain. Seems a claim was filed for a silver mine in 1910 over there." Charles pounded his fist into his palm. "Which means our plans have changed. AIDA needs to fly low and barely skim the treetops or we're not going to get into the box canyons and find that silver."

"Can't be done." Basua raised a bushy eyebrow and frowned. "We are already at four hundred feet and scaring the rancher's cattle. It's got to be bloody bad for the large steers to run so far and so fast, afraid like they are."

He didn't stop, just drew in a breath. "Besides, drones were not designed to fly that close to the ground or skim treetops."

He closed the toolbox lid and wandered over to stand by Charles. "The first unmanned aerial vehicle—the UAV squadron in the Air Force—provided long-endurance, aerial reconnaissance, and surveillance with the Predator MQ-1 UAV back in Vietnam and flew as low as two thousand feet." His hands waved in the air as he spoke. "Like the Ramirez' RQ-4 device from 1994. They both flew very high, very far, and very long. They did not skim the trees."

Charles gritted his teeth, wishing he could strangle Dr. Basua. "Ours is not the same size as the Predator or the RQ-4, it's a miniature version. West side of Sunrise Mountain has deeper canyons than this side. We're not finding our target because we're too damned high." He uttered some other colorful words.

Basua winced.

"How do you think I could do my drug cartel spy work back in Brazil with a plane that shoots pictures from fifteen hundred feet up? The guerillas would shoot it down." Charles banged his fist on the desktop. The massive computer monitors jiggled. "I need to see the eyelashes on a squirrel."

Basua chuckled. "Perhaps the squirrel won't appreciate having his face photographed."

Charles shot to his feet, gripped Basua by his lapels, and got in his face. "You'll get that damned plane to skim the trees and go into the deep canyons, or I'll ram the thing down your proper British throat."

Though bigger than Charles, the kid trembled. However, he still snickered. "Perhaps we could put the propeller on the top of AIDA like a helicopter."

"I don't give a rat's ass how you modify the thing." Charles snarled. "Get it done. I want that silver mine now. Got it?"

CHAPTER FOUR

Shadow Pines—Two Stop Signs and a Bar

J **OE'S GUT CLENCHED** as he drove his rig toward the sleepy little town of Shadow Pines and the much-dreaded Sheriff Cody Warner. Any time spent in that man's company, was time better spent elsewhere.

The sheriff still blamed him for stealing Cindy away and marrying her, and eventually causing her death. Cody Warner was a fool. He'd done a damn good job of crushing his relationship with Cindy by cheating on her before Cindy switched cowboys and staked her claim.

Shadow Pines, no more than a wide spot in the road, lay about sixteen miles due west from the ranch as the crow flies. Today though, wandering down the extremely narrow winding Mosquito Ridge Road hugging the switchbacks of the American River and sheer thousand-foot drops took about thirty minutes. The river, flowing with icy spring runoff from higher up and the sky a cloudless, robin's egg blue, was a sight he never passed up. He loved meandering especially if Cindy sat beside him. She made even the most mundane thrilling.

Joe clutched the steering wheel of his Ford F350 dually and his eyes burned. "Dammit, Cindy. Why'd you leave me?"

His pride and joy, the 1965 turquoise and white Ford F150 pickup Cindy persuaded him to buy, stayed behind today. Too many memories for him to mentally wrangle, especially after his dream of her last night.

He thumped the steering wheel as memories came unbidden anyway.

1971. Right after Joe had mustered out of the Army in San Francisco, ending his military career and three brutal tours of duty in Vietnam, he had wandered the country on foot. He considered going home to his pa's ranch in Texas, but couldn't work up the desire to see them. Both parents had been cruel and abusive to him in his youth. There was no love lost between them before he escaped at seventeen and enlisted in the Army. Why return for an encore?

For days now, Joe slept where he could lay his head and hoofed it plenty of bitter miles.

Somehow, he got on the road outside Auburn north of Sacramento and ended up in the once thriving gold town of Shadow Pines, now nearly a ghost town.

A short burly, friendly fellow at the steakhouse told him some cattle ranches east of town might be hiring. Ranching he knew. He wandered that way and ran across a rock wall nearly hidden in a grove of pines, and a sign that read: **SUNRISE RANCH**. He arrived at the farmhouse lean, gaunt, and somewhat shell-shocked.

At Sunrise Ranch, Bert Johnsen, an embittered, impaired man who hated soldiers because of his rejection from the Army during World War II, grudgingly took Joe in. He offered him a job as a ranch hand, a hard bunk, and three square meals a day. Despite Bert's gruff, hardened exterior, Joe found a home with a friendly family.

Bert was a hard boss probably because of his painful injuries. Joe believed Bert pushed him harder than the other ranch hands because he'd served in Vietnam. The hard, back-breaking work helped Joe work out some of his emotional suffering from the horrors of war and his abusive childhood.

Over time, he proved to Bert he was a hard worker and became solid friends. He treated Joe like his own son. Bert depended upon him to run the ranch and the cattle.

At the time, Bert's seventeen-year-old daughter, Cindy, looked at him as if he was a hero. She followed him around the ranch hanging on every word he spoke like they were God's honest truth. To him at the time, she was little more than a cute, blonde-headed pest, something to be shooed away from your picnic lunch. The four-year difference between their ages made him cautious.

Though mostly annoyed with her constant adoration, he soon found out she'd gotten herself entangled with the captain of the football team and star quarterback of the high school, Cody Warner.

That pissed Joe off. Part of him desired to rip Warner's throat out. Everyone in town knew Warner was a womanizer—everyone except Cindy. Rumor had it Warner had gotten Beverly Harding pregnant while dating Cindy. He was eventually forced by Beverly's daddy to marry the poor girl even as she went into labor with Warner's baby boy.

He knew he didn't have the right, but Joe shouted at Cindy to stay away from the philandering swine. She only pursued Warner harder. Later, Cindy confided in him, she was in love with Warner and intended to marry him.

Joe's heart cracked and bled.

When Cindy found out about Beverly's pregnancy, she cut Warner off at the knees and left immediately for college.

For the love of Pete, Joe had missed his little pest around the ranch.

Because Warner popped a knee during the last game of his senior season, he never received a scholarship to play football at any college. Eventually, he became the sheriff of Shadow Pines.

When Cindy returned four years later, Joe hardly recognized her. She had flowered into a gorgeous woman. Tall, curvy, in control of herself, and for some reason, still idolized Joe.

One night after her college graduation in 1975, Cindy stood just inside the stables watching him mucking out the stalls. She didn't say anything to him for a long time. Blasted woman made him jumpy.

"If you stay around the ranch much longer," Cindy said, "you're gonna need reliable transportation."

"I don't need a truck." He stopped shoveling, leaned on the handle. "I don't go anywhere."

Her peach-pale skin turned a lovely shade of scarlet. She gazed at the ground and laced her hands together behind her back. "What if you have designs to take me out for a drive up the American River?"

Dumbfounded that Cindy—a much younger and educated female—could have any feelings for him, a saddle bum, a mere ranch hand, Joe couldn't find his voice.

"You want to take me out driving, don't you?" she asked.

The question hit him between the eyes. He hoped he didn't look like he was facing down old Diablo, Bert's favorite bull. Though he'd had images in his head about Cindy and how beautiful she was, how delicate, Bert would've staked him to an anthill and poured honey over him for even thinking such things let alone acting on them.

"Don't you?" she asked again.

He toed the ground afraid to look at her. "Whoa, Cindy. Why would you think such a thing?"

"Because you treat me like I have a brain. You've always respected me."

"That's a long way from going out driving together. I'm too old for you."

"Bunk." She laughed and laid her small hand on his sleeve. The jolt from her touch was immediate and shocking. He backed up, considered running. She held him in place with her hand and a glance. "A woman knows when a man is interested."

"A woman?"

"Yes. A woman." She pinched her lips together.

And wow, what a woman. "But I thought … Warner … Cody's coming around again, begging for your forgiveness." The swine was sniffing around like a dog in heat—even as a married man with a kid. Joe would love some target practice on his backside.

Cindy's expression turned indignant, her lips pursed. "Do you think I could be the woman who would break up a man's marriage? I'd never do such a thing to Beverly. She never deserved to be the rebound from the relationship I had with Cody." She shook her head. "Besides, he's a slimy womanizing porcos to me."

"A what?"

"Swine." She grinned.

She sure pegged Warner. This was Great. Just what he wished. However, what would Bert think of him driving out with his daughter? Would he kill him?

Before he could say so, she spoke again. "Now let's take all the lovely money you've saved since you started working for my father. Hey, don't go shaking your head at me. I know you don't spend any money, so you must be socking it away somewhere. Let's go into Sacramento and find you a suitable truck so you can date me properly and drive me to town on occasions."

What could he say? Joe never needed transportation. If he needed to go into town for something, all he had to do was wait. Eventually, one of the other hands, Ricardo, or one of his sons would drive into Shadow Pines for supplies with the ranch rig. He didn't need a lot of money and saved all his pay. How did she know about that?

Cindy had other ideas for him. She'd give him that sideways glance with those baby-blues, and he lost the power to speak, let alone resist.

That time had been no different.

He had bought his Pride and Joy and dated Cindy until the fall of 1975 when they married.

Warner hadn't taken Cindy's final rejection well. He held onto his grudge like a grizzly with a thorn in his paw.

A dazzling flash of sunlight bounced off the windshield of a black SUV and into Joe's eyes from his rearview mirror. It jolted him back to the present.

He took the curve at the road's highest spot above the river, holding the rig tight to the white-striped center line. In the mirror, a black SUV—no it was a black Jeep—was coming up fast. It had to be exceeding the speed limit. Joe had another mile to go before there was a turn-out for slower vehicles to pull over and let other cars pass, but this guy was going to move on by regardless.

Joe checked the road ahead of him for other cars. None. He stayed atop the white line on the edge of the road, but not too close. Taking a one-thousand-foot plunge into the river below the cliff wasn't on his schedule today.

As the Jeep approached, it revved its engine and sped up like it was going to pass, but didn't make a move. It was going to hit his bumper.

Joe instinctively swerved right. His tires spit up dirt and rocks off the narrow shoulder of the drop-off.

The Jeep rammed his bumper, jolting him, sending him closer to the edge. "Dammit."

Joe jerked the wheel, holding the rig to the road and sped up.

Again, the Jeep accelerated and collided with Joe's bumper. The crunch of compressing metal sounded exceptionally loud in Joe's ears.

Sweat broke out on Joe's forehead. What the hell did that jerk want with him? Was he trying to kill him?

Considering the size of his rig compared to the Jeep, he could win in a head-to-head contest. However, it might cause him to lose control. The third time the driver of the Jeep prepared to slam into the rig, he hit the rig's brakes, fishtailing to a stop.

The Jeep's driver slammed on his brakes, also fishtailed, and came to a stop sideways across the highway.

Joe threw the rig in park, grabbed his rifle from the gun rack, and opened the door. Time to confront the bastard. His heart thundered in his chest as he brought the gun up and prepared to get in the guy's face.

However, before he could reach the Jeep, the driver threw it in reverse and shot backward until it disappeared around a bend in the road.

"Dammit." Joe lowered the rifle and strode to the back of the rig. The bumper was mangled. He'd have to replace it. Thankfully, the frame wasn't bent. More than likely, Sal could replace the bumper. He kept all the vehicles on the ranch in smooth, operating condition.

He stood for a moment glaring in the direction the Jeep had retreated. Should he flip around and follow?

With an ear-scrunching shrug, he climbed back into the rig and slammed the door.

Nearing the last turn before the outskirts of Shadow Pines, the black Jeep once again popped up in Joe's rear-view mirror. "Damn it to hell," Joe said out loud. "I gotta get the license plate number and then pound the bastard into the dirt."

Still, nowhere to pull over to get out from in front, Joe sped up.

So, did the Jeep—matching his speed.

This time the driver meant to hit him full in the back, ram him hard enough to send him either spinning out of control or into a roll-over.

The Jeep roared toward him. Joe's hands trembled on the steering wheel. He didn't want to die even though he was eager to be with his wife again. "I won't let this bastard send me to meet you, Cindy. Not yet."

At the last possible moment, Joe noticed a wide spot. He pushed the gas pedal to the floor, hit the loose gravel at the edge of the road and jerked his wheel to the left. The giant rig spun around until Joe faced his road-rage opponent.

The driver of the Jeep hit the brakes, his back end lurched toward the edge of a deep cliff along the side of the road. The driver managed to pull the vehicle back on the road and squealed the tires to roar away before Joe could get a good look at his license plate.

"I'll be go to hell."

Hands trembling, Joe struggled to pull in air to calm his galloping heartbeat. His breath came fast and raw in his throat. He could have been killed. Who the hell pegged him for death? Well, besides Sheriff Cody Warner?

Joe battled to get his composure back as he continued to sit in his truck facing oncoming traffic on the wrong side of the highway. Experiencing that kind of fear had only happened once before in his life. It wasn't something he wanted to relive.

Across the road from where Joe sat, Shadow Pines Elementary School signaled the town's limit. Joe watched the young children race around the play area. Must be lunch time. Had anyone seen his brush with death, or the Jeep?

Someone in a red ranch rig honked, pulled alongside Joe's rig, and rolled down his window. One of the other ranchers who lived out his way.

"Are you all right, Joe?" the rancher asked after Joe rolled down his window.

"Not really." Joe's hands still shook.

"What happened? I saw a guy in the black Jeep racing away from here. Did you have some trouble with him?"

"Yeah. I'm headed to the sheriff to talk to him."

The rancher shook his head. "You'd better get that rig turned 'round or someone else will finish the job."

Joe waved as the man sped off. He made a wide U-turn, headed into town. At First Street, he turned right and parked in front of the Shadow Pines Sheriff's Office. Joe strode inside still trembling from his run in with the black Jeep. He dreaded his confrontation with Warner.

Sheriff Cody Warner, standing next to the receptionist / dispatcher's desk, glanced up at the sound of Joe opening the door. He scowled, his body stiffened, and he puffed out his broad chest.

"What the hell do you want, Mack?"

CHAPTER FIVE
Sheriff Cody Warner

JOE SMILED AT WARNER'S dispatcher / receptionist, Barbara Cook, sitting at her desk behind the raised counter. She smiled back. Barbara was about fifty, Joe's age, a pleasant woman with silvering red hair, faded freckles, and a mole the size of a walnut on her chin.

"Why are you here, Mack?" Warner shifted his stance, glared at Joe.

Sheriff Cody Warner, part Mexican heritage, part English, still had the brawny muscular upper body of a quarterback and long run-toughened legs of a sprinter. He made sure everyone knew he'd kept his high-school physique by how tight he wore his sheriff's uniform. The damn thing looked painted on, even the trousers. At forty-four he resembled a middle-aged Latino lover from a *Telemundo* soap opera.

His short black hair was graying slightly at the temples. His squared off jaw sported a close-shaven bad-boy beard, with a little sprinkled in gray. No wonder women lost the good sense God gave them.

The irritating jock attitude kept him from resembling a human being. Like Ricardo said, Warner continued to play the "womanizing swine." Whenever Warner was out and about, the women of the town would slip him a half-wink come-on when they figured their men weren't looking.

However, the pig was still married.

Joe cleared his throat and stared Warner down. "I need to report an incident out at my ranch. Something is stampeding my cattle and horses."

Warner folded his arms over his massive chest and continued to scowl. "What do you want me to do about it?"

Joe fought hard not to bring up his fists. "I figured you'd wanna do your job and investigate the incident before I do."

Warner's frown deepened, but he said nothing. He didn't have any more affection for Joe than Joe had for him. Warner made Joe's life miserable over him "stealing" Cindy. Not so much since Cindy's passing. However, they would never be friends.

"Should I take his statement and fill out a form for investigation?" Barbara pulled some paperwork from her drawer and grabbed a pen.

"Nah. Let him talk to Deputy Sayer." Warner pointed over his shoulder to Sayer, a black uniformed officer who sat at a metal desk in the central office. Warner spun around, stomped into his office and slammed the door.

Joe's stomach clenched. He clamped his jaw shut. Not that anything was wrong with the deputy. "How ya doin' Pat?"

Pat rose from his chair. "Can't complain. You?"

"Fair to middlin'." With a half-smile, Joe motioned Pat back down. "I've come for the sheriff, and I will speak to the sheriff. Sorry."

"No skin off my nose." Pat chuckled. "Have at it."

Barbara smiled, but her cheeks glowed red. "I'm sorry, Joe."

"Not your fault."

He shoved open the swinging gate next to Barbara's desk and marched to the door. The doorknob turned in his hand. Pushing the door inward, he entered Warner's office.

"What the hell?" Warner shot to his feet from behind his desk. "I told Sayer to handle this."

"I need you to handle this."

"You're a son-of-a-bitch, aren't you?" Warner sneered.

"So, I've been told."

"What makes you think I will help you?"

Joe shook his head. "You probably won't, but I gotta ask anyway."

He glanced around the tiny space to fight down his urge to lay the sucker out in his office. Warner decorated his small office like a high school football locker room. Trophies of gridiron heroics littered his bookcase and filing cabinets. Photos of long-ago games and teams covered the dull beige paint on the walls. The office smelled faintly of Lysol and heavily of sweat.

On his paper-strewn desk sat a small portrait of his lovely wife, Beverly, and their son, Cody Jr., also a football player some years back. Joe didn't have many occasions to visit the sheriff's offices and hadn't been inside Warner's office.

Joe's calm seemed to unnerve Warner. He sat in his office chair and leaned back. The chair protested loudly with a whine. "What do you want?"

"So many things, Warner." Joe took one of the two hard chairs and faced his nemesis. He fought the turmoil in his gut to ask this guy for help. "SRM has been flying a small recon plane over my property. It's already caused two stampedes, and this morning's flight nearly killed Ricardo and me."

Warner's eyes widened at the word "killed." "Really?"

Joe could almost hear the next words, "too bad," come out of Warner's mouth, but the guy didn't utter them.

"What are you gonna do about it?"

Rocking back in the squeaking chair again, Warner steepled his fingers. "I don't know if I can do anything. The government doesn't answer to anybody, especially local law enforcement."

"Isn't there someone at the facility you can call to ask what's going on and put a stop to it?" Joe asked. "If the cattle continue to stampede, I might lose cows and calves, and some of the older steers. They'll lose whatever fat they've gained on their spring feed. Plus, I'll lose money come sale time." He took an impotent breath. "There's got to be someone you can call."

Warner remained quiet for a moment.

Joe fidgeted with the edge of his jean jacket and waited.

"You know SRM is only a research facility doing experiments in conservation and land management for the Federal Forest Service. You don't think they'd be into spying on you, do you?" Warner chuckled without humor. "Perhaps it's an old enemy, someone you pissed off who is sending the plane to cause you trouble."

Joe fisted his hands. "I don't know why SRM is sending a miniature plane to crisscross my land up to Sunrise Mountain peak, but they are, and it's causing me a lot of trouble." Joe paused, swallowed. Hell, it hurt to admit he needed Warner's help. He might as well tell him the rest.

"On the way into town today, I was also nearly run off the road by Little Mad Canyon by a black Jeep."

"What the—"

"The Jeep followed me clear into town hoping to hit my bumper to force me into a roll-over when they couldn't push me off the edge of the cliff and into the river."

"What does this Jeep incident have to do with the plane?"

"I don't know, Warner, that's for you to find out. I think they're searching for something on my ranch. Can you think of a better way to search my ranch than if I'm dead?"

Warner shook his head. "I still don't know what you think I can do about it. There are tons of black Jeeps in the valley and over in Tahoe."

Joe could spit nails. "As the sheriff sworn to protect the citizens of the county, I demand you come out to the ranch and check on this plane, then find the bastard who rammed my bumper."

Warner looked ready to reach for his sidearm. After a long moment, he leaned forward, opened his drawer, and searched for a pen. He held it over a similar form to the one Barbara had pulled from her desk. "Did you get the license plate of the Jeep, and when did you first notice the plane?"

For the next few minutes, Joe filled Warner in on the details from Ricardo, the stampede yesterday, and again this morning, and told him about the car chase down the canyon.

After ten minutes, Warner flipped over the form and glanced up at Joe. "I don't think there is much I can do, but I'll make some calls."

Joe's shoulders relaxed. Releasing his clenched teeth, Joe said in a flat voice, "I'm obliged for whatever you can do."

"Do I have a choice?"

"Just do your damned job."

"You think I don't?" Warner raised his fist.

"I haven't cared what you did until now. I need the services of the sheriff. I don't like being here anymore than you want me here, but I made a promise to my wife." He emphasized "my wife" just to drive Warner crazy.

"I'm only doing this because of Cindy, Mack." There was no warmth in the sheriff's voice, just cold bitterness. "Otherwise I wouldn't give a damn if that spy plane dropped a bomb on your whole enterprise."

"Go to hell." Only Joe and Warner's promise to Cindy on her deathbed kept Joe from slugging him right here in the sheriff's office.

Joe spun around, stormed out of the sheriff's office, and slammed the door. He didn't trust Warner to do anything for him. If he wanted to solve the mystery of the flying silver demon, he'd have to do it himself. The goal was to protect his ranch—the ranch Cindy and her father begged him to care for and safeguard until his dying breath.

To hell with Sheriff Cody Warner. This mission called for someone with military training and jungle cunning.

CHAPTER SIX
Red Ruby and Wild Bill

JOE THRUST HIS KEY into the ignition as his stomach growled. It was nearly two in the afternoon. He'd missed breakfast and lunch. Luckily, down the same block as the sheriff's office stood the Red Ruby Saloon and Steakhouse, owned by Ruby and Bill Green. It was pretty much the only fancy place to eat in Shadow Pines.

During the day, Ruby served more café style food. At night, she served a delicious fare of steaks, seafood, and fabulous desserts. He could use a good bacon club sandwich before stopping at the general store to pick up a new hat and heading down to Auburn to have his saddle repaired.

He parked his rig in front of the restaurant and climbed the stairs to the front door. The glass and metal door to Ruby's opened into a black and red decorated foyer. A tastefully covered naked lady with her back to the door graced the wall behind the bar in the saloon.

Ruby's husband, Bill Green, ex-Navy Chief Petty Officer, ran the bar. The black and red wall-papered café had been added to the original saloon Ruby's great-grandfather built in the 1850s gold-rush days. The café and steakhouse stood on the left of the saloon. Delicious scents of roasting meat beckoned Joe.

When Joe walked to the server desk, he noticed Bill behind the bar running a white cloth over the highly polished slab of live-edged Ponderosa pine.

Joe raised a hand in greeting. Bill glanced up and waved back.

Bill resembled the Chief Petty Officer he'd been in the service—squatty, solid, and barrel-chested. He had a scar over his left eye and tattoos all over his beefy arms. Today he wore a too small t-shirt that read, "Sailors do it on the high seas."

"Comin' in for a beer?" Bill asked. "Got your favorite on tap."

"Not today," Joe said. "I gotta drive to Auburn."

"Too bad." Bill grinned. "Catch you next time."

Joe nodded and ambled into the steakhouse. Ruby Green leaned on a bar chatting in her high-pitched voice to a tourist, who had a camera strapped across his body and wore khaki shorts and a plaid shirt, sleeves rolled up.

When Ruby saw Joe, her whole face lit up. "Well, looky what the cat dragged in."

Joe grinned. No one could feel stressed around Ruby.

Not a bad looking woman at fifty, Ruby wore her color-boosted golden-blonde hair short and sassy. It fit her thin, long face, and pointed chin. She had delicate crow's feet around her eyes and generous mouth. When she smiled, her dimples widened and were deepening with age. She wore a red-checkered blouse like the tablecloths on her tables, but she left a few too many buttons undone at the neckline. Not that Joe was above glancing, but Bill would beat him to a pulp if he did.

Patrons sat at most of the tables. Joe nodded at a couple of folks he recognized. He waved at them and moseyed toward Ruby.

She said something to the tourist who turned and left. With hips swinging, she meandered over to Joe.

"How you doing, sweetie?" She gripped him by the arms, leaned in close, and pecked Joe more passionately on the cheek than Joe considered proper. A lesser man might have turned into the kiss, but Joe was a one-woman man.

He stepped out of reach, so her hands fell away. "Got some bacon cooked for a nice BLT?"

"Sure thing, sweetie. Anything for you." She glanced over her shoulder toward the kitchen door and hollered. "Say, Bella, fry up a little pig and slap some grass on it for our fine-looking, ranch hand here."

Bella Taylor from Georgia, Ruby's cook, poked her head out the door to the kitchen. "What did you—" Her hazel eyes opened as wide as a bowl of her good sausage gravy. "Damned if it ain't Mister Joe come to visit us. Heavens be still my heart." She laid her hand on her plentiful bosom.

He chuckled. He'd missed getting a shot in the arm of pure Bella lovin'.

Bella's skin was a warm brown. She was as wide as she was tall. She'd served nineteen years in prison for chatting up a child molester with a baseball bat. Tough as cowhide and tender-hearted as Mother Teresa. Joe loved her better than his own mother.

"How's my best gal?" Joe paced over to give the woman a big squeeze.

"You're more handsome than two skunks mating." She squeezed him back. "How you doin', you hound dog, without that lovely woman around to keep you sane?"

Joe's heart pinched, his breath stalled. After a long moment, he said, "I'm good."

"The hell you say." She shook her head stepping out of his embrace. Her hairnet over her mostly bald head didn't hold back the sweat. Some dripped in her eyes. "Ain't no good woman to cook for you no more, is there?" Bella pulled him over to a table and shoved him into a chair.

"I got Lettie Sanchez. She cooks for me."

"Pooh. She don't know nothing but all that hot and spicy Spanish cookin', do she?"

Joe huffed. He knew coming here after his run-in with the sheriff would lift his spirits. "She makes a killer mac and cheese."

"Go on with you now." Bella frowned and shoved his shoulder. He was glad she didn't have her baseball bat. "It would have to be something to beat mine."

"Say, you got some bacon cooked for a nice BLT?" Joe asked.

Bella glanced over at Ruby. "Was that what you screamed at me?"

Ruby laughed. "If you weren't so hard of hearing, old woman, I wouldn't have to scream."

"You just wait, Mister Joe, I'll be back in a jiff with the best BLT you ever had." She pinched his cheek before swaying away.

"The place looks good, Ruby," Joe said when Ruby dropped a bread basket on the table and took the chair across from him. The walls looked freshly painted, and new tablecloths graced the tables.

Ruby waved over a young waitress. "Take the couple at table twelve some more bread and fill their water."

"Yes, ma'am," the girl said and scurried away.

"New?" Joe buttered some of the fresh, yeasty-smelling, molasses bread.

"She's cute, isn't she?"

"I hadn't noticed." He didn't like that Ruby believed he was the same as all men who couldn't keep their eyes off the young ones. "I'm not Cody Warner."

Ruby thrust back her head and bellowed out a laugh. "You are a card, sweetie, I'll give you that." Some of the lunch crowd stared at Ruby. She didn't seem to mind.

Joe's face heated. He hunched his shoulders and nibbled on his bread.

"You seen the sheriff today?" she asked.

Small town gossip spread fast. Ruby didn't need to know why. "Had some trouble at the ranch. Hoping he'll investigate."

Ruby leaned in close. "What sort of trouble? Cattle rustlers?"

That was as good of an excuse as any. "Probably."

"You think Barney Fife will be able to find them for you? He hates you, you know?"

"I hadn't heard."

"Jackass." Ruby grinned. "That's why I love you."

Joe squirmed. What if Bill, the bartender, heard his wife talk to him like that? Not good.

Before he could reply, the waitress hustled out of the kitchen with his sandwich and fries. After dousing the fries with Bella's homemade ketchup, he shoveled them in his mouth, leaving Ruby to chat by herself while he just nodded. There was no need to answer, she never asked any questions requiring more than a nod.

"I just don't like it that you're living out there all alone with rustlers picking off your cattle," Ruby said. "You be careful, sweetie."

He nodded.

After Ruby went back into the kitchen, Dr. Samantha Stone strolled in. His gut did a slow, sweet somersault, and the back of his neck itched. When she noticed him, her eyes lit up, and a smile rippled across her lips, lighting her angelic face.

Buffalo chips.

"How are you, Joe?" Sam paused by his table, reached around him for a warm hug. Flabbergasted, he didn't know what to say and held himself stiff. Certainly, he couldn't hug her back, not while holding his knife and fork, anyway.

"Mind if I sit?"

He opened his mouth, but nothing came out.

She sat. Her long, black hair was wound up in some knot at the back of her head. She'd worn a black checkered blouse and black jeans. She always wore her manure-kickers, but they were clean and shiny.

"Looks good," she said pointing at his sandwich.

He glanced down, unable to meet her gaze and fidgeted. Why did she make him nervous?

"What brings you to town?" she asked after she gave the waitress her order—the same as his.

"Meeting with the sheriff."

She leaned toward him, curiosity in her gaze. "Why?"

He finished off the last bite of his sandwich. Tilting forward so Ruby wouldn't hear, he briefly explained about the plane and the cattle stampede.

Sam looked visibly shaken. "I'm so glad you're all right. You could have been killed."

"I hope Warner will help."

She chuckled. "Good luck."

"I make my own luck," he said.

"You're going after the plane yourself, aren't you?"

When he didn't say anything, she blew out her breath and frowned. "Promise me you won't do anything stupid."

Joe couldn't make that promise. "Would I do anything like that?"

He didn't like it when Sam frowned. She was much prettier when she smiled. "It's almost branding time, you comin' out to make sure our calves are healthy and give them their shots?"

She smiled when the waitress set her sandwich and fries before her. "You got another vet working here I don't know about? Of course, I'll come. Jess, as well."

"You're the best, doc." Embarrassed at saying so much, he stood, rifled through bills in his wallet and tossed some on the table to cover his and Sam's sandwiches. "Lettie and her daughters-in-law are going all out cooking their specialties for this year's branding to feed the visiting ranch hands. I trust you'll stay, er … to eat with us?"

Rosy highlights appeared under her flawless golden skin. "Wouldn't miss it." She nibbled on a fry. "Say, I heard your boy Robbie's coming home this weekend for his mother's birthday."

Robbie Meyers. Some years back, Joe saw a young boy shuffling along the side of the road up the canyon. When he stopped the rig to question the kid on his plans, solemn brown eyes met his, and the boy announced, "I'm off to see the forest and catch me a big black bear."

"Don't you figure you'll need a good rifle to bring down this bear?"

The boy chewed his bottom lip. "Guess I didn't figure on that. You got one I can use?"

Joe nearly split his side laughing so hard. Since he knew the boy's mama—a hardworking gal who worked two jobs just to keep food on the table, he offered him a ride up the road to find a bear. "I happened to have two rifles right here. I reckon we can bring down an old black bear if you're a mind to?"

Robbie only hesitated a moment before climbing into the rig and fastening his seatbelt. "Can't be too careful," he said.

Joe chuckled and sped up the mountain to a spot known for bear activity. He pulled his rig off the side of the road and loaded both rifles and together they set up on a quest through the pines. Two hours and twenty mosquito bites later, there was no sign of a bear, but Joe had formed an attachment to Robbie and his brilliant mind.

He took the boy home for supper because Bonnie Meyers, his ma, had to work the night shift at the café in town. Cindy fell in love with the boy right off. Arrangements were made for Robbie to ride the bus out their way after school and then he'd stay with Joe and Cindy until the weekend. Took a heap of burden off Bonnie's shoulders and let Cindy be a mom—something she'd prayed for and craved her whole life.

Robbie had been away at CSU Chico and would come home for a short break and celebrate his mama's birthday.

Robbie, a computer genius, might be Joe's ticket to protecting the ranch. They'd keep that buzzin' menace and the black Jeep bastard from invading his privacy.

CHAPTER SEVEN
Doing His Duty?

March 20, 1998—Friday

"**D**AMNED ORNERY COOT."** Sheriff Cody Warner smacked the top of his desk. He wouldn't lift a finger to help Joe Mack, the S.O.B. who robbed him of his only true love. If not for Mack, he could've been married to Cindy Johnsen and been the one to inherit the prosperous Sunrise Ranch.

He hadn't worried about the guy or his case since he came in two days ago. "Spy plane harassin' him, my as—"

"Are you all right, Sheriff?" Deputy Pete Vargas, his third shift replacement barged into the office interrupting him.

Eight p.m. and Pete just punched in for his twelve-hour night shift.

"Yeah. It's nothing." Cody rubbed his scratchy beard sadly in need of a trim.

"Is there anything you'd like me to check on during my usual rounds tonight?"

Cody leaned back in his chair. The thing squawked like a chicken getting its throat slit. "You could drop round Joe Mack's ranch come sun-up."

"What the hell for?" Pete narrowed his dark eyebrows and sat in the chair Joe had occupied on Wednesday.

"He claims someone's flying a plane over his ranch early in the morning stampeding the cattle and his stock horses."

"So?"

"Exactly." Cody rubbed his knee where he'd been hit hard the last game of high school football. The sideways hit had ended his bid to play college ball and his high-faluitin' ideas of going pro. Still ached when it rained, or he was stressed—like over Mack. "Unfortunately, I told Mack I would check it out."

Pete frowned. "So, I have to check it out?"

"Aren't you a deputy sheriff 'round here?"

"That's what my wife told me this morning when she left to take the kids to school."

"Then your duty," Cody said, "is to go by Mack's farm and see if you notice anything strange flying around on his side of Sunrise Mountain before you head home."

Pete nodded and brought two fingers to his forehead in a mock-salute. "Aye, aye, Skipper."

"Jackass."

"I take after my boss."

"Smart mouth, too."

Pete chuckled. "What will we do if something flies over Joe's ranch stampeding his cattle?"

Cody stared at his trophies sitting atop his filing cabinet. He wished he was still back in school and the most significant deal on campus alongside his golden girl, Cindy Johnsen. Dirty, thieving, Joe Mack.

Finally, he glanced back at Pete and snickered. "Nothing. We're not going to do a damned thing."

Pete nodded and left his office. Cody heard him say goodnight to Deputy Sayer before walking out and driving away in his patrol Jeep. He didn't know what he hoped the kid would find out on Mack's ranch. Too bad his old rival hadn't bit the big one Wednesday morning when his cattle stampeded. Too late for him and Cindy, even if Mack did bite it. She'd died three years ago from cancer. Also, Mack's fault.

Mack had stolen so much from him.

He promised Mack he'd make a call. That's the least he could do. The very least.

Cody flipped open his cell phone, located the number of his buddy, a Marine Sergeant working as a guard at the SRM Facility. Career man. Perhaps he knew something about the mysterious plane. Maybe he could meet him at Ruby and Bill's saloon for a beer.

Much later, Cody sat at the bar in Red Ruby's Steakhouse Saloon nursing a beer. Someone grabbed him by the shoulder in a death grip, pinching a nerve.

"What the hell?" He flipped around, fists at the ready.

Aleksander "Chip" Kowalski roared a laugh. "You think you could take me, Sheriff? That's Bravo Sierra, sir."

"Chip. You dirty jarhead. Sit yourself down here. I'm a beer ahead of you."

"We can't have that." Chip flung his leg over the next barstool and held up a single finger at Bill Green.

Chip was an upstanding, handsome, solid kid from Shadow Pines. He'd played football at the high school like Cody. When Cody helped the team as an assistant coach, he and Chip had hit it off.

Tonight, Chip wore his camo uniform, or his "civvies" as Cody called them, including steel toed boots and desert camo cap.

Bill, behind the bar, tipped his head in response to Chip's order. He twisted the cap off a cold beer, and placed it in front of Chip, who took a long draw, nearly drained the thing.

"I see you were thirsty." Cody laughed.

Chip wiped his mouth with the back of his hand. "Sure tastes a hell of a lot better than that swill they sell at the Facility commissary."

Cody laughed and patted him on the back. He signaled for Bill to replace Chip's empty beer. "Speaking of the Facility, what they got you doing over there now?"

"Mostly, I embrace the suck." He chuckled at Cody's blank expression. "Boring time spent in the military police working the guard gate sucks. It's checking on the credentials of the government's best and brightest who do research up in the lab complex. The labs are filled with government types and corporations doing experiments and creating new products for governmental or private sector use."

Chip took another draw from his new bottle of beer. "Sometimes I do perimeter guard duty at night. Not much exciting ever happens at the Facility." He placed his empty bottle on the bar and signaled for another. "I've caught up, dude, and then some."

Cody chuckled. "Say, you ever see anything suspicious, like something doesn't belong at the facility?"

Chip narrowed his eyes. "Like what?"

"Like something that might fly?"

"Sheriff, that's a secret squirrel—I'm not at liberty to discuss what goes on at SRM." Chip downed his second beer.

Cody held up a finger for another beer. He needed that information.

"Thanks," Chip said when Bill put another beer in front of him. He chugged back half of it.

"Surely there's something about a miniature plane flying around Sunrise Mountain you could tell me."

Chip drained the last of his beer, held up another finger for Bill. "I suppose I could tell you the unclassified stuff."

"Nothing you can't reveal now, you hear?" Cody grinned.

"I think there's a lab working on forest fire detection," Chip said. "I've seen a little plane that sweeps the mountain peaks—like you said. I think they're testing it for longer flights and to replace or be used by fire spotters out in the forest. It certainly would be cheaper to fly a radio-controlled plane around the wooded areas to check for fires than keep paying a couple of men to sit in a cabin high up in the mountains like at the old Duncan Peak Fire lookout." He hiccupped. "Excuse me."

Bill frowned as he set another cold one in front of Chip.

"What does SRM do exactly for the forest service?" Cody held up a finger for another beer.

"Some"—he swallowed half of the new bottle—"of the labs design, build, and test equipment for surveillance…" Chip trailed off as he polished off his drink. "Some for quick containment of forest fires and … and to keep an eye on those famous California earthquake faults." Chip wobbled some on his barstool.

"That would explain a lot. One of our ranchers in the valley has a fault line running through his property along the foothills where he likes to spring and summer his cattle. I supposed this little plane would only be looking for cracks in the fault lines or something like that?"

Chip shrugged a shoulder. "Possibly." He nodded at Bill who was more than willing to ply him with more beer.

"Do you know the name of the lab or government agency working with the plane?"

Chip's blond eyebrow lifted as he considered and raised his glass. "I can't tell you that. Secret squirrel, remember."

Cody put a hand on Chip's beer preventing him for taking another sip. "I'm gonna have to ask you to come to the jail and sleep off your beer-buzz. Isn't that your fifth beer?"

"I'm not drunk." He hiccupped.

"You can't drive over the mountain to the facility after five beers. I won't allow it." Cody frowned. "I could run you in for a DUI, but that would go on your driving record."

"So … I should tell you … you about the facility to keep my record clean?"

Cody laughed. "Whatever works."

"Okay, okay. You got me. I could use some rack time." He grinned. "There's an intense major dude who's the government man working in a lab. I can't remember his name, but an Indian guy is a scientist. A Dr. Basua." He finished off his new beer. "You won't believe this," Chip whispered, "…but the name of the project is the Peter Pan Project." He spit on the three Ps.

Cody couldn't fight his bellowing laugh. Some people at the bar turned to frown at him. "No kidding?"

"This is no Bravo Sierra, sir. I wouldn't … kid about a thing like that." Chip blushed some under his tan. "We've had stranger names. It's … appropriate. Why do you wanna know about the plane anyways?"

"A rancher in the valley say's it's frightening his cattle."

"Don't know about that. Could be." Chip tossed some bills on the bar, slid off the barstool, wobbled a bit. "I gotta get some sleep. Where's your jail cell?" He turned to Bill. "Thanks for the beers, Pops."

The older man pushed the bills back toward him. "Your money is no good here, Marine. Thank you for your service. You come back anytime."

Bill pointed to a picture of himself in his Navy uniform. Chip glanced across the bar, saw the photo, and saluted Bill. "That's very generous of you, Chief Petty Officer Green. Thank you and thank you for your … service."

45

Bill's face turned bright red as he returned Chip's salute. He turned aside quickly and wiped down the bar.

Chip extended his hand to Cody. "I hope I helped you out."

Cody shook Chip's hand. "You've been a big help."

After they both left, Cody tucked Chip into bed in a jail cell. Cody strolled back to Ruby's and ordered another beer. He wasn't much of a drinker, but figured this had to be a special occasion— he'd done something for Joe Mack, the boil on his behind.

He took the last pull from his bottle, thought about ordering another and held up a finger.

"Time to slow down, Sheriff." Bill warned. "You won't be able to drive home."

He chuckled. "Who's gonna arrest me for a D.U.I., huh?"

Bill said nothing.

"Quit being a nagging mother. I don't need a mother. I had one." One that took off on him and Pa when he was only ten. She didn't want to be a mother anymore and found a new lover.

Speaking of lovers.

He glanced around the noisy place. Friday night. Easy pickings. Everyone in the saloon section was having a cocktail before their tables were ready in Ruby's Steakhouse.

He gazed through to the steakhouse and noticed Doctor Samantha Stone, the town's veterinarian sitting at a table with a girlfriend. She chatted with her friend and nursed part of a beer in a glass, the foam sliding down the inside as she'd just taken a sip. Dainty drinker.

Good golly, she was a looker.

She was half-bred Native American—politically correct way to refer to her—and blessed with straight black hair hanging to her behind. She kept those dark eyes that could stare right through a man hidden behind dark-rimmed, doctor-looking glasses. Typically, she had a ready smile for everyone she met, just not him. He couldn't remember how long he'd yearned to hook up with Dr. Sam. Even back in high school while dating Sam's friend, Cindy Johnsen.

Sam's companion got up and strolled back toward the restrooms leaving Sam alone. Now was his chance.

Cody laid down some bills, grabbed his long neck beer, and slid off his stool. He moseyed through the saloon and into the steakhouse. Perhaps he'd get lucky tonight. He'd been hammering away at Sam for years. She was bound to give in eventually. Might as well be tonight.

He pulled out the chair opposite Sam, watching her whiskey-colored eyes widen even as she scowled at him. He leaned in close and whispered, "Say doll. When are you and me gonna dance the horizontal rumba?"

Sam's laser glare could've cut him in half. "When Sunrise Mountain blows its top."

"Could happen." Cody drained his beer. "We live on some mighty sketchy fault lines."

"Sheriff, you're the only one who's sketchy. You'd better leave before my friend comes back." Sam crossed her arms over her chest, leaned back as far as her chair would allow. "Go home to your wife, Sheriff."

CHAPTER EIGHT

Goin' Fishin' with Robbie "The Geek"

March 21, 1998—Saturday

J OE SIPPED HIS HOT CUP OF COFFEE and leaned back in the wicker chair Cindy made him purchase on one of their trips into Sacramento. The early morning sky above the east porch just outside his front door was a husky navy blue—the pre-dawn beginning to lighten the sky. Right before the sun burst over Sunrise Mountain Peak was Joe's favorite time of the day, even better than the sunsets on the master bedroom side of the house.

The menace plane problem hung heavy in his mind. He grated his teeth. He should drive up the old logging road and see where there was a good spot to break the radio frequency and bring that nuisance down. But then what would he do with it?

After Cindy's passing, mornings became his quiet time of reflection … and grief. Today was no different. But one bright spot illuminated his mind. Robbie Meyers, "The Geek," would be heading home today from California State University at Chico for a weekend visit and be here through Sunday for his mom's birthday. Joe couldn't wait to see the kid he and Cindy practically raised.

Robbie's old man was still in jail for nearly killing his mom when the kid was five. His mom, Bonnie Meyers, had waitressed for Ruby and Bill at the Steakhouse during the day and flipped hamburgers at the drive-in at night. She worked like a dog and left the little kid with kind strangers most of the day by necessity. Mostly the kid roamed all over Shadow Pines.

Finding Robbie on the side of the road was the best thing that happened to Joe and Cindy. For Cindy, who'd suffered through the loss of two miscarriages at that time, having Robbie around had been a godsend. Cindy spoiled the kid rotten, though.

He taught Robbie about ranching. There wasn't a piece of electronics on the ranch that Robbie hadn't taken apart and somehow figured out how to put back together. He became Joe's fishing and hunting buddy, horse-exerciser, and cow-puncher. Somehow the kid decided computers were his future and yearned to go to college.

Joe took another sip of the hot brew. The strong, earthy, scent of richly ground Chilean coffee beans hit his nose. Grinding his beans for a unique blend was something Cindy introduced him to, that and tea. He found tea distasteful, but Lettie, consistently made him iced tea for warm afternoons.

The German Shepherds sat at Joe's feet, their noses up in the cold March breeze, their ears circulating back and forth like antennas.

Joe raised Shep from a puppy. He carried the usual characteristics of a Shepherd—patches of brown and gold on his coat, with the usual black down his spine to his rump. Spike, pure black, was a stray Joe found wandering around the mountains without dog tags. After a search for owners with no response, Joe kept him. The dogs bonded like littermates.

Cindy's grandfather, Elmer had raised Shepherds. Her Pa, Bert Johnsen had as well. Joe's two dogs descended from Elmer's original pair. He spent years training them to work cattle and to patrol the ranch grounds. Isolated as he was out here among the mountain, deep river valleys, and thick pine trees, he needed all the protection he could muster.

Shep growled low in his chest.

"What is it, boy?"

Shep stood, his nose pointed toward the gravel lane to the front gate. Spike got to his feet, too, his nose in the air. Someone was coming down the long drive from the cattle guard gate, the entrance to his ranch compound.

It wasn't long before Joe heard the rumbling of an old engine—really old. Could it be The Geek?

He jumped to his feet and leaned on the porch's railing. "Well, whaddya think, guys. I think it's Robbie."

In the dim light of the early dawn, Robbie's 1978 Mercury Comet chugged down the driveway spewing gravel and smoke. Poor kid needed new transportation. Good thing Cindy wasn't here. She'd make Joe go out and buy the kid a new car, one of those fancy foreign jobs. Joe took pride in knowing his and Cindy's secret trust fund kept Robbie in college. Not that he or his mom knew about that. That's the way Cindy and he had helped.

Joe had worked with the banker in Shadow Pines, and Robbie believed the money came from a town fund. So, the boy thought the whole town had helped.

The belching car pulled up to the hitching post in front of the ranch house, and Robbie killed the engine. Joe could see his smile though the sun wasn't quite up yet.

"How you doing, Mr. Joe?" Robbie said as he opened his squeaking driver's side door.

"Better than your car." Joe chuckled and removed his new hat to run his hand through his freshly washed hair. He wished he'd shaved. Probably looked like an old reprobate to the kid. Like he should be standing on a city street corner with a tin cup in his hand.

Robbie leaped up the four stairs onto the porch. He rushed to Joe and swallowed him up in a giant bear hug, nearly broke Joe's ribs. "I'm so glad to see you, Mr. Joe."

"Why are you here so early in the morning? Where's your mother?"

Robbie leaned back but didn't let go of Joe. "I knew you'd be high-tailin' it up to the mountains early and Mom's already at the café cooking for the tourists." He shrugged. "Since she purchased that place, she's been working non-stop. I figured right now would be a great time to catch up with you."

Joe stepped out of Robbie's grasp, sat back down. "You figured right, son. Sit. Tell me all about school."

"There isn't a lot to tell." He dropped into a chair like the one Joe chose. "I like college, but it's a lot harder than I imagined. I love my classes, don't get me wrong, especially the computer classes, but the professors really pile on the work, and I have to spend a lot of time in the lab working on projects and learning how to program the computers."

"We're … I'm proud of you." Joe swore under his breath. He wasn't part of a "we're" anymore.

"Yeah, I miss her, too."

They were both quiet for a moment, each lost in their memories of Cindy. Right about now Joe could see her strolling out of the kitchen wearing her blue gingham apron. "Come to breakfast, you two."

"Yes, ma'am, Miss Cindy," Robbie would say and bounce into the kitchen for her famous flapjacks and bacon, or biscuits and sausage gravy. Didn't matter what she fixed, Robbie ate like his entire body was empty. "Sure is the best, Miss Cindy."

Cindy would smile and caress his cheek, just like she would have done if he were her son. Sweet memories. It wouldn't do any good to shake his fist at the heavens and shout, unfair. Unfair. She should be here, growing old with him.

The backs of Joe's eyes burned, but he would not cry.

Robbie sniffed and laid a hand on the sleeve of Joe's plaid flannel shirt. "She was a beauty, wasn't she?"

Joe couldn't answer, just nodded.

"She made the best flapjacks in the country. Light and fluffy, tender and delicious."

Joe's tongue stuck to the roof of his mouth.

"She could make a deer roast taste like the finest beef from Texas," Robbie said.

Joe "Mm-hmm'd."

"You wanna go fishing before I head back to town? Dawn's a great time for trout." Robbie looked eager.

Damn kid had grown up on him. Where once before the kid Joe took in resembled a stalk of summer corn, thin and stringy, Cindy's home cooking had put some muscle on him. Today, he'd filled out like a body-builder and had cut his thick, shaggy black hair into a businessman's style—clean sides, tapered back, and curly on top.

He was a man, and Joe respected him like a man. "Let's go fishing, Geek."

Robbie shook his head, but his smile was huge. "Do you have to call me that?"

"Want some breakfast first?"

"Not if you're cooking."

51

Joe and Robbie took Joe's pride and joy—his rig—the turquoise and white 1965 Ford F150 to their favorite fishing hole. The old thing did the back roads better than his newer truck.

"Is the river still running high and clear?" Robbie bounced on the clean row seat of his rig as they jostled along on the old logging road to the north of Joe's ranch.

"You bet."

Robbie rubbed his hands together. "Fish dinner tonight."

Though still early, perhaps he and Robbie would be fortunate enough to see the plane flying over the mountains. Then Joe could track its movements, understand where the thing went.

He parked the truck at the sloping side of the rapidly moving river. Robbie reached Joe's tackle box out of the truck bed and a couple of small folding chairs. Joe grabbed the two fishing poles that hadn't seen much action since the Geek fished here the last time, and a mesh bag filled with drinks. Was that before he went to Chico?

They negotiated their way through the thick pines, over boulders, and above ground roots to the river's edge. They'd fish in a perfectly round backwater section of the river below the rapids but away from midstream. Right now, the river water ran high with winter runoff from the snowpack around Tahoe. Fish congregated at the pool to catch their breath.

"Chilly down here this morning." Robbie shivered.

"Perfect."

"You're thick-skinned, Mr. Joe."

"Fresh kid." Joe laughed.

Robbie unfolded the two chairs and placed them near the shore of the backwater. He wiggled his long body into the small chair and rooted around in Joe's tackle box for hooks and some bait.

Joe laid the two poles down next to Robbie's chair and managed to lower himself into his chair. His body still ached from the early-morning bareback ride on Checkers in front of the stampeding cattle.

The sky, a bright sparkling blue and the river smelling clean and fresh, looking a bit icy, filled Joe with peace. He tied a mesh bag with sodas in it to a tree branch and tossed the net into the cold water. They could make a day of this.

For a while, neither spoke. They didn't have to.

Joe heard that miserable sound first—the buzzing of a small engine.

Robbie looked up. "What's that?"

Joe locked his back molars together. "A menace."

"A what?"

Joe stood, looped his pole through his chair, and secured it. "Come on. I need to show you something."

Robbie climbed out of his chair and did the same thing with his pole. "What?"

Joe didn't wait to answer. He climbed the side of the bank until he stood in a clearing of trees facing Sunrise Mountain. The sunburst over the mountain cast its shimmering glow on his valley and the ranch compound beyond. Thankfully, Ricardo and the boys had moved the cattle closer to the ranch yard. He wouldn't have to worry about another stampede.

Robbie stopped beside Joe and stared up at the mountain. "Where're the cattle?"

"Because of the nuisance, I had Ricardo move them closer to the house."

"What is this nuisance?"

"Look." Joe pointed to the peak. Just above Flat Ridge, the silver demon glided, propeller whirring.

"It's a UAR drone." Robbie shielded his eyes and stared at the approaching plane.

"UAR Drone?"

"Yeah, an unmanned Aerial Reconnaissance plane," Robbie said. "They call them drones because of the droning sound of their little engines."

"How do you know about these?"

Robbie pointed to his head and grinned. "Smarts, Mr. Joe."

"Say, Robbie?"

Robbie turned to stare at Joe. "You don't usually call me by my name."

"There's a first time for everything." Joe chuckled. "How is that thing controlled?"

As the plane flew closer, the noise grew louder.

"Normally, radio controlled." Robbie raised his voice.

"Like radio waves?"

"Yeah, sort of. But not like music over radio waves, signals that control the power of the plane."

The plane dipped into a canyon about four hundred feet from the ground.

"Do you know what the plane is looking for?" Robbie asked.

"Not really, but it's been stampeding the cattle and stock horses, and nearly killed Ricardo and me a couple of days ago."

"Oh, my gosh. Did Ricardo get hurt?"

"No. Thanks for asking about me, Geek."

"You're standing, aren't you? I just figured you were okay." Robbie chuckled. "You are okay, aren't you?"

"I didn't get hurt, but my saddle and hat were destroyed."

"Wow!"

Joe examined Robbie's bright face. "How could someone, ah, take down a plane like that?"

The plane flew up and out of the canyon, back across the face of Sunrise Mountain, and Flat Ridge. It circled back again and returned.

"Why don't you ask the owner of the plane what they're looking for?" Robbie asked.

"I would, but I don't know who the owner is." Joe rubbed his sore neck at the half-lie. "Might be someone from those multi-million-dollar cabin-mansions between here and Tahoe. Damned fool kids have nothing to do but play with the toys rich mommy and daddy lavish on them."

Robbie stroked his chin sporting a five-o'clock shadow. Who knew the kid could grow facial hair? "Could be privately owned."

"If it is, how could someone take it down?"

Robbie's eyebrows drew together. "You'd need a special box to disrupt the radio frequency."

"How hard would it be to find a box like that?" Please don't ask why.

"I could build one, but the person thinking about taking it down would need to find the correct frequency the owner uses for his plane."

Joe knew the Geek was curious, he could read it in his eyes, but he never asked, and Joe would never tell him his plans.

"If someone takes the plane down after severing the frequency, how could they do that?"

The Geek's eyes widened. He flipped around when the plane buzzed low overhead. "I can see why someone would want to get rid of that. How often does it buzz your ranch?"

Joe blew out a breath. "Every day, sometimes twice."

"Wow, man. That sucks."

Stoking his chin again, Joe could see Robbie's mind whirling.

"I think you could find something like a net gun in a sporting goods store in Sacramento. I could find one for someone who might be ready to try and take out the plane." Robbie snickered. "You could hold it hostage until the owners come and tell you they won't fly over your place anymore."

Joe knew who the owners were, and they would not be happy when he took their plane down.

The plane disappeared over Flat Ridge.

Gotcha.

CHAPTER NINE

Mike Sanchez, Agronomist with the Green Thumb

March 22, 1998—Sunday

WORK ON A CATTLE and horse ranch where agriculture grown for feed and for sale didn't stop on the Sabbath day—no rest for a rancher.

Joe, up before dawn, gulped down his favorite roast coffee and ambled out of his house. He'd only been married to Cindy for five years when she decided the renovation of her parents' ranch house needed another redo.

Partial to everything turquoise and decidedly western-themes, she wanted a home dedicated to ranch life in the American West. She called it shabby-Western. Joe called it bunkhouse style. The only concession he got was replacing the weathered and hard to care for clapboard siding with newer vinyl in a pale off-white.

He stood a moment on the wraparound porch facing the east to Sunrise Mountain. He and Cindy didn't want an obstructed view between them and all that beauty, so he and Ricardo cut down a number of pines for pastureland and the view, and milled the logs for the casitas, fence rails, and other building material.

Joe's new barn replaced the one Elmer rebuilt after the original barn burned to the ground from a lightning strike in 1915. It stood one hundred feet from the southeast corner of the house.

Joe's barn was a grand red building with three stories, one story was a bunkhouse complete with a kitchen for his ranch hands, the middle floor for grain and hay storage, and the bottom filled with stalls for milking. They still had twenty head of cows to supply the compound with fresh milk.

Because his horse population and the demand for storage of grain had grown over the years, Joe built a larger stable to the west of the barn and grain silos. The loft above the stalls was filled with hay. The new stalls were as modern as he could make them, everything a discerning horse could require. From the end of the stalls to the front gate of his property bordering the road to Shadow Pines, was a spacious corral, which also had to be cleared of the thick stands of pines. Sal sectioned parts of it off for horses and mules in various stages of training.

Joe stretched and yawned. He jogged down the porch steps and turned to his left, facing the north road leading to the orchards and fields of grains. He was ready to meet up with Miguel "Mike" Sanchez, Ricardo's youngest boy, who also had a casita down the row of modest homes along this road.

To his right, he passed the garage where Sal Sanchez tinkered with his farm equipment and Elmer's old stake-bed truck, circa 1933, and his 1948 Olds sedan. Next came the chicken coops, the hog sheds, and Lettie's fabulous garden plot. The dark, rich earth had been turned over in preparation for her early planting. She grew the biggest, sweetest tomatoes this side of Mexico, even cultivated lemon and avocado trees for her famous guacamole and salsa come fiesta time.

To his left was the remnant of a garden plot Elmer had planted for his wife, Olina. The size of the garden had grown with each new wife. Bert Johnsen's wife, Frances, doubled the size of the plot, and added additional rows of watermelons, cantaloupes, and pumpkins which she sold in town. Cindy had added carrots and potatoes.

Next along the road, was the original two-bedroom casita Elmer built for his new bride. The ranch house he'd won with the ranch in a poker game, turned out to be an abandoned and vermin-invested log cabin. It mysteriously burned down a few months after they took ownership. Seems he had some trouble with a big-wig in Shadow Pines.

Bert and Frances used it as a guest house, but he and Cindy shared the little white house with the picket fence just north of the garden plot after they married in 1975. Seeing it now gave him a special happy/sad ache in his chest.

He strode on.

Sweeping his gaze back across the road, Ricardo, Sal, and Mike had built casitas for their families. Joe loved the vibrant colors Mike's wife insisted they paint each of their cozy homes. The lively coral, yellow, green, and red reminded him of a fiesta.

"Good morning, boss," Mike said with a yawn as he opened the door of his home and stepped on the narrow porch.

Mike, who'd earned a master's degree in Agronomy—the science of horticulture and growing vegetation—from the CSU at Chico, became Joe's right-hand man in charge of farming on the ranch. The money crops he cultivated and raised to maturity kept the ranch afloat until the sale of the cattle each September. What grain, hay, or straw they didn't need to stock for their own cattle and horses, Joe sold to the local feed store in Shadow Pines and Auburn. Some grain shipped by truck to Roseville near Sacramento.

Joe glanced at Mike, nodded. "You ready to go turn out the irrigation water before I head off to church?"

"Let's go."

Today, Mike wore a Levi jacket over a checkered shirt, sturdy jeans, and waders. Like Joe, he hadn't shaved. "I'll get the rig." Mike strolled over to the garage.

Mike, not any taller than his father or older brother, didn't resemble either one of them. Handsome kid. He didn't have the darker Spanish coloring or the weathered look of hard ranch work. He resembled Lettie's side of the family, light tan skin and bourbon-colored eyes. Mike had an innate sense of all things growing. Joe let him practice his art with the fertile land of Sunrise Ranch, and both had prospered.

Joe removed his new hat, ran his hands over the edges to keep working the curl into the rim. New hats needed to feel old.

After Joe climbed into the rig, Mike drove along the rutted dirt road between the acres of rich, black earth awaiting the insertion of oats, barley, and alfalfa. Some ground fog lay on the fields before the warm morning sun could burn it off.

"The winter wheat is about ready to cut, and the durum wheat on the north side will follow in a couple of months," Mike said. "I think we'll have another couple of tons for sale and shipment."

"Good," Joe grunted.

He remembered the days of Cindy's dad struggling to raise even a pitiful hay crop. Until Joe studied up on the yield, how to plant correctly and cultivate, the ranch barely grew enough to feed their cattle, let alone sell any extra.

Opening the chute on the irrigation levy off a tributary of the river running through Joe's property took both struggling together.

"I don't remember it sticking like this before," Mike grunted as he manhandled his side of the enormous wheel-valve.

"Rust." Joe laughed.

They eventually worked the chute up, and icy cold water flowed into the channel that Mike had dug on the slope. The water cascaded down rolling hills to the hayfield rows and eventually into the orchards of almond and mandarin orange trees.

Almond production was Joe's big money crop and the Satsuma mandarin orange trees second best. The air was heavy with their orange-blossom fragrance. The first trees had come to the valley back in the days when the Chinese worked the railroad. The groves were Mike's big idea about ten years ago.

Auburn held a Mandarin Festival in November, and Mike usually took top prize for his splendid orange citrus fruit. The almonds Joe sold to a national almond-selling corporation for peoples' snacks. Selling something people could enjoy, Joe got a real boost of pride. He'd also took pride in pleasing Cindy's dad. He remembered a day before Bert passed when they spoke in the fields.

"I'm making the ranch pay, Bert," Joe had said to Bert while gazing out at the fields of oats and wheat.

Bert had smiled and patted Joe on the back. "You're the son I always wanted."

Joe missed Cindy and her dad.

Taking shovels from the truck, Joe and Mike worked the water all the way to the end of the long row of hay. They would leave the water flowing most of Sunday and come back later to replace the chute. Irrigated crops did better than rainfall-water crops, Mike told him.

Joe stopped, his back aching and rested his hands on the shovel handle. "Looks like a good crop."

Mike pointed to the acreage just beyond the hay fields. "Normally, barley would be planted over there. I think I'm going to plant oats and rotate out the barley this year to control for root-knot nematode."

Joe squinted. "What's that?"

"Root-knot nematodes are plant-parasitic worms. They exist in soil in areas with hot climates or short winters. But rotating the crops shakes them up, keeps them from destroying the crop."

"Glad to hear it. The farming side of the business is your baby," Joe said.

Mike smiled. "I'm real grateful to you for allowing me to farm your land."

"I'm the one who's grateful, and we all prosper."

Later that Sunday morning—**The Pastor Does Standup**

In his Lettie-fresh-pressed Sunday suit, Joe settled himself on the back pew in the little Shadow Pines Christian Church run by a high-school friend of Cindy's, Pastor Benjamin English. He made the service by one minute to ten. He hoped God would forgive him. All the other members of the congregation took seats before he arrived. Some turned around to smile at him. Joe tipped his head at Bella, Ruby's cook. She beamed her five hundred-watt smile at him.

The community constructed the little church out of Ponderosa Pine and the wood paneling smelled fresh and woodsy like sitting in a grove of lengthy Ponderosa and Sugar pines on Sunrise Mountain.

The choir was singing, "How Great Thou Art," Cindy's favorite. For a moment, she sat beside him, clutching his hand, and singing slightly off-key. He rubbed his chest where the grief hit him the hardest.

Why Cindy? Why did you have to leave me?

Joe hummed with the third verse, and the congregation was encouraged to sing the fourth.

When Christ shall come, with shout of acclamation,
And take me home, what joy shall fill my heart.
Then I shall bow, in humble adoration,
And then proclaim, "My God, how great Thou art!"

Tears welled in his eyes as a soft, gentle pressure built around his hand. Was she here? Was Cindy aware of him, his struggles to remain sane without her?

He glanced to the side when someone sat beside him. Dr. Samantha Stone, the town veterinarian. His heart did a little bump. A thin draping dress covered her slender legs and curvy body and shifted when she sat and crossed her legs. Had she always been so shapely?

He shook himself. Don't even go there.

He ran his finger between his collar and his strangling throat. Too tight.

"Good morning," she mouthed to him.

He nodded, crossed his arms over his chest, and tried not to think about attractive Sam and her long legs.

Pastor Benjamin English stepped up to the pulpit and looked out over the congregation. He was the same age as his Cindy, had been the cut-up of her high school. He had a quick wit and a keen sense of humor. Everyone was sure he'd head to Hollywood or go out on the road as a comedian. No one could have imagined Ben would put on the white collar and black shirt and trousers and preach about Christ.

"My good brothers and sisters, welcome to the Shadow Pines Christian Church. It's a glorious morning to be a faithful member of the congregation." He paused and looked at each member individually.

Joe could count on the reverend to open his sermon with a joke. He didn't have to wait or be disappointed.

Pastor Ben smiled. "I heard a story about a minister who told his congregation, 'Next week I plan to preach about the sin of lying. To help you understand my sermon, I want you all to read Mark 17.

"'The following Sunday, as he prepared to deliver his sermon, the minister asked for a show of hands. He asked, How many have read Mark 17? Every hand went up. The minister

61

smiled and said, Mark has only sixteen chapters. I will now proceed with my sermon on the sin of lying'."

The audience glanced around blankly as if they didn't know if they should laugh or not. Joe, however, belted out a laugh and besides him, Sam chuckled softly. The rest of the congregation eventually laughed, too.

Much too aware of the woman sitting beside him, and mad at himself for noticing everything about her, he strained to listen. By the end of the service, he couldn't remember what subject Pastor English taught. Had it been about lying, like his joke? Joe desperately needed some fresh air and to get back his level head.

He was a one-woman man.

"It's okay, Joe. Sam is my friend."

"Did you say something?" He leaned toward Sam.

"I said 'amen'." Had Sam's eyes always been a dark gray, nearly a gray/green surrounded by an even darker circle of black? "The sermon was especially filled with the spirit today, don't you agree?" she said.

"Sure. Great sermon." Liar.

He lifted his chin to ease his tightening collar. Blasted tie. He couldn't wait to get home and shed this noose around his neck. Dear Lord, he wished himself anywhere but here sitting next to someone who stirred his blood and made his mouth go dry. He hadn't felt that way since….

"Can I come out to the ranch today?" Sam asked.

Joe nearly swallowed his teeth. "W-what for?"

She stood, chuckling. "Shep and Spike are due for their annual checkup and their DHPP shots." She tsked. "You haven't brought them to the clinic, so I need to come to you."

"Why do they need shots so soon?"

"You know, for distemper, hepatitis, parvovirus, and parainfluenza. They're due."

"Are they really necessary?" He felt like a drowning man looking into her eyes. Hell, what was the matter with him? He was swearing in church.

She took his arm, and together they walked out into the brilliant sunshine and cool March Sunday of Shadow Pines. Her hand felt right on his arm, different from Cindy's touch, but right.

"I'll follow you to the ranch after I stop by the clinic and get my bag."

What could he say? Stay away, you're too tempting to a man who's sworn off women.

"Sure." He gulped. He was in big trouble.

CHAPTER TEN

Doctor Samantha Stone, Veterinarian for the Ranch

SAMANTHA LOVED ANIMALS. They didn't get drunk and beat the crap out of you for no reason. Or treat you with disrespect. If she got bit or kicked, she'd done something to annoy the animal.

After changing out of her Sunday dress and into her comfortable blue jeans, cotton blue-plaid shirt, and cowgirl boots, Samantha was ready to get down to business.

She adored the drive out to Sunrise Ranch. Today, the clear sky glistened like a diamond. Sometimes she dawdled and stopped to admire the crystal sparkles shimmering on the surface of the river hundreds of feet below in the gorge. She wished Joe was beside her to enjoy it.

After arriving at Joe Mack's ranch and parking, Samantha removed her doctor's bag and headed to the horse barn. He was mucking out stalls in the stable. For several minutes, she stood just out of the late afternoon's warmth and watched this rugged man work. Oh, Joe was rough around the edges—tough and bull-headed, but he was also tender like when he gentled a horse.

So much strength and power lived in that tall, lanky body of his. He'd lost some weight since Cindy's passing and was too thin. Lettie needed to beef up his diet, help him fill out a bit. He was one handsome, masculine cowpoke with his hawk-like facial features, lake blue eyes, and deep dimples. However attractive all those sinewy muscles were—and Samantha wished like nobody's business he'd hold her in those arms—it was his kind eyes that could float her boat.

Mostly when he looked at her, he frowned. Samantha figured it was just him figuring out if he could still be true to Cindy and let himself love her. He didn't smile enough, in her estimation to really detect his dimples. He did, however, give a huge laugh at the pastor's joke this morning. That tickled her, and she couldn't help but laugh as well.

This afternoon, Joe wore his six foot-two like a determined man with places to go. His cotton plaid work-shirt couldn't hide his broad shoulders, or his jeans his narrow hips. His thick brown hair gently sprinkled with a tiny bit of gray around the edges, had grown a little long and shaggy. It was perfect for him—perfect for her fingers to smooth down.

Joe threw on the last shovel of manure in his wheelbarrow and noticed her watching him. Busted. "Good afternoon," Samantha said.

His warm welcome was to raise his chin in greeting before hoisting the heavy wheelbarrow and sauntering away. Stupid man.

He whistled for the dogs who came running.

Samantha knelt to be eye level, as they approached her, however cautiously.

Shep and Spike never had to be told "at ease" before they allowed her to touch and examine them, even giving them their shots. Shep, the larger of the two was also the gentler, though neither could be considered pets. Spike, not as large, but black as night looked dangerous as a cobra. He allowed his shots, but Samantha watched him.

Calling to Shep, he stepped forward. She stroked Shep's head and checked him over and gave him his annual shots. He didn't stir or wince. "Good boy. You don't mind your checkup and shots, do you?"

Shep scanned her with soft brown eyes. His tongue lolled out of his mouth in a doggy grin. She chuckled. "What a sweetheart." She stroked his coat.

"Don't let anybody hear you call him that," Joe said nearly grinning. "It'll ruin his rep."

Samantha's gaze flew to Joe's scowling face and yet tender eyes. "His heart is safe with me," she said, with a double meaning. Her heart thudded behind her ribs. She hadn't heard that many words at one time come out of Joe's mouth in like forever. Hesitant for a moment, she pushed an errant lock of hair behind her ear. Maybe he was coming around.

Spike padded over to her and held motionless as she examined him and gave him his shot. "You're not such a tough guy, are you?"

Spike examined her as though trying to decide if she were friend or foe.

Joe leaned against the open-door frame with his arms crossed over his chest and his feet crossed at the ankles. Anybody would think he was protecting himself from her. She couldn't help but laugh. He looked so serious. He'd been nervous in church when she sat next to him. Jumpy as a male rabbit in spring.

"Don't let your guard down around him, Sam. He can be unpredictable."

So, can you, she wished to say but held her tongue.

Back before Cindy and Joe married, Samantha had been jealous of her friend's good fortune—a ranch the size of Sunrise Ranch and a good, strong man for a husband. Did he know she'd had a big crush on him, had long before he married Cindy—not that she'd tell him though?

When Joe brought Cindy home to die in her bed, Samantha looked after her while Joe worked the ranch during the day. She'd slept in one of the spare bedrooms at night to be close. A hospice nurse slept in the other room. When Cindy had groaned in pain one afternoon, and the nurse was on her lunch break, Sam had run to her, held her hand, and turned up the morphine drip.

"I need you to look after Joe when I'm gone," Cindy had choked out.

Sam gritted her teeth, shoving a lock of hair behind her ear. "You're not going anywhere yet, missy."

Cindy smiled a bit lopsided. "Promise me. He'll need you."

Samantha kept her eye on Joe, but it wasn't easy. Her little crush had grown into something that rang like a song in her chest when he was near. Luckily, she could shower his animals with her love and affection and wait for him to open his eyes and see her.

Oh, well. She could hope and pray that day would be soon. She wasn't getting any younger.

She gave Spike a doggy treat which he swallowed whole. "Chew, please. I don't want to have to operate on you out here in the barn."

Joe snorted. "That's how he eats."

"Do they hunt for little animals around the ranch?"

"If I tell them to, otherwise, no."

"Good. I don't want them eating rabid animals. Rabies has been detected in the smaller animals of the forest."

Joe uncrossed his arms and feet. "You heading home now?"

Was he that anxious to get rid of her? Stupid man. "I figured you could serve me a glass of iced tea before I have to make the hot drive back to town."

For a moment, his eyes darted back and forth as if he were thinking of an excuse why he couldn't do that, couldn't have her in his house—Cindy's home.

"Never mind," she murmured and dropped her gaze to her boots.

"That's ... that's a good idea. I think Lettie left a pitcher of iced tea in the refrigerator. I'll go set up some ice and glasses." He turned to leave and stopped. "On the porch okay?"

Sam moved like she was going to rise from her kneeling position. Joe double-timed over to her and offered his hand. Did he think she was too old or might fall getting up? Touching him would only kick-start her heart again, but she placed her hand in his open palm.

When their hands slid together, a jolt like a mule kick took her breath away. She glanced into Joe's eyes to judge his reaction. For a moment, he looked as if he'd stepped on a rattler.

Sam chuckled as he dropped her hand.

Stretching out her aging, aching back, she said, "I'm getting too old for this job."

His brow wrinkled. "You. Too old. Never."

"How sweet." She sighed. "Can I help you with the iced tea?"

Joe barely nodded as he spun and strode toward the ranch house. Stubborn, stupid man. He was going to be harder to crack than one of his almond shells.

The front door to his farmhouse stood open, the closed screen door kept the bugs out. Joe tugged the screen open and held it for her brush to by him. She smiled at this chivalry and chuckled when he sucked in his breath, leaning away from her like she was contagious.

"Thank you." Samantha stepped into the cool living room.

Cindy had loved her western theme home from the furniture to the knick-knacks. She had the walls painted a soft turquoise before she got sick. Since she was quite an artist, she'd painted three pictures. One of her horse, Ivy, one of Checkers, Joe's buckskin, and the other of cattle grazing on the range. She also made the gingham and lace curtains hanging at the windows. Joe hadn't changed them.

A large, comfortable tan leather L-shaped sofa with Indian patterned throw pillows dominated the room, along with Joe's substantial brown leather chair facing a big screen TV on a dark walnut stand. Out here Joe had to have a satellite dish to get any TV programming.

Cindy's grandfather had built the massive river-rock fireplace in the corner. Cindy's dad had replaced the mantle with a blackened railroad tie he'd found in the mountains by an abandoned gold mine.

A large square coffee table which was a cedar chest with a double-folding lid stood in front of the sofa and held Cindy's prize possession—a Remington sculpture, the bronco buster—a twentieth anniversary present from Joe.

Samantha caressed the rough metal as she passed on her way to the kitchen.

Cindy redesigned the kitchen after her parents passed. She'd painted the old cabinets a turquoise blue and distressed them. The old wood-burning stove was replaced with a modern range with a grill, and where the old ice box stood, a side-by-side refrigerator took up the space. Joe crafted the countertops out of pine he'd stained and sealed against blemishes.

They were stunning. Cindy loved her kitchen and became the best bread maker in Shadow Pines. She won blue ribbons at the county fair for her molasses bread—a secret recipe handed down from her great-grandmother.

A large square oak kitchen table and four chairs also painted turquoise sat to the side of the kitchen with only one place setting on the tabletop.

Samantha would change Joe's eating alone if he'd let her.

Someone, no doubt Lettie, had placed fresh sunflowers in a turquoise vase and a plate of gingersnaps on the table. Samantha wondered if Joe even saw them.

"Glasses." He pointed to the cupboard above the sink.

She reached for two tall glasses, also clear turquoise and placed them on the counter. "Cindy loved this kitchen."

Joe winced, and ice cubes clinked against the glass of the iced tea pitcher.

"I'm sorry," she murmured.

He didn't say anything, just moved to the counter and poured the two glasses with the light-brown liquid. "Sugar and lemon?"

"I'll get them." She stepped to the cupboard she remembered from her stay with Cindy that held the sugar and grabbed the bowl shaped like a boot with a tiny spoon shaped like a Colt .45. She must have offended Joe by the scowl on his face.

"Have you seen the plane again?" Samantha asked.

Joe halted, shifted to look at her. "Yesterday. The kid was here."

"I'm sorry it's bothering you. Do you think it's a neighbor's?"

"Oh, yeah. It's a neighbor's, all right."

She nearly laughed. If the plane belonged to the government, they were going to regret flying over Joe's property testing their spying capabilities. He was overprotective of the ranch.

"Has Sheriff Warner done anything about contacting the owner?"

Joe huffed and stared at her.

"I didn't think so." She sighed. "I'm sorry about him."

Joe took the two glasses and stomped back through the doorway, through the living room, and back out on the porch.

In the vegetable drawer of the refrigerator, Samantha found a lemon and sliced it for the tea. Carrying the sugar, spoons, cookies, and lemons in a hand-made turquoise bowl, she wandered through the living room and outside. The screen door slapped closed behind her.

In his huffing mood, it was going to be tough to talk to him about his wife.

Samantha stiffened her spine, totally up for the challenge.

Joe placed the two drinks on a small wicker table between the high-backed wicker chairs. Samantha sat and set the items next to the glasses. Not a tea drinker, doctoring her tea with four heaping teaspoons of sugar was necessary.

Inclined back in the chair, she studied Joe as he leaned against the post of the porch, gazing out toward the solid line of pines and the forest to the south.

"You're going to have to talk about her sometime," Sam said.

Nothing.

"She was my friend. I lost her, too."

He shifted until his back was ramrod straight, remained silent.

"Do you think you're the only one who grieves for her?"

Joe's face hardened into his famous scowl. "She was my wife." Bitterness hardened his raised voice. "No one misses her more than I do."

"I knew her longer than you. She and I grew up together. We went to college together. She was more of a sister to me than my own sister. Cindy nursed me back to health when my husband beat me senseless." She took a drink of the sweet liquid, letting it coat her parched throat. "You don't have a monopoly on sorrow and pain where Cindy is concerned."

Joe hung his head like he regretted his outburst. "She loved you like a sister."

She wasn't sure she heard him right. "I loved her. Don't you think I would have gladly traded places with her when she got sick? If I could have stepped into her body and taken on that wretched pain, I would have."

His shoulders relaxed. He approached a chair and sat. Nothing passed between them for a few minutes.

Samantha watched the horses milling around the corral. She needed to make sure they were doing all right before she left.

"I keep blaming myself." Joe blew out a shaking breath.

"Why? What for?"

"I keep thinking if I hadn't gotten her pregnant four times, this … cancer wouldn't have gotten her."

"You don't believe that, do you?" Samantha asked. "Cindy wanted children like she needed air. We're all born with the seeds of cancer. None of us know when they will develop." She put the glass down. "She loved you so much. You were her life."

"She comes to me, you know."

Stunned, Samantha could only stare at Joe, hand trembling. Was he losing it? "I didn't know."

"Sometimes at night or when I'm sitting on the bedroom side of the porch," he whispered." I feel her next to me. Most times she talks to me. I know she's around."

Samantha always wondered where the life-giving, animated spirit of a person went after fleeing from the body leaving behind a cold, clay-like shell. Could they be close to us humans? Her Native ancestors believed in an afterlife.

She leaned back in the chair, unexplained comfort seeped into her bones. Believing that Cindy could be close wasn't a stretch of her imagination.

"Do you remember the day she returned to the ranch after her college graduation?" she asked. "What a special day that was."

Joe stared out into space as if living that time over again. He eventually smiled. "Ricardo and I had spent a whole year repairing fences, painting the barn and outbuildings, fixing broken farm equipment, and the crop of hay and alfalfa never looked so good."

He chuckled. "I had this idea to surprise Cindy with a new horse. Ricardo and I went to the government stock auction in Auburn a couple of months before she returned.

"As you know, we found that frisky little filly, the one-year-old palomino with the white mane and tail and four white stockings," Joe said. "Wild as the wind."

"I remember. Cindy was sure surprised."

"It took all those months to gentle that wild spirit without breaking it. Ricardo had a way with gentling and training a horse to be a cutter for cattle. I picked out the name Stockings."

Samantha smiled. "I remember her whole family was there, most of her friends from high school who were still around, and Ricardo, Lettie, and their kids. Also, several of the other farmers in the area and the ranch hands."

"It was the year before Elmer passed, in 1976. He nearly made eighty-six years." Joe frowned. "He loved cake and ice cream."

He paused, lowered his voice. "You were there."

Samantha had a crush on him even though she'd married that drunk, Stone, right out of high school. Did Joe know that?

Joe leaned forward, clasped his hands together. "Ricardo told Cindy he needed help with something in the barn. Before she got there, I told her to close her eyes—we had a surprise for her. We'd tied the palomino to one of the stalls, had repaired Cindy's old cutting saddle, and had the filly ready for a ride."

"I remember her face when she opened her eyes," Samantha said. "She screamed, and jumped around, and cried at the same time. She was so happy. I've never seen such love shining from someone's eyes before she hugged you and kissed your cheek." She chuckled. "You blushed."

Joe glanced away. "We went riding that day, out over the towering hills and deep arroyos. After that, she'd pack a picnic sometimes, and we'd ride out and eat up at Flat Rock, watch the cattle grazing on the range. She won a couple of barrel racing events at the local rodeos on her little palomino. She named her Ivy because she wasn't happy with Stockings."

"She made you buy that old truck then, didn't she?"

Joe's eyes got glassy. "She said she'd drive out with me. I knew I loved her then."

He fell silent after that, sipping his tea and nibbling on one of Lettie's cookies, letting his gaze roam over his compound.

After Bert passed, Joe turned the ranch into a thriving enterprise. Because of Cindy's passing, he became stuck in neutral. Ricardo and his boys, along with several ranch hands did much of the work. He needed to be shaken up, awaken to life around him, and to her love.

Samantha had to tell him how she felt even if he balked and threw her off the ranch for good.

She drew in a shuttering breath and held it. Now or never.

"Joe?" She exhaled, closed her eyes, unable to bear seeing his dismissal of her. "I lov—, ah … you need to know I care about you."

CHAPTER ELEVEN
Ricardo and Salvador Sanchez—Working the Ranch Hands

March 23, 1998—Monday

ALVADOR SANCHEZ—Sal to everyone—rose early. He saddled Chaco, Papa's pinto, and his horse, a chestnut named Casi, in the stables. They were heading out to check on the cattle. Papa moved the animals closer to the compound last week, so they wouldn't be run off by the "flying silver demon," but cattle wandered where the grass and their bellies led them.

Finished with the saddles, he led the two horses over to Papa and Mamá's casita. He couldn't wait to see this demon of Papa's.

"You cinch up tight?" Papa said when he strolled out of the main house he shared with Mamá. Sal, Miguel, and their sister Leandra had grown up in this home.

This morning, Papa carried a leather satchel hopefully loaded with tender, flaky empanadas filled with shredded beef, chipotles, adobo, and onions for their lunch, as well as a canteen of water. Better be some of Mamá's homemade salsa in there as well.

Papa yawned and looked at the still dark sky. "We make sure *ganada* move close to home."

"Sure, Papa, we'll move the *cattle* closer. Should we bring our rifles in case we need to shoot down the demon?"

Papa frowned. "You should take this *amenaza*, this threat seriously."

Not about to put his rifle back in the house, Sal shoved his Winchester .30-30 into the scabbard. He stepped up into the stirrup and swung his leg over the saddle. *Dios mío*, he loved riding. Much more than his younger brother, Mike, the smart-ass Ph.D.

Papa swung up into his saddle, his old bones creaking as bad as the hand-tooled leather saddle Sal'd made for him. He smoothed his thick green wool poncho around him, the one

73

Mamá made for him. Papa loved green, and this one was warm. Perhaps that was why he also loved the ranch.

"You okay, Papa?"

Papa stretched his back, his leathery, weathered face puckered. "*Que*? Why not okay?"

Sal snorted. "You're too tough an old bird to be anything but okay."

"You believe it."

Sal and Mike worried about Papa and Mamá. The family, taken in by Elmer, had seen hard times. Ruined crops, cattle rustlers, harsh winters, forest fires, and low cattle prices, had tested their spirit. Living here in America and working for Elmer and Bert was their life.

Papa had been born to ranching having worked with his father in Baja, California before coming across the border to pick fruit for American farmers. At the tender age of seventeen, he struck out on his own and wound up on a truck to Sacramento to pick fruit. He and Mamá met at a dance in Auburn and fell in love.

When work ended, they headed northeast for Tahoe and ended up on the canyon road that passed by Sunrise Ranch. Elmer saw them—young, frightened, poor, and pregnant with Sal. He took them in. Sal, Mike, and Leandra, their baby sister, loved living on Joe's ranch.

But Papa's back was bent, and his legs bowed from time spent bending over in the fields and most of his life on the back of a horse, so they worried about him.

Together they rode into the pre-dawn, Shep and Spike running after them, when Papa whistled. Shep was a good dog, but Sal was cautious of Spike. An all-black dog held superstitions for him. Still, they were great to have along when moving the stubborn herd. They were loyal, intelligent, and had strong protective natures toward Papa and Joe. A lot of people didn't know they were bred for herding cattle.

Dew lay heavy on the short grass of the rolling hills. His horse, Casi, high-stepped like she didn't care to get her hooves damp. "There, there delicate lady." Sal patted her neck, and she calmed.

After a mile or so, Papa stopped. He gazed out over the pasture land. "Some of the *ganada*, they wander away. Not all here."

Crap. A roundup. Sal silently cursed. "We'd best get at it. I don't want to be out here all day. The new headlight came in for Elmer's old stake bed truck. I want to get it installed today."

"You and your autos." Papa shook his head. "Look to your work."

"Yes, Papa."

Papa whistled for the dogs. "Boys round up *ganada*."

They watched the dogs work the cattle.

After a while, Sal heard something. Over the din the cattle made as the dogs barked and nipped at their heels, he recognized the low moan of an engine. Didn't sound like a car or a ranch rig, but something smaller.

He shaded his eyes and glanced toward the sunrise. The sun glinted off something shiny crossing over Flat Ridge heading in their direction. The cattle stopped moving, their ears perking up to listen.

"*Demonio de plateado*," Papa shouted and spurred Chaco toward the approaching plane—if that's what it was.

"Papa wait." He heeled Casi's side, and she flew over the grassland. Fool old man would fall off and break his neck. "Stop, Papa."

The silver object—the small plane—took a sharp turn and skimmed the face of Sunrise Mountain heading north. Nothing up there but sagebrush and scrub oaks, no trees of significant size. If they were scanning for forest fires, that wouldn't be the place he'd look.

Sal heeled Casi harder in the sides and laid low over her back. "Fly, Casi, fly."

Why didn't the people controlling the plane skim the dense forest region east of Sunrise Mountain toward Tahoe? Last twenty years had left that area bone dry. They hadn't had a deep snowpack until this year.

Before they reached the foothills—the first group of small hills before the mighty Sunrise Mountain range—the plane dipped. Sal didn't think a drone could fly that close to the ground.

75

He yanked on Casi's reins and she clambered to a stop beside Papa who'd reined in Chaco.

The plane skimmed the lower mountains below Sunrise Peak. It was approaching their position quickly. Sal reached for his rifle, aimed, and fired. The little plane dipped its wing but didn't go down.

"I got it," he yelled.

"Holy mother of God, no shoot it," Papa said, his voice in a rage. "*El gobierno*—the government will be angry."

"They damned well better keep their spy plane away from Joe's land." Satisfied, Sal stuffed his rifle back in the scabbard. "Let's get the cattle back down the range before they stampede again."

Ricardo shook his head. He watched the plane circle a couple of times, disappear in some of the box canyons around Mesa de Salvia and return to pass over Flat Ridge. Government property. How could Salvador, be so *¡estúpido!* to shoot it? What if he had shot down the *demonio*? The *gobierno* would come to take him away. Prison. Ricardo could not have his oldest son in prison.

"*Vámonos, mi hijo.*" He nudged Chaco with his knees and bounded into a gallop.

Together they dashed back to the scattered herd. From a sweeping arroyo to the west, Ricardo heard the bellowing of a cow. "Perhaps a cow got herself tangled up in vines," he said when he calmed down enough to speak to him. "We look."

"Sure Papa." Salvador's tanned face reddened.

He should look ashamed. *¡Estúpido!*

The scene inside the arroyo scrambled Ricardo's breakfast in his stomach. The cow must have run from the noise of the demon, trampled her calf to death. She had then fallen and broken her leg. She lay at the bottom of the arroyo. The smell of death curled in his nose. He crossed himself. "Ah, Querido Dios. Señor Joe, he no be happy about this."

"I'm so sorry, Papa." Salvador slid off his horse. He crouched, placed his hand on the small calf, its neck oddly bent. "At least the calf died instantly."

Ricardo shook his head and uttered some Spanish curses. "This should not happen. *Gobierno* killed them." The mother thrashed around and bellowed. "She will have to be put down and skinned, the meat frozen."

Salvador straightened and frowned. "Such a waste."

"I hate to tell Señor Joe. He will be *furioso*." He turned to Salvador. "Return to garage and get rig and flatbed trailer. Bring back Miguel and some of the hands."

"Do you want me to tell Joe?"

Ricardo rubbed his aching neck. He was getting too old for all the bad of ranching, the storms, the dead cattle, the ruined crops. Not so much since Joe took over from his father-in-law, but some wore on the soul. "Bring him as well. We'll need all hands to lift the cow."

The death of the cow and her calf would send Joe into the mountains after the demon for sure. Ricardo would not let him go alone. Joe could not go to prison, also. Not if he, Ricardo, could stop another hombre from doing something *¡estúpido!*

Ricardo watched his oldest son ride off toward the compound. The boy was so much like himself. Impetuous, bull-headed, *¡estúpido!* Ricardo chuckled. "I would have shot the demon as well, *mi hijo*."

SRM Facility—**East Side of Sunrise Mountain**

Dr. Paul Basua examined AIDA after it returned from its morning search for the silver mine. What would his defense contractor client say if he knew the major was on the take—using the plane as his personal search for riches?

Paul had long since proven the plane maneuverable enough to patrol the jungles of South America looking for drug smugglers unseen. The only thing left for him to work out was making the plane's motor quieter. Not an easy task given the low drone of the tiny engine.

His two assistants, who knew nothing but what Paul told them, helped him lift it onto the examining table.

"Doctor Basua?" one of his assistants said, his hand on the wing. "I think someone shot AIDA"

Paul scurried around to the other side of the plane. He pushed his assistant out of the way. He uttered some choice curse words in Hindi. "Sorry. Pardon my French. The major will go off and blame me. I cannot have this."

He felt along the light aluminum wing. A bullet hole went clean through the soft metal. It was a wonder the plane had not gone down. He would have to review the tapes of the flight, see if there was anyone out there on the rangeland interfering with the flight of his plane.

"What do you want us to do, Doctor?" the second assistant asked. "Should we call the major?"

"Bloody hell, no." Paul slapped the table. He had to think. Could he patch up the hole before the major returned from his trip to Sacramento? "Take an early lunch. No, take the rest of the day off. You are not needed anymore, at least for today. I have to consider all of my options."

The two assistants removed their lab coats and left. When the door closed, the phone rang. Please don't be the major.

"Dr. Paul Basua here."

"Dr. Basua, you don't know me, but I'm the sheriff in Shadow Pines. Sheriff Cody Warner."

The blood rushed from Paul's head. He stumbled over and sank into his rolling desk chair. "What can I do for you, Sheriff?"

"I heard talk you might be testing some type of military spy plane over Sunrise Mountain," Warner said.

Paul winced. "I'm not at liberty to say."

"So, you are testing a military plane used for spying over the mountain range?"

"I cannot say one way or another."

"According to one of my ... citizens in the valley, a small plane has been harassing their ranch and cattle on the west side of Sunrise Mountain. I was hoping you might know something about this," the sheriff said and paused. "Maybe you could tell those responsible not to fly on the west side anymore. Cattle are this rancher's bread and butter."

"Pardon." Paul scratched his head with a trembling hand. "Bread and butter?"

"You know, his livelihood, his income."

"Of course. I understand. A real bugger of a problem."

"Yeah, a real bugger," the sheriff murmured.

"I do not know how I can help."

"I'd appreciate it if you would pass a message along to the person or group in charge of the plane and let them know the problem it's causing one of my … citizens. I would hate to have to investigate further."

Paul coughed. Was the Sheriff threatening him? Major Donald would be furious. They did not need a copper snooping around their operation. They could not lose their grant money or have the project removed from his grasp. If Major Donald did not get his mercenary hands on the other end of the silver mine, he'd be angry in spades.

"Can you do that for me, Dr. Basua?" the Sheriff asked.

"I will certainly look into it." The words were out of Paul's mouth before he could cut them off. "If I knew of anyone flying such an object on the west side of Sunrise Mountain, that is."

"Glad to hear it. I'll be checking back. I wouldn't want to hear from this particular citizen your plane is still harassing his cattle." The Sheriff hung up before Paul could answer.

"Bloody hell."

Paul was going to have to be economical with the truth with the major if he didn't want to get it in the neck and find himself in a research facility in Alaska, or at the bottom of one of Sunrise cliffs in a deep ravine.

The damaged plane would throw a spanner in the works if Major Donald found out.

He would flail the skin off Paul and not give two hoots about him.

CHAPTER TWELVE
Dying Cattle on Sunrise Ranch

March 24, 1998—Tuesday

SLEEP WAS IMPOSSIBLE. Since Joe's run-in with Dr. Sam on Sunday and the dead cow and calf Sal and Ricardo found Monday morning, sleep eluded him. He sat on the side of the bed he'd shared with Cindy. He buried his head in his hands as his feet hit the cold hardwood floor.

"I could've used your advice Sunday, sweetheart. I only seriously dated one woman in my life. Sam scares me some." Sam was permanent. None of the other women sweeping in and out of his life before Cindy or during his military career was the type you wanted in your life.

He listened for Cindy's sweet voice to tell him what to do about Dr. Sam.

Nothing.

Perhaps Cindy was busy helping others in heaven this morning. She used to help friends and neighbors. If she wasn't baking bread or making a casserole for someone who was sick or an elderly shut-in, she was volunteering with Pastor English to care for the widows of the church or helping with the youth program. She told him she felt close to the Savior when she helped other souls.

He raked a hand through his bed-messed hair. "I lost one of my best breeding cows, sweetheart, and her newborn calf. The government is gonna pay for this. Your little camera came in handy." He'd shoved it in the glovebox of the truck before he drove Sal, Mike, and a couple of his ranch hands to haul the murdered cow and calf back to the farm for skinning and butchering. Photographic proof of the cow and calf's deaths would go a long way to getting the government to back off. At least he hoped it would.

The loss of the calf was upsetting enough. After weaning, the calf would have brought in about four hundred dollars at summer auction. He'd paid six hundred and fifty for the cow, and she would've produced calves for some years yet.

Now the sale of many calves was history.

Joe stood and stretched his aching spine. Dragging the cow back to the compound and hoisting it with the block and tackle in the shed, had been back-breaking work. Skinning and butchering the cow and her calf had chafed his backside. Today, he would take the hides into Auburn to the tanner who'd make it into a rug and wall hanging for his living room. Seeing them would remind him of his loss and his righteous anger with the government.

"I guess we should have had a barbeque, cooked one of the halves, and invited the neighbors. You would've done that, wouldn't you, sweetheart?"

He studied Cindy's self-portrait hanging over his dresser. His favorite. She painted herself with the sun shining off Sunrise Mountain behind her shoulder and the mountains blue and purple in the early morning light.

Her "Mona Lisa" smile had captured him. Her dimples deepened when the corners of her mouth pulled up like she remembered something amusing. She was never one to burst out laughing. Joe loved her quiet, serious sense of humor—and the cool blue of her eyes, her pale skin, and her thick blonde hair.

Joe wandered the dark house, stepping lightly to avoid the legs of tables and edges of furniture that Cindy loved and crammed into the living room. He made it to the kitchen, ground some beans and set the coffeepot to percolate. The clock shaped like a wagon wheel showed not yet three a.m.

What would Sam be doing this morning?

Damn. Why would he think about her? "I'm sorry, Cindy."

Joe sat in one of Cindy's turquoise-painted chairs, cupped his coffee, and let his mind drift into the past.

Cindy had wrinkled her nose at the hearty sludge he drank for breakfast when he lived in the bunkhouse. "How can you drink that stuff?" She'd come to ride her favorite horse, Ivy.

Joe stood by the corral sipping from his coffee cup and watching her.

He took a swallow and winced. "I'm used to it." He rested his foot on the lower board of the corral's fence. "Aren't you supposed to be doing your chores?"

She made a face at him. "I'll have you know I've been doing chores around this ranch since I was four," she said, an angry bite to her words. "Ma and Pa made me gather eggs from the chickens, feed and water the pigs, milk a cow—every day. I collected the strippings off the milk to churn fresh into creamery butter, and inside the house, I washed the morning meal dishes, dried, and put them away. All this happened before I went to school. At night, I did it all again."

"Oh, poor baby." Joe mocked her. She'd swatted him. She couldn't be angry at his silly jabs.

Cindy had a sweet heart and she was never afraid of hard, back-breaking work. That was another reason he admired the young woman.

A few months later, after they were married, she had said, "When I did my chores, my only companion was an old shaggy sheepdog I'd named, Sunrise, like the ranch and the mountain."

He blinked, and the memories flitted away.

The family buried the dog, Sunrise, and all of Elmer, Bert, and Cindy's dogs in the family plot on the first rise below Flat Ridge among the peaceful pines. Her parents, grandparents, and Cindy were buried there, too.

He needed to talk to her before heading up into the mountains to chase down the menace. "Sweetheart, I need your advice before going after the plane. Also, about what I should do with Dr. Sam."

Joe finished his cup of coffee and stared at it for a while. The first glow of the coming morning fell across the front window in the living room. He stood, rinsed his cup, and placed it in the drainer.

Glancing at the clock again he saw it was nearing five a.m.— the beginning of the ranch day came early. Lettie would be coming in a moment to fix him breakfast. He didn't know if his stomach could handle her huevos rancheros with peppered potatoes and crumbled bacon this morning. The spy plane, the dead cattle, the incompetent sheriff, and Dr. Sam, had his gut churning with anxiety. Although thinking on Sam, the churning was sweet.

Before walking from the kitchen to get showered for the day, the phone rang. Who'd be calling him at this hour?

He checked the caller i.d.

Sam. Hell.

"Hey," he said keeping it cool though to hear her voice warmed him.

"Hey, yourself. How are you this morning?" Sam asked.

"Tired." He grunted.

"I had to call and tell you something."

"Okay." Please don't let her try to blurt out that she loved him again. He'd been too stunned to reply on Sunday evening after she'd confessed having feelings. He'd hurt her.

"I'm on the east side of Mesa de Salvia this morning. I had to stay the night with one of those wealthy cabin owners back up in the hills." It sounded like she took a big breath. "His mare was going to foal at any time."

"Did she?"

"Yes," Sam said. "Right before dawn. A beautiful little roan, as red as the sunsets over West Mountain."

He could hear the joy in her tired voice. "You okay?"

"I'm fine, thank you for asking. I saw your menace."

He stiffened. "Where?"

"Flying back and forth just above the Mesa. What are they looking for?"

"Damned if I know."

"I'm sorry about the cow and her calf." Tenderness in her voice touched him. "Sal told me last night when I saw him in town."

"Yup."

"Joe?"

Here it comes. "What?"

"Thanks for Sunday afternoon."

Curse the woman for making him feel all gooey and warm inside. He needed some hard work for a distraction. "You're welcome." It irked him that he meant it.

"Goodbye Joe." Sam practically purred like a barn cat. "Perhaps we could have dinner some night at Ruby's."

She didn't give him time to refuse, just hung up.

After a tepid shower, he dressed in jeans and a plaid flannel shirt.

Lettie stood at the stove frying up some chorizo. The smell was divine.

"Hay, Lettie." He waited for her to turn from the stove.

"Good morning, Mr. Mack."

"When are you going to call me Joe?" He chuckled.

"Ricardo calls you *Señor* Joe, doesn't he? It wouldn't be proper." She stirred the sausage in the cast iron skillet. "What would you like for breakfast?"

"If that's chorizo, can you make me a burrito for lunch instead of breakfast? I think I'll skip it today." He needed to be hungry and angry when he drove up the canyon to SRM Facilities.

She quickly loaded up a sizeable hand-made tortilla with sausage, eggs, onions, and peppers, covering the whole thing with her special pico de gallo, and wrapped it up tight. "I pray you don't starve."

He chuckled. "With your delicious cooking, how could I?"

In the mudroom next to the kitchen, he slipped on his sheep-skin jacket, opened the back door, and strolled down the side porch steps near the garden plot.

The garden still had winter vegetables to be harvested like Brussel sprouts, cabbage, broccoli, and cauliflower. Carrots even grew through the cold, and some sweet peas came on early. Supplementing his groceries and the others who lived here with him with fresh vegetables pleased him.

In a small greenhouse near the garden, Mike Sanchez had started seeds for eggplant, potatoes, peppers, and tomatoes for planting in April and May depending upon frost dates. The greenhouse was Mike's idea, and he usually had plants at various stages of development inside.

Glancing east, the sun was barely visible over Sunrise Peak. He stretched and headed toward the stables and his horse.

When Joe became the owner of Sunrise Ranch, his chores changed. He no longer plowed the fields sitting on an old tractor, hand planted crops, or tended the family's vegetable garden. Mike had taken on the responsibility for the garden, money crops, and orchards—he and his two boys were hard workers. Having their help cut Joe's worry by half. He still rode herd on the cattle with Ricardo and Sal.

Salvador and his older boy trained the horses and repaired all the farm equipment. They helped Joe rebuild old cars and tractors and kept the ranch rigs running smooth.

Joe was stuck with ranch finances and making ends meet.

He sometimes felt at loose ends with less to do. However, he continued to ride fences and manage the significant yearly branding of the new calves. He'd scheduled the branding to take place the end of March—the week Robbie would be home for spring break to help. Right now, he needed to get into the canyon south of Flat Ridge and see how close he could get to SRM Facilities side, and the spot where that plane landed.

Earlier in his office, Joe typed out an invoice for the death of the calf and its mother on the computer Robbie had set up for him. He would present it to SRM along with a copy of the photo showing their brutal deaths because of a stampede. Hopefully, it would wake them up and make them realize the destruction their plane had caused. If not ... well, it didn't matter. He was taking that menace down and soon—sheriff or no sheriff.

After starting the ranch rig, Joe headed down the graveled and tree-lined lane to the front gate. He paused under the wrought iron sign that read "Sunrise Ranch." The sign hung from a log of Ponderosa Pine fastened to two large Ponderosa Pine uprights. Under the sign, he'd installed a cattle guard to keep the cattle from wandering off the property. If he got into it with SRM, he would need to install a security gate system.

Rubicon Road ran along the south edge of Joe's ranch along the Rubicon River. The road rose quickly from the ranch level to that of Flat Ridge, about forty-two hundred feet above sea level. His ears always popped, and Cindy would make fun of him.

At the summit, Joe noticed a cave on the ridge about one hundred feet above the narrow road. He'd forgotten about those old bear caves at the south forest end of his place. They might make an excellent spot for holding the plane. It wouldn't be on his land, so Warner couldn't accuse him of stealing the menace. Excellent.

An old logging road intersected the highway, meandering through the tall trees. Joe turned onto it. He'd been up here many times for firewood and replanting trees—a sustainable crop if he replanted, which he always did.

Elmer taught him that after clearing most of the ranchland of trees for grazing land. "Don't allow all the trees to be cut down without plantin' more."

As it was, trees nearing eighty- to one hundred-years-old, if not older, grew undisturbed as well as some as young as three years—the ones he'd planted for Cindy before her passing.

The potholed, dusty road wound through the trees climbing ever higher. The intense blue above showed through the pine branches. The smell of damp undergrowth still covered with snow, filtered in through Joe's open truck window. The path was the way up to Flat Ridge Mesa. Often, he and Cindy took this road on horseback for picnics.

It wasn't long before the dirt road petered out at the base of the rocky granite cliffs spanning the foot of Sunrise Mountain. He hadn't taken the Flat Ridge cut-off, just stayed on the road. He parked his rig and shut it off. Ahead of him, plenty of trees had filled in making the walk challenging. But he had to see how close he could come to the mountain.

When he was about a mile in and still hadn't reached the old deer path leading into the mountains, he figured he'd better turn around. Could he get into SRM Facilities before heading down to Auburn to deliver the cow and calf's hides? He ground his teeth at the disheartening, expensive waste.

Tramping through the undergrowth of the old forest, Joe lost his footing a couple of times and went down on his knees, scraping his hands and arms, even his legs through his jeans. He should have brought a machete.

He stood and swiped the dried pine needles and dark forest dirt from his clothes and hands. He still hadn't come out of the forest to the east of his ranch.

The sound of cattle mooing drew his attention. He trudged on.

After another half hour, Joe burst through the forest about fifteen feet below the sheer cliffs of Flat Ridge mesa. The scene to the west was of the rolling ranchland that had gotten into his blood. His cattle and stock horses grazed peacefully with heads down oblivious to his presence.

He stood for a long time just absorbing the gift Bert left him, a drifting war vet. Bert, who was turned down for the service, had grudgingly taken a liking to him because he worked damned hard and didn't complain. Bert gave him a room in the old barn and good food. He paid a scant but fair wage, the old skinflint. Joe had saved every penny, except for when Miss Cindy made him spend his money on a used 1965 Ford F150. Other than the clothes on his back when he stumbled upon Sunrise Ranch, he'd never owned anything. Soon he had a new rig, a home, and a wife.

He spun around from the sight and his memories and fought his way back to his rig. Damned if he didn't have to take his horse and pack mules if he wished to get up into the mountains. No roads led in, not even poorly constructed logging roads.

Jumping into the rig, Joe backtracked to the highway and continued toward the turnoff to SRM. It had been about a mile down the other side of the summit. He made a left onto a dirt road.

At a guard shack, a marine sergeant named Kowalski stopped Joe's rig.

"Can I help you, sir?"

Joe's right hand twitched to salute. It had been over thirty-three years since he left the Army and he still felt the pull. "I'm looking for the outfit that flies a small recon plane, Sergeant."

"Sorry, sir. I can't tell you the name of that group."

Joe raised an eyebrow. "This is a matter of life and death."

The sergeant shook his head. "I'm right sorry, sir, but most of these labs are off-limits to civilians unless you're a civil contractor or were invited." He stepped back into his shack and grabbed a clipboard. "Perhaps your name is on the visitors' list?"

Joe snorted. "Nah, I don't think so." He reached over and picked up the envelope with the invoice and photos in it. "Could you give this to the people responsible for the spy plane for me? It's imperative."

The sergeant's eyes narrowed. "What's in it?"

"That would be on a need to know basis, Sergeant." Joe smiled at his witty words.

"If this is a threat—" The young man reached for his sidearm.

"That recon plane has done a lot of damage to my herd."

"Are you from Shadow Pines, a friend of Sheriff Warner's?"

Joe chuckled. Never a friend. "Yeah."

"I'm sorry, but I'm not sure I should give this to them."

Joe clamped his back molars together to keep from swearing. He thrust the envelope into the sergeant's hands. "This is an invoice for a murdered cow and her newborn calf."

CHAPTER THIRTEEN

SRM and the Envelope—Time to Pay Up

March 25, 1998—Wednesday

MAJOR **D**ONALD **HAD TO WAIT** for a man driving an old turquoise and white truck to back up and turn around before he could approach the guard gate. "Stupid jerk," he said to his aide.

The corporal driving grinned as they approached.

"Sorry about that, Major," the guard said through the window.

Charles waved him off.

"I have something for the lab techs of the Peter Pan Project." The sergeant handed a sealed envelope through the window and opened the gate.

Charles took it. "There's no return address on this."

"He just dropped this off," the guard said. "Didn't tell me his name."

Could he be the rancher he'd tried to run off the road? The same rancher who owned the property butting up against SRM's? He hadn't recognized him because he'd driven a different vehicle today.

Charles motioned his driver forward without thanking the sergeant. He fingered the envelope. Crackpot. He shoved it in his pocket.

Gotta get into the facility and inform Basua of his good fortune, because he'd found the deed to the "Lady Olina Mine" right on the other side of this mountain. County recorder told him the mine was played out, as far as she knew. Would it be as productive as the mine on the government's side also believed to be "played out?" He would have that silver mine with all its cha-ching veins of silver and to hell with his government contacts and the arms manufacturer from Texas. The mine was his baby, and nothing or nobody would stand in his way.

He found Basua leaning over the little fortune-finder in the back, his assistants missing.

"Where are your lab rats?" Charles asked.

Basua jumped at the sound of his voice. He clutched his chest with one hand and hid the other one behind his back. "You should not sneak up on me." He took up a position in front of the plane. "You are back early."

Charles clutched the copy of the deed in his hand. "I only had to go to Auburn, not Sacramento." He narrowed his eyes at Basua's posture. "Something wrong, Doc?"

"Oh, my no. N-nothing." He dragged a finger between his collar and throat. "What would make you think there was something the matter?"

"Don't bug out on me now, Doc, we're this close."

When Basua didn't move and kept shuffling his feet, Charles' gut clenched. "Get away from the plane." He marched over and shoved Basua out of the way. "What the—"

Basua backed away. Charles gripped him by the lapels and dragged him closer. He got in his face. "What happened to this plane?"

"I do not know."

"It's been shot."

"Yes. It appears so." A bead of sweat ran into Basua's eye. He rubbed it away

"Were you going to tell me?"

"Of course. I was waiting until you got here." Basua swallowed. "It is an easy fix."

Charles gritted his teeth. "Someone shot my plane."

"Your plane?" Basua choked.

"Yes. My plane." He released Basua. The doctor stumbled gripping his throat. "Did the plane fly this morning?"

"Of course, Major. I believe I might have found something in a box canyon near the upper mesa."

Piqued, Charles stared at him. "Photos?"

Basua let out a deep, shuddering breath. He ought to be afraid. The toad.

On a TV monitor, Basua queued up the video of today's run. Sure enough, in the back wall of a box canyon, there was a black indentation, like a cave entrance. "That could be the Lady Olina Mine. Finally." Charles swore. "Make a longer, more defined sweep of that area tomorrow. Fly it later in the day."

"Later?" Basua gasped.

"Sun will be in a different position." He glared at the English-Indian royalty. "Gotta a problem with that?"

"No sir, Major, sir. I do not have any problem with that. I am about finished with my repairs of the wing."

"Get at it then."

Charles sat at his desk in the corner of the room and remembered the envelope the sergeant had given him. He retrieved a letter opener from the desk drawer and slit it open. Out dropped some pictures and two folded pieces of paper. Unfolding them, he read the letter.

> To the proprietors of the Peter Pan Project and whom it may concern,
>
> Your miserable recon plane has been stampeding my cattle and nearly killed my foreman and me. On Sunday, on your flight over my ranch, you scared a cow and her new calf causing them to run and fall to their deaths.
>
> Attached is a copy of the invoice for the cow and the calf, and photographic proof of their deaths.
>
> Please remit to the sheriff of Shadow Pines, Sheriff Cody Warner, with a cashier's check made out to cash.
>
> Signed: Your unhappy neighbor

Uncontrollable heat built in Charles' gut as he slammed the letter on the desktop and snatched up the photos. He had to calm himself, or he wouldn't be able to stop the violence he could cause. The gruesome photos showed a dead cow and a calf. That stupid rancher couldn't blame this on Charles' plane.

He picked up the invoice. "What the hell." The bill was for one cow at $1,250.00 and fifteen promised future calves, including the dead one, at $400 apiece for a total of $7,250.00.

Below that line the invoice read:

On average a cow can have thirteen to eighteen calves in her life. You have cost me a bundle on new yearlings at auction. I'll split the difference with you and only charge you for fifteen. Consider yourselves lucky I didn't push the amount to the real value of what I've lost.

"Who does he think he is? He's just SOL if he thinks he's getting something from me." Charles picked up a geode paperweight and hurled it across the room, narrowly missing Basua's head. It smashed against the wall. "I could kill him with my bare hands, and no one would find his body."

"Major? Are you all right?" Basua's brown face turned a little pale at the close call with the paperweight.

"Nothing I can't handle."

Hawke, one of his private security buddies, could deal with this situation quickly and quietly with no links back to him or Peter Pan.

Charles bolted to his feet, shaking his fists. He'd forgotten his good luck. "Basua, I located the deed to the claim on the other side of the mountain." Charles waited until Basua looked at him. "There is silver over there."

CHAPTER FOURTEEN
Lettie Sanchez, Harry Truman, and Dwight D. Eisenhower

March 25, 1998—Wednesday

J**OE DIDN'T GET BACK** from Auburn until late because he stopped in Shadow Pines and had dinner with Dr. Sam Stone. He shouldn't have invited her to eat with him, but there was something about her...

They'd spoken about Cindy and Cindy's love of animals. It was nice to have someone who remembered and grieved as well. He'd been selfish in his grief believing he was the only one who deserved to mourn his beloved wife. Guess he didn't have a monopoly on pain.

Up this morning before four a.m., Joe found a large UPS package on the kitchen table. Had it been there last night? He couldn't remember. The return address was the Geek's. Ah, his tools from Robbie to fix his menace problem.

The back door of the kitchen opened and in stepped Lettie.

"*Buenos días,* Lettie." He smiled at her.

"Good morning, Mr. Mack," she said with hardly a trace of a Spanish accent. So, unlike her husband. All her kids receiving their college degrees was her doing. She tied on an apron that hung by the back door. "How did you like your burrito yesterday?"

"It was fantastic. But then all your food is *muy bueno.*"

Lettie's warm tanned face radiated joy from within even though she lived a hard life. Joe could hardly believe she was sixty already. She didn't look it. She wore her long black hair pulled away from her face, but loose down her back. She had a bright smile for everyone and love shined from her dark eyes. Not much shorter than Ricardo, she managed to keep herself at a good weight, but some of her delicious burritos had found their way to her waistline.

Today, she'd worn a lively yellow floral cotton dress and the apron Cindy had purchased for her that read: "Kiss the Cook."

He smiled as he cut into the box with his pocket knife, opened the flaps, "I'm going up into the mountains for a few days," he said. "I'll need some meals packed."

"How many days?" she asked. "You'll take the cooler?"

"Through Sunday, and yes." He'd stay in the mountains as long as it took to learn the pattern of that flying slaughterer and bring it down.

She removed a cast-iron skillet from a cupboard and lit a burner under it on the stove. "I'll make some more burritos and biscuits. I made jerky from the cow." She glanced up as Joe, frowned. "*Lo siento mucho, mi amigo.*"

He fought a wince. "Yeah, I'm sorry, too, Lettie. I'm grateful for the food. Thanks."

She got a mischievous glint in her eyes. "I see Dr. Sam's coming around. She's good for you." Bacon sizzled in the pan filling the kitchen with its heavenly aroma. "It will be good for you to find some peace. You've worked like a dog since Miss Cindy passed away."

Joe didn't say anything because it was true. He'd had to do something. Working the ranch and staying away from the house as much as possible kept him sane. The house was Cindy's domain. Her spirit walked the halls, sat on the porch, and invaded his sleep. Lettie kept the home as if it were a shrine. Maybe he needed a redo.

Even now he could remember the day the doctor from Sacramento called with the news of the Silent Killer.

They'd been sitting at this table drinking her special coffee blend. He'd been holding her hand telling her it would be okay.

He watched her eyes as she spoke to the doctor. The bright, sparkling blue of them faded as she took the news. Then the blue had faded behind a sheen of tears. Finally, her lip trembled, and she gripped his hand so tight he thought his fingers might break.

"What is it? What's wrong?" Joe asked.

She sniffed. "Thank you, Doctor. Yes, I'll be there."

Cindy stared into Joe's eyes for a long time before she spoke. He knew she was trying to get a grip on her emotions. "He told me I have stage-four breast cancer. I'm to begin chemo next week."

He couldn't breathe. His free hand curled into an impotent fist he could shove through the wall. For a moment, it was as if the fault line on his property opened and swallowed him.

Hell no. Joe wished he could shout, curse, call the doctor back and make him say he was lying or wrong. But he did none of those things because his wife needed him.

Cindy had worked hard all her life and had been in terrific health. After the miscarriage loss of their fourth child, a boy this time, she had some bloating and abdominal pains which the doc in town suggested was normal after losing so many children to miscarriage.

After that, she couldn't eat and was distended all the time. Fatigue set in and the torturous back pain. She couldn't do her chores anymore or clean the house. Lettie had stepped in then, Sam as well.

They did the chemo. Radiation. Nothing.

The doctors in Sacramento eventually told Joe to take Cindy home and make her as comfortable as possible.

"Let me take you to another specialist. We'll go to Los Angeles, down to Cedar Sinai. I hear their cancer program is top notch."

Cindy put her hand over his while they sat at this very table. "Let's not waste the time we have left. How about I pack a lunch and we'll ride up to Flat Ridge and have a picnic?"

No. Joe screamed in his head. I'm supposed to die first. You're a child still.

The local doctor had sent an in-home healthcare nurse to stay with Cindy—hospice they had called it.

After Cindy had died, Lettie stepped in to care for him, keeping his house spotless, and cooking for him so he wouldn't starve. As depressed as he had been, he might have just skipped eating altogether. Lettie, like a rose blooming in an unrelenting desert, wouldn't let him quit.

Joe tore into the cardboard package and found a black metal case resembling his satellite box, and shotgun with what looked like a bullhorn attached to it. "What the hell?" he mumbled.

"What?" Lettie turned and stared at him.

"Just something from Robbie."

"I sure love that boy." She sighed.

Joe did too but didn't voice it. He picked up the note and read.

Dear Mr. Joe,

You'll have to adjust the frequency until you find the correct one the plane's handlers' use. When you do, you won't have much time after the engine is cut and before the plane hits the ground. As soon as you see it taking a nosedive, shoot the net gun at it. Be sure the rope is attached to the net or the whole thing will be for naught. Maybe you could practice taking some birds down or some calves. Ha! Ha! Rob

Funny kid. But a good suggestion. Joe would spend the first few days charting the flights of the plane and making his plans to bring the menace down.

Ricardo found him at the corral before the sun breached Sunrise Mountain. "Where are you headed, *amigo*? Tell me you no go after the *demonio*?"

"To the mountains to do some fishing."

Ricardo shook his head. "*¡Estupido!*"

"Hey." Joe hated lying to his best friend, but he couldn't chance Ricardo's life, and he was fishing, in a way.

He'd just finished saddling Checkers with additional saddlebags filled with personal items: two changes of clothing and thick wool socks, a bright yellow rain slicker, his warm coat, water bottles, purifier tablets, and his first-aid kit. The mules would carry his other supplies.

Finally, he strapped his old scabbard and new shotgun to Checkers' saddle. The bullhorn-shooting net attachment didn't fit. He tucked that safely into the panniers—the large canvas bags attached to the mule, Harry Truman, along with his camping gear.

On the other scabbard, a newer one, he stowed his Winchester .30-30 and lots of ammo. Who knew what creatures he'd encounter in the mountains?

Ricardo dogged him as he located the mules' harnesses. "I no see why I cannot go with you."

He typically took his red mules, Harry Truman and Dwight D. Eisenhower into the high country. Once the harnesses were located, he looped the first harness over Harry's head.

Both Harry and Dwight were docile creatures, easy to pack, and even easier to lead through the mountains. Harry was a product of Bert's old mare and a male donkey and carried on the tradition of Grandpa Elmer's uncle, Hans, naming the mules after presidents of the United States. Dwight liked to think of himself as a jumping champion.

Joe and the Geek bred good pack mules for some of the resorts at Lake Tahoe. Sure helped with putting college money away for the kid. He'd sold Kennedy, Johnson, and Nixon, to a dude ranch at Tahoe. Carter was too passive to be a good pack mule, and Reagan and Bush weren't trained yet.

"You go alone into the mountain?" Ricardo said from behind him.

"Yes."

"Why?"

"It's safer." Joe tossed the soft cowhide blanket he'd tanned himself over Harry's back. The mule didn't blink. Joe hooked up the hand-tooled pack harnesses and the wooden decker harness Ricardo and he had constructed out of pine. Ricardo did the same for Dwight.

"*¿Puedes dejar de decir sandeces?*" Ricardo swore as he picked up the soft canvas panniers. They'd been stained from many camping trips smelled of numerous campfires.

"I don't want you involved in this."

The weight in each bag Ricardo was filling would be distributed equally with fishing gear, flashlight, folding-handled ax and saw, toilet paper, small shovel, the soft food cooler with Lettie's food, snacks, his kitchen pack, feedbags and oats, and various items needed for the mules and Checkers. On the top, crossing the back of Harry Truman, he tied his bedroll and covered the whole thing with an old canvas tarp.

Ricardo moved to the other side of the mule and helped Joe tie a perfect diamond knot across its back. *"Es estúpido. I am involved."* Ricardo cursed some more in Spanish.

"Doesn't matter. I need you here." The mule, Dwight would carry his tent and food. Ricardo and he covered his pack as well. Joe pulled the last loop tight across the mule's back. He took off his cowboy hat and ran a hand through his matted hair. "I need you to stay here so if someone comes around asking questions, you don't have to lie to them."

Ricardo swept his straw hat off his head, worried the edges with his narrow, gnarled, somewhat arthritic fingers. "What are you going to do with the *demonio?*"

Joe walked around and squeezed his friend's shoulder. "I fear danger will come to the ranch. You, your boys, and the ranch hands need to think of ways to protect our homes, the farm, and the cattle."

Ricardo shook his head back and forth. *"Los problemas."*

Joe couldn't agree more as he whistled for Shep and Spike.

At a walking pace with the pack animals in tow, the trip felt interminable. From the ranch compound to Flat Ridge where Joe used to camp with Cindy, took about two hours if he were galloping at a good clip. But this slow pace had his back aching, his knees giving him fits, and other parts of him complaining about sitting on a horse for too long.

He was getting too old to be traipsing through the wooded mountains in search of a government spy plane. It was apparent the sheriff had done nothing about it because it continued to fly over his ranch. It was up to Joe to rid himself and his property of this menace before more cattle were lost.

About two in the afternoon, he reached the flat, semi-open camping spot that butted up against some tall Ponderosas. It was his and Cindy's favorite place for camping. Above the trees, Sunrise Mountain shone in the afternoon sun like a bright diamond—the sun glistening off the icy snowcap. A small creek ran cool and crisp not more than twenty feet from the old stone fire ring he'd built of smooth river rocks—blackened now with the multiple fires he'd sat in front of, his arm around his sweetheart.

The memories were swift and painful. Joe forced them away.

"Time to set up camp and get a fire going," he said to the dogs, Checkers, Harry, and Dwight. Unloading the supplies and camp set-up went quick. The forest was dense with underbrush and small dried limbs. Soon he had a roaring fire built inside the ring of blackened stones. He placed the small cast-iron griddle on a rock to heat up one of Lettie's burritos and shivered in his light jacket. At this altitude, they could still get snow in March. Thank God he remembered his long johns.

Above him from Flat Ridge, he heard the low moan of an engine. He glanced at his watch. "That plane shouldn't be flying around this time of day."

The dogs' ears perked up, Shep whined.

He patted the dog's head. "I know, buddy. Wrong time of day." He was going to have to watch this thing like a hawk, record flying times to be in the right place to take it down.

Joe trotted out to a clearing where he could see the mountain's face. Sure enough, that little spy plane swept back and forth in broad daylight then dipped into some smaller box canyons. What in the hell were they looking for up here? There wasn't much danger of forest fires among the granite cliffs. There was no need for a fire-watching plane. Something else drew their concentrated interest.

CHAPTER FIFTEEN
That Menace is Going Down

THEY CHANGED THE FLIGHT pattern of that damned demon plane. For Joe to find the right position and the right time to take it down would be a challenge. He brought enough food for five days. If he killed an animal and cooked it, he could last many more days. If the plane flew over Flat Ridge first, then so be it. He might have to camp on the side of a cliff.

The falling of night surrounded Joe's camp as the fire blazed to warm him. The dogs stood like sentinels at his sides. Joe commanded them to "guard" the area while he was unpacking mostly to keep unwanted critters away from his camp and set up a warning if something larger should approach. Still, he had his rifle nearby.

After tin-foil dinner of steak and potatoes Lettie packed him, he tied the rest of his food high into a hundred-year-old pine hoping any bears would be discouraged from stealing it from thirty feet up.

Before losing the light altogether, he attached a highline between two sturdy pines and tied Checkers, Harry, and Dwight's lead ropes to it. The stream was within reach as was a clear patch of dirt for them to sleep on. When they finished their ration of grain, he'd stowed away the feedbags and gave them both a good brushing. Dwight sloshed in water and drank. Harry nipped at the brush as Joe moved down his legs.

"Behave, you brute." Joe laughed.

Finished, Joe settled next to the fire. This complete dark of night was the time he and Cindy would tell each other their secrets. Joe never told another soul, except Cindy, about his ghastly tours of duty in Vietnam. No one understood the horrors he'd witnessed, committed by both sides in that war. She understood and loved him despite what he'd done and lived through.

After a while, he yawned, stretching his aching arms over his head. He'd always loved sleeping under the stars. The smells, the sounds of the forest, and the wind singing through the pines lulled him to sleep.

"Guard," he said to the dogs, and they stood on either side of the tent door. During the night, they would lie down to sleep, but they were ever on guard.

Once tucked into his sleeping bag still dressed in everything but his boots and hat, he drifted into an uneasy sleep.

It was anything but dreamless as he heard Cindy's voice in his dreams.

"I'm cold." She had thrashed about in the blackness of the tent.

Groggy from sleep, Joe opened his sleeping bag for her. "Climb in."

Her small feet were ice cold—as usual when she placed them on his legs. "Oooh, your feet are like ice."

She kissed his beard-roughened chin as he wrapped his arms around her. "You can warm them for me."

Thank the Good Lord he always ran a little hot. Soon her feet were toasty warm, and both stopped shivering. "Warm enough?" he asked.

"I'm always warm in your arms, my darling." Cindy ran her hand across his flat stomach.

How he loved this girl, this woman, with all her charms and her soft, silky hair he could wrap in his hands. He leaned down and kissed her ... and loved her.

Later, curled against his chest, she whispered, "I love you, Joe."

He kissed the top of her head as she drifted off. Too happy to sleep, he held her until the sun broke over

Sunrise Mountain. Little had he known this was their last camping trip.

March 26, 1998—Thursday morning—**Scouting the Hunt**

Joe woke with a start. Where was he? For a moment he had to stare at the tent roof to orient himself. He rubbed his stubble-covered jaw. He heard Shep and Spike whine. "Don't worry, boys, I only had a dream."

Outside it was still dark. The dream about loving his wife was too vivid, too intense. It left him shaking. Tears trailed from the corners of his eyes and wet his pillow. She'd gotten pregnant with their little boy on their last trip into the mountains. He blamed himself for causing her miscarriage and eventually her cancer. Sam told him that was nonsense. Could he let it go?

Too awake to drift back to sleep, Joe unzipped his bag and shoved his feet into his boots. Still chilly, it was time to get moving if he planned to spy on the spy plane.

Joe cleaned up his trash, tied it and his food back up into the tree. He left Harry and Dwight tied to the highline by the stream with cool, green grass growing on the banks. He departed camp before dawn to ride Checkers into the steep mountain pass up to Flat Ridge. The plane had to fly over again in the morning time.

A small notebook he kept in his shirt pocket was for recording each year's harvest, livestock counts, and weather reports. Today, he recorded the plane's route of last night, the time the thing swept past him, locations of the search, and where it had disappeared to after the flight.

At six a.m., he first heard the whine of the motor. He jotted down the time in his notebook. Sure enough, the menace flew over the southeastern edge of Flat Ridge and on toward where he hid in a grove of pines and scrub brush. Wouldn't pay to be seen by the plane and its invisible pilots, not until he could net it out of the sky. Not even then.

He watched it swoop into some box canyons north by Mesa de Salvia.

The low, tree scraping flight of the plane amazed him. Why didn't it get hung up in the canyons or tall trees? Some canyons had very high, extremely steep walls of sheer granite cliffs on one or all four sides. He'd been over most of this country at one time or another, searching for gold and silver mines he believed were still hidden on his property.

His tiny pencil flew across the page of the notebook as he filled in the times and areas the plane searched. It seemed to concentrate on several box canyons below the north mesa. Most of them had jagged rock-faced walls, and treacherous loose shale paths leading down into them. Some had no trails down to the bottom at all. If someone searched for something there, they'd need rock-climbing equipment to in and get out.

A thin deer trail lead from Buena Mesa, another flat area above him, through a ravine back toward the more prominent Flat Ridge. That had been Cindy's favorite ride. The view of the valley and the ranch from the top of Flat Ridge was spectacular. However, traversing the steep, crumbling sandstone sides on a narrow path was perilous, especially for a rider dragging a mule.

Perhaps if he took the better traveled switch-back path up the face of Sunrise Mountain, he could wind his way down to Flat Ridge from the top. The route would bring him toward the back of the mesa where the bear caves were, on the SRM Facilities side. He'd hide that menacing plane on their property right under their noses.

Before heading Checkers up the steep path, he paused to scout out the hunting trail winding up the face of Sunrise.

The plane was heading back toward his position. He removed his binoculars from his saddlebag and pressed them to his eyes. He struggled with the focus, thanking the Lord he only needed reading glasses and hadn't lost his long-range sight.

Several patches or labels covered the plane's belly. One looked like a NASA symbol, but he couldn't be sure at this distance.

The plane swooped up not more than fifty feet above the ground, turned and dived into another box canyon, this one nearer to where he sat on his horse. On the underside of the plane, Joe also noticed a black box. Likely the camera which Robbie said a drone would have so the pilot could see what was happening on the ground. Joe prayed it was always pointing forward and wouldn't notice him if he attacked it from the side.

Checkers' ears perked up, flipping back and forth. He snorted and tossed his head. "There now, you're safe." He patted Checkers' neck when the plane drew near, and the sound grew louder. "Don't let that menace frighten you."

The horse shook his large head, his mane flying in Joe's face. "Hey, what's the big idea?"

Beside him on the ground, the dogs whined.

"Not you, too." He laughed. "I'm in the mountains with a bunch of scaredy-cats."

At the mention of cats, both dogs stood at attention, noses in the air. They had chased some big cats in these mountain canyons. No doubt they remembered.

He nudged Checkers in the sides and reined him toward the wider, more comfortable path through the tall pines and scrub oak. The smell of rain hung in the air. Just what he needed. He peered up at Sunrise peak. Sure enough, fat white clouds rolled over the snow-covered top threatening to burst. If his aching knee was any indication, he didn't have much time to scout out the back way up to the Flat Ridge mesa and get back to camp before the rainstorm hit. This late in March, he might get snow.

Checkers, nearly as sure-footed as a mule, still couldn't make that climb. "Checkers, buddy, there's no way I can ride you and pull Harry Truman up the steep sidewalls of Flat Ridge in the rain. It would be suicide."

Checkers bobbed his head in response. He didn't think so either.

Standing in the doorway of Cody's office, Deputy Sheriff Vargas gazed at him. "Sheriff, you ever gonna tell Joe Mack what I saw up on his mountain or what you found out from your contact at SRM?"

Cody leaned back. "It's not high on my priority list."

"I can certainly see why Mack would be worried about his cattle. That thing is a nuisance," Pete said.

Cody figured so, too. Especially after Mack called in Monday morning with the report. The plane had frightened his cattle enough to cause a cow to trample her calf and fall, breaking her legs. She needed to be put down.

He should make it a higher priority. But hell, he hated knowing the S.O.B. was right about something and needed his help as the law in town.

Pete folded his arms over his chest. "Should I drive out there before I go home tomorrow morning and talk to Mack?"

"Nah, it's out of your way." Cody rubbed his aching neck, twisting until he heard the pop of a few vertebrae, jerking back into alignment. If he knew Mack, and he did, the jerk would already be planning something stupid. Cody wondered if Joe'd already gone over the mountain to SRM to talk to the Indian scientist. Not that he could blame him, but still. Investigating was his job. "I'll get Sayer to take a run out there today and chat with … Joe."

CHAPTER SIXTEEN

Camping on Sunrise Mountain—The Takedown

March 30, 1998—Monday

T**HE HOWL OF A WOLF** startled the dogs. Their ears twitched. Shep whined and turned worried brown eyes on Joe. "It's okay." He'd kept his animals close tonight, especially the horses. Rainwater was a conductor of electricity, and they'd be in danger if he'd left them too close to the stream during a lightning storm.

Luckily, near the bear caves, they found shelter under an outcropping of rocks. Since Joe's move up the canyon closer to Sunrise peak, he'd seen some bears. He couldn't take any chances with his horse or mules. They had to get him off the mountain.

Checkers neighed low, but Harry and Dwight kept munching on the grass near the campfire as if they were in his pasture at home.

Joe huddled in his yellow rain slicker over his heavy coat, though the fire was burning in a new ring he'd built. The storm had come Friday afternoon before he'd gotten back to camp and had turned into light snow. It snowed and rained off and on for two more days. He hoped the storm would be pulling out soon, so he could carry off his mission and get off this forsaken mountain. It was beautiful, but not a sweet mistress in her tempers.

Shep curled close, his paw touching Joe's leg. Spike was on his other side but didn't lie as close. He kept lifting his head and sniffing the cold air.

"We'll get through this, my friends," he said to his animals. They eyed him with skepticism. Joe laughed. "You don't trust me, do you?"

Checkers shook his head and whinnied. The mules stamped the ground but resumed eating. Shep and Spike looked wary, but content. "Ah, it's good to be loved."

That afternoon, he found a crowded "dog-hair" stand of lodge-pole aspen trees. Regularly, he and Ricardo or Miguel would thin out the trees at the end of autumn for firewood. He'd missed this grove. Good thing. Those tall, thin trees, some of them reaching about twenty feet into the air, would make a quick travois, or a Native American traveling bed, for Harry to carry the plane once Joe brought it down.

With his folding ax, he cut down three lanky, skinny trees, stripped off the scraggly limbs. Two would make the long poles Harry would drag, and the other tree would make the cross bars. There was no telling how much that flying demon weighed, and he had to haul it about three-quarters of a mile back down to Flat Ridge and one particularly deep bear cave.

When he found the rock ridge that hung above a deep, thousand-foot crevasse, he also noticed enough cover from a grove of Ponderosa pines to hide him until he was ready to net the plane. An overhang of limestone shale would conceal him on the south from the plane's camera. He wouldn't be seen by the plane unless they focused the plane and flew directly at him. It was perfect. He'd tested some of the lower frequencies and found none of them interfered with the plane's flight.

Joe had tested the net gun on a rabbit, a crow flying above him, and one of the dogs. It worked perfectly. Shep wasn't too happy about it, but at least Joe'd practiced. Everything was ready in case he found the correct radio frequency. He'd fastened the attachment onto the shotgun and secured the travois for the plane to Harry Truman, so he could do the heavy lifting.

Before dark, he'd hid the shotgun/net gun and black box interrupter behind a boulder along with the travois he'd constructed. Tomorrow was D-day. That menace was going down.

Returning to camp, he fried up the last of Lettie's burritos and fixed a small cup of instant coffee. Blah!

If the plane didn't come down tomorrow, Joe'd have to hunt or fish down by the Hell Hole Reservoir near Flat Ridge to lay in a new food supply. He wished he could go home to his bed.

Joe rose from the log he'd been sitting on, laid another piece of wood on the fire. Hopefully, it would take all night to burn through. Satisfied, he crawled into his tent. Shep and Spike both whined.

"You two are getting soft," he said before opening the tent flat for them. They stood long enough for him to remove his boots and crawl into his sleeping bag and laid down next to him. The temperature in the tent did rise a little even if it did smell like wet dog.

"Good night, my friends." He patted both on the head and rolled over.

The next morning, a long time before dawn, Joe gave Dwight an extra helping of oats. Then he walked Checkers and Harry Truman up the sheer, vertical trail to the top of the ledge where he'd planned the takedown. Shep and Spike brought up the rear, sniffing through the underbrush for rabbits. Joe couldn't take the chance of riding Checkers, fearing he'd lose his footing in the darkness of early morning and the loose shale of the cliffside. They still had two hours until the first light would glow from behind them over Sunrise Mountain.

Time to set up for his one-chance shot.

The snow had stopped sometime in the night, and the sky was a bright, navy blue, the stars twinkling like gems in the heavens. It was bitter cold this morning, but no wind. He missed starting a fire and making a cup of coffee, but he had the jerky Lettie oven-dried from his cow.

With each chew, Joe grieved for the cow and her calf. He couldn't help but wonder if the people of the Peter Pan Project had taken him seriously and sent a check to Sheriff Warner. If they weren't on the up-and-up, they probably wouldn't. Maybe they'd send someone over to talk to him. Or worse.

He jerked to a stop. Checkers bumped his back. What if a goon from the government came while he was away and messed with Ricardo or his family? Damn. This was the government after all. They could make people disappear without a trace. With no way to contact the ranch or Ricardo, Joe prayed his friends would be safe.

What was he thinking? No one messed with the government.

Maybe this was a bad idea.

Joe climbed the steep path again, the horse and mule stepping cautiously behind him.

By the time he reached his takedown spot, the sky in the east had warmed them with a glorious bright glow. Not long now. Every day since he'd arrived in the mountains, the plane had flown over Flat Ridge at precisely six a.m. even through the light dusting of snow. He didn't think it would change its routine now. He prayed it wouldn't, anyway.

He tied the horse and mules inside a grove of trees out of sight, told the dogs to "guard." A big boulder overlooking the thousand-foot crevasse became his lookout spot. He waited. Any misstep too close to the edge and it would be so long for him.

The sun broke over the mountain peak. With binoculars in hand, Joe scanned the morning sky. He didn't have to wait long before he heard the whine of the engine, though it was different today. Not as loud. Perhaps where he was, the air was thinner, and the sound didn't travel as far. Or, the government made modifications for a quieter engine. The thing would be practically invisible, and the government could spy on anyone, and they wouldn't know it.

Joe felt his heart thumping hard and not from the altitude.

He had to get rid of this demon.

Before long, the plane came into the view of his binoculars. Unfortunately, it did not follow its regular pattern of sweeping across the face of Sunrise and settling into the box canyons around Mesa de Salvia. It headed for his lower rangeland … toward his cattle.

Joe swore viciously. He stood and clenched his hands into fists.

Through the binocular lenses, the plane dipped and swirled toward his cattle. Was Ricardo tending them this morning? Or Salvador? Or his unsuspecting ranch hands?

Lowering the binoculars, Joe could see the plane purposefully head for the grassland where his cattle fed. He swore more and colorfully. Cindy would be appalled.

The demon flew directly through the center of his cattle and stock horses. Animals took off in all directions. Some toward the ranch compound, some toward the thick forest on the south, and still some cows and their calves toward the east and the sprawling, low hills before the cliffs and box canyons of Mesa del Salvia.

Joe ripped his hat off his head and slapped it against his thigh. He raised his free hand into a fist and shook it at the plane. "This is too much, you S.O.B.s. I'll destroy that plane. You'll never see it again."

The plane rose above the scattering cattle and returned to its original flight plan, swooping into the canyons below the mesa. If Joe was right, the plane would make a swing past his location once before returning to the plateau and then on its last flight before disappearing over Flat Ridge and the way home.

He had two chances.

Adjusting the frequencies on the black box had been easy. Finding the correct one had not. But Joe would take the menace out of the sky if he had to wait all week. His gut churned on the jerky.

Joe squatted, picked up a small rock, and hurled it as far as he could. Rounding up his cattle and horses would take several days. They could be lost up in the deep ravines and box canyons of the lower mountain and up into the pines near the north mesa. Some might be dead.

What a nightmare.

"I guess I have my answer to dropping off the invoice," he said to his animals.

Heat still pulsed at the back of his neck. He gazed at the dogs. They stared at him. He could almost hear them thinking he was a fool to believe this would end reasonably.

This was war.

By now the sun was high over the peak, the snow melting fast. He positioned Checkers in a little alcove near the edge of the drop-off, but out of sight. He tied one end of the heavy-duty nylon rope of the net gun to the saddle horn. The plane had made a turn and headed back his way for the first pass. He dropped behind the boulder he'd been sitting on and hid, still fiddling with the radio frequency interrupter. He had the net gun poised for when the right frequency stopped the engine from receiving commands.

The demon swooped overhead. Joe clicked the knob on the interrupter box. One frequency, two, three ... four. Nothing. The plane flew by.

Dammit. Next pass for sure.

Frustration had Joe locking his teeth together. He had to relax his aching jaw.

Lifting the binoculars again, he watched the plane bank, gliding back toward the ledge he laid on. "One hundred feet." He turned the knob. Click. One hundred twenty-one. Click. One hundred forty-six. Click. One hundred fifty-five. Click. Four hundred forty-six.

Silence.

No more engine noise.

Joe laid the binoculars on the ground, watched in delight as the plane propeller stopped turning and the plane began to glide downward. Luckily, the breeze held it aloft.

Joe raised the shotgun, steadied his arm against a boulder.

He held his breath.

Steady.

Steady.

Bang.

The shotgun kicked back into his shoulder, but he turned with it.

The net flew up, up, up and surrounded the hunk of government junk like it was a jackrabbit in the sky.

"I got you, you son of a bitch."

The nylon rope uncoiled fast out of the gun. Joe ran for Checkers, gripped his reins in his gloved hands.

"This is gonna be a jolt, old friend. Hold steady. Steady, boy."

Shep and Spike looked from him to the horse to the rope— their ears twitched. The mule set up awful noises from the tree line.

"I brought it down, boys. No time to bellyache about it."

The rope jerked taut as the plane swung over the brink of the ledge. Joe felt the jolt through the body of his horse and his hands. Checkers reared his head as the rope yanked on the saddle.

"Steady, steady. Hold tight, boy." He held onto Checkers' reins until he was sure the horse wouldn't back up toward the edge and go over.

Joe released the breath he didn't know he was holding and straightened. "Let's pull up that piece of crap and get rid of it."

Checkers' head bobbed up and down.

"Hold on," he told his horse.

The plane swung in the net about thirty feet from the edge of the cliff. Joe attempted to pull on the rope, but nothing doing. He walked back to Checkers. "Okay, buddy, it's all up to you."

He tugged on the reins. The horse struggled forward. After the first resistance, his horse pulled hard, the rope taut. Foot by foot, the plane began to rise.

"Keep pulling, Checkers. That's it. Good boy." He looped the reins onto the saddle horn and spoke softly to encourage the horse. At last, the plane topped the ridge, crumbling some of the soft sandstone off beneath its belly.

"This blasted thing is heavy." He patted Checkers on the rump, and the horse turned and looked at him as if to say, "You didn't do any lifting."

"You're right, old friend. Thank you."

Joe saw a round USAF sticker on the side of the plane. United States Air Force. Damn government property.

The plane was bigger up close than he first imagined. He'd have to turn it sideways to accommodate the wingspan. He checked the thing over. Other than a couple of scrapes on the wings, it sustained no damaged. The camera appeared unharmed. He didn't care who was behind the plane and its deliberate attack on his cattle. They didn't have the right to mess with him. Now let them try and find the damned thing.

Checkers fought to pull the plane onto the thin log poles of the travois. As long as Joe had horsepower, he'd use it. Next, he bound the plane to the poles and got Harry Truman in position to secure the pine-pole travois to his decker saddle. He congratulated himself on his ingenuity.

The hard part was to come. Joe hauled himself up on Checkers' back, the mule's lead rope gripped in his hand, and headed up the trail leading to the backside of Flat Ridge and the extensive bear caves.

Two hours and a few stumbles later, Joe located the biggest bear cave. He'd made sure the bears had vacated. He didn't want any surprises. This one was deep, going back into the mountain about two hundred feet—way into the government's side.

Stupid people wouldn't know the thing was right under their noses.

Joe checked the plane for a tracking device. When he found none, he yanked the wires out of the camera, so it wouldn't transmit.

He laughed out loud as he untied the plane, walked Harry Truman forward, and let the little demon slip off the travois.

CHAPTER SEVENTEEN

Deputy Patrick Sayer—Trouble at SRM

March 30, 1998—Monday

DEPUTY **PAT SAYER DROVE** the Sheriff's patrol SUV the sixteen miles to Joe Mack's cattle ranch. Why had the sheriff passed off this responsibility to him? Warner told him he'd spoken to the lab over at SRM and the guard at the gate. Pat didn't know anything other than what little the sheriff told him to tell Mr. Mack.

Oh, well. This assignment got him out of the office and away from Vargas, who was a pain in the neck, and Warner, who was a slacker. Pat was grateful he didn't work the same shift as Pete. It was bad enough taking his ribbing in the mornings when Vargas clocked out, and he clocked in.

Pat had paid his dues, and when the sheriff retired, he would naturally step into his job. It was about time. Only Warner had been at the small office longer. Vargas was a hothead and in trouble with Warner for his less than by-the-book antics and his schoolboy attitude.

Most of the complaints in the small community of Shadow Pines were speeding tickets, domestic disputes, and a bar fight now and then. Only one murder happened since he signed on as deputy. One of the wealthy cabin owners up near Tahoe had disappeared from his home. They found him later beaten to death on this side of the mountain.

Since Pat took his police training down in Dallas, he knew all the modern techniques for finding clues and had solved the case. But the sheriff had taken the credit.

Didn't matter. Pat wasn't a glory hound like Warner.

He turned up the volume on the jazz CD playing in the SUV. "Sing it, Ella." He thumped the steering wheel in time with the upbeat song. A sweet spring breeze blew the scent of pines in through the open window. He breathed deep.

After mustering out of the Marines, he went to the police academy and worked as a patrol officer in Dallas. On the fast track of promotions, he became a homicide detective working the most horrific of cases for two years before his ma took ill and needed him home in Shadow Pines to care for her. He'd moved his wife, Danette, and his little girl to this peaceful community and loved it.

The sun glistened off the Middle Fork of the American River as it rushed over boulders, millions of years old. Sometimes the narrow road came dangerously close to the edge of the cliff falling straight down to the rushing water. A couple of tourists driving the back way to Tahoe had skidded off the road and plunged into the river a few summers ago. Luckily, Joe Mack had happened along at the same time and fished the driver and his wife out of the freezing water.

Mr. Mack hadn't wanted a fuss over his heroic efforts. Pat never forgot the gruff man with a heart of gold.

When Pat retired from police work eventually, he'd explore the canyons and mountains of this area and catalog the rocks and geological formations. He loved geology.

He saw the big sign hanging over the turnoff to Sunrise Ranch as he came around a bend in the road.

When Pat discovered the rancher had served his military career in Vietnam, they'd had lengthy discussions about the military over cold beers at Ruby's Saloon. Mr. Mack was a fair, honest man who had treated Pat like a fellow brother-in-arms.

He stopped his SUV in front of the gate to the ranch, got out and pushed open the wide gate. A small sign read: *If you let 'em out, you chase 'em down.*

He laughed. "Okay, Mr. Mack. I will."

Jumping back into the SUV, he pulled forward and got out to close the gate. Once in the vehicle, he jammed it into drive and sped down the gravel road to the ranch house.

Several horses ran along the fence in the pasture area. Mr. Mack raised good quality horses and mules for sale. Pat'd bought an Appaloosa for his daughter, Talia, for her sixteenth birthday. Now with Talia at Chico, he rode the horse.

The foreman, Ricardo, strolled out of the barn as Pat pulled to a stop. The older man raised a hand in greeting. Ricardo's face was brown and looked as tough as old leather from his work in the sun. But now a smile split his face.

"*Hola, amigo*," Ricardo said as Pat exited the vehicle.

Pat extended his hand and Ricardo shook it. "The place is looking good."

"*Sí.*" Ricardo glanced around the ranch yard. "*Señor* Joe, he expects us to look professional."

Pat chuckled. "It does at that." He glanced around. "Where is Mr. Mack?"

Ricardo removed his straw hat and wiped his brow. "He is up at Sunrise Mountain."

A stone dropped into Pat's gut. Hell. Joe might be taking matters into his own hands. "What's he doing up there?"

Ricardo glanced away. "Camping, *amigo*."

Pat didn't believe it for a moment. "I have news about SRM Facilities for him."

The old foreman searched Pat's face. "You tell me."

Pat glanced up at the mountain standing majestic against the stunning blue of the mid-morning. *Where are you, Joe?* "The sheriff called the lab doing the experiments with the small search plane and told them to stop circling Mr. Mack's property."

"You believe they will stop?" Ricardo chuckled. "*Lo siento, amigo*, sorry, they no stop."

SRM Facility—**AIDA is the mission**

Paul Basua covered his ears. Major Donald turned the air in the lab blue with his string of foul words. He flung a stack of Paul's research files on the floor scattering the papers everywhere. The major had lost the plot, as his British mum would say. Paul had never seen the major so gutted before. His face was crimson red, his fingers white as he balled them into fists.

Paul feared for his life and cowered in the corner. Maybe he should not have told the major he had lost communications with the plane.

Major Donald slapped his hands down on the desk. "You're telling me the plane is gone?"

Paul flinched. "I am not sure if it is gone, exactly. I lost communications with it. One second it was flying over Flat Ridge, and then the screen went blank. No more radio signal."

Major Donald gritted his teeth. "What was the last thing recorded before communications were down?"

Paul walked over to the plane's control panel sitting on a workbench. He queued up the video of this morning's run. He had already watched it over and over, looking for someone or something in the camera's view. He had seen nothing.

"Did you buzz the rancher's cattle like I told you?"

"Yes." Paul felt awful about that. Mother cows with their babies ran off in all directions. He hoped none of them were hurt. Cattle were sacred to his people.

Together they watched the first footage of this morning's flight. The descent into the ranchland where the cattle grazed peacefully, and the terrified reactions of the horses and cattle, and their run in all directions.

Major Donald laughed. "Serves him right, the bastard."

Paul winced.

The plane rose from its shameful duty and swung north to sweep the box canyons again. The dark spot in a sheer rock canyon face just below Mesa de Salvia was still there, still looking like a cut in the granite, maybe an entrance. But three of the walls were sheer rock face. Only a tiny crack with straight granite walls led in and out of the canyon.

Major Donald folded his arms over a massive chest. "I still believe that's the mine entrance. It's almost parallel with our mine on this side."

"Should I send in our geological expert?" Paul asked.

"Wouldn't hurt. He can search that end of the range for the plane as well."

Paul said nothing.

"Do you think the plane crashed?" Major Donald asked.

"The electronics on board would have sent a signal if it had crashed." Paul pointed to the video monitor. "See, it is just

117

sweeping back to Flat Ridge, and it is still aloft. I do not believe it crashed, Major."

"Then it must have lost power or signal and gone down in that area." The major pointed to a small outcropping of rocks at the north end of Flat Ridge.

"It might have glided somewhere, held up by the mountain breezes."

"When did this happen?" the major asked. "What time?"

Paul glanced at his watch and then at the clock on the wall. "Perhaps around six twenty this morning."

"No other readings from the box?"

"None, Major. The readings halted when the video did."

"I'll bet my last dollar that rancher had something to do with the plane's disappearance."

"How?" Paul asked.

Major Donald shook his head. "Is the other plane ready to go? We have to get it up in the air now."

Paul stalled. "I received a call from Sheriff Warner from Shadow Pines yesterday."

"What the hell did he want?" Major Donald stormed away from the screen. He dug his fingers through his close-cropped hair.

Paul swallowed the lump in his throat. This would end badly. "He said to tell the people or group responsible for the plane to quit flying over the rancher's property."

Major Donald uttered some bad words. "I want that other plane up in the sky today."

Paul took a few steps back, glanced behind him at the other spy plane missing its wing, camera, and other electronics. The major stepped around him. All the veins in the major's forehead popped out. "You took the other plane apart?"

He nodded, his blood pressure spiking dangerously high. He needed a pill.

A hurled stapler barely missed Paul's head. He ducked in time. "I don't care what you have to do. I want that plane found, *now*!"

Charles stalked away from Basua and picked up the handheld phone. Staying too close might result in the doctor's untimely demise. Damn Limey. If he didn't need his help so badly, he would have dropped him weeks ago. He didn't like taking chicken-hearted civilians into his operations.

The phone rang. Someone answered on the fourth ring. "Yeah?"

"Code Red. SRM Facilities. Town Shadow Pines. Missing experiment."

"How soon?"

"Yesterday."

Charles clicked off and placed another call.

Jim Ports answered on the second ring. "Hiya, Chucky. Whaddya need?"

"Don't call me Chucky. I need The Chameleon to help me locate my missing experiment."

"She's deep in New Orleans," Ports said. "Human trafficking case."

"Get her out. New assignment—rancher using California ranch for drug-smuggling operations. Mexican cartel connections. Deep cover."

"Aye, aye, Captain."

"Major. Just call me Major, and I need you to come as well."

Ports chuckled. "How soon?"

"A.S.A.P."

"I can't pull her out right now."

Charles smacked his hand against his forehead. "Just get her—NOW!"

*March 30, 1998—Monday—***New Orleans***

Special Agent Ana Penn pushed the squealing shopping cart filled with dirty and disgusting blankets and clothing around the corner of Calliope and Tchoupitoulas. Filthy industrial area—plenty of buildings to house those wretched women fresh off the boat. Most came from China or Mexico or South America on their way to become the sinful, sexual pleasure of some bastard fat-cat American businessman, a Saudi prince, or worse.

At times she hated her job.

The deceased homeless woman she'd taken the full cart from had died of alcohol poisoning about three weeks back. Everything smelled of Southern Bourbon and death. Her nose should be used to it by now, but it wasn't. She didn't smell much better.

This assignment was the last one she'd take. She was sick to death of seeing these scared, abused women and the filthy bastards who sold them into slavery. She needed a vacation. Her mole told her today the sale was going down in a warehouse on Terpsichore Street where the girls were being held.

The earpiece beneath her grimy wig squawked. "Penn, check in."

"I'm almost to Terpsichore now."

"Be careful."

"Aren't I always?"

"No." Her partner chuckled. "I don't want to call Reed with a report of your death."

"Copy that."

Ana sucked in her breath. Reed Jin-ho Penn. Her husband. She hadn't thought about him in … oh, about five seconds. They'd been so much in love, but their assignments split them up—him in San Francisco and her out of the Washington, D.C. office. The long-distance marriage hadn't survived. She still loved him more than life.

In his last letter with the signed divorce papers, he'd told her he still loved her, and when she was ready to move to the Omaha, Nebraska office, he'd be there. She nearly jumped at the chance. But she was lead on this case and looking to move up in D.C.

The bureau had nicknamed her The Chameleon because she was damn good at what she did—hiding in plain sight. Like today as a homeless woman of considerable years. But the Glock .22 and Smith & Wesson .40 pistol were safely tucked under her mounds of body-odor-enriched blouses, and her smaller Glock .26 9mm was nestled in her ankle holster ready for a quick grab.

She paused at the entrance to the dead-end street, pretended to straighten up her belongings and watched. It didn't take long to see a fifty-five-foot moving van turn right on Terpsichore Street and head toward the harbor. Like most homeless people in The Big Easy, this city of hot jazz, she was ignored.

Crouched over, feeling every one of her forty-six years and with the cart squealing, she crossed the road slowly, ignoring the honks of cars and trucks. She mumbled to herself. Something about the stupid government and aliens with death rays. People went out of their way to walk around her. One of her teeth had been painted black which she found quite amusing. Her partner called her Billy Joe Jean after a cousin of his.

Her informant told her the big boss of the operation was personally overseeing the sale today. If she could only lay hands on the bastard, she could receive her promotion and move away from the down-and-dirty field work.

Her cell phone vibrated against her leg. She should have turned it off. Leaning against a building, she reached for her phone. "Yeah. What do you want?"

"I need The Chameleon. Drug smuggling rancher. Undercover."

"Ports. That you?" Ana asked.

"Hiya, Ana."

"When?" She thought she'd get a rest between cases. She figured wrong.

"Soon."

She scratched her head under the itchy wig. She'd probably get lice from this assignment. "That sounds low-key. I'll take it."

"Call me when you're free."

"Copy that."

"Good huntin'." Ports rang off.

Ana pocketed her phone, yanked her Glock from her shoulder holster, hid it in the folds of a smelly blanket on the top of her cart. She sang, "The Boy is Mine" off-key as she waddled down the sidewalk in front of the warehouses. At the end of the street, several burly men offloaded rope-tied, malnourished women, and scurried them into the warehouse. Dirty rotten bastards.

"I'm in position," she whispered into the headset.

"Copy that."

121

Her heart beat loudly in her ears. She wasn't nervous. The excitement of the capture rushed warm and delicious through her veins like hot fudge sauce. "I'm going in."

"We're right behind."

If the men offloading the women saw her, they paid no attention to her. She could walk right up to the truck. It wasn't hard to slip inside. Men in hand-tailored suits, some in Saudi garb, stood next to a raised dais. Pigs. Boils on the ass of humanity. She could kill them all and not lose any sleep.

When she was well hidden behind a stack of boxes on pallets, she said, "In position."

All the women stood against the wall, most of them dirty, with tear-stained faces, wearing just enough to cover their essential parts. Ana braced herself. Her team would be right outside. She drew in a large breath through her nose and out through her mouth. "Now."

With her gun held solidly in both hands, she raced around the pallet and braced her feet. "Federal agents. Stay where you are and put your hands up."

Chaos ensued.

CHAPTER EIGHTEEN

Jessica and Dr. Samantha Stone, Veterinarians

April 4, 1998—Saturday

"I'm IN LOVE WITH Robbie Meyers," Jessica Stone said.

Dr. Samantha Stone put down her stethoscope to glare at her daughter, Jessica. The Labrador on her steel examining table whined and turned his head to stare. "Sorry, champ. My daughter just blew my world apart."

Jessica, who just arrived home from school, blurted out a declaration of her love for Robert Meyers, Robbie, the local computer geek, while helping her mother in the vet's office. Samantha couldn't catch her breath. She shook her head. "You're still a baby.

"Mother." Jessica sighed. "I am nearly twenty-one and you know I've always liked him."

"I was hoping when you got to Chico, you'd find a nice vet student to fall for."

Jessica plopped her hands on her slender hips. "What's wrong with Robbie?"

Sam closed her eyes, calmed her breathing. "Nothing. It's just that—"

"It's just what?"

"Can we not talk about this now? Mr. Blanding's coming in for Rocky, and I still haven't given him his shots."

"Can I do it?" Jessica asked eagerness in her eyes.

"I don't…" Samantha hung her head. Her daughter had grown up before her eyes. "Have you gotten that far in your training?"

"Mother."

"Okay." She held up her hands. Her daughter had always been a livewire, and now she was a woman—a woman Samantha didn't recognize.

123

She patted Rocky on the head, sat on the rolling stool. "Do you remember where I keep my needles and vials?"

Jessica smirked but didn't say anything. With the finesse and expertise born from years of working with her here in the animal hospital, Jessica washed her hands thoroughly in the sink and dried them. Finding the box of latex gloves, she slipped them on her hands and walked to the cupboards where Sam kept all the vaccines. Jessica opened them, read each label until she came to the DHPP vials. She located a new syringe and loaded it up.

Jessica resembled Samantha so much, Samantha's her heart ached. Thank God she hadn't taken after her drunken father. The girl had cut her straight, black hair into a short, swinging bob. It made her dark eyes luminous against her pale skin—the only contribution from her pasty criminal father.

Her smile for Rocky, the Lab, was full-wattage and lit up the small grayish-green room smelling of animals and antiseptic.

Jessica straightened her tall, thin frame clad in jeans and a Chico t-shirt sporting their mascot, Willie, the Wild Cat. Samantha wished she still looked like that. Too many of Ruby's great ribeyes were to blame for a couple of extra pounds on her hips and thighs.

Jessica approached the dog slowly, speaking in soft tones. Rocky swung his head around and glanced at her. "There, there old fellow. I'm not going to hurt you." She stroked the dog, scratched under his chin until his tongue was lolling.

When the dog was putty in her hands, Jessica squeezed some of the dog's skin above his shoulder and plunged in the needle. "There, that wasn't so bad, was it?"

Rocky wagged his thick tail.

Sam's heart swelled with pride.

"That's my girl, the new veterinarian of Shadow Pines." She walked over and gathered up her daughter in a hug. "Now tell me about you and Robbie."

April 4, 1998—Saturday—**Ruby's Steakhouse and Saloon, The Mysterious Stranger**

Bill Green swept his damp rag across the polished rough-edged bar top in the Red Ruby Saloon. He'd built the bar and shelves underneath as well and kept them well stocked.

Ruby's famous ribeyes grilling in the back over open flames could be smelled in the saloon, making everyone hungry. A current country tune blared out of his new sound system. Three couples two-stepped on the dance floor near a small bandstand he also constructed.

Friday and Saturday nights, he and Ruby featured live music and dancing. Even folks from Tahoe came to some of the shows for the high caliber of entertainment they signed to perform.

Bill hesitated a moment to admire the rest of his saloon, his half of the business he shared with Ruby. He glanced toward the steakhouse. Ruby must have seen him staring at her because she glanced up from chatting with Dr. Stone and her daughter, Jessica, and gave him a saucy smile. His Ruby was still a looker. His old heart beat a little faster.

Ruby fluffed her blonde hair and winked at him. As far as he knew, she hadn't colored her hair yet. Always a natural beauty, her soft, pale skin grew rosy under his intense stare. What man wouldn't gawk at her and wonder if she was available?

How was it that he'd been able to snap her up—a short, Jewish, retired navy guy like him? Bill still pinched himself. They'd enjoyed twenty-five wonderful years together.

He tore his gaze from his wife only because a trio of cowboys from a dude ranch up the road sauntered in bumping shoulders and talking loudly.

"Hey, Bill. Set 'em up," the tallest one said. Dewey or Donnie something. Bill wasn't sure.

They swept their cowboy hats off and hung them on the deer antlers secured to the wall for such a purpose. There were lots of ranches in Auburn area of California where cowboy could find work.

"Sure thing. Beers all around?" Bill asked.

The short one with long sideburns grinned. "None of that light crap neither and keep 'em comin'."

The third cowboy was a quiet one. He laughed at something his companion said. They all trooped to one of the raised, round tables with the pine stools, and mounted up.

Bill flipped the tops off three long-necks and skirted the bar. He placed three coasters down on the small table-top and then the beers. "Here you go."

"Thanks, Bill," Dewey or Donnie said. Yep, Dewey.

He left them to enjoy their drinks and their loud conversation, which centered on a couple of young ladies and a spring-fling dance coming up in town. Bill hoped they couldn't see into the restaurant and notice Dr. Sam's daughter, Jessica. She was a looker, growing up to resemble her Native American ma in so many ways. If they spotted her, those cowboys would be on the prowl like baying wolves.

After walking back to the bar, he tossed the bottle caps into the trash. A tourist on the end of the bar ordered one of those little fruity numbers with a tiny umbrella. Where did she think she was, the Caribbean?

Bill shrugged and mixed one up for her.

He'd almost finished concocting a Bahama Mama when the front door opened. He glanced up, his hands froze in midair with the shaker. What the hell….

A man with leathery, dark-skin stepped up to the reservation desk of the restaurant, cigarette clenched between yellowed teeth. Halting beside the host's station, he surveyed both the restaurant area and the saloon with hooded eyes.

Not tall, the man carried himself like ex-military. He dressed all in black except for a multi-colored scarf wrapped around his thick, bearded neck. He favored his right leg and hobbled some as he stalked toward the bar.

The sight of the Scarf Man gave Bill the heebie-jeebies. He'd seen any number of bad dudes during his time serving drinks at the saloon, and when serving in the Navy as a Chief Petty Officer. He'd bounced a good lot in the brig. But this man looked like he could slit your throat before you hollered, "Halt."

Bill finished the tourist's drink and placed it on a napkin in front of her. The woman's eyes opened wide as she stared at the Scarf Man. Her hand shook as she picked up the drink for a sip.

Bill couldn't blame her. Even the rowdy cowboys stopped yapping to stare at the man.

At the other end of the bar, Scarf Man jerked his bearded chin in Bill's direction. "Bottle of Jack and a glass," he said in a deep-throated smoker's rasp. Leaving the bar, he hobbled over to a table in half-shadow at the back corner and sat. Of course, he'd keep his back to the wall and make sure there were at least two means of escape. Standard special ops M.O.

Bill reached behind him for an unopened bottle of his finest Jack and a clean shot glass. When was the last time he'd served an entire bottle to a customer? Maybe he needed to put in a call to Sheriff Warner.

Bill set the bottle and glass down in front of the stranger, smacking the table a bit hard. "That'll be sixty."

The man scrutinized Bill out of squinty eyes, but whipped out a hundred-dollar bill and tossed it on the tabletop. "Keep the change."

"T-thanks." Bill swallowed hard. "Say, where you from—?"

Scarf Man cut him off. "Who're the birds sitting at the front table in the restaurant?"

Bill couldn't tell this … this psycho, maybe a murderer, about Dr. Sam and Jessica. He feared for their lives. He was about to open his mouth and tell him so when he noticed the long hunting knife strapped to the man's thigh. No doubt he was proficient with it. "That's our town vet and her daughter."

"Names." He demanded.

"Dr. Samantha and Jessica Stone."

The man grunted and took a shot of whiskey, wiping his mouth on the back of his scarred and tattooed hand.

Bill escaped, hiding behind his bar. Thankfully, he wouldn't have to attend to the man until he left, and he retrieved Scarf Man's bottle and glass, and cleaned the table.

The cowboys took up their conversation again. "I heard tell Mr. Mack's cattle has been scattered by some secret military spy plane," Dewey said.

Sideburns shook his head. "Killed one of his best cows and her calf."

"A real shame," the quiet one said.

127

During this short conversation, Scarf Man perked up, all his attention focused on the cowboys.

The tall one scowled. "We're gonna go there on Monday to help with the roundup and branding. I'm thinking we're gonna be chasing cows and their calves clean up by Mesa de Salvia."

"That's some rough country," Sideburns said.

"Good pay, though," the quiet cowboy said.

The stranger rose from his chair, shot glass in his weathered hand. "Howdy boys," he said in a phony Texas drawl. The cowboys leaned away from him. "Y'all know the name of this here rancher bothered by that there spy plane?"

Dewey, the apparent leader of the group, took a pull from his beer, probably to find his courage. "Who's askin'?"

The psycho stiffened. "I am."

Dewey's bottle quaked in his hand for a second. "That'd be Mr. Joe Mack on Sunrise Ranch."

"That be southeast of this here lovely town?" The stranger fingered the handle of his large knife.

Bill's heart beat wildly in his chest. He'd just polished his hardwood floors, he didn't need blood on them.

Needing to act, he turned around and pushed through the swinging doors at the side of the bar. He had to call the sheriff.

April 5, 1998—Sunday: **Mr. Hindi Comes to the Ranch**

Robbie's old Mercury sputtered and wheezed before he reached the gate leading into Sunrise Ranch. He couldn't believe he had a whole week to spend with Joe on the ranch. Robbie sure hoped Joe had left the roundup and branding until he could get home. He could hardly wait to get on the back of a horse again and ride hell-bent for leather across Joe's green ranchland.

Earlier, he stopped by the Shadow Pines café to see his mom. She told him he was too thin. He couldn't bring himself to tell her about Jessica yet. She'd practically lost him to the Macks during his growing up years. He didn't have the heart to tell her he was going to marry Jessica Stone after college, and maybe not return to Shadow Pines.

Ahead of him, a black sedan, late model, turned onto the gravel road leading to Mr. Joe's ranch house and compound. He stopped in front of the gate. Who was this man coming to see Joe? He didn't like salespeople.

Robbie pulled up behind the black car to see who got out.

A tall, stout man with jet black hair and dark skin climbed out of the sedan. He wore a navy polo shirt, tan khaki multi-pocket pants, and hiking boots. For a moment, the man didn't look as though he knew what to do with the gate. Robbie needed to install a camera at the entrance, or at least an intercom so Joe could buzz people in. That way they wouldn't have to worry about shutting the gate behind themselves.

"Can I help you?" Robbie asked as he climbed out of his car.

"What?" The man flipped around, placed a hand over his heart. "I did not see you there." The man's speech was British, but his face was Indian, and not like Jessica's Native American mom, Sam.

"Let me open the gate for you."

"Oh, yes. Thank you. I did not know what to do."

"Can I ask why you're visiting my…" What was Mr. Mack to him? He always pretended Joe was his dad. "What business do you have with Joe Mack?"

The man clutched his hands together. "I am Paul … Hindi, a geologist from…" he pointed to the label on his polo shirt. It read: University of Calcutta, Geological Department. "I need to do some research on the fault lines running across Mr. Mack's property."

Yeah, that wasn't going to fly. Robbie knew what Joe would say. "Get the hell off my property."

Robbie grinned. "Well you can try, but I warn you, Mr. Joe is one ornery, stubborn cuss."

"Cuss?" The man's dark eyes narrowed in question.

"Dude."

"Ah, dude. Yes."

Robbie opened the gate and stood aside to wait for Mr. Hindi to drive through. Once the gate was secured, he jumped in his sputtering car, which Sal needed to look at, and followed.

Mr. Hindi parked in front of Joe's house and got out. He surveyed the ranch buildings nervously like someone watched him. Another thing Robbie would install for Joe was cameras. Set him up with surveillance cameras and motion detectors. Couldn't be too careful with all those rustlers about, and small military spy planes.

Robbie parked over by the garage but didn't see Sal or Ricardo around. He had to see Joe boot the scientist off his property or pull the shotgun he kept by the front door. It would be something to tell Jessica.

Nervously touching his face, Mr. Hindi trudged up the stairs to Joe's front door. Robbie wasn't even sure Joe was home. He could be anywhere. Up on the mesa or in the east pastureland, or north in the orchards and farm-fields Mike managed. He could just be riding Checkers up through the canyons searching for ... peace. He hadn't had much since Miss Cindy passed.

Mr. Hindi knocked on the ranch house door. He waited.

Robbie walked over to the corner of the porch railing, leaned against it. He crossed his ankles, and his arms over his chest.

The front door burst open. Joe looked like he'd been asleep. His clothes were rumpled and dirty, and he hadn't shaved in days. He squinted through hawk-like eyes at the stranger on his porch. "What do you want?"

"Good day, Mr. Mack. I am Paul Hindi from the University of Calcutta, Geological Department and I'm in your beautiful country on assignment from the U.S. and British government to do a seismic study of the surrounding areas of Lake Tahoe. They are worried about a large earthquake rocking this area and causing a tsunami on the lake which could affect you down here below the lake."

Joe rubbed his eyes, appeared to refocus on the man.

Hindi rushed on pointing up at Sunrise Mountain. "You have an unnamed quaternary fault running right through your property from the Tahoe-Sierra frontal fault zone, which is only secondary to the West Tahoe Fault. I need to set up monitoring equipment—a seismometer, which is an instrument that measures the motion of the ground, including those of seismic waves generated by earthquakes to take seismic readings. It is very dangerous, and it is imperative I get up to Sunrise Mountain and the lower canyons to inspect this fault and take core samples."

The man didn't even take a breath.

By now Joe appeared wide awake, his mind racing.

Joe straightened up to his full height and glared at the man. "Are you the people flying the small spy plane over my land?"

Mr. Hindi sputtered. "I cannot answer that."

"Get off my ranch."

"But you do not understand, Mr. Mack. I am from the governments of two countries, and I need to gather this information. It is a matter of life and death."

Joe leaned back. The next thing Robbie saw was the working end of the shotgun pointed at Mr. Hindi's chest. The dark man stumbled back a few paces. "I'd say you're coming on my ranch is a matter of life and death. Now get off my land."

"But Mr. Mack—"

Joe lifted the gun, his finger on the trigger. "One."

"Wait!"

"Two."

"I'm going." Mr. Hindi ran down the stairs and jerked his car door open. He practically dove into the car.

"Three." Joe aimed and shot the ground in front of the sedan's tires.

Mr. Hindi, his expression resembling a scared rabbit's, roared the car to life and it spit gravel as he raced the car out of the yard.

Joe placed the gun back inside the door and turned to grin at Robbie. "Welcome home, Geek."

CHAPTER NINETEEN

Robbie and Jessica and the Roundup

April 6, 1998—Monday

J**OE WOKE BEFORE DAWN** to the smell of Lettie's flapjacks and bacon caressing his nose. He had no appetite since running off the government flunky, but today was roundup day, and he needed his strength.

Stiff from sleeping on the ground while camping, he struggled to sit up. Carefully he swung his aching legs over the edge of the bed. Not hard to believe the government already sent someone to search his property for the plane. Scratching the thick stubble on his jaw, he probably shouldn't be surprised.

They'd be pissed off when the plane didn't return home.

Why send someone pretending to be a geologist? No fences stood between his property and that of SRM's side. A lot of rugged country, yes, but no rails. They could hike through the backcountry of his property without anyone being the wiser.

Maybe they figured he'd hidden the plane here on the ranch compound instead of back up in the mountains. Joe pushed off the bed and lurched into the bathroom for a shower and shave.

"Good morning, Mr. Mack," Lettie said when he strolled into the bright kitchen about half an hour later.

Robbie had taken his place at the table and stuffed a four-layer bite of pancakes dripping with syrup into his mouth. He nodded his greeting as he chewed.

Joe sat. Didn't say anything. Happy morning family scene in a warm, homey kitchen. Only one thing missing from making it perfect—the love of his life. Cindy hadn't come to him since the night in the tent. He missed her with a heavy ache in his chest.

Robbie sliced through another massive stack of pancakes. "Jessica and I'll take the canyons and arroyos below Mesa de Salvia."

"Jessica?" Joe murmured.

"Dr. Sam's daughter."

At the mention of Sam, Joe's heart bumped, and he stabbed into his pancakes with his knife. Since they ate at Ruby's Monday night, he hadn't seen or talked to her. It irked him that he felt terrible. He should have called her back and scheduled another time to get together, maybe invited her to the ranch for a quiet dinner.

"Anyway," Robbie went on. "Jess and her mom are coming to ride the roundup and vaccinate the new calves."

Damn, he'd forgotten. Could he have Sam this close and not desire to touch her hand or her hair? Cindy, where have you been?

"That dude coming here pretending to be a geologist was whack." Robbie stuffed in some more pancakes.

"What?" Joe pushed his pancakes around his plate. "How did you know he wasn't a geologist?"

Robbie shrugged and slugged back his orange juice. "I think he was. There was something government about the dude. He knew his geology, but he wasn't here because of either."

"He said he represented ours and the U.K.'s government."

"True. But Mr. Hindi was fishy."

Joe frowned. "Fishy?"

"When I met him at the gate, he almost didn't know his last name, like he had to think one up. Hindi." He laughed. "That's a language, not a last name."

Joe held a hand up when Lettie put two more pancakes on his plate.

"You need to eat. You're still weak from your time in the mountains," she said.

He scowled at her. "Yes, Momma."

She chuckled. "Don't you forget it. Miss Cindy said to feed you well."

The pain of grief hit below his ribs, but not as intense as usual.

Robbie stood, gathered up his dirty dishes and placed them in the sink. "I'm right thankful to you, Ms. Sanchez, for a wonderful breakfast."

She touched his arm. "You be careful out there among the cattle. They can spook easily, especially after the one mother and her baby died."

"Thank you. I'll remember." Robbie turned to Joe. "You coming?"

Joe took one last bite, having eaten less than half of his pancakes.

Lettie grabbed a sheet of plastic wrap, twisted up his left-over bacon in it, and handed it to him. "For later. We'll serve dinner for the cowhands at one."

He nodded, mashed his hat down on his head, slipped his arms into his Sherpa jacket, and followed Robbie out into the darkness.

Robbie bumped down the porch steps and out into the yard, Joe at his heels. Gosh, he loved roundup day, even if they started before sunup. They would get their assignments from Joe and Ricardo and head out over the grassland in search of the herd. Joe told him he'd seen the little spy plane purposefully dip into the herd and scatter them in every direction. He and Jessica would ride together into the foothills and arroyos looking for strays, up to Robbie's favorite spot.

"Say, Robbie," Joe said from behind him.

Robbie jerked to a stop and spun around. "What's up?"

"You and I need to talk about securing my property."

"I was thinking the same thing when Mr. Hindi dropped in. Just anyone can drive onto your property, and you wouldn't know until it was too late."

"How much do you think it will cost?"

"I'll get you a good deal and won't charge you labor."

Joe shook his head. "I can't do that. I owe you a lot."

Joe wouldn't like him to hug him. He was a proud man, not one for affection, so Robbie smiled. "The feeling is mutual. How about you drive to Sacramento with me when roundup is over?"

Joe nodded and kept walking toward the stables.

Robbie studied him. His shoulders appeared more hunched, his step slower, as if he carried some heavy burdens. Missing Miss

Cindy had taken a toll, but Joe was coming out of his despair, getting on with life. What he needed was a woman.

Bright lights flickered over the dirt around the corral interrupting Robbie's thoughts. Rigs pulling horse trailers jolted up the gravel road toward the compound. Some of the local ranchers showing up to help and had brought their mounts. The place would be hopping with cowboys and high-stepping horses itching to get into the rangeland and collect the cattle.

Dr. Sam and Jessica would ride some of Joe's stock. Robbie couldn't figure out why Joe looked surprised when he mentioned them coming. And why didn't he remember Dr. Sam's daughter, Jessica?

"Hey, gringo," Salvador called to Robbie from the stable door. "Who you riding today?"

Robbie grinned. He'd taken a shine to Sal, mechanic and horse wrangler. "I'm taking Garfunkel. Jess will ride Simon." Remembering when twin chestnut colts were born one spring that Joe had let him name, he chuckled. Joe'd been sorry ever since.

"Jess, your girl?" Sal asked when he fell into step with Robbie.

He was glad it was still too dark to see his red face. "Maybe."

"She coming to ride the range with you?"

"Maybe."

Sal chuckled. "You sound like the boss."

Robbie grinned. "Maybe."

Sal slugged him in the arm. "Geek."

"Don't you forget it."

Jessica Stone found Robbie saddling her horse, a slender three-year-old chestnut inside the stable, named Simon. Garfunkel already saddled, waited loosely, tied to a stall board. She leaned against the weather-roughened door to watch Robbie work.

A lock of his dark, wavy hair fell over his forehead in his concentration. Her fingers twitched to slide it back into place. He crouched down and reached under Simon for the cinch and threaded it through the rigging ring and pulled it up tight, the muscles in his arms flexing. Her heart thumped loudly.

"Suck it in, boy." He slapped the horse on the side. Simon swung his head around to take a nip out of Robbie's hand. He jerked it back and laughed. "Nice try."

Jessica covered her mouth to keep from laughing. Who knew she'd fall for the handsome geek, the chess club champion from their senior year? So many jocks had asked her out and were confused when she turned them all down to walk and talk with Robbie. He was super smart and funny, though shy. His exceptional mind kept her captivated and engaged. None of the jocks could hold even the most straightforward conversation. She had loved Robbie since middle school.

He finished with the back cinch and stepped away from Simon to grab the reins. That's when he turned and saw her. "Jess?"

"You caught me."

His eyes lit up. "I sure did."

He pulled Simon over toward her. Before he handed her the reins, he looped his hand around her neck and pulled her to him for a stunningly, rad kiss. When they separated, she sighed. "Hmmm."

"I like your t-shirt," Robbie said pointing to her black tee.

She laughed. "I like yours, too."

Both shirts said: "I love my Geek."

"You ready to hightail it for the mountains after those wanderin' bovines?" Robbie asked.

She chuckled. "As long as I'm with you, I don't care where we go."

He grabbed her again and held her tight for a sweet kiss, but at the sound of a cough behind them, they jumped apart. Mom had walked into the stables to saddle the horse she'd be riding.

Jessica's face flamed. "Busted."

Mom's mouth opened and closed as her face turned a blotchy red. Jessica couldn't blame her. After all, she'd just told her she was in love with Robbie. It had to be a shock to see her and Robbie kissing. However, she'd been in love with him for years and being together at college had cemented their relationship.

"I'm sorry, Mom."

Mom waved her hand in the air like she could make the kissing scene disappear. She didn't speak.

Robbie inclined his head toward the open stable door and tugged on Garfunkel's reins. Jessica had no choice but to follow him. They needed to go since they had the farthest to ride today.

Jessica's gut churned. She'd do anything for her mom not to be upset with her, or to be disappointed in her. But she loved Robbie and wanted Mom to accept him. With any luck, they would get married soon.

Mom had been through so much with Jessica's drunken father and the abuse she suffered at his hands. He was serving time in prison for assaulting Mom. He nearly killed her before Jessica could get to Robbie's house and call the sheriff. Jessica still had nightmares.

Maybe she wasn't marriage material. Once up in the saddle with the reins in her hands, Jessica considered she might be making a colossal mistake—much like her mother had.

CHAPTER TWENTY

Gettin' Stoned—And Not in a Good Way

April 6, 1998—Monday

ROBBIE REINED in his horse, Garfunkel, when they reached the bottom of the foothills at the base of Mesa de Salvia. Lots of box canyons to search before making the treacherous trip up the side of the Mesa. Jessica hardly spoke the entire ride. Having her mom see them kiss must've messed with her head.

"You okay?" he asked.

She shrugged, but wouldn't meet his eyes.

"I'm sorry," he said. "I shouldn't have kissed you in front of the others."

"It's not your fault. It's mine."

Robbie's neck warmed. "Why would you say that? We're in love, so kissing is allowed. Do you think she's mad you're seeing me?"

Jess turned her head away. "She wasn't happy."

"What? Why?"

Tears glistened in Jess's eyes when she turned and gazed at him. "She wasn't happy when I told her I loved you."

"I'm sorry."

On the cliff above them, Robbie heard someone moving around. Small pebbles tumbled down the sheer rock face. "Quiet."

Jess' eyes widened. "What is it?" she whispered.

"I'm not sure. Let's dismount and go in on foot."

He slid off Garfunkel, and Jess did the same off her horse. They walked them over to a tall aspen grove and tied them there. Robbie removed the pump action, .280 Remington hunting rifle from its scabbard and took her hand. Jess trembled.

"It's going to be okay," he said.

She allowed him to pull her behind him. Together they skirted the base of a hundred-foot wall of limestone shale, hugging the other side of the box canyon. Small rocks and gravel tumbled down from the top narrowly missing them. Jess jumped closer to him, gripped his arm with her hand. Someone was up on the ridge and may or may not have sent the crumbling edge down where they stood on purpose.

What if someone was purposefully trying to hurt them? Robbie had to find shelter.

Murderer

"Ah, sod it." Dr. Paul Basua swore. He had only leaned over the edge of the canyon when he heard someone moving around down there. However, he had sent small rocks tumbling from the top edge side to the bottom and alerted them to his presence. Did the young man know he had snuck back onto the Mack ranch? Would the boy and his girl turn him in to the sheriff?

He was not a murderer, and he was cheesed off at the major for sending one of his wanker lags, Hawke, a squint-eyed assassin, to babysit him. Guess Major Donald didn't think he could follow through with the rough stuff. The major was correct. Hawke, dark-skinned and vicious, always looked a tad narked—scary, and gave Paul the willies.

Paul asked himself what Major Donald would do?

The major would kill the boy and girl, leave no trace of their bodies. But Paul was not a murderer, and he would not harm those two young people.

"Don't get buggy on me, Basua," Hawke said in a gravelly voice. "I should've come here alone. I knew you didn't have the stomach for killing."

Paul gulped but said nothing. This henchman of the major's was a rotter.

He figured Hawke had no compunction about murdering someone. This man was a bloody butcher. He probably sent many a person "to the farm" where no one would ever find them.

When this project was completed, Paul would need an extended holiday in the South of France.

139

When the cliff edge crumbled away under his weight, Paul backed away. Unfortunately, Hawke told him he had a brilliant idea.

"Who's gonna question a rockslide in this area of loose shale and crumbling cliff faces?" Hawke grinned. "A boulder slipping from its spot ain't gonna be so unusual. So what if two twits get caught underneath."

Paul brought his walking poles with him in case he had to traverse rocky patches like the one he was standing on.

The assassin eyed his poles. "These'll make terrific levers to pry out this boulder. No one would be the wiser," he said. "Give 'em to me."

"I am not a murderer." Paul gripped the poles to his chest. "This is not right. They are innocent kids."

"In this world, nobody's innocent." Hawke shoved him aside. "Get out of the way if you can't stand getting your hands dirty, or I might just send you over the cliff with 'em."

Paul watched in horror as the arse dug the sandy gravel and soil out from beneath the giant boulder.

The young man he saw at Joe Mack's ranch house and the girl would walk directly under the cliff where Hawke dug out the boulder. Only a few stomps with Hawke's boots were needed to dislodge the large rock and send it thundering down the cliff.

Paul prayed for forgiveness from all the gods he could recall—Shiva, Vishnu, Shakti, Ganesha, the elephant god, and Surya, the sun god, for good measure as he walked away from the edge of the box canyon.

"Shut your trap, so we can go our merry way," Hawke said from behind him. "I'm gonna search some of the canyons to the south. You take the top of the mesa." He spun on his heel and disappeared into the forest.

Paul regretted being a part of killing those young people. He wished he had never signed on to work with Major Donald and what they were doing at SRM. He would find the mine, tell the major and that would be that. He would wash his hands of the major and SRM and have a clear conscience. At least that is what he told himself as he walked through the ponderosa pines to the top of the mesa.

The major would be happy Hawke performed his bloody duty so well.

April 6, 1998—Monday—**Near Death Experience**

Robbie saw a small shelf-like opening in the canyon wall at the same moment he heard the thundering of much bigger rocks slipping from their position on the cliff above them.

Someone caused a rockslide.

He gripped Jessica around the waist and tossed her into the open outcropping, tumbled in after her, and covered her with his body.

A large boulder, the size of one of Mr. Joe's one-ton bulls, fell exactly where they'd been standing. Other smaller boulders and rocks, still deadly, fell around the bigger one.

They would have been killed for sure.

Jessica's body quaked.

"It's okay, babe. We're fine," he said with more peace in his voice than he felt.

"S-someone tried to kill us. Why?"

"I don't know, but I intend to find out." Robbie hugged her close and continued to whisper into her ear they were okay. He listened until the canyon grew quiet and no movement came from up above.

"Do you think they're gone?" Jessica asked.

"I haven't heard anything for a few minutes. Perhaps they think we're dead and took off."

"Oh, I hope so," she whispered and clung to him. "Oh, I mean gone not us being dead."

They lay together for another few minutes. Robbie told himself it was to make sure whoever had attempted to kill them was gone, but it was more than that. He loved being this close to the woman he was going to marry.

He gently kissed her trembling lips. "Are you all right now?"

She gave him a half grin. "This is opportune for you, isn't it?"

"I don't know what you mean."

Jessica kissed him, turning him inside out.

"Shall we go get the murdering S.O.B.?" he asked.

Robbie shoved aside several small boulders and jagged rocks, so he could scoot out. He thanked God they'd seen the break in the rock and dove into it.

Jess' mom would be furious with him.

Robbie's rifle had fallen out of his hands when he dove under the small ledge, but it wasn't damaged in the slide. He picked it up and took Jessica by the hand. "Let's get the horses and circle around to the top of the cliff."

Fear filled Jessica's eyes for a moment, but she blinked it away. "Okay. Let's go."

CHAPTER TWENTY-ONE

Dr. Paul Basua—A.K.A. Mr. Hindi—Captured

April 6, 1998—Monday

THE RIDE WITH JESSICA through the trees around the box canyon base and up its steep side took about an hour. Robbie had his doubts they would be able to catch the would-be murderer now. Hopefully, they might find evidence the rockslide hadn't been an accident of nature.

"Do you think whoever did this left evidence?" Jessica asked.

"I hope they were stupid enough to leave boot prints or marks in the ground at the edge. Although matching evidence with a person might be a lot harder."

Steadily the temperature rose as they climbed through the forest. Robbie forearmed the sweat from his face and gulped down water from his canteen.

The top of the box canyon was a stone's throw from the foot of Mesa de Salvia and covered with loose rocks. Only a handful of trees dotted the top. Robbie dismounted and walked to the edge of the cliff. Jessica sat on her horse and watched from the tree line.

He slowly approached the edge, careful to notice any disturbance in the sand and gravel. Sure enough, the area looked like an army had trampled through the sand.

"Do you see anything?" she asked.

"Footprints in the sand here and there." He pointed to several clear prints.

"I have my disposable camera in my saddle bag. I meant to take some pictures of our ride today. Do you want to use it?"

Robbie grinned. "I knew you'd come prepared for anything. Bless you."

He ran over to her and took the camera from her hand. He pulled her down for a quick kiss. "I love you."

Jessica blushed. "I love you, too."

He took several pictures of the footprints and of the edge where it looked like the giant boulder once was. Pry marks crisscrossed the sand. "This was no accident."

"Who would want to kill us?" Jess asked.

"I don't know." Robbie found the footprints leading away from the cliff face and decided to walk his horse to track them. "The boulder falling toward us was a clear case of attempted murder, and now that we have proof, we'll call in the law. We just have to find this murdering jackass and turn him in to the sheriff."

He glanced back at Jessica. By her pursed lips, she appeared eager, but a little afraid. Her rifle lay across her lap. Having practiced with him on so many occasions, he knew she was a crack shot. But could she shoot a human being?

Robbie paused before following the footsteps into a thick stand of ponderosa pines. "Do you want to tell me why you were upset?"

She glanced up and met his eyes. "Mom thinks I'm too young to get involved with anyone."

"Especially me?"

"She doesn't know you like I do."

"I think you're both afraid I might end up being like your dad, aren't you?"

She placed a hand over her heart. "How … how would you know that?"

"I saw it in your mom's eyes. She was afraid, not mad." He looked at the blinding blue sky and then back at Jessica. "She married young, didn't she?"

"Yes. Mom was seventeen."

"You aren't seventeen. You should know your own mind." He took a breath. "And … I'm not your dad."

He dropped Garfunkel's reins and meandered back to her. Reaching up, he gripped her hand. "I would never hurt you. I'd as soon hurt myself."

"I know that, Robbie. For a few moments, I couldn't trust myself."

Still holding her hand, he reached into his pocket where the little velvet box pressed against his leg. He drew it out and worked up the lid. Jessica sucked in her breath and stared at him, and then at the dazzling diamond in the box. He'd gone without a mid-day meal for three months to purchase this token pledge of his love.

"I wish this were a more romantic setting, but up here in the mountains with the wind blowing your hair around your gorgeous face, I couldn't wait." He knelt on the rocky ground. "Jessica Stone, will you do me the honor of marrying me?"

Her mouth hung open for a second before she giggled. "Yes. Oh, yes, dear Robbie Meyers, I will be your wife."

The footsteps leading away from the edge of the cliff disappeared into the forest at the tree line. Someone with long narrow feet made tracks in the dirt. The two of them walked their horses on foot through the woods so Robbie could track the footprints. Thankfully, the man hadn't been very good at covering his tracks. He probably figured they'd been killed in the slide and wouldn't be following him. Jerk.

"How much further do you think he'll climb?" she asked.

Robbie stopped walking near a downed tree resembling a place where the would-be murderer stopped to rest. He knelt and fingered the earth, something Joe had taught him. "He stopped here to take a drink because the ground's wet. I don't believe he's too far ahead of us."

Jessica gripped the rifle until her knuckles went white. "I wish we could get this over with and get back to the cattle search."

"It won't be long now."

The narrow trail up the side of Mesa de Salvia was treacherous. Robbie opted to go around. It might take a few more minutes, but they could sneak up on the idiot from behind and see what he was doing. Then Robbie'd take him down.

Coming out of the trees above the mesa left him and Jessica in the darkness, while the man they were pursuing stood on the plateau inspecting a small box canyon in the full sun. Robbie's advantage.

He tiptoed back to Jessica now standing beside the horses, her rifle gripped in her hands. "I need you to stay here and keep your rifle trained on the guy."

"Okay. Be careful. That man tried to kill us."

Robbie spun around to glimpse once more at the man. Shock rattled him as he recognized the Indian/English geologist from the government. He figured the guy quite harmless. Who knew he was capable of such a horrendous act? "It's Mr. Hindi, or whoever he is."

"The geologist?"

"Who knows? He could've been lying through his teeth." Robbie tied the horses to a small aspen tree. "Stay here. He doesn't appear to be armed. But keep him covered. I may need you to shoot off a warning shot to show him we mean business."

She nodded, although he could tell she was trembling. "You're a strong woman, Jess. Remember I love you."

With a crooked smile, she pulled the rifle up in front of her. "Ready."

Keeping an eye on Hindi, Robbie held to the tree line as he circled the mesa. The man looked cocky and completely at ease. What a shock he was going to get. With the man's shoeprint captured on Jessica's camera and clear evidence someone pried the rock off the cliff side, they had him nailed.

The small box canyon Hindi inspected had shorter sides and the back wall towered about two-hundred feet. Robbie crouched behind a large boulder at the entrance and waited for him to walk by him. He turned and gave Jessica a thumb's up. She returned the signal. They made a great team. Perhaps they would go into criminal investigations after graduation.

Rocks scattered when Hindi walked around the canyon. Robbie heard the man mumbling to himself something about "no cave at the back." What was that about? Was he searching for a cave up on Joe's property? A cave of what?

Lightning struck.

Maybe the fool was searching for a gold or silver mine on Mr. Joe's property. Were there any mines left that hadn't been tapped out? Surely Joe would know if there was a mine on his property. Or perhaps Miss Cindy's pop or her grandfather dug out one. Must be some record of a mine up here in the mountains at the county clerk's office in Auburn.

Hindi turned and headed back toward his position. Robbie steadied himself.

The man walked past his hiding spot behind the boulder. Robbie leveled the rifle at his back.

"I wouldn't move if I were you." With a quick pump action and the gun pressed into Robbie's gut, he loaded the first shell into the chamber. But in the thin, clear mountain air, the ominous, cold clack-CLACK of the pump action caused Hindi to spin around and clutch his chest.

"What the bloody hell?" Hindi sputtered, his dark face turning a sickening shade of pale. "Who are … you're that college kid. But I thought you were—"

"Dead? No thanks to you. Hands up, Mr. Hindi, if that's your name. You're going to answer for your attempt to murder my girlfriend and me."

"Look, it wasn't me. I was walking along the fault line, and some rocks fell. But the big boulder crashing down wasn't me," Hindi said.

Robbie moved his finger to the trigger, waved it at Hindi's heart. "Now why don't I believe a word coming out of your mouth?" He shook his head. "I said, put 'em up."

Hindi made a quick move with his hand as though he was reaching for a gun. A shot rang out peppering the man's legs with tiny rocks.

"Don't shoot." His arms sprang upwards. "I was only kidding. I did not want to hurt you, but I was…." He clamped his mouth closed.

"You were what?" Robbie stepped closer to the man. With the gun barrel, he urged him to continue. "Don't let me stop you from confessing."

"It was … the other man … left me to take the blame. I cannot say what I have been doing up here."

"Mr. Joe told you to get off his land and stay off. Do you know the penalty for trespassing in this state?"

Hindi shook his head.

"Since you not only trespassed on land clearly marked as owned by Mr. Joe and threatened to injure us in the worst way possible, I do believe you're looking at felony attempted murder charges here, not just felony trespassing. That means jail time."

Hindi clasped his hands in front of him. "I'm the victim here." He continued to babble.

None of it made sense to Robbie. Hindi the victim?

"Jess, my rope," Robbie shouted.

She appeared next to Hindi, rope in one hand, rifle in the other.

"Secure his hands behind him. Nice and tight. We're going to head back to the ranch and have a chat with the sheriff."

CHAPTER TWENTY-TWO
Roundup Complications

April 6, 1998—Monday—late afternoon

D OCTOR SAMANTHA STONE CHECKED
her watch a second time. Hours had passed since
her daughter and that boy, Robbie Meyers, went
into the foothills by Mesa de Salvia. Even if they
had to swing back and forth in most of the small box canyons,
they should have been back by now.

She sat on her horse at the tree line edge of the ranch. She
and Joe had rounded up three cows and their newborns. The little
ones were gangly creatures on spindly legs—so adorable. She
chewed on her bottom lip.

"What's the matter?" Joe asked from beside her. She
flinched, not having heard him approach on that stealthy horse of
his. The dogs, Shep and Spike, stood at attention on either side
of Checkers, but not too close. Wise animals.

Samantha frowned. "I would have figured Jessica and …
Robbie would have been back by now."

He glanced toward the mesa. "You're right. It's getting dark.
Most of the other hands have moved their cattle into the valley
close to the compound."

"Do you think I should ride up into the foothills and look
for them?"

Joe rubbed his chin as he considered her question. He
glanced behind them toward the compound, then back up at the
foothills. "Robbie's as good a horseman as I've ever known. He
wouldn't let anything happen to Jessica."

She bristled. "I'm not afraid of Robbie as a horseman.
I'm—"

"You're upset he's seeing your daughter."

"They're not right for each other."

"Why don't you let them decide that?"

149

"Don't you see," she said, then paused to calm herself with a huge breath. "Their backgrounds are completely different."

With a frown, Joe leaned on his saddle horn as Checkers shifted his feet. "Who says so? You're a single mom, and so is Bonnie Meyers. You both married men who were skunks."

He held up his hands. "Sorry. I didn't mean any offense. You're both strong women who did what you had to do to raise your children and you survived. Thrived as well. The kids are bright as the stars and have found each other. I think it's wonderful. Why don't you give them a break?"

Samantha stared. She'd never heard Joe string so many words together since she'd known him. "What if he takes after his dad?"

"Ah, that's it. You're afraid Robbie's a drinker and will beat on Jessica."

"Bluntly put."

"Sam." His voice was calm like he was taming a wild horse. "Not all men are bastards. Sorry. Even those sired by one." He sounded like he had firsthand experience, though he never spoke about his upbringing.

She gripped the horse's reins tight in her hand. Finally, she was able to gaze at him locking her eyes to Joe's blue/gray ones. Could he see the love shining from her eyes? "I know that, Joe. I know you're not." She sighed. "I don't know Robbie all that well."

Joe straightened in the saddle appearing uncomfortable. "He's a good kid—kind, generous, and so damned smart. As you know, Cindy and I did a considerable amount of raising of that child. He'd never hurt Jessica. I'd stake my life on him."

"Would you hurt a woman?" she whispered.

He didn't answer. After a moment he removed his cowboy hat and speared his narrow fingers through his hair. "I'm sure Cindy's 'feelings' were hurt a time or two."

"I'm not talking about feelings. I mean would you hurt a woman—physically?"

Joe glared at her, his eyes troubled that she would ask him such a question. "Never. And neither would Robbie. I taught him to be a gentleman. He's never had a bad temper, his nature is gentle and inquisitive."

"How can you be sure? I … I couldn't tell Brad had a temper. It only appeared when he drank—and he drank all the time after we got married."

This time when their eyes met, Joe's held only sympathy. "If I'd have known what that bastard was doing to you, I would've gladly taken him out."

Samantha chuckled. "I would've loved to have seen that." Why couldn't she have caught Joe's eye before Cindy snatched him up? She hoped it wasn't too late for them. "I loved watching how gentle you were with Cindy. She really loved you."

He clamped his eyes closed, and she felt him pulling away, disconnecting.

Samantha hurt for him. How could her love help him?

Neither one spoke for long, awkward moments.

Joe eventually opened his eyes, looked heavenward and then up at the Mesa de Salvia. "Look," he said after a while. "I think that's them now."

"What?" Her gaze shot over the green, rolling hills of the grazing meadows to the foothills. Sure enough, a cow and her calf trotted over the small rise of a hill, Jessica right behind them walking her chestnut. She moved the cow and calf along with a coiled rope which she circled over her head and whistled. Samantha's heart beat steady again. Her daughter was safe.

Next, Robbie rode out on his chestnut twin, his rifle cradled on his lap and one hand holding a rope. Attached to the rope was a tall, dark-skinned fellow trussed up like a Thanksgiving turkey. He stumbled along behind Robbie's horse.

"Oh, my gracious."

"Damn it all to hell," Joe said his voice filled with fury. "That no good trespassing liar, Mr. Hindi. I chased him off my property the other day."

"Hindi?"

"That's probably not his name. He came here claiming to be a geologist and asked to hike back up into the mountains to check on fault lines." Joe huffed.

Her hand trembled on the reins. "You didn't believe him."

151

"Not a chance in hell. He was a lying son-of-a-gun, and now Robbie must have found him trespassing. I'm gonna run him in to the sheriff and press charges."

"You don't think he might've hurt Jessica and ... Robbie?"

"Come on, let's see what the no-good rat's done." He spurred Checkers forward.

Samantha nudged her horse and followed.

Joe couldn't believe how close he'd come to losing Robbie, and Sam's daughter, Jessica. They sat on the porch in evening's cool shade as Robbie and Jessica told them about their near-death experience in the box canyon. Indignation burned in his gut and he clutched the arms of his Adirondack chair so firmly, he nearly splintered the wood.

It was probably a good thing it was against the law to hang a man for trespassing and attempted murder in these parts, or he would have strung up Mr. Hindi in the ranch compound.

Joe tied the law-breaker in the back of his rig. He'd get the facts straight before heading into Shadow Pines and the no-account sheriff.

"We're going with you." Sam insisted.

Joe didn't argue. He'd needed her gentle strength right now. "All right. We'll take the dually."

Sam shook her head. "Jessica and I will drive into town in my rig because we're going home tonight."

"But the branding and the immunizations?" Joe jumped to his feet, strode over to her, disappointment warring with good sense. "I'd hoped you'd stay the night here ... er. ... in the casita and work the branding at daybreak—like always."

Sam fisted her hands on her narrow hips, glared at him like a bull sizing up a bullfighter. "You figured wrong."

"Mother." Jessica stood as well, pleading in her voice. "I want to stay here—you know—to help out in the morning."

Sam cocked her head—examined her daughter then Robbie who stepped up to Jessica's side, clutched her hand. "I'll bet you do."

"Mother, it's nothing like that." Jessica's face reddened.

Joe wondered about the two young people, how well they knew each other. From the red-faced Robbie, he didn't have to wonder anymore. What would Sam do now?

He chuckled under his breath hoping she wouldn't bite his head off.

Sam closed her eyes for a second and took a huge breath in and blew it out with force. "All right. We'll go with Joe ... and Robbie to see Sheriff Warner. I'm only doing this because I need you to tell the sheriff your testimony against that English monster and put him away for good."

Jessica leaned into Robbie. Oh, yes. These two had been bitten by the love bug pretty good and hard. Sam obviously hadn't seen the enormous diamond on her daughter's finger yet. Joe predicted a wedding in the next year or two, or maybe they'd wait until after Jessica graduated. Hopefully not too long. He wished for grandchildren.

"Now that's settled," Joe said, "let's get going. I don't want to be all night in town."

Sheriff Cody Warner's day had been hellish. A big-rig on the two-lane just south of town had collided with a camper truck around noon today killing the male camper driver and a small five-year-old girl. The wife, badly injured, had to be life-flighted to Sacramento. It took hours to clear the road from Auburn into town. Drivers on the warm spring day had short tempers.

The semi-driver was cooling his heels in Cody's jail cell at the rear of the Sheriff's Station, not a scratch on him. Damned D.U.I. reminded him of Dr. Sam's husband, Brad. Cody couldn't count the number of D.U.I.'s the drunken bastard racked up before he finally killed someone as he fled arrest for spousal abuse and nearly killing Sam.

Brad Stone was doing time in San Quentin for vehicular manslaughter with a double count of spousal abuse and one for attempted murder. Terrific place to house the S.O.B.

Cody glanced at the clock on his wall. Six o'clock. Time for a beer and to head home. He shuddered as he considered going home to his timid wife of twenty years, and her usual, but pitiful attempt to cook him dinner.

He loved Beverly, even if he had been forced to marry her because of Cody, Jr. She'd been a calming influence on his moodiness and volatile temper, but she wasn't Cindy Johnsen.

Beverly should have been strong and independent, like Cindy, not act subservient to him like a slave. Though he never raised a hand to her, often he knew his words sliced through her heart quicker than a sharp sword. Although Bev never cried in front of him, he'd seen tears gloss over her eyes. He should treat her better.

A commotion of loud voices coming from the entrance drew Cody out of his melancholy. "What the hell?" He heard Barbara—his receptionist and dispatcher—attempting to restore order. Damn. He was this close to putting a cap on this frustrating day.

He stood, gritted his teeth to keep from ripping his hair out, and plodded out his office door.

Joe Mack stood front and center at the counter, his hand holding a rope tied to a dark-skinned fellow, who resembled a scared rabbit. Behind Mack was Dr. Sam, her daughter Jessica, and Robbie Meyers.

"What's the problem here?" Cody ambled up beside Barbara.

Deputy Sayer walked up to the counter as well, interest and amusement in his eyes.

"Joe said this man trespassed on his property," Barbara said, "and caused a landslide that just about killed Robbie and Jessica."

Cody rubbed the back of his aching neck. "You pressing charges, Mack?"

"You bet your a— Yes, Sheriff. I'd like the book thrown at this... He says his name is Hindi, but frankly, I doubt it." Joe shoved the man forward until he bumped the counter and winced.

"What's your story?" Cody asked the man.

"I cannot say, Your Honor."

"I'm not a judge, so don't call me 'Your Honor.' I am Sheriff Warner."

The man's eyes widened as if he recognized Cody's name, but he clamped his mouth shut.

"Do you know me?" Cody asked.

Hindi shook his head, pressing his lips together.

The front door opened and in strolled Deputy Pete Vargas. His eyebrows shot up into his hairline. "What gives, Sheriff?"

Relieved help had arrived, Cody pointed to Vargas' desk. "I need you to take Dr. Sam and Jessica and interview them."

He raised a finger and motioned Deputy Pat Sayer over. "I need you to interview Joe and Robbie. I'll take Mr. *Hindi* and have a chat."

"Can you please make them untie me?" Hindi asked.

"Absolutely. Joe?" Cody whipped his hand behind his back and gripped his handcuffs. He stepped through the swinging half-door and spun Hindi around as Joe untied Hindi, then before the man could move his hands, Cody snapped on the cuffs.

"I beg your pardon. I wish to be free to go," Hindi said his voice raised. "What is happening? I have done nothing wrong. I am the victim here."

Cody gripped Hindi's arm and hustled him through the gate. "Barbara, bring an arrest form, we're gonna explain to Mr. Hindi how the American justice system works in California."

"Right away, Sheriff." She dug into her desk and pulled out a form, hurrying after him.

A half-hour later, Cody glared at Hindi. "Now let me get this straight." He stared at the English/Indian who was clearly lying to him in spades. "You're just a humble geologist casually hiking up Mesa de Salvia with a friend looking for a supposed fault to document for the government? Neither one of you noticed the two young people at the bottom of a crumbling wall of rocks and boulders, you say your friend accidently caused to fall on them?"

"This is correct." Hindi insisted one more time. "My ... friend might have leaned a little heavy on the boulder. I am the innocent victim here." He swiveled his head around to gaze out the door of the sheriff's office as if hoping someone would walk in and rescue him. There was nothing to see.

"Do you know the penalty for attempted murder?"

Hindi's dark skin paled. "I would like to make my telephone call now, please."

CHAPTER TWENTY-THREE
Major Donald's English Screw-up

April 6, 1998—Monday Night Late

T**WO FULL DAYS PASSED** since Major Charles Donald had heard from his bright Indian scientist. Where was the British screw-up? They'd discussed the plan for Basua to slip onto Mack's ranch and pretend to be a geologist. Something must have gone wrong. Had the rancher killed Basua for trespassing?

Charles chuckled. He would have.

It was late and the lab empty tonight. Charles trudged around the vacant crypt-like room unable to sleep. Their time allotted for the completion of his assignment was drawing near, and the second plane was far from air worthy. He stopped walking when he found himself in the back of Basua's lab.

The second AIDA lay in pieces on the large table—stripped of parts. That dope Basua had removed the wing and used it to fix the original plane. He'd also replaced the camera with the newer model. Unless Basua got back to work and ordered new parts, they'd never find that exact canyon with Joe Mack's silver mine. Charles had to have that silver. He had a buyer waiting impatiently for the pure metal.

His buyer owned an aviation manufacturing company in Texas and would use the high-grade silver as a critical component in his jet engines. Its high melting point allowed it to withstand high temperatures of jet engine function.

Charles had to have that mine even if he had to kill the rancher to get it.

The phone rang startling him. He was getting soft. Getting back into the jungles of Brazil or Columbia to bare-hand kill people is what kept him sharp. He needed to be sharp.

"Major Donald," he shouted into the phone.

"Good evening, Major Donald. It's Paul Basua," Basua whispered from the other end of the line.

"Where the hell are you? And why are you whispering."

Sheriff Cody Warner wasn't supposed to listen in on the phone conversation between his prisoner and the man he called, but he wasn't above using certain tricks to ascertain the truth. Lifting another phone in the office, he heard the bulk of the conversation. This one was a doozy.

Hindi was none other than Dr. Paul Basua of the SRM Labs, working on the Peter Pan Project. The man he called turned out to be the mysterious Major Donald. Chip, Cody's friend, the sergeant over at SRM Facility, told him all about this major.

Basua had to be the one who'd developed or was developing the small spy plane buzzing Mack's land and killing his cattle. This guy was dirty to his eyeballs, especially since he'd attempted to kill Dr. Sam's daughter and Robbie Meyers.

The major shouted at Basua about being arrested on an attempted murder charge. After barking some obscenities into the phone, the major sounded disappointed Basua had failed to "take out" Robbie and Jessica.

What kind of government contact was this? Cody had his doubts it was a legitimate operation. Anything could be going on at the SRM Facilities, and the real government might never know anything about it.

Basua pled with the major to be set free, saying he couldn't live behind bars.

Cody shook his head. An attempted first-degree murder rap could carry the penalty of a life sentence, with a range of five to nine years in the state prison. If it was a crime of opportunity, then a little bit less. But given the right circumstances, any man could be driven to commit first-degree murder.

Cody was tired and hungry—just not hungry enough to go home to Beverly's cooking tonight. He'd stop at Ruby's for a ribeye.

"Come on doc, it's time to go to jail." Cody stood and gripped Basua's arm. "You might find our accommodations to your liking. I'll have our steakhouse owner bring you a nice, juicy ribeye."

"Oh, I do not eat meat," Basua said as Cody dragged him to the back and the two cells there. The D.U.I. truck driver was passed out on a cot in one.

Basua balked. "You cannot possibly suggest I occupy this dirty prison cell."

Cody jerked open the door. "I most certainly do suggest it, and our cells are not dirty."

"But it smells like a saloon in there."

Cody chuckled. "Meet your cellmate, Mr. D.U.I."

"Mr. D.U.I.? Is he Hindi?"

"He's a drunk who murdered a father and his daughter this morning."

Basua gasped and resisted Cody's efforts to shove him into the cell. "Please, you cannot put me in this cell so close to a murderer."

Cody unlocked Basua's cuffs, pushed him until he stepped inside the metal box. He slammed the barred door behind him. "You two have something in common, then. You're both murderers."

"But wait." Basua sputtered, gripping the bars in his large hands. "This is not fair. American justice, indeed. It is cruel and unusual punishment. I shall sue the county for false arrest and imprisonment."

"Shut up, Basua." Coby clenched his hands ready to give the guy a knockout punch to settle him down.

"How did you know my real name?"

*April 7, 1998—Tuesday—***Branding and Immunizations**

A delicious smell drifted through Joe's sleep-fogged brain. Someone was cooking breakfast, but it wasn't a smell he knew. Smelled like vegetables cooking, not his usual bacon or his favorite egg and beef dish, machaca con huevos.

Rising from bed, Joe trudged into the master bathroom Cindy designed with its trough-type sink, gooseneck faucets set up on a galvanized-steel covered counter. After remodeling pains, the bathroom space looked like his old Army barracks with a communal sink—not that he would have told Cindy that.

The whole sink get-up sat on some old wooden beams removed from Grandpa Elmer's original barn that burned to the ground in the 20s. Cindy said it was cool. He said it looked like an old barn. Thank goodness she had the shower walls tiled with limestone cut from their mountain and the shower floor covered with tiny flat river rocks from the Middle Fork of the American River. Cindy said it reminded her of showering in nature. Her idea of bathing was a colossal copper bathtub.

"I feel like a queen in my tub," she'd told him one day. He was glad he spent the extra money to install the thing.

"You deserve it." He had joined her.

He turned the water on in the shower as hot as he could stand and stepped under the scorching spray letting it wash away the horror of what might've happened yesterday. What if Hindi or whoever he was, had succeeded in killing Robbie and Jessica?

He shuddered—cold to the bone even under the hot spray.

That's why when it came to bed assignments last night, he could have put Sam and Jessica in the casita north of the main ranch house, but he'd needed them near—in case of another attempt on their lives.

Who knew if the SRM division would send anyone else to "persuade" him to tell them where their plane was? They might use people he cared about to twist the point home. He couldn't take chances with their lives. He felt responsible for Jessica. Sam would never forgive him if anything happened to her daughter.

Joe desired Sam here on the ranch for another reason. Having her inside his home with her black hair hanging down her back and her natural fragrance of jasmine filling him with guilt and pleasure, was hard to resist.

"I've asked Sam to look after you, dear," Cindy said a few weeks before she passed. Her health had deteriorated to the point of her being unable to walk. The doctor confined her to bed and sent a retired nurse to take care of Cindy's needs. Joe had resented her intrusion into the sanctity of their home. Even though he figured he could care for Cindy himself, Joe'd found out how wrong he'd been. She'd taken a turn for the worse and needed to up her dose of morphine. He would've frozen with indecision and made Cindy suffer needlessly.

As he pulled on his comfortable jeans and his blue checkered cotton shirt, he remembered Cindy said the color brought out the color of his eyes. Would Sam notice?

He strolled into the bright kitchen feeling mellow, as Robbie called it.

Jessica and Robbie sat at the small kitchen table for four, and Sam stood near the stove poking at a delicious-smelling creation in the cast-iron frying pan. Her back was to him, so he could admire her shapely, trim backside.

He shook his head. "What's for breakfast?"

Sam spun around, her lovely face animated. "I'm fixing something for you to try besides beef and pork this morning."

He narrowed his eyes in irritation. "What is it?" He was curious and ambled over to look in the pan, but she shooed him away with her spatula.

"Promise me you'll try it," she said.

He felt his stomach turn. He hated food he hadn't tried. "I'll try it." He turned his head, so Sam couldn't see him cringe, but the kids did and laughed.

"I know you, Joseph Mack." Sam waved the spatula around in the air. "Don't you lie to me."

He moved to her and placed his arms around her slender waist. He felt an immediate and powerful connection, a jolt of energy. "I never would lie to you," he said in a solemn voice for her benefit only. He was afraid he might kiss her in front of Robbie and Jessica, so he removed his arms and stepped back. His face heated.

What the hell was happening to him? His heart thumped double-time. Cindy was the only woman for him. Wasn't she?

"Sit. Eat." Red-faced, Sam pushed him toward the table and shoved a plate in front of him.

"It's great, Mr. Joe," Robbie said with a smile and an arched eyebrow.

Robbie and Jessica held hands under the table. Young love. Did anything make people more nuts, or feel more wonderful?

Joe looked down. The thing on his plate looked like an omelet, but green stuff hung out the sides and where was his cheddar cheese? He poked at it. "What is this?"

Sam brought her plate over to the table, pulled out a chair, and sat. "You mean this looks like something only folks in San Francisco would eat?"

Jessica and Robbie laughed.

Sam shot them an irritated glance and turned to Joe. "It's called a village omelet—fresh eggs and some added whites for protein, along with spinach and Swiss cheese. Eat it. It's good for you."

He made a strangling sound. "I didn't know there was spinach in my fridge."

"Eat!" Sam slapped her hand on the table.

"Who knew you were such a bossy woman." With trepidation in his gut, he cut a small corner of the omelet and popped it into his mouth. Sam had done something creative with the spices. The egg/spinach/cheese concoction melted on his tongue. He swallowed. "This is ... okay." It was fantastic, but he wouldn't tell her that. Didn't want to fatten her ego.

Sam grinned. "I told you."

For the next few minutes, they ate and chatted—just like a real family in Cindy's cozy kitchen. Even though it felt right, comfortable, Joe's heart felt off-center.

After breakfast and the kitchen clean up, Joe strolled out to Sam's SUV with her to check on the supply of immunizations. Joe didn't know precisely how many calves needed to be branded and receive their shots, so she stocked up on everything.

For most of the dark, chilly morning and into the early afternoon, Ricardo, his sons, the ranch hands, and neighboring ranchers, separated the bawling calves from their mothers for branding and shots. Samantha and Jessica took turns injecting the adorable little animals and watched as they received the Sunrise Ranch brand.

"How did you learn where and what to inject into the calves?" Jessica asked.

Samantha smiled. "They'll eventually teach you that at school. For now, I'll give you some pointers." She grabbed the injection gun from her bag, loaded the vaccine. "When possible, select vaccine products which can be administered subQ, or subcutaneously, and inject them in front of the shoulder." She knelt beside a little guy barely three or so months old. Miguel and Salvador Sanchez held down the bawling red and white calf. "Thanks, Mike and Sal."

"You're welcome, Dr. Stone." Mike smiled at Jessica, keeping his gloved hands firmly in place on the calf's front hoof with the snout between his legs. Sal extended his back leg so Joe, doing the hot work, could easily apply the fire-red branding iron.

"We don't want to produce lesions from the shot, or scar tissue which remains for life. Doing so would decrease meat quality." Samantha demonstrated with her injection gun shooting the liquid into the calf's shoulder with one swift move. The calf bawled, but afterward, licked her hand. "It's okay, baby. You'll be fine." She patted his head.

Samantha straightened. "If the calf has loose skin around its neck, that's the best spot for the injection.

Joe held the hot iron to the calf's leg. The calf bawled.

"Looks so barbaric." Jessica cringed.

"I thought so, too. It might hurt for a moment, but they recover."

Jessica shrugged. "I don't like them to get sick or die, or worse, get rustled, so I guess mixing the shots and the branding are necessary."

"They are. Lots of critters out here on the ranch carry all kinds of diseases." Samantha filled the vaccine gun with the second dose. "If a product goes intramuscularly, inject it into the muscles of the neck in front of the shoulder, and insert the needle into the raised fold of skin. Some are administered at the base of the ear."

Standing next to the long tunnel-like fence, the cow-catcher, Robbie, inserted colorful plastic tags into the ears of other calves. The tag contained their mama's name, birthdate, and other information necessary to identify the calf later.

"It's just like getting their ears pierced," Robbie said to Jessica when she stood up and walked over to where he was working.

While he secured the larger calves in the head grip, the cowboys approached with the hot iron. Sam hoped one day some inventive people would create a more painless form of marking the calves. Perhaps by freezing the area first.

The stench of burning cowhide sizzled up from the branded area. The calf bawled. Now that the tagging, vaccinations, and branding were completed, the calf was released back into the larger corral to find his momma.

Jessica wiped sweat from her brow. "This sure is an involved procedure."

Samantha chuckled. "When you take my place as the county vet, you'll be doing a lot of these injections."

Jessica frowned. "I can't wait."

CHAPTER TWENTY-FOUR

Securing the Ranch from Dirty Rotten Skunks (not the animal kind)

April 8, 1998—Wednesday

ROBBIE WAS UP before the sun, showered, and ate one of the breakfast burritos Lettie prepared for Joe's lunch. Joe appeared done-in last night, so Robbie let him sleep this morning.

He strolled out of Joe's house in darkness and climbed into his '78 Comet. Darn thing was noisy. He prayed Joe wouldn't hear him crank over the engine and drive away. Sal had looked at it, said it needed a tune-up and took care of it. Sal didn't charge Robbie a dime.

The car turned over with a purr. Bless you, Sal. Robbie drove down the graveled road toward the front gate whistling along with K-Ci and Jo-Jo and their hit, "All My Life"—his and Jessica's song.

He'd been disappointed Jess took off her engagement ring when Joe noticed her wearing it. She told him her mother wasn't ready yet. Last night before saying goodbye, she'd kissed him and said she would tell her mother when they were alone. Why did he doubt that?

Were her misgivings still eating her up? Did she think he could treat her like her dad did her mom? What could he do to prove to her he wasn't a drunk or a mad-man and wouldn't hit her in a fit of drunkenness or stupidity? It wasn't in his nature, not after he'd seen what his old man had done to his mom.

He thumped the steering wheel in time to the slow, haunting melody. His heart crushing. What if Jessica changed her mind and didn't wish to marry him after all? Perhaps she just needed more time.

He couldn't let Joe come with him this morning and be seen purchasing security equipment in Sacramento. Word might get back to the murdering creeps at SRM. Joe told him a little bit about the problem including how Mr. Hindi turned out to be a British scientist named Dr. Paul Basua.

Friday, the county judge would be in town to arraign the D.U.I. guy and Dr. Basua. Robbie didn't know what was going on, exactly, with SRM and Joe, but Joe was in trouble. What other explanation could there be for putting in a security system?

Robbie visited a ranching supply store in Sacramento on the off chance they might have wireless CCTV—closed caption TV cameras with wireless transmitters for the barn. The company claimed they had a three-mile-line of sight. He bought four—two for the barn and stables, one for the forested area south of the ranch, and one for the top of the barn. With them, Robbie and Joe could record one hundred and eighty degrees of comings and goings around the ranch compound on Joe's VCR. Maybe he should also upgrade the ancient 1990 IBM computer he helped Joe learn.

Robbie located an Apollo swing gate opener system with a receiver and antenna. He bought extras remotes for all the ranch vehicles and his car. By now, his credit card was screaming. He'd have to stop eating lunch for a month, so he could pay for all this. Keeping Joe, Ricardo, and his family safe, was his only concern.

With Joe, Mike, Ricardo, and Salvador's help, Robbie spent the rest of Wednesday through Friday installing the cameras, the motion detectors, and the gate opener.

"*Que Bueno.*" Ricardo patted him on the back. "Now *Señor* Joe protect his property."

"Exactly." Robbie smiled. Just try and sneak on the ranch now, you thugs. Joe'll be watching for you.

April 10, 1998—Friday—**Sentencing of the Murderer**

Sheriff Cody Warner called Joe Mack to come to court on Friday morning to see the proceedings with Basua and the judge. They met on the porch of the old assessor's building now used for a makeshift courthouse. Mack nodded to Cody as they entered the building. No words were exchanged. Cody liked it that way.

Deputy Sayer dragged the nervous scientist into the courtroom and plopped him down at the defendant's table across from the district attorney, Javier Castaneda, already in his seat. Only the blasted Public Defender had yet to show and chat with Basua.

Deputy Vargas led in the sorry and sober D.U.I., who continued to say he'd done nothing wrong. Vargas shoved him in the second row and sat beside him.

Sayer was acting bailiff today, and he strolled through the side door leading to a small office the presiding judge occupied when in town. Cody wondered which county judge had been sent to oversee the arraignment of these two skunks.

With a determined step, Sayer marched back into the makeshift courtroom. "All rise for the honorable Judge Beauregard T. Langstaff, Shadow Pines District of the Placer County Courts."

The black-robed, white-haired judge, strutted in, head high, back straight and meandered to a chair behind a large table. He sat and straightened the already straightened paperwork lining the tabletop.

Cody leaned toward Joe. "Pretentious bastard," he whispered.

Joe nodded and folded his arms.

Judge Langstaff looked up and focused on Basua. "Do you have representation, Dr. Basua?"

Basua stood, knotted his hands. "I believe so, yes. I believe a barrister is coming, Your Lord Justice."

"In the United States, we call them 'lawyers,' and you can call me Your Honor, Doctor. You're not in the U.K. now."

"My apologies, Your ... Your Honor." Basua tanned face reddened.

"Are you aware of the charges against you, Dr. Basua?"

"Yes, I am innocent. Your Lor—Your Honor."

"Don't—"

The door to the courtroom banged open. In marched a giant of a man sporting a precise military buzz cut. He wore an impeccable black suit, dark glasses, and a murderous scowl on his pockmarked face. He strode to the front of the courtroom and leaned over to address the scientist.

Cody couldn't hear what Buzz Cut said to the doctor, but Basua's eyes blinked non-stop and his face pinched.

"Can I help you?" the judge asked the man.

Cody had seen men like this—disgraced military, unable to get a real job. Most took the finger-busting, head-bashing work with private mercenary security companies sometimes dealing with illegal operations. He'd seen such a man in Ruby's Saloon the other night. For Pete's sake, the man had a Bowie knife strapped to his thigh and looked like he would decapitate someone for looking at him the wrong way. Perhaps the man in the saloon, the doctor, and this major worked for the same people. Cody would have to keep his eyes open.

"Who are you?" the judge asked. "And what are you talking to the defendant about?"

The incredible hulk turned around. Damn. He had to be about six three—six four, fullback sized, and intimidating. "I'm sorry, Your Honor. My name is Major Charles Donald. I'm an associate of Dr. Paul Basua's. I've come to post his bail."

So, this was the infamous Major Donald. Big scary S.O.B.

Joe stiffened beside him.

The judge didn't bat an eye. "I'll ask you to remove your sunglasses when you address me in my courtroom."

"Sorry, sir." Major Donald whipped off his glasses. The S.O.B. had black eyes, squinty and beady, more intimidating than his size.

"Well now Major, we haven't decided what the bail amount should be yet. You're just in time to wait for his defense attorney to join us. Why don't you have a seat by your associate and wait for me to decide if I'm going to let this man out on bail at all?"

Facial muscles bunched along Major Donald's jaw. "May I have a word with you, Your Honor?"

"Highly unusual, but might as well, we're not headed anywhere." The judge stood up.

Cody fisted his hands. "What the hell?"

The major followed the judge out of the courtroom.

"Can he do that?" Joe asked. "Who is that guy?"

"I would suspect he's the muscle for the Peter Pan Project. I guess if the judge allows it, he can do anything he pleases. Who'd stop him?"

Joe rolled his eyes. "Hell of a huge S.O.B., isn't he?"

"Yeah, he is." Cody exhaled sharply.

Joe crossed one leg over his knee. "Can the judge release Basua on bail?"

Cody resisted the urge to punch the bench in front of him. "Yeah, he can."

"Can't I do anything to prevent his release?" Joe asked. "When he returns to SRM, they'll probably send up another plane to scatter my cattle or worse."

"Don't you think I know that?" Cody's anger burned in the back of his throat.

The side door opened and in strolled the major and the judge. The major returned to his seat next to Basua.

The judge sat and picked up the file containing Basua's arrest information. "There now, let's see what your good doctor has done to warrant such a scene." He read silently to himself.

"You think the major used his governmental influence on the judge?" Joe whispered.

"Damned if I know," Cody said.

"Do you have something to say to the court, Sheriff Warner?" the judge asked smirking.

Cody's neck flamed. "Not at this time, Your Honor."

"Do you mind if I continue reading?"

"Not at all, Your Honor."

"Thank you." The judge focused his attention on the paperwork.

The door opened again, and a flustered man in a rumpled suit entered and faltered down the aisle balancing a briefcase, dark glasses, a file overflowing with papers, and a bottle of water. Ah, the county public defender, Marvin Ludlow. Cody'd called him to make sure Basua had representation, although Basua said he didn't need a "barrister," as he put it.

"I apologize, Your Honor," Ludlow said as he made his way to the front and sat by Basua and the major. He gave the major a once over and then focused on the file in front of him.

"We have all day for you to confer with your client," Judge Langstaff said. "Don't let us stop you."

Ludlow had the decency to turn red. "I'm sorry, Your Honor. My car wouldn't start."

"Now that you're here, proceed. How long will you need to confer with your client?"

"By all means, Your Honor. Not long." Ludlow motioned for Basua to rise and together they were led out of the room by the bailiff.

Damn. Cody gritted his teeth. He wasn't getting out of here anytime soon.

After fifteen minutes, Ludlow strolled back into the courtroom, Basua behind him with a hang-dog expression on his brown face. Anything could happen now.

"We're ready to proceed, Your Honor," Ludlow said, rustling through his paperwork.

After the D.A. read all the charges against Basua, he called Cody to the stand.

Cody stood, walked to the table and sat in a designated chair. Sayer swore him in, and he explained some of the charges, displayed the physical evidence he'd collected at the scene along with Jessica's pictures, and told the judge Basua was caught dead to rights up on the mesa after the attempted murder.

The judge dismissed him, and Cody returned to his seat.

For a few minutes, Judge Langstaff ran through some preliminary legal jargon and then glanced at Basua. "According to your arrest report and the testimony of our honorable Sheriff Warner, Dr. Basua, you've been a busy boy. You tried to kill a young couple at the bottom of a box canyon by jimmying a huge boulder to crash down on them. Tsk-tsk. How do you plead?"

Basua rose to his feet along with Ludlow. "According to the counsel from my … attorney, I plead not guilty, Your Honor."

The judge sat back, steepled his gnarled fingers together. "These are serious charges, Dr. Basua. You do understand them, don't you?"

"Yes, Your Honor," Basua said, head down.

"However, Major Donald has assured me that you are not a flight risk and will be more than happy to present you back here again when you and the clerk set your court date. Is that correct, Doctor?"

Basua glanced at the major.

Major Donald lifted his chin.

Basua turned and faced the judge. "Certainly, Your Honor."

The judge took a huge breath. "By the authority of my position in Placer County, I set bail at $50,000. I do hope that you, Dr. Basua, will not skip town or return to India. You need to stay at SRM Facilities until your trial."

"Yes, Your Honor."

"You're a free man, Dr. Basua until our next meeting. Schedule that date with my court reporter on your way out." He slammed his gavel on the tabletop. "Court will resume for the D.U.I. after lunch."

"Fifty thousand dollars!" Joe stiffened in the chair next to Cody. "That's a damnable pass. That S.O.B. nearly killed my son and Jessica. Bail should be a million."

"Now, Joe." The look in the rancher's eyes alarmed Cody. "I don't want to arrest you for attempted murder. Don't take the law into your own hands."

Joe shot him a murderous glance, jumped to his feet, and stormed out of the courtroom.

After the judge's court reporter recorded bail, and the trial date, Major Donald and Dr. Basua headed in Cody's direction.

"May I have a word with you before you leave?" Cody asked standing in the center of the aisle, so they couldn't pass.

Major Donald eyed him like he was lint. "Make it quick. We have responsibilities to attend to."

Cody straightened to his full six foot two. "I'll be checking on you, Basua."

"I tell you, Sheriff," Basua said. "I am an innocent man."

"Be that as it may, don't leave town. I'll be watching, and about that plane, I asked you not to fly on Joe's side of Sunrise Mountain—look what happened. Keep that damned thing on your side. There's no reason to fly over Joe's property."

Deep red suffused the major's neck and cheeks. His jaw tightened to the point of cracking some teeth. "And I'll tell you, Sheriff, not to interfere with government projects. We will fly where we damn well please when we please. Nothing stands in the way of my projects."

He moved in close, got in Cody's face. "Nothing. Not a small, hick-town sheriff or an S.O.B. rancher."

Cody's eye twitched, but he wouldn't show this gorilla any fear. "You've been warned."

The major shoved Dr. Basua toward the door but turned around before stepping outside. "So, have you, Sheriff."

CHAPTER TWENTY-FIVE

A Better Plan

April 10, 1998—Friday

"**H**OW THE HELL** did you get arrested?" Major Donald asked Paul Basua as soon as they sat inside his black Jeep.

Paul's neck heated with embarrassment. He felt knackered, exhausted from his ordeal. "I am gutted by the whole situation. I was not to blame. I was gobsmacked when Mr. Hawke proposed the idea to kill those young people. I warned him to stop. I knew it would not end well."

The major pounded the steering wheel as he sped out of Shadow Pines. "I didn't ask you who attempted to kill those kids. I just asked how you got yourself arrested."

Paul explained what happened after Hawke disappeared into the forest leaving him behind.

The major uttered very unpleasant words. "I asked you to do a simple task, and you can't even do that. I'm gonna have to call in some favors."

"But … you already have Mr. Hawke. I supposed he … that he came to help you." Hawke was doing the major's dirty work, so he would not get his hands filthy. The whole thing was getting dodgy.

"Now I don't have just the rancher to worry about, I've got a county sheriff on my back. This situation will take some finesse. People will have to disappear," Major Donald said.

Paul recoiled. He could not stand the idea of other people dying for this stupid plane or a possible hidden mine. "Why don't we just purchase the land from the rancher? Do it legally, so nobody else has to get hurt."

He held his breath. He never crossed Major Donald before. With friends like Mr. Hawke, he could find himself on a slab at the undertaker's, or his body chopped into a million pieces and fed to the wolves. It would kill Mum if he died.

173

The major said nothing.

The drive back to SRM didn't take long with the major at the wheel.

After they took the elevator down to the lab, the major paced for a few minutes, his fingers drumming on his lips. He stopped when he reached Paul now sitting at his desk. "That's not a bad idea, Basua. I'll call a real estate broker in town and get them out to Mack's ranch. I've got some money stashed away. Who knows? Maybe I'll settle down and raise me some cows."

Chuckling to himself, Major Donald strode back into the area of the lab where the other plane laid in pieces. "Now, my good doctor, will this plane be up and flying within the week?"

Paul flinched. He rose from his desk and trudged back to where the major stood. He would soon walk over hot coals like his ancestors than tell the major the parts would not be here soon. Time to be a man as his father instructed him to be.

"I have ordered a new wing and a new camera," he said.

"What did you tell the supplier?" Major Donald's expression was a mask of fierceness.

"I told them we had a bit of a sticky situation with the plane, that it had a dodgy flight and the wing and camera were the victims."

The major ground his teeth. "And?"

"They will construct and send a new wing, and a new camera."

"How soon?"

Paul glanced at the ceiling of fluorescent lights. "They will be sending the replacement parts in a fortnight or a little longer."

"How the hell long is that?"

"Two or three weeks."

Major Donald blistered the room with his obscenities.

Paul backed up two or three steps fearing for his life. Luckily, Major Donald didn't have anyone else to fix the other spy plane.

Without another word, Major Donald grabbed up the portable phone and headed through the door, slamming it behind him.

Paul was in for a bollocking now. He was sure Major Donald would call Hawke to pay him a visit.

"What a bloody hell of a mess."

Major Charles Donald needed the skills of a sniper and his rifle. His friend from the Army and exploits in South America, Gunnery Sergeant Butch Henry, had returned home to Naples to visit his mother dying of cancer. Charles made a call to Italy.

Butch answered on the fourth ring. "What do you want?"

"Code Red at SRM Facilities. Fly to Sacramento, California."

"How soon."

"As soon as you can get a flight."

"Mama's dying."

"'Let the dead bury the dead'." Charles believed himself a real funny guy for quoting scripture. He was taking a chance. Butch loved his mama.

"You're a bastard," Butch growled. "I'll get there when I get there."

"This is an order, Gunny."

"Screw you, Donald."

Later Friday afternoon, Joe, antsy, with nothing to do, roamed the ranch and ended up in the barn. Everything was in its place, neat and tidy. The silence rang in his ears. Thanks to Ricardo, the cattle peacefully grazed in the tall grass pasture between the house and the road to town. The horses were fed and watered—a nod to Sal. The crops grew fast and plentiful under Mike's supervision. He rubbed the back of his neck. Even his hired hands attended to their chores, leaving him at loose ends and experiencing overwhelming uselessness. His ranch operation ran without him having to lift a finger.

Joe paused to stare into his office. Nope. He'd paid all his bills for feed and supplies. With the sale of two more quarter horses to the dude ranch in Tahoe, he'd be able to buy a new seedstock bull.

Something was gonna hit the fan. He felt it in his bones.

Though still burned because the judge released Dr. Hindi or Basua, not much he could do about it now. Time to check his computer monitor for anyone trying to sneak on his property. The major and that dolt, Basua, were probably planning something major?

"Major all right." Joe chuckled as he meandered through the barn door and stopped to face his and Cindy's home. "We did it, sweetheart. Made your dad proud."

Fighting his premonition of doom, he strolled over to the wrap-around porch Cindy loved so much, stepped up the stairs, and wandered over to a chair to sit. Shep and Spike joined him and sat at attention near his and Cindy's chairs, so empty without her. He'd experienced loneliness before, but this time he didn't have to be alone.

Lingering grief caused hot tears to well in his eyes. He closed them, allowing tears to flow down his cheeks.

"Don't keep fighting this. Samantha will be good for you, darling." Cindy appeared next to him in her chair.

Joe jerked. His eyes flashed open, and he swiped away the moisture from his eyes. "Where have you been? I've missed you."

"I know, but I've been close. You've been busy." Her blue eyes were sunken, her skin pale, and her long blonde hair a limp mess—just like the day she passed away.

"It's not like I don't think about you all the time."

Cindy chuckled. "Not all the time. I'm glad you're seeing Samantha."

Joe shook his head. "I won't if you don't like it."

"Don't be silly, darling. Samantha is my friend, and I love her dearly. You know I told you to take care of her, marry her."

He groaned. "I'll never marry again. You're my one and only."

"Don't ever say never." She coughed, blood came away on her fingers when she removed them from her lips. The cancer had spread to her lungs from her breasts then metastasized in her liver. "I want you to be happy. I want Samantha to be happy."

"Why are you making me do this?" Pain knotted behind his ribs.

Cindy reached out and took his hand in hers—her touch so real, so comforting. "Promise me you'll love and take care of each other. Don't wait any longer. You know I told you the same thing before I passed away."

"I promise, but I don't have to like it."

She chuckled. "Oh, my darling, you'll like it. Samantha adores you." Her face grew pale. "Call her Joe. Find a way to bring happiness into both your lives."

She faded away leaving him alone—again.

"Cindy, dammit, please don't go."

Joe sat in the chair for a long time after Cindy drifted away. He rubbed at the painful grief under his heart. She was right about one thing. He didn't have to be alone anymore—neither he nor Sam. They could be together.

Rising from his chair, he briskly walked inside to the kitchen. With the number already in his head, he dialed the kitchen phone. "You doing anything for dinner tonight?" he asked when Sam answered.

"Hello to you, too," Sam said. He could hear the laughter in her voice.

"You know I'm not good at small talk." He found it natural with Sam.

"I'd love to eat with you. Will you pick me up for Ruby's at six-thirty?"

"I'll be there."

Cindy had been right—again. Sam would complete his life.

Elated Sam said yes to dinner, an idea popped into his mind. His needs were few, his wants nearly all fulfilled. Well, practically all. If he could convince Sam to join him on a short weekend trip to South Lake Tahoe—Nevada side—he'd have all his needs met. He'd have everything. Time to call and make a reservation for a quick and quiet wedding ceremony. He decided this coming weekend at Regan Beach, South Lake Tahoe would fit his plans perfectly. He couldn't wait to take Sam there.

Time to move on with his life.

Joe was a mess by the time he finished showering, shaving, and dressing. He'd changed his shirt about five times and finally chosen his best non-ranching slacks, his black wool trousers. He couldn't remember the last time he'd worn his brown corduroy blazer. Was it at Cindy's funeral? Nah. He'd worn his black suit. His chest ached for a moment. No more sorrow tonight. Fresh start time.

Digging through his chest of drawers, he located the shoe polish and put a gleaming shine on his Sunday-go-to-meetin' boots. Now dressed to impress, he strolled through the house whistling.

Sam looked like a dream when she opened the door of her house in Shadow Pines. Joe was afraid his jaw smacked the porch. "You look sensational."

She'd worn a form-fitting black dress with a beaded neckline. It sparkled under the porch light. She grinned and looked him up and down. "Thanks. You look mighty fine, Joe Mack."

Embarrassed, he hung his head. "Yeah, well, it's about time, I suppose." He doffed his hat. "Shall we mosey on down to the saloon and have us a hog-killin' time?" Joe smiled.

She laughed and threaded her arm through his, tugging him down the steps and toward his rig—which he'd spruced up and sprayed with a fancy can of deodorizer.

Joe helped her climb into the passenger seat.

Ruby's Steakhouse was crowded and hopping. Joe led Sam to a table back in the corner of the bar and ordered two white wines from Bill.

"What's the occasion?" Sam asked over the noise of the bar crowd. She took a sip from her condensation-covered wine glass. "Hmmm, nice choice of wines."

"California grown. The best." Joe was momentarily at a loss for words. Sam's eyes shown like black diamonds in the twinkling lights of the bar. On stage, a country duo played a quiet love song. For Pete's sake. His foolish heart threatened to gallop out of his chest with anticipation. "Let's dance."

Her brows knit together, but she stood and allowed him to pull her onto the floor. The way she swayed against him, opened his eyes to his three-year-long, self-imposed prison. Why the hell not. Cindy had been right—he was lonely for no reason. And … he was in love with Sam already.

Joe led Sam off the dance floor to their little table. They said "howdy" to people as they passed. Seemed everyone in town was eating out tonight.

After he shoved her chair in for her, he sat and grabbed up his courage. "And the occasion…" Could he tell her Cindy told him to see her, invite her out? He'd better not. "The occasion is…" He gulped. "I … really like you, Sam."

She put down her glass and glared at him. "Like?"

"Damn. You know what I mean?"

"Do I?" She enjoyed his discomfort too much.

He leaned closer, caught a whiff of her perfume, something spicy mingled with flowers. He breathed deeply. "You're gonna make me say it, aren't you?"

Sam leaned closer. "You know it." She smiled—a little too cheeky.

Joe gulped wine for fortification. Before he could speak, Ruby called their names for a table in the steakhouse.

"Saved," Sam whispered.

After being seated, they both ordered ribeyes, medium rare with the works. Joe, in relationship-hell—wanting Sam in his life yet fearing for her safety—didn't know how to ask. Danger surrounded him. Major Donald could use Sam to get to him.

"Where do you see us heading?" Sam asked him as she pushed the half-eaten steak around the plate.

"I think we're on the same road." He'd attempted non-committal, shooting for funny.

She was not amused. "You know I have feelings for you, Joe. Deep feelings."

He took a quick glance around the steakhouse to make sure no one could hear. Unfortunately, the other diners appeared to strain to listen to their conversation even though they sat in the dimly lit corner booth. "I know Sam." He didn't say anymore.

She implored him with her eyes.

179

He frowned, feeling like dog meat. Time for some truth. "Yes, Sam. I feel … something very deeply for you."

"But it hurts. I get it. You don't want to be unfaithful to Cindy." She wiped her mouth with her cloth napkin glanced everywhere but at him. "It's only been three years since Cindy passed and you were terribly in love with her."

He didn't want to talk about Cindy, especially not to tell her Cindy wanted them together.

She reached across the table and laid her hand over his. He shuddered with a thrill of her touch. "I'm not trying to take her place."

He hung his head, placed his steak knife down. "I know."

"I need my own place in your heart, my darling."

His face heated. It was all in or nothing. "And I … want you there, too."

"But?"

"I'm involved in a war right now, and I would be devastated if something worse happened to you and you got hurt." Or worse, but he didn't say that.

Sam crinkled her nose. "And you believe I would turn tail and run? That I wouldn't grab my shotgun and stand beside you? Is that it?" She glanced around the dining room. "You don't have to protect me like everyone or everything else you protect. I'm not fragile. I can handle myself."

Gosh, he admired her spunk. "I know that. I know you'd stand by me. I have a target on my back, and I don't want you anywhere near me until this thing blows over." He took a huge breath. "SRM wants something on my property and are willing to do anything—even murder our kids—to get it."

"I understand. You need my help. I'm not a faint-hearted woman, Joseph. I've been kicked by horses, stomped on by cattle, and scratched by mountain lions. I can shoot the eye out of a squirrel at five hundred paces and ride better than most men."

With each determined word, Joe's love ramped up. Nobody messed with Samantha Stone. Hell, he loved her more for her single-minded tenacity.

She leaned closer, her full, silky lips less than inches from his. "You need me, Joseph Mack and I love you, I have forever."

He had plans to wait, but why? "I do love you Samantha Stone. Let's get married."

They passed on dessert.

*April 12, 1998—Sunday morning—***Congratulations and Best Wishes...**

Lying in the big tree-trunk crafted four-poster bed at the lodge on Lake Tahoe, Joe smiled to himself.

He shuddered, so damned impossibly happy. Cindy had been right. Sam fit in his life perfectly—wholly made for him.

Snuggled next to him in the big bed, Sam sighed. She'd slept like a rock.

"Good morning, Mrs. Mack." He drew a finger down her spine.

She shuddered, turned and flopped her arm across his chest. "Good morning to you too, Mr. Mack." She stretched and cuddled close to him. "I'm so happy."

Who knew his heart would expand to include Sam? "So am I. You ready to go home?"

"Home. That sounds so nice." She frowned. "How are we going to do this—moving in and telling everyone?"

He sobered, hadn't thought that through. "We'll play it cool, for a while. You can move things in a little every day. We'll tell the ranch family, Robbie, and Jessica, of course." Major Donald and his lackey, Basua flashed in his mind. "Perhaps we'd better wait for an announcement, just in case ... you know. We'll work it out."

"Okay. We'll keep a lid on it in case ... you know." She chuckled. "But why don't I move in some stuff this week and we'll have a big celebration—"

He stiffened, cutting her off.

Stupid man. "Okay, we'll wait and celebrate when this all blows over."

He exhaled, grinned, and kissed her again, losing himself in her. "That works for me."

CHAPTER TWENTY-SIX

A Rich and Criminally Insane Investor

April 13, 1998—Monday

"**M**ISTER JOE, THERE IS A TELEPHONE
CALL** for you," Lettie called to Joe from the
ranch house kitchen window.

Shep and Spike, sitting on their haunches
just outside the garage, glanced at him with concern in their dark
eyes. Joe stepped away from the old tractor he had been working
on with Sal. Stupid carburetor was stuck open. Damn new one
could cost a couple of hundred bucks. No tractor meant no
harvesting. "I gotta take this call, Sal."

"No problemo, boss." Sal waved him away, screwdriver in
his hand.

"I'll take it in the barn, Lettie," he yelled toward the house.

Joe tramped into his office in the barn, the dogs on his heel.
He picked up the office extension. "Hello," Joe growled, still
standing.

"Mr. Mack? Mr. Joe Mack?" a woman asked with a high-
pitched, annoying whine of a voice.

"Yeah, this is he."

"Joe. I hope you don't mind if I call you Joe. This is Sophia
Devereux-Melancon from the Home Town Realty in Shadow
Pines. How are you today?"

"I'm extremely busy. What can I do for you, Miss Devereux-
Melancon?"

"It's Ms., thank you."

Pretentious woman. She'd been a significant player who
gobbled up repossessed ranches and farms from hard-working
families in the valley. She then sold them to equally pretentious
celebrities who built multi-million-dollar cabins which they rarely
stayed in or visited.

Joe rolled his eyes. Shep whined. He patted the dog's head.
"Good day, Ms. Devereux-Melancon. What do you want?"

"I have just received a fabulously generous offer for the purchase of your ranch, Mr. Mack—Joe, much more money than the property is actually worth. It would be—"

"Look, Ms. Devereux-Melancon." He cut her off. "I'm not interested in selling."

"But once you hear this offer, you'll be able to fulfill all your desires of travel and relaxation. You can retire from your hard work and do what you've always dreamed of doing. Live a life of ease. You could buy a home in Sacramento, a fabulous home, or move out of state. Whatever you like."

Hell of a fast talker. Joe gritted his teeth to keep from swearing.

She didn't take a breath. "I've never actually seen an amount like this for a property in and around the Shadow Pines area, or the Sunrise Mountain area. These people are serious, and they said they won't change a thing. They'll be cattle ranching as well."

Fire blazed in Joe's gut. He hated the bum's rush. It was all he could do not to reach through the phone and grab this woman by the throat. "This ranch is not for sale—at any price."

She went on as if she hadn't heard. "At least come in and hear the offer. These are quite influential people and they will pay you top dollar to keep your ranch intact. You should at least hear me out."

Why did Major Donald's face flash into his mind? "Did you not hear me, Ms. Devereux-Melancon? I told you. This. Ranch. Is. Not. For. Sale."

"You can't imagine what a blessing to the town and our community an influx of cash and substantially influential people could bring. You'd be serving your community and raise the standard of living for your friends and neighbors."

Joe's free hand curled into a fist which he banged on the office desk. "I don't give a damn if the president of the United States is interested in my spread. I'm not selling this ranch. You can tell this influential buyer to go to hell!"

"Please, Mr. Mack, Joe—"

Joe slammed the phone down, sucking wind like he'd run for miles up Sunrise Mountain's face in the thin air. "Damned pushy female."

"Are you okay, *amigo*?" Ricardo asked from behind him.

Joe swung around, his fists sprang up before him. He relaxed his shoulders when he saw Ricardo's concern, and dropped his arms. "I'm thinking SRM facilities might be trying a different tactic."

"*¿Cómo?* What you mean?" Ricardo asked.

Sal ambled into the barn and stood by his father to hear what Joe had to say.

Joe glanced from Ricardo to Sal. "I believe SRM has been in contact with Home Town Realty and told them to buy me out."

"You think they'd take such drastic measures?" Sal asked.

"Right now, I think Major Donald would do just about anything to find that stupid plane." Joe muttered some expletives. He wished Sam had come home with him last night. "I'm going for a drive."

"Sí," Ricardo said. "We will not let anyone on the ranch while you are gone, amigo."

Joe nodded and stalked back to the garage. The dogs followed him.

He opened the tailgate of his pride and joy—his '65 Ford Truck.

"Ride." Joe commanded. Shep and Spike jumped in the back of his truck, tongues wagging in eager anticipation.

He drove through the ranch compound and out the gravel road.

The morning was clear and cool. It was just warm enough at these higher elevations to go without a jacket.

He paused outside his gate debating which way to head. He wanted to wander the backroads of the Sierras before Tahoe, maybe take his favorite hiking trail to the Big Trees Grove, a collection of gigantic sequoias located among the pines. He could go north and drive up to Duncan Peak Fire lookout, or up to Chipmunk Ridge not far from Sunrise Mountain. He'd have to take Sam up there, introduce her to the land he loved.

He gazed out his truck window. "Sorry, Cindy, sweetheart. I hope you don't mind. I married Sam."

Nothing. Only the wind. He turned right.

Taking a severe curve up the Middle Fork of the American River, Joe realized it had been a long time since he and Cindy had discovered a nearly grown-over, logging road cutting through the forest to the backside of Mesa de Salvia. They'd gotten lost one Sunday after services and found this old truck-trail which topped out in the forest in a section cleared of old growth. He and Cindy later planted new trees there to build the forest back up. He hadn't returned in ages.

When there was a dip in the highway, the small, barely seen dirt road appeared at the right. Joe slowed the truck and made the turn. By the look of the tree growth, he might lose some paint. The dogs huddled together in the center of the bed behind him to avoid the slap of branches. He opened the sliding window between them. "Don't worry, boys. All is well."

Shep stuck his nose through the window and snorted.

"It's okay, boy. It's just trees." If the forest encroached too much, he'd have to bring them inside.

The overgrown path ended about four miles in the middle of old growth forest, near where he and Cindy had planted the new trees. That had to be about fifteen years ago.

Joe grabbed his jacket from behind the seat, just in case. The temperature at this altitude could change with a wind's breath. He stopped to fill his lungs with the sweet scent of pine and the rich brown mulch under his feet. Dear God in heaven, he loved his property. So much variety and lushness. Not far from here was the cornerstone of his property line with SRM.

He pulled his old Remington off the gun rack. He liked the fast shooter even when deer hunting. After loading the rifle, stuffing extra shells in his pockets, he took off to hike through the undergrowth. The dogs trailed behind him sniffing the air. "It's good to get out and hike, huh, boys?"

Shep's tongue lolled out to the side, a sure sign he was enjoying himself. Spike just sniffed the ground. Sometimes Joe wondered about him. Though obedient to a fault, Spike had his own sense of when to do something or if he'd do it at all. Sort of reminded Joe of himself.

"Those dogs are absolutely yours," Cindy had told him one day while hiking around this same area. "They sure don't listen to me."

"They obey Ricardo, Sal, and Mike," he said with a grin.

She punched him. "They obey me, too, but they always look at you first for permission. It's like I'm not good enough to tell them what to do."

"As long as you know the commands, sweetheart, you'll be okay."

She'd smiled that honeyed-smile of hers and he'd melted inside.

Now a different smile that greeted him every morning—a warm, curl-your-toes grin with seductive dark eyes to boot.

He rubbed his chest. The normal debilitating pain, however, had lessened. Sam's doing?

Sam.

He tramped around a massive pine, the bark scratching against his palm as he passed.

Sam had been a trooper through all this nonsense with the doctor from SRM and the scare of the kids nearly dying. They still had so much to learn about each other, but she was going to install herself in his home. He wouldn't be lonely anymore.

Before Robbie, and Jessica, left to go back to school, he'd have a barbecue for them this Sunday after church. Sal had some friends with a small country band. They could clear out the barn and have a barn-stompin' dance.

Sam felt right in his arms all weekend long.

She was different from Cindy.

Joe pulled to a stop in a small clearing as memories of his first wife came, but shadowed now without the bitter pain. His wife—Cindy, had been petite, pale, blonde, calm and wise. Sam—much taller—her almond skin and laughing dark eyes made him feel like cutting loose, grabbing life by the horns.

Cindy's lips had been rosy and sweet. Sam's branded him, so smoking hot he'd nearly forgotten himself when she kissed him goodbye last night.

He walked forward again.

"She's right for you, Joe." He heard Cindy's voice whispering through the pines. *"I'm pleased for both of you."*

He found himself smiling, the painful sorrow slowly evaporating. "Thank you, sweetheart. I'll still miss you."

"I know," Cindy whispered back as her voice faded on the wind.

Shep padded around Joe, whined. Spike put his nose in the air, his ears at attention.

"What is it, boys?" Joe paused to listen.

Only birdsong twittered in his ears, along with the breeze rustling the needles and leaves above his head. Then he heard what sounded like footsteps over rocky ground. "Find." He commanded the dogs and jogged after them as they dashed through the undergrowth.

They darted through the bushes and scrub trees heading south, noses in the air. Intruder. They knew better than to bark.

Running and the thin air was doing a number on Joe's lungs. He paused to catch his breath, leaning against a thick old-growth tree. Somewhere near here was the backside of Mesa de Salvia, probably where that no-good Dr. Basua gained access from a different route. If Joe saw that snake again, he'd tear him apart.

Someone was running hard and fast over rocky terrain. It didn't sound like the dogs. Joe cocked his rifle.

When Joe cleared the edge of the thickest forest, a view onto the topside of Mesa de Salvia and the valley below opened before him. A narrow path led down off to the west and over the mesa's side. A less used deer track meandered east into the granite canyons. Had he been that way before? When he had more time, he'd come back and follow that trail.

He heard the dogs scrambling down the path to his right and followed.

When he reached the tree line, he saw a man charging across the mesa. He was dressed all in black except for a billowing multi-colored scarf, and a dungaree hiking hat. The dogs nipping at his heels.

Joe brought his rifle up to his chest, sighted the man's backside and prepared to fire. "Stop, or I'll shoot," he shouted.

The intruder stopped for a moment and turned his head to locate Joe. With no further hesitation, he leaped forward. Joe's shot missed wide, kicking up tiny rocks and dirt.

"Halt, boys." He whistled for them. They remained poised on the treacherous rocky path.

Breathing hard, Joe struggled over the edge and stopped next to the dogs. The intruder continued to scale the steep trail hugging the sides of the mesa. "Don't come back on my property, or I'll shoot to kill."

Joe readied his rifle and fired again. Gravel spewed into the air and showered the man's feet and calves, but he didn't go down. He'd hit the guy, but he kept descending the treacherous mountainside without a jerk or a limp.

At least he knew Joe was serious.

Damn. Joe was so sure he'd shot the guy. Why didn't he react?

The man stopped before he disappeared around a bend in the rocky trail, turned, and fired a small handgun in Joe's direction.

"Oh, Dear God," Joe shouted as a sharp pain ripped through his shoulder and he crumpled to the ground.

CHAPTER TWENTY-SEVEN

Deadly Skunk on the Ranch

April 14, 1998—Tuesday

J**OE'S INJURED ARM**—the shot grazing him at the shoulder—hurt like hell even though he had it propped up on couch pillows. He'd never let a skunk like his intruder get the drop on him before. Was he getting too soft and slow?

After stumbling home and calling Sam, she'd and the town doc showed up. After patching up his "scrape," the doc said, they insisted he recover by lounging on the couch watching basketball and soap operas for at least two days. Not that he minded, but hell, he didn't have a disability. He'd gotten grazed on the upper arm, not his legs, and hadn't been killed. His arm felt okay. He needed to get up and get busy.

Sam checked his bandage before she left that morning, gave him some pain pills, and kissed him goodbye rather passionately. He'd come close to asking her to stay, but she and Jessica had appointments in the vet clinic all day, and several ranches to visit that afternoon. She promised to meet him for dinner at Ruby's—hopefully they could get through dessert tonight. It was time to tell Jessica and Robbie what they'd done over the weekend.

Joe needed to check his security systems before he showered and got dressed for dinner.

He rose stiffly from the couch, his arm throbbing, and rambled through the kitchen to the little storage room. He'd converted the room into his office at the back of the house. Robbie had set up the CCTV's monitor next to his computer to check the video feed from the barn cameras. From his chair in the office, Joe could look out over most of his ranch and inside his buildings. He could remotely position the camera on the top of the barn if he saw a disturbance in the compound, and dial for help immediately on a new phone system Robbie had installed.

Joe Mack, Texas cowhand, and California cattle rancher had finally gone high-tech.

He was about to push shut down on the computer when he saw a shadow in the stables on the camera monitor.

Someone was moving around among his horses. There it was again. Definitely the shadow of a man.

He focused on the camera's view. Though it was dim in the stables, he saw a man dressed all in black except for a multi-colored scarf climbing the ladder into the hayloft. Joe swore colorfully. "Thank you, Robbie."

Joe killed the lights in the office locking the door behind him.

He marched through the house, determined to catch this intruder before he could cause damage, or harm his ranch hands, or himself.

The dogs stood at attention on the porch, their noses sniffing the air in the direction of the stables. Shep eyed the stables and whined. Joe couldn't let them warn the guy or perhaps get hurt.

The man snooping around was dangerous. Who could race down the side of a cliff with no fear of injury or death, even perhaps wounded himself? He'd have no problem taking out a couple of dogs.

"Stay," he said to them.

Shep whined, but Spike sat back down on his haunches, prepared to wait for another command.

"I'll whistle if I need you."

Joe crept across the ranch yard and into the open garage. He could enter the stables through the west door unseen. He should've grabbed his shotgun by the door. Right now, he didn't want to kill anyone, however. Although all his instincts learned in the jungles of Vietnam screamed at him to kill. He would control those urges. Neither Cindy nor Sam would be happy if he got himself hurt or killed in the process. He wasn't an eighteen-year-old boy in the Army anymore. His movements might be compromised by his age and his blasted injured arm.

From a dark corner by the tack, Joe watched the man poking through the loose hay in the loft. He was limping on his left leg. Joe'd bet his last bull he'd managed to shoot the jackass in the leg.

The horses in the stalls nervously neighed and stomped around. Joe couldn't calm them, or he'd give away his position.

Joe couldn't reach his .35 Remington by the door. Off to his side, the pitchfork hung from a post. He had to remove his sore arm from its splint to grab it and inched toward the only ladder to wait.

Checkers' stall was closest to the ladder. He calmed his buckskin with a hand on his nose and opened the gate. He'd crouch inside the stall and wait for the intruder to walk past. Then surprise.

After poking around, the trespasser put his foot on the ladder and climbed down. Joe saw the long Bowie knife strapped to his thigh. This man was a stone-cold butcher, and Joe had to take him out before he harmed anyone.

The man limped slowly by the fence of Checkers' stall. Joe waited, anxious, his hand trembling on the handle of the pitchfork. He could sink the tines into the man's heart, but that would land him in jail for murder.

He decided something more in line with his military training was appropriate.

After the man passed, Joe stood, opened the gate noiselessly, and swung back with the handle of the pitchfork. "Looking for me, you bastard?"

The man spun around, shock written across his bearded face. Joe swung hard, the handle catching the man on the jaw. He went down to the cement floor, out cold.

About ten minutes later, Joe poked the intruder with a stick as the man lay on the ground. "Wakie, wakie." He chuckled. He'd heard that line from his favorite movie *Crocodile Dundee*.

The man shook his head, a blood trail from where Joe clocked him, spread across his left cheek and had rolled down through his beard and neck to his chest. "Wh … where am I?"

Joe sat on his haunches in front of the man. "You were trespassing on my property with the intent to do bodily harm. You've been found guilty, and sentence is about to be carried out on your sorry hide. What do you have to say for yourself?"

The man swore bitterly.

"Watch your mouth."

The man tugged on his secured arms and inclined his head up to look around. "What's happening? Where are my clothes?"

"Don't worry about your clothes." Joe had stripped the man of his black costume, scarf, and old hiking hat, and left him in his skivvies. His body, covered with tattoos from Army service, also sported multiple scars and gunshot wounds. He now had a new leg injury from where Joe clipped him with his rifle shot. "You've been a busy man, haven't you?"

The man swore again.

Joe tied a rope securely around the man's left ankle and left wrist and stretched the rope lines to the harness of one of Joe's two large draft horses. He did the same with his opposite ankle and wrist. The horses faced away from the murdering thug, pulling tight on the ropes as the man squirmed on the ground. Though the horses were docile as purring kittens, both Shep and Spike sat at each of their feet to keep from moving.

"With just a voice command, I can have my dogs nip at the horses sending them in opposite directions at a fast gallop."

The man's cold, gray eyes opened wide. "You don't have the guts to do that."

Joe drew a figure of a man much in the same position as his intruder in the dirt with a small branch. He spoke in a serene tone. "You ever see Bob Hope in *Paleface* or *Son of Paleface*—I forget which one? When I need a big laugh, I watch both."

"What's that got to do with anything?" the intruder asked, tugging on the ropes.

"I wouldn't do that if I were you, pal. Though tranquil, those horses can pull hard and quick. Wouldn't want you to be ripped apart too quickly." He chuckled. "Where's the fun in that?"

The man's scarred face paled. "You can't do this. You're only trying to scare me."

"You wanna bet?"

"What do you want?"

"Tell me who you are and who sent you?

"Go to hell."

"Probably." Joe huffed. "I think in the movie the Indians used young, tender pine trees pulled taut to the ground then secured the victim. Do a number on you when those trees sprang back into place. I saw it in a Tarzan movie as well. Don't remember the title. This way you'll only lose an arm or two." Joe raised his stick like he was going to tell the dogs to act.

"No. Wait."

"I'm waiting."

The ex-military thug pulled on the ropes. The horses moved forward an inch to counter, jerking the man's arms and legs further until he was stretched out stiffly, nearly doing the splits like a cheerleader. "Make them stop."

"You're frightening them. Just tell me what I need to know, and I'll cut your ropes."

Sweat poured from the man's nappy black and gray hair. "My employer'll kill me."

"Not if I beat him to it." Joe rose to his feet. "Time to spill your guts. Tell me why my ranch is so important to the government. I can wait all day. I don't know how long my horses will stay steady, though."

To prove his point, one of the horses shifted forward. The intruder yelled. "Please. I don't know much."

"Tell me what you know."

"My employer … Major Donald said you had something of his. He wants it back and sent me to find it."

"Did you try to kill my boy and his girl?"

The horses moved.

"Yes," the intruder cried out.

"Basua was with you."

"Yes."

"What's your name?"

"Hawke." He laid his head back, the pain from his tied wrists and ankles must have been awful.

"Well, Mr. Hawke. You wait right here while I shower and shave. I have a date."

"You can't leave me here. What if something spooks the horses?"

"That's your problem."

After Joe was showered, he replaced the bandage Sam put on his shoulder. He shaved and splashing on vibrant bergamot cologne. Whistling, he strode out of his bedroom and through the house. Time to see if his captive was still in one piece.

He pulled the ranch rig around and parked it in front of Mr. Hawke. He got out of the truck. "I see you survived."

"No thanks to you." Hawke swore viciously.

"We're going for a little ride."

"Where?"

"Your new home for the next few years."

"You can't turn me in. I can't go to prison. I won't go back."

Joe grinned. "You'll need to make peace with that since you've obviously lived a life of chaos and murder."

He whistled for the dogs. "Come." They brought the horses toward Joe, lead ropes in their mouths.

Hawke's ropes loosened, and his body slumped, but he couldn't stand. Though his shoulder was weak, Joe forced him to turn over and lay face down. He tied his legs together then thrust his hands behind his back and tied his hands to his feet. "Calf roping style," he said. "Nothing less than you deserve."

"You can't do this," Hawke yelled.

"I just did, now shut up, or I'll have my dogs attack. They're well-trained."

Hawke fell silent except for a groan of pain as Joe struggled to lift him by his ropes slide him onto the tailgate of the rig. Breathing heavily, Joe shoved him into the bed. The dogs hopped up beside him.

"My dogs are going to keep you company until we get to town. Don't make them mad."

"Where are my clothes, my blade?"

"Souvenirs for me." Joe laughed. "Hang on tight."

Joe stopped the rig in front of the Shadow Pines Animal Hospital and Sam's little house. Sam, wearing a clingy dress of deep red and looking gorgeous, came running. Watching her move drove him nuts. He ran a finger under his too-tight collar.

She paused when she saw the dogs and looked over the side of the truck bed. "What's this?" Her shapely black eyebrow winked up.

"A present for the sheriff. Caught him trespassing. He's the one who almost killed Robbie and Jessica."

"Well, by all means. Let's deliver the package to Sheriff Warner. Too bad you don't have a big red bow."

Joe chuckled as he jogged around the truck to open the passenger door for her. "You think they have them at the general store?"

Sam laughed, the sound filled him with sunshine. "We could ask."

However, they didn't stop at the general store, just turned the corner at Ruby's Steakhouse and headed to the sheriff's office. The lights were still on in the Sheriff's Office which meant Warner was still there.

Joe wouldn't go inside. He'd leave the present on the grass outside on the lawn.

He pulled parallel to the sheriff's office, flipped a U-turn and backed up in front of the door. He put the truck in park, honked, and jumped out of the rig.

"You can't turn me in," Hawke said again. "I'll die in captivity."

"How many people have you killed?" Joe gripped the ropes and pulled the man out of the truck. He dumped him on the lawn.

Joe looked up as Sheriff Warner opened the door.

"What the hell is this?" Warner asked.

"This is me doing your job, Sheriff," Joe said. "This is Mr. Hawke. Don't know if that's a last or first name. This is the man who shot me up on the mesa. He's also the person who attempted to kill Robbie and Jessica in the box canyon. I found this ... criminal assassin this afternoon tramping around in my stables with the intention to do bodily harm."

Sheriff Warner stood on the sidewalk shaking his head. "Where are his clothes?"

"Casualty of war."

"Joe, you can't take the law into your own hands."

Sam stuck her head out of the truck window. "Evening, Sheriff."

"Sam?" Warner looked a little green.

Joe walked to his truck door, pivoted toward Warner. "Any chance you could do your job, so I don't have to?"

CHAPTER TWENTY-EIGHT

What's the Secret of Sunrise Mountain?

April 15, 1998—Wednesday

IT WAS VIETNAM ALL OVER AGAIN. Another government snafu. Why would the SRM take such an interest in this steep, inaccessible area of his property? They were looking for something and sent a spy plane. When that failed, they sent murdering butchers to search and destroy.

Joe reined in Checkers at the forested edge on the mesa. The mules, Harry Truman and Dwight Eisenhower, loaded with his supplies for camping, halted as well. Immediately the mules stuck their faces in the tender grass shoots springing up between pine needles to nibble.

He rubbed his sore shoulder. Joe'd chased one of Major Donald's thugs, Hawke, the Bowie knife butcher, a few days ago up here and got shot for his efforts.

This morning, instead of heading right for the break above Mesa de Salvia like he'd done with the dogs when pursuing Hawke, Joe nudged Checkers up the barely seen deer path and through a thick stand of pines around the northern point. This path led directly east and would take him deeper into the granite cliff sides of the mountains. To what, he had no idea. He couldn't believe in all this time on the ranch, he'd never scouted out this spot among the sheer-faced granite walls, not even for missing cattle.

Checkers stepped deftly on the needle-covered ground broken only by new deer prints. Joe contemplated his life with his new wife, the lovely Samantha Stone ... Mack, and dinner last night. It'd been nice after the stress of telling the kids they'd gotten married and swearing them to secrecy.

Robbie and Jessica had shared a knowing look like the announcement didn't come as a surprise. The mercenary intruder beforehand and confronting the government's assassin had added to the excitement of the evening. However, being with Sam had him acting like an awkward teenager.

The sun was at its zenith this morning as Checkers and the mules plodded along. Some areas of the trail disappeared into thickets so concentrated, no one could follow.

The dogs shifted and soon picked up the trail again. His little caravan trooped on.

Close to the peak, they came upon a beautiful old growth forest nearly impossible to ride through, but they slogged their way between the tall pines. The mules followed without complaint, his pack sometimes brushing against two-hundred-year-old trees on either side of him.

Joe dismounted at one point and tugged Checkers' reins behind him. He knelt to find the trail in the overgrowth. This forest of tall pines at noon cast murky shadows on the path and blocked enough light to seem dim as twilight.

"Not long now." He patted Checkers' neck. The dogs whined, and Harry raised his head and let out a loud whinny/bray. "I know it's time to eat, Harry."

Harry bared his teeth. Dwight simply stared at him. Joe chuckled and continued to work his way through the pines and close-growing aspens.

Up ahead, sunshine engulfed an opening in the forest. "See. Almost there. And you guys were worried."

They burst through the forest after the dogs. Joe searched the clearing. Checkers jerked his head up, whinnied. Joe heard the splashing of a stream. Water.

Before them was a small, snow-ringed lake not more than a hundred feet across. Surrounding the lake, a granite wall rising hundreds of feet into the sky. All but concealed along one wall, was a small depression, or cleft in the escarpments. The split in the granite wall looked as though a small stream eroded through over time creating a cleft.

Curiosity burned.

Nearing the entrance to the cleft, Joe saw a narrow animal trail alongside the stream. It led through the high walls of a tapered ravine—a canyon leading to another canyon. "Why haven't I ever seen this before?"

Checkers shook his head. He chuckled. "You don't know, either?"

The horse nickered.

They walked along the trail, in most spots only wide enough for the little stream and the deer tracks. "I'll let you drink when we get out of here." He gazed up at the sheer cliff face. "I don't want to get caught in a rockslide."

He pulled the horse and mules through the narrow passage. At the end, the walls opened into a small box canyon with high granite cliffs. Tall pines growing at the top of the canyon's edge hid the whole thing from view. That's why Joe'd never seen the canyon before. Like a secret ravine.

Along one side of the canyon, the small stream babbled over rocks. It appeared fed by a falls trickling over a rock shelf at the canyon's back wall. Snow lay in clumps on the east side of this canyon still untouched by the warm sunshine.

He led Checkers and the two mules over to the water and a grassy area and let them drink.

Shep and Spike stepped into the stream and lapped up water while cooling their paws. "That does look like a fine idea." Joe crouched down and scooped up a handful of the clean mountain water. "Ahhhh."

After unloading Harry and Dwight's packs, he decided to refresh his own feet. The stream wasn't more than a foot deep and ran crystal clear and ice cold.

He gazed around his new discovery. Scrub and sage bushes grew everywhere. It wasn't a rock quarry-type chasm like most of the box canyons in this area, layered with thick chunks of granite. The walls were reasonably smooth granite rock impossible to climb. Some of the sidewall rocks had fallen into the little stream diverting it. Situated as it was back behind Mesa de Salvia, it was a pleasantly cool, forest-lined box canyon, not visible from the mesa or the air.

Not visible from the air.

"Well, I'll be damned."

This had to be the canyon The Peter Pan Project people were searching for. Directly through the mountain from here was the SRM Facilities. Did they think this gorge held something special?

After a brief, invigorating soak and clean socks, he slipped his feet back into his hiking boots. The dogs heeled next to him as he walked through the scraggly, prickly scrub bushes overgrowing the floor. Basketball sized boulders, and some the size of his dogs, which had fallen from the side walls, lay scattered around. Joe had to pick up his feet to avoid tripping on the sharp splintered rocks. This crevice was maybe twenty feet wide and about sixty feet deep. Hidden, never before discovered.

Movement behind bushes and some skittering noises caught the dogs' attention. Possibly a ground squirrel. Shep whined and scooched on his belly to military-crawl toward the sound.

"What the hell?"

Spike followed his friend, his nose to the ground. "It's just an animal. Leave it alone."

Both dogs barked, the sound bouncing off the high walls.

"What have you found? What is it? If this is just a squirrel..."

Joe ripped the scratchy bush from the graveled soil with his gloved hands, tossed it aside.

About four to five feet back, under more bushes, the dogs stopped to whine. After he pulled the last bush out, Joe discovered a broad, flat stone jutting out of the ground. He straightened up. "What's this?"

Shep pawed the dirt around the stone. "There's writing on this stone. It's a headstone of some sort."

Joe crouched down and pulled his handkerchief from his pocket to wipe the years of gravel dust and dried mud from the face of the hand-carved stone.

Leaning back, Joe studied the carved letters as best he could without his reading glasses. Damned old age.

"Best dog I ever had. R.I.P. Plata." He gazed at the dogs. "Well, what do you know?"

Shep walked over to him and laid his head on Joe's shoulder. "You knew, though, didn't you?"

He stood as a memory surfaced.

Joe had been digging through some old notebooks he'd found in the barn belonging to Cindy's granddad, Elmer. He had fallen on hard times after winning Sunrise Ranch in a poker game, and a first lousy winter. He'd managed to pull through somehow and purchased some acres to expand the ranch—even bought more cattle.

How could a man without means accomplish that? Elmer had also written about raising Shepherd pups to sell and use as cattle dogs. "Wasn't one of them named Plata? And didn't Plata mean silver in Spanish?"

The dogs gazed up at him as if to say, "Well, duh. We found Plata."

He patted them on their heads. "Good work. I suggest lunch. Then we'll make Plata's grave look good again."

Why had Elmer buried Plata so far from the house? Crazy Old Elmer.

After lunch, he staked Checkers, Harry Truman, and Dwight Eisenhower, near the stream. They didn't need much beyond the small patch of fresh grass at the water's edge anyway, but he gave them a cup of oats.

The dogs seemed hyper, galloping back and forth across the width of the canyon chasing small mice or a rabbit or two.

Joe spread out his sleeping bag near a large log and laid down for a rest. His weary bones were screaming. It was difficult to breathe at this altitude, slowing him down some.

About an hour later and still light out, Shep barked at a rock formation at the back of the canyon. "Quiet down," he shouted. But the dog kept barking. Perhaps he found another grave.

Joe slowly shoved his feet into his boots and moseyed through the sharp rocks.

Not more than thirty feet from where he built their camp, Joe saw why Shep had barked. He stared at what looked like a man-made structure. A round wall consisting of tall, thin stones surrounded a lower circle of flat, level stones.

What the hell?

In the center of the circle of stones was a round log structure like a cylinder with a rusted wheel attached to its top. Two gray-faded logs connected at the center of the wooden cylinder and the wheel with a large railroad spike.

Chains hung from the logs and connected to massive stones that looked like someone dragged them along the smooth rocks to crush something. The whole thing resembled a mechanical horse walker only constructed closer to the ground. What would it be doing in this canyon and who built it? Obviously, someone had been here before him. Possibly, Elmer Johnsen.

Spike stood at the back wall of the canyon as though he were in a hole. "Come, Spike," Joe demanded. The dog ignored him. Joe stomped over to him, leaving Shep by the curious stone structure.

"What is it, Spike? Don't want to be left out of discovering new stuff?"

Spike pawed at some of the denser bushes growing there. Once again, Joe tore out more thorn-ridden bushes. "Maybe this is a pet cemetery."

Shep joined them and sat next to Spike. They watched Joe struggle with the plants, tongues lolling. "You could help."

They both cocked their heads. "What good are you?" he asked them.

This section of bushes had grown tall and thick from the water nearby making them harder to remove. Joe was about eight feet from the canyon wall when he stumbled and fell into a divot carved out of the ground. "Damn," he said bumping his chin against some granite.

More bushes. Yanking hard, he managed to clear to the last bush. When it came out in his hands, he stopped—open mouthed and stared.

"Well, well, well. Crazy Old Elmer had himself a mine."

Before Joe was a marker, the writing long gone except for the words "Olina" and "mine." It stood in front of a small jagged opening in the canyon wall big enough for a man to crawl through. Jogging back to camp, he dug his flashlight out of his pack and returned.

Joe turned to the dogs. "You coming?"

They whined but didn't move. "Cowards."

He glazed into the dark abyss. Turning on the flashlight, Joe bounced the beam off gray rock walls of the cramped tunnel. A real tight fit crawling on all fours. "If Elmer could do it, so can I." Joe crouched down and crawled into the mouth of the cave.

About six or seven feet in, the small shaft opened into a much more extensive cavern. Joe struggled to his feet and gazed around. Rusting picks, shovels, and a metal-wheeled wheelbarrow littered the smooth rock floor. Elmer's crude mining equipment. No wonder he never told anyone about this. He had his own bank right here on the ranch.

The thought paralyzed Joe.

What if someone found out about this mine, or at least believed there still might be working mines in this area? What if that someone owned a small spy plane and searched non-stop in this area for the opening?

Joe leaned against the wall as the implications sunk in. Major Donald and Dr. Basua were searching for Elmer's mine. Had the old man staked a claim and was it on the books in the county offices? What if the government imbeciles found the mine? He'd seen the plane flying in a grid pattern across the land up here searching. No wonder they were willing to kill to get their hands on Elmer's ... no, wait ... *his* silver.

Elmer had constructed a crude type of timber framing consisting of vertical logs on either side of the diggings, like ribs, capped with a third horizontal member to support the roof.

That structure of rocks he'd seen outside must be how Elmer processed the ore. Perhaps he'd attached his mules or horses to the logs and had them drag those heavy stones across the rocks to crush out the silver.

Joe picked up the rusty pick and ambled back into the mine shaft. He wondered if Elmer had dug out all the ore. He crisscrossed the flashlight beam on the shaft walls. Streaks of sooty gray rocks lined the walls.

Old Elmer wasn't crazy after all. He'd outfoxed the whole family. Joe bet Cindy's father, Bert, didn't know about this mine. He'd always seemed financially strapped. Except, now and then, a check from some bank in Sacramento would arrive and save the day. Hadn't Bert known it was his father's money? Would he have been angry at his father for not telling him about the mine? Maybe he left clues in his paperwork, and Bert ignored it or didn't know what Elmer meant.

Joe laid down the flashlight, directing the beam at the rock wall looking more like regular granite than high-grade ore. He swung the pickaxe. The effort was taxing with no immediate reward. Then, on about the tenth swing, a chunk of the wall broke loose and tumbled down at Joe's feet.

He picked it up, but couldn't tell if he'd found anything of value.

After a few more swings, he dislodged some more rocks but left them on the floor of the shaft. He'd examine the first, larger stone outside in the light of day.

Crawling back through the hole even carting some of the rocks was a breeze. The dogs waited at the mouth of the entrance always on guard duty. Thank the good Lord that plane wasn't searching anymore. They might have found the mine by now.

In the sunlight, Joe turned the rock around in his hand. His eyes widened. The stone not only had silver streaks running through it, but a peppering of gold particles. "Gold," he whispered.

He'd heard of some mines producing silver mixed with gold. He examined the rock again, his heart thumping wildly. Sure enough. Gold and silver, possibly some copper colored the stone in his hands. He didn't know the value of gold and silver these days, but he'd bet the ranch, the government needed pure-grade silver to build electronics and use it in aerodynamics. He had to get to the county offices in Auburn and make sure Elmer had claimed this mine.

"Eureka, Elmer, you crazy old dog. I've found your safety deposit box."

CHAPTER TWENTY-NINE
"Thar Be Gold in Them Thar Hills"

April 16, 1998 – Thursday

JOE LEFT FOR SACRAMENTO at four a.m. He didn't want to answer any questions from Sam or Ricardo about where he was going or how long he'd be gone. It was time to haul the raw ore he'd dug out of his mountain to Sacramento to see if it was worth anything.

He'd driven into Auburn yesterday to check with the county offices on Bell Road to see if Elmer had filed a claim. By golly he had. The man in the office told Joe he needed a lawyer to legally make sure his name got transferred to the mine documents as an inheritor of the property. He'd done all that and the mine was officially his. Now he could cash in.

Finding an assayer in 1998 had been a trick. Many of them closed around the end of the 19th Century and moved the concerns over to the government, which controlled a big part of the mining industry.

Taking as many of the mine's rocks as Harry and Dwight could carry, Joe had hidden them in his old rig and planned his trip to Sacramento.

Joe slid out of his and Sam's new king-sized bed in the dark and left her with a kiss on the lips managing not to wake her. He didn't want to tell her anything in case the rocks were a bust. Also, she could deny any knowledge of a mine if asked.

In Auburn, he pulled his rig off the Foresthill Road and parked at the Black Bear Diner for some out-of-this-world pancakes. He'd never let Lettie know their pancakes were just a little better than hers.

He ate the sweet melt-in-your-mouth flapjacks, slices of thick bacon, sausage, ham, hash browns, and drank his French-roast coffee.

What had Major Donald planned for him now? Joe prayed Sam would be okay while he was out of town. The last thing he'd wanted was to involve her in any of his troubles.

That's what husbands and wives did—they shared their troubles and their happy times.

He tossed some bills on the table after swallowing down the last of his coffee, not sure how long it would take him to find the California Department of Mines and Geology. After that, he had some provisions to buy at a more sizable ranch supply store in the outskirts of Sacramento.

Joe glanced at the burlap bags of rocks he'd dug from the mine and stuffed on the floor of the rig. The dogs sat beside him on the seat ever watchful. No wonder Major Donald was in a hurry to locate the mine. He'd possibly net a small fortune if Joe were out of the picture.

On "K" Street in Sacramento, Joe pulled into the parking lot of the Department of Mines and Geology. Nerves had his heart thumping loud. What if they told him his ore was no good? This long trip would have been for nothing.

An older, whiskered gentleman manned the front counter and looked like he could still be scouring the hills of Placer County working his own mine.

"My name is Marshall Hammond. How can I help you today?" the gentleman asked as Joe approached. He held one glittering rock in his hand.

"I need some help with assaying this rock I found."

The older gentlemen's eyes widened. "May I see it?"

Joe clunked the rock on the counter.

Marshall held the rock turning it this way and that. "My goodness, it's a heavy one." He moved to where it caught the early morning sunlight streaming through the glass windows. "Magnificent. Haven't seen ore like this since the Jenny Lind closed down." Gosh, he was old.

Joe's heart skipped a beat. "How long would it take to assay the mineral content?"

"Today's advanced equipment analyzes a variety of samples by the atomic absorption test or mass spectroscopy." He glanced at Joe, grinned. "These tests measure the concentration of the elements down to parts per billion of a gram." Marshall chuckled. "It's very accurate. We charge upfront for the test, and there's no guarantee your sample will verify as pure."

"How long?"

"About four weeks. Our labs are very busy."

"Four weeks." Joe should have taken it to Nevada. "How much?"

"For this rock, about forty dollars."

Joe clenched his teeth.

"Do you mind if I ask where you found this particular rock?" The older man's eyes glittered.

"Yeah, I do mind."

Marshall chuckled. "It was worth a shot."

"How do I know you won't take all the gold out of it and cash it in yourself?" Gold did funny things to people. Just ask Elmer Johnsen.

"You don't." Marshall laughed. "Sorry. Assayer's humor. I can assure you we are an above-board facility and are certified. We have only the client's best interest in mind." He rifled through a drawer and came up with some paperwork. "I'll have you sign some papers. Then I'll take a 3-D picture of the rock—for your protection."

"All right." Joe dug cash out of his wallet. No way would he use his credit card. He rattled off his cheap cell phone number. Robbie had him purchase a new phone to contact only him. He gave the name of Mack Johnsen with the Auburn address of the Black Bear Diner.

Marshall wrote down his information. "Call us in about three and a half weeks, Mr. Johnsen. We might have pushed our work forward."

Joe nodded and spun around.

He traipsed out of the office, disappointment nipping at his heels. He had to know now what the rock was worth.

What if he'd found real silver or ... gold.

He'd make Sunrise Ranch something special for Sam.

April 19, 1998—Sunday after Easter—**Semana de Pascua (The traditional Mexican celebration after Easter)**

Dr. Samantha Mack met her husband in church, and they held hands during the service. After that, she'd floated to her house behind the vet clinic to finish her preparations and pack up her food. Most of her furniture—which was older—would remain. Her assistant rented her house and would keep watch on the vet hospital.

At the same time the beans sputtered in the frying pan, she changed from her Sunday dress into her best black slacks and cowgirl boots, a body-hugging jersey tunic in red. She would leave a lasting impression in Joe's mind.

"Yeah, he can't live without me," she told her fluffy tabby, Max, who ignored her in favor of curling up in the sunny spot in the windowsill. How would Max get along with Shep and Spike? They'd soon find out.

Food prepared and boxed, Sam loaded up her 1996 Suburban, her behemoth Vet wagon, Robbie called it, with potato salad and her unique Mexican-seasoned ranch-style refried beans. She also made her specialty, a Tres Leches cake, a traditional Easter coconut cake soaked in sweetened condensed milk, evaporated milk, and heavy cream. She made the dessert specifically for her new husband, even if it wasn't good for him.

Today would be the last time she cooked at her house. Samantha paused for a moment to look around. The little house never felt like home without Jessica there. She'd been biding her time waiting for Joe to get over Cindy. None of that mattered now—she would be the lady of Sunrise Ranch.

After she loaded all her dishes, she slammed her front door, and climbed into her well-stocked SUV. Her pulse thumped rapidly as she considered the quiet, stoic cowboy with a heart of gold. He'd always treated her with kindness and respect—now he loved her as she wished to be loved.

Nothing could mar her happiness today. She was going home.

Samantha pulled onto Main Street behind several vehicles loaded with other church families headed to Sunrise Ranch. Lettie and Ricardo were hosting a combination Easter Celebration and the local Mexicans celebration of the end of *Semana de Pascua*, Mexican Holy Week after Easter, with a fiesta. Although Sam wouldn't have Joe entirely to herself, she didn't mind sharing him for a short time. She'd be the one remaining after everyone else left.

The late spring morning was crisp and cool, the sky a robin's egg blue above her head as she headed her rumbling SUV east along the highway. About two miles from the turnout to the ranch, a black Jeep appeared in Sam's rearview mirror. It came up on her fast and didn't look like it was going to slow.

At this section of the highway, the road wound closely between a rock-faced cliff and a drop off, several hundred feet to the Middle Fork of the American River.

The driver of the Jeep honked and tailgated. Samantha's hands trembled on the steering wheel. What was the matter with him?

She pulled as far to the right as possible, hoping he'd take the hint and pass. However, the road was narrow, and he continued to ride her bumper, honking that gosh-awful horn.

Sam rolled down her window and signaled for him to pass.

The driver sped up and pulled into the opposing lane, but didn't pass. The windows were tinted too black for Sam to see inside.

Even with her vehicle now, the Jeep swerved at her. Sam tugged the wheel to the right, nearly scraping her Suburban on the rock-faced cliff.

"What the hell?" Her hands shook as she brought the Suburban back into her lane.

Dread choked her, and her heart galloped. The driver was forcing her off the road, or to send her smashing into the jagged rock wall to kill her. She offered a prayer.

The Jeep veered again, this time swiping the side of her SUV, and shoving her toward the jagged rocks at her right. The sound of screeching tires, and the tinny scrape of metal on stone grated on her ears. Her back-passenger window shattered with an ear-splitting explosion, splintering into jagged pieces.

She fought the wheel to hold the big vehicle steady. Up ahead was an outcropping of rocks jutting out into the road's shoulder. If this jackass kept at it, he'd force her into the stone wall and kill her.

This road rage must stop.

Her fear calmed. A new emotion hit her like a wave. Anger. Her SUV was the same size as his, perhaps bigger and heavier.

Feeling stronger and defiant, she hit her brakes, jerked her wheel toward the Jeep, caving in the back-passenger door with her much larger bumper. The black vehicle veered to the left. Its skidding tires kicked up the gravel on the non-existent embankment above the river.

"Take that, you jackass," she shouted.

She watched the Jeep slam to a stop on the wrong side of the road, gravel spraying out from behind it. Ramming her foot on the gas pedal, and screeching tires on the asphalt, she bolted.

Not more than two miles further up the road was the turnoff for Joe's ranch. Thank the good Lord.

She slowed so she could take the turn without flipping her vehicle. The Jeep had nearly caught up to her. However, as she turned down Joe's lane, the Jeep hurled down the road.

Too wired to continue, Samantha pulled next to the gated entrance and slumped in her seat.

CHAPTER THIRTY
Food with Friends

April 19, 1998—Sunday

SAMANTHA'S HAND QUAKED when she raised it to punch the gate keypad. Robbie installed the thing when he was here at Spring Break hoping to secure the ranch. Though she wasn't happy about Robbie dating Jessica, she had a new-found respect for the boy.

Breathing hard like she'd run the entire way from Shadow Pines, she steadied her finger to push the key-code Joe gave her. She waited for the large metal gate to swing open, so she could drive through.

Joe stood on the porch of his ranch house looking robust and handsome—his dark blond hair combed neatly, his beard carefully cropped. He still wore his Sunday-go-to-meeting clothes, except the constricting tie. She pulled her Suburban to a stop, killed the motor. Still shaking, her clammy hands refused to release the wheel.

Joe's eyes widened as he frowned at her SUV. Swearing, he raced down the stairs.

"What the hell happened?" She heard him yell before the driver's door jerked opened. "Are you all right?" Joe reached for her, tugging her from the driver's seat and into his arms, wrapping her up snug.

"You're shaking." His tone was simultaneously protective and furious. "Tell me what happened."

"Someone … tried to run me off the road." Even her voice wobbled.

His whole body clenched. "Did you see who it was?"

"No. I couldn't see inside the Jeep because of the tinted windows.

"Black Jeep."

She nodded.

"Dammit," he said.

211

"I was scared, then I got angry."

"Good girl." He stroked her hair, but his hand quivered. She rested her head on his chest, felt his heart beating steady and quick beneath her ear. He was her rock. "It's probably someone from SRM," he said.

She leaned back so she could look into his gray/blue eyes, so wise and kind. "Why would they come after me?"

He hesitated. "As I told you before, they want something from me, and you're a target."

He gritted his teeth and shook his head "I know that Jeep. It tried to run me off the road a few days ago."

"Oh, Joe. Why didn't you tell me?"

He crossed his arms. His closed-mouth, tough guy thing had to end as they went further into their marriage.

Joe released her, stepped away, and turned like he was heading to the garage.

"Where are you going?" Samantha asked.

"I'm gonna call on SRM."

"No, Joe. No." She ran after him, gripped his arm to stop him. "Don't do this. It's not worth getting killed over. I'm fine."

He touched her shoulder, his eyes blazed with a frightening angry light. "You could have been killed."

"But I wasn't." She glanced over her shoulder. "You can't leave because your guests are arriving."

He glanced over her head and watched as two more cars filled with families arrived. He blew out a ragged breath. "I'd forgotten. I'm sorry."

"Shall we put this incident behind us for now and enjoy the Easter celebration?" she asked him.

With a resigned smile, he hugged her one more time. A moment later, he took her arm and led her back to her SUV to get her food. They then strolled to the fiesta in the middle of the yard.

Joe, Ricardo, and his boys had set up several four by eight sheets of plywood between barrels to serve as tables in the center of the yard. Folks brought their chairs. Pastor English was in his element, greeting all the parishioners and seeing to their needs with food and a kind word.

Off to one side, a portable dance floor had been set up, and people were whirling to the waltzy music of a Mariachi band. Several *piñatas* made to look like an effigy of Judas Iscariot dangled from tree limbs for the children. Samantha loved the traditional celebrations of the Mexicans who honored the death and resurrection of Jesus Christ. They warmed her heart.

Lettie, her daughters-in-law, and some of the Mexican women from town had spread out delicious traditional Mexican Easter foods on a large serving table. The smell of the traditional *cabrito*, the young spring lamb, roasting over a spit filled the air with heavenly aromas making Samantha's mouth water.

"Looks like Lettie made all her traditional Easter foods," Samantha said.

Joe squeezed her hand. "She's been using my kitchen to cook and set everything up. I can't walk through without dipping a finger to sample it all."

Samantha laughed. She loved it when Joe let loose.

Lettie's creations lined the table. Delicious *pambazos*—chicken or cheese filled rolls bathed in a spicy salsa. *Molotes*—Oaxacan masa *empañadas*—a tortilla made with fresh masa filled with a chorizo and potato filling, fried, then topped with salsa, crema, queso fresco. And Samantha's favorite, the shrimp potato cakes swimming in cilantro, guajillo chili, chipotle, and cactus sauce—a treat the Mexicans ate in the celebration of Lent.

She and Joe strolled over to the dessert table. It also contained a delicious spread of other traditional Mexican sweets. *Capirotada*—Mexican Bread Pudding, which reminded the Mexicans of the suffering of Christ on the cross. It was a pudding made with cinnamon, piloncillo, cloves, raisins, bread, and cheese. *Biscochos*—Mexican wedding cookies. *Plátanos*—fried plantains topped with sweetened cream. She placed her tres leche on the table.

She pointed to the cake. "I made this especially for you."

Joe dipped a fingertip into the sweet whipped cream topping. "Hmmm. Save me a big piece."

Gratified, Samantha squeezed his arm.

Some of the children were guzzling aguas frescas at a table manned by Salvador's wife. Lettie had worked most of the week

213

infusing gallons of waters with pineapple, melon, tamarindo, and chia seeds. Other refreshing drinks made from jamaica, horchata, melon, and other seasonal fruits were ladled out from large, clear glass containers.

"The spread looks wonderful." Samantha pointed to the array of salads, hot dishes, and breads. "Do you think Lettie prepared any of her special Bloody Marias, those drinks with serrano-infused tequila this year? I remember it was a big hit with the ranch hands." She fanned her mouth.

"It better not be this year." Joe laughed. "I need them sober. But I do believe you are correct. Right this way, m'lady."

Joe led her to a smaller table where Sal was ladling up the bright red concoction garnished with a sprig of fresh cilantro.

She and Joe got their drinks and headed for the main table.

Ricardo and Mike were carving up the lamb, placing large slices on a platter held by Lettie. She was smiling, probably happy to be at the center of her celebratory feast.

"Did you help roast the lamb?" Samantha asked Joe.

He nudged her shoulder. "Who else?"

"I can hardly wait to eat."

"Elmer began these Easter-Sunday-after-services supper years ago, and then Bert continued it." Joe grinned. "Ricardo and Lettie added their traditional Mexican foods. I wouldn't let the tradition die out."

"I'm glad you didn't. Traditions are important." Samantha loaded her huge, platter-sized paper plate with all of Lettie's treats and some rich baked beans, creamy potato salad, fresh homemade tortillas, and slabs of homemade bread and creamery butter. When she got to the lamb, she asked Lettie for three large pieces. "I'm starved."

"I like it when a woman isn't afraid to eat a good meal." Joe laughed. His plate was heaped higher than hers.

"There comes a time when we all must cut back, though, because of our health. Don't you agree?" Samantha asked.

"I'm not that old yet."

He led her over to where he'd propped two of Cindy's kitchen chairs against the plywood table and righted them. She sat and grinned at Deputy Pete Vargas and his female companion.

"Howdy Pete," she said and nodded at his friend.

"Hi, Doc. This lovely lady is my date, Karen."

"How do you do?" Samantha asked.

The girl blushed. "Fine, thank you. What a wonderful celebration."

"A tradition of Joe's wife's family and the Sanchez family." Samantha pointed to Joe. "This here is our host for the evening, Joe Mack."

"I'm glad you came." Joe nodded and smiled. It warmed Sam's heart to see his sincere smile. He frowned though when the sheriff drove up with his wife, Beverly. Samantha clutched his arm and told him to get over it.

So many people came, Samantha thought they could have called it a "town" Easter Fiesta. Even Ruby and Bill Green, from the Steakhouse, came and seemed to enjoy the lamb Joe'd roasted.

They ate and chatted. Pastor English gave his pronouncements about Easter. A week late, since last Sunday was the actual day of Easter, but it had rained hard last Sunday, postponing the party until today. Not that anybody minded.

Around four p.m., the partygoers cleaned up and gathered children who had run around the barns and stables chasing cats and riding the gentler horses in the corral with Sal's assistance.

After washing dishes and cleaning up Joe's kitchen, Samantha stood on the porch watching the families pack up their vehicles. Someone wrapped an arm around her waist, the hand resting on her hip.

Joe whispered in her ear. "Did you have fun?"

She turned to smile up at him, her heart tripping over itself. "The best."

Pastor English ambled over to the porch stairs and glanced up. "Thank you, Joe, for hosting this year's Easter barbecue, even if it's a week late."

"Better late than never, Pastor." Joe grinned.

"Yes, well, we're all mighty glad you've kept up the tradition. The Lord bless you and … your friends."

Joe nodded but didn't say anything. Did the pastor know she and Joe were already a couple? People would've noticed them at Ruby's, the hand-holding in church, and him standing with his arm around her now. It was silly not to tell people. She'd waited so long to be Mrs. Joe Mack.

Four cars headed up the graveled road to the ranch gate, more were getting ready to depart. Joe ran his fingers through her hair. Shivers ran from her neck to her toes.

"You have the softest hair." He snuggled close, dipped his head and inhaled. "Smells like strawberries."

Her tongue tied up in knots.

"I've been so lonely since Cindy died."

"I know." Samantha sighed.

"She did everything for me." His hand stilled.

"Yes, she did."

"She was delicate and frail even when she was younger."

Samantha knew that.

He drifted forward until he was facing her. "I married Cindy at the Shadow Pines Christian Church with Pastor English performing the vows."

"I know. I was there." She'd been Cindy's only bridesmaid.

Joe glanced out over the buildings of the ranch. Where had he gone?

She'd always desired a proper wedding surrounded by her friends, but that skunk Brad, had insisted they run away to Reno.

"I was thinking." Joe paused. "Perhaps we could get officially marri—"

"*Señor* Joe," Ricardo shouted from the edge of the barn. He ran toward them waving his hands above his head. "Dark smoke, she rise from the east range. Forest fire."

"Holy hell. Forest fire." Joe ran down the porch stairs, Samantha on his heels. "Ring the bell," he shouted at Ricardo.

Ricardo jogged over to the entrance to the barn where a large bell hung since Elmer's time. It was used to call cowboys to supper. A specific number of rings were for trouble. Ricardo rang the bell vigorously.

Joe pointed to the mountains. "Looks like it started up on Flat Ridge."

"The cattle." Fear gripping Samantha's stomach. "How can I help?"

"The cattle are settled in the front pasture. Don't worry about them. Worry about a range fire racing toward the compound or racing up the mountain."

"We'll take up where we left off when the fire is contained." He pulled her close and kissed her. "Can you call the fire department and find Lettie and her daughters-in-law? Have them stand by with hoses for their houses."

"Okay. What else?"

Joe's serious gaze met hers. "Pray."

Joe ran toward the garage and the large water truck he used for watering the cattle when they were out on the range. The truck was old, and it took a few moments for the engine to kick over.

Sheriff Warner sprinted over to the house. "Can I use Joe's phone to call the fire department and the local hot shots for a water drop?"

"Yes, of course." Samantha ran inside the house behind the sheriff.

Cody'd already dialed the number to the fire department. "Yeah, captain, we have a forest fire southeast on Joe Mack's ranch at the top of Flat Ridge ... What? You already know. You say someone else already called it in?" Cody scratched his head. "So, they'll send in the wildfire air tankers from Tahoe? ... It's already on its way? Thanks. We don't want this blaze to spread to the trees or along the face of Sunrise Mountain. Right. Gotcha. I'll coordinate from here." Cody rattled off his cell phone number. "Thanks, Captain."

Cody hung up and whirled around. "Did Joe tell you to prepare the hoses and wet down the houses?"

"I'll coordinate with Lettie and her girls."

"Great." He whisked past her on his way outside.

Samantha chewed her fingernails, but jumped into action. Someone had already called in the fire. Who?

Outside, the men who hadn't left yet with their families snatched hoes and shovels from the equipment shed and ran for Joe's long-bed rig. Pastor English drove the truck, and they all headed through the compound toward the rangeland and the canyons beyond, each one of the men still dressed in Sunday clothes. What a mess.

"What do you want us to do?" Ruby Green asked.

"I'd stick close to your cars, but if you want to help, you could follow me and help use hoses to wet roofs."

Ruby nodded, and some of the women without children jogged behind Samantha as she mumbled a prayer and ran for the row of quaint cottages that housed Ricardo and his family. She knocked on doors and told the women to grab their garden hoses and water down roofs. The town women stayed behind to offer their help.

Joe kept a much more substantial hose in case of fire in the barns or stables. Had he taken it with the water truck? She raced across the compound to locate the hose and find the connection to the water system.

The hose was coiled right where it should be, the connection to the pipe leading into the ground not far away. The wrench to open the water valve hung next to the shut-off. Sam struggled to connect the hose and opened the valve with the wrench. She tugged the heavy hose to an excellent spot to reach the whole roof of their home—her home. She wouldn't allow the fire to take away her new home. All she could do then was wait breathlessly, and to pray the smoke wouldn't shift in their direction.

The black smoke billowed up over Flat Ridge. There hadn't been a lightning strike, and the pasture land was still too damp to burn from a cigarette butt thrown from a passing car up on the mountain road to SRM.

Someone set this fire intentionally.

Was Joe about to propose they get hitched formally in front of their friends if it hadn't been for the fire?

What if he sent her back to town to stay because he was afraid for her safety? Her heart sank. She couldn't leave him. Not now. They were husband and wife and would face the adversities together—no matter what, even if they didn't have a formal wedding ceremony and celebrate with their friends.

"Oh, dear God. Please don't let anything happen to Joe." Samantha prayed as an intense and horrible feeling washed over her. "Please, dear Lord, bring my husband home."

CHAPTER THIRTY-ONE

Where There's Smoke, There's Forest Fire

April 19, 1998—Sunday

DOCTOR **PAUL BASUA** had been into Shadow Pines and had a delicious dinner at Ruby's Steakhouse and Saloon. The young woman who waited on his table had flirted with him, and he'd stayed much longer than intended. She was sweet and curvy with dancing blue eyes that flashed a come-on sign when she'd served him a breadbasket, then again when she returned to deliver his barbecued vegetables. Cows were revered in Hinduism and were not to be eaten even though his English mother had no problem eating red meat.

He'd dined with one eye on the waitress and the other on the door lest Major Donald catch him here. None of the patrons recognized him from his arrest the other day. In fact, there weren't many people in town at all. The young woman had told him most of the town was at a barbecue and fiesta out at Sunrise Ranch.

Paul winced when he remembered being caught bang to rights upon Sunrise Mountain. He suffered emotionally since coming to do his work at SRM. It was embarrassing. He did not want to end up as a lag in the U.S. prison system. His parents would disown him.

When Paul finished his dinner, he had lingered. The waitress, who had few customers to wait upon, sat down next to him and they had spoken of many things. She was a delightful person. He was captivated by her loveliness.

However, it was getting close to check in time with Major Donald. Reluctant to leave, he left a generous tip. On his receipt, the young woman wrote, "Tiffany, 555-2323. Call me." Paul strolled to his green government sedan with a spring in his step.

The drive up the canyon had been warm, the trees lining the winding road were green and smelled of pine. Paul drove with the

219

window open, the mountain breezes wafting around him. He knew he would face a heated argy-bargy with Major Donald over the spy plane. The parts had been delayed another week. He could already feel the major's hot breath down his neck as he shouted at him. The major was bent as a nine-bob note, as his very British mum would say. Paul had to agree.

He drove around one of the last curves before his descent into SRM's side of the mountain, when he saw a column of billowing black smoke. Forest fire. And him without a spotting plane. Bloody hell.

Paul pulled his sedan over to the side of the road, gripped his government-issued cell phone and ran across the highway. He dialed 9-1-1 when he got to the edge of a cliff before Flat Ridge requesting one of those fancy water-dropping aeroplanes. He'd given them the coordinates but refused to give his name.

Sweat poured off Joe's face, running down to soak his favorite Sunday shirt. No time to worry about it now. He leveled the water truck's hose and sprayed the fast-burning grass and trunks of dry trees. The smoke billowed up into the clear air, thick and choking.

Ricardo had one of the other hoses and attacked the fire from another spot. Sal approached wearing a bandana over his mouth. He handed another one from his pocket to Joe. "Here. Wear this. It will help."

Joe took it and covered his nose and mouth, tying a knot behind his head. "Thanks."

Sal pointed to the east. "The fire is burning north toward Big Tree Grove, but the down-drafts from the canyons on Sunrise are blowing the fire back into the open range."

The roar of the fire made it hard to hear. "I think we've got a good handle down here. I won't allow it to spread to the cattle's feed."

Sal jogged away and helped some of Joe's guests who'd remained to help fight the fire with shovels and hoes. He'd always been impressed with the people in the community who came together when there was an emergency. He was lucky and blessed.

Overhead, Joe heard the low rumble of an engine. Too large to be another spy plane. He glanced up. One of those giant tanker airplanes from Lake Tahoe flew over the peaks above Mesa de Salvia and headed for the fire.

Men cheered.

"We need to move away from the fire," Joe shouted. "Everybody back."

The men helping him grabbed up tools and ran away from several thousand pounds of water dropping from the sky.

It amazed Joe how accurate the water dropping could be as a load of water hit the fire, snuffing parts of it out in an instant.

After what seemed like an eternity, two more drops from the tanker plane, and the emptying of the water truck, the burnt ground steamed, but the black smoke finally blew away on the late afternoon breeze.

Joe walked the fire line. He figured he lost several acres of pastureland, but couldn't account for the amount of acreage lost up the canyon or on Flat Ridge.

"Walk with me," he said to Ricardo and Sheriff Warner. "Let's see where this started."

They hiked to the top of Flat Ridge with other men joining them including Deputies Vargas and Sayer. They poked through the burnt grass with their shovels looking for clues. At one point, Joe noticed a rutted set of tire tracks and the distinct smell of gasoline.

He crouched down, fingered the grass, and brought his finger to his nose. "Just as I thought. Gasoline."

"What the hell?" Warner said from behind him. "Someone deliberately set this fire? Why?"

Joe stood, wiped his fingers on his Sunday trousers. "A man is sitting in your jail cell who'll probably know why."

The other men blackened from the smoke and fighting the fire stared at the sheriff.

"He's not very talkative," Sayer said.

"No one has come to talk about bail, and he never placed his one phone call," Vargas said.

Warner shook his head at Joe. "Whaddya do to piss off these people?"

221

Darkness fell before Joe reached the ranch compound. Warner had taken statements and sent Sayer back to the sheriff's office for the official photographer to take pictures. All Joe figured was Major Donald, or one of his henchmen had set this fire intentionally. If they couldn't buy him out, they'd burn him out. But it was worse than that. They'd threatened everyone's life at the fiesta, especially Sam's. He wouldn't tolerate that.

Her big Suburban was still parked outside his house when he drove the old water truck back into the compound. The truck needed to be refilled, but not tonight. He had to tell Sam they couldn't be together at the house until things settled down. She had to return home for her safety.

Tired and weary beyond exhaustion, Joe trudged to the house. The family room lights burned cheery and welcoming from the windows. A fire blazed in the immense rock fireplace in the corner. For a moment, he imagined Cindy might be waiting for him. "That's nuts. She's gone." And he would be alone tonight. He couldn't endanger Sam's life.

He found her curled up on the couch, his colorful Mexican blanket from one of Ricardo's trips home, wrapped around her. With her hair like a dark wave over the blanket and her face soft in rest, she looked angelic.

Joe sat in his big easy chair and stared at Sam. So beautiful, kind and spirited. She hadn't taken anything from the goons ready to hurt her on the highway. She'd fought back. He was proud of her courage, but he couldn't ask her to risk her life by staying at the ranch.

A log snapped and dropped in the fireplace. Joe stared at the fire for a moment, gathering his thoughts.

*April 20, 1998—Monday—***Don't Put Words In My Mouth**

Morning found Joe stiff and sore having slept in his chair all night. He smelled his favorite brand of coffee brewing in the kitchen. Sam was no longer asleep on the couch. He leaned forward and stretched out his back. He needed a long, hot soak in Cindy's copper bathtub and a half-bottle of aspirin.

"Good morning," Sam said from the doorway of the kitchen. "You looked comfortable. I didn't want to wake you."

Joe stretched his arms over his head and regretted it when his muscles screamed. "Sleeping sitting up isn't all that comfortable."

"I must have drifted off. What time did you come in from the fire?" Sam didn't move from the doorway. Something was off in her expression like she didn't dare come close.

"The investigation took until well after dark to complete."

"Was it arson?"

"Yeah." He didn't want to tell her to go back to town, at least for a while. He needed her. "I gotta get out to the range and see if the cattle are all right."

Her shoulders slumped, and she frowned. "I see."

No. She didn't see. "Look, Sam—"

"No. Don't." She held up her hand. "I get it. We had a nice time in Tahoe. Eating at Ruby's and talking, and just being together, but…." She bit her lip in a most becoming manner.

Damn him. Joe took a couple of steps toward her.

She backed up. "I've got to change into my work clothes, then drive out to a farm on the south end of town. Two mares are ready to foal." She ducked into the kitchen.

He slapped his hand on his thigh. He was no good at this relationship stuff—always making a fool of himself. Did Sam think he wasn't happy they had married?

Damn.

With every joint and muscle in his body screaming, he shuffled into the kitchen. Sam was pouring him a cup of coffee and didn't look up. "Please Sam, let me explain."

She lifted her head. "There's nothing to explain. You changed your mind about me … about us. I get it. I really do."

"No, you don't get it. This—" Joe twirled his finger in the air "—thing we've got going is wonderful—"

"But you weren't ready for marriage and family and the whole living together."

223

"Stop putting words in my mouth." He hadn't meant to shout. "I'm sorry." He had to sit again before he fell. "What's going on right now is dangerous. You were almost killed yesterday, and that freaked me out, and then the fire meant to destroy my ranch. If you get hurt because of me, I'd never forgive myself."

She crossed her arms. "And I told you, I fought back. I won't allow anyone to hurt me."

"That doesn't matter, Sam. I … I care about you—"

"Care?" Her laugh was brittle. "After all we've been through, and finally getting married. When did you stop loving me?" A tear leaked out and trailed down her cheek. She plopped in a kitchen chair opposite him.

"You know I love you." He felt lower than a pig's belly and reached out only to have her draw away as though she was afraid of his touch.

She tossed an icy glare at him. "Do I? And how would I know that?"

Women. They could be so thick when it suited their needs. He lifted the cup of coffee to his lips to sip. The aromatic steam did nothing to settle his nerves. "If you'd just stay in town for a little while until this blows over, then we can be together."

"Bull crap!" she shouted. "I'm not running away from a fight, and you have no right to decide anything for me, taking the decision out of my hands.

"But … I don't want you hurt."

"You don't get to make that decision for me. We're married, for Pete's sake. We make decisions together. I will not be chased out of my new home by anyone. Not with fire, or with an attempted car accident, and certainly not with a gun." She took a deep breath, scorched him with her scowl. "I'm staying."

"I can't—"

She raised a single finger. Mule-headed woman wasn't going to listen to him. "Tell me you don't love me, and I'll go."

Moments passed. The clock shaped like a chicken on the wall ticked off the seconds. Joe scrubbed his hands down his unshaven face. "I love you," he whispered.

"What was that?"

"Hell, woman. You know I love you. I'm just not much for talkin' is all. Do I have to keep repeating it?"

"You betcha, husband dear. I wanna hear it often and from your heart." She finally grinned at his distress.

"I. Love. You." There. He said it with emphasis.

"Oh, Joe." She pulled her chair closer to his, caught his hands in hers. "I know you muttered it at dinner last Friday night and then … at the hotel, and while we—" Her face reddened. "Do you know how long I've waited for you *really* to say it to me?"

Joe had no answer.

"I've loved you since high school."

Now he really had no answer.

"Cindy just got to you first." She grinned slowly. "I was so jealous of her. You were the kind, rough, protective man I'd always wanted. Because you chose Cindy, I chose Brad. Marrying him was the biggest mistake of my life. Having Jessica is what saved me, and … finding you again."

He stared at her.

"I know you're worried about my safety. What happened frightened me as well, but we can't give in to fear from these people, or they've beaten us already."

Damn. Strong, stubborn woman. So determined.

"Let me be by your side through this," Sam said. "I can help."

Joe shook his head slowly. "I can't lose you, too."

She leaned forward, pressed her lips against his. Her lips were tender and insistent. She tasted of toothpaste and smelled like lavender soap. Her lips lingered, moving against his, then he wrapped his arms around her and drew her close, deepening the kiss that seemed to spiral out of control. This woman filled up the empty, lonely hole in his heart.

When she drew back, love shined from her eyes.

He was a skunk. "I don't want you to get hurt."

"I'll be careful."

They stood. Joe reached for her, drew her close and kissed her with his whole heart.

The ringing of the cordless wall phone had them breaking apart. He yanked it from the wall. "What?" he snapped.

"Mr. Mack, this is Sophia Devereux-Melancon again. I have another offer that will sweeten the deal for you. A corporation is interested in taking over your ranch and will pay two hundred thousand over the last price I quoted you. This offer is fantastic. I sure hope you won't want to pass on it."

Joe was ready to pitch his coffee cup across the kitchen. "I told you I'm not selling. I don't care how much money the government offers."

He heard Sophia's sharp intake of breath. "I've said nothing about it being the government."

Joe smiled at Sam, squeezed her hand. "You tell Major Donald to come here himself, and we'll talk."

CHAPTER THIRTY-TWO
Trouble Comes Home

April 21, 1998—Tuesday

SAL **S**ANCHEZ **HELD CHECKERS'** hoof between his knees and scraped out the dirt and muck of the range. "For the horses, we will need hoof complex and pellet vitamins," he rattled off to Joe who stood inside the stable holding a pad of paper, his head bent over his pen. He seemed distracted after the ranch fire, seemed older, too. That worried Sal, Mike, and their papa. "We also need two hundred pounds of pig feed with calcium, and about one hundred and fifty pounds of chicken feed, as well as a couple of gallons of liquid Omega 3-6."

"What was it Mike needed for the almond grove?" Joe asked.

"He said his order of nitrogen and organic fertilizer is in at the feed store."

Joe scribbled something on his pad. "You only need the complex and pellets?"

"I'm pretty well stocked for now."

"Thank you … ah … for all you do around here." Joe's face turned red. He flipped around to hurry off in the direction of his house.

Sal released Checkers' hoof and stared at Joe's retreating back. The boss didn't give compliments often. He already praised both him and Mike a lot during the past two days. He gave special admiration to Sal's papa, Ricardo, as well. Something was up with stoic Joe Mack.

Sal shrugged and went back to work.

About ten minutes later, he heard the ranch rig pull up to the stable door and stop. His brother, Mike, was back from checking the south fences.

Sal wiped his hands on an old cloth and guided Checkers back to his stall. "Your manicure is complete, sir."

227

The horse nickered and bared his teeth. "You're such a lover."

"You always talk to the horses?" Mike asked him from the door. "I always knew you were the loco brother."

Sal huffed. "Thanks, *perro*. What did you find out about the fencing up by the river?"

Mike took off his straw hat, beat it against his thigh. "About a ten-foot section has been cut and pulled down. I don't know if any of the cattle are missing."

"That's a damn shame. Joe will be fuming over this."

Mike leaned against the old tractor. "Say, some guy at the gate just said he had to talk to Joe about maybe buying the ranch."

"You didn't let him in, did you?" Sal gritted his teeth when Mike nodded. "Someone from a real estate agency already called with an offer to buy the ranch and Joe had told them vehemently NO, and various other instructions. *¡Estúpido!*"

"What?" Mike shrugged his shoulders. "Who you calling stupid?"

"You. Now get your rifle." Sal grabbed the rifle Joe kept by the stable door and gazed out into the yard at the same time a black Jeep Cherokee pulled up to the house. Its passenger side had been bashed in and carried a long gash of blue paint—the same color as Dr. Sam's lumbering Vetmobile. The suit driving was probably the same *carbón* who tried to run Joe off the road by Dead Man's Curve, and Dr. Sam last Sunday. *"¡Estúpido!"*

What climbed out of the Jeep's driver's side had Sal's heart galloping. A huge man dressed in a black suit, dark glasses with an ultra-short buzz cut over a severely pockmarked face.

Out of the passenger side and the back door exited two other massive goons with hulking bodies and who had a just-escaped-prison look about them. One black, one white, both wearing the same type suits as the driver. Sal swallowed hard.

Before they saw him, Sal ducked back inside the garage. He slipped out the north side and circled the back of the pens. He could come up on the wraparound porch from the garden side, in case Joe needed him.

When he reached the walkway between his and Mike's casita, he motioned for Mike, who came out with his rifle, to circle the other way.

Mike nodded in understanding. He skirted the coops and pig pens and crouched down behind the garage.

As Sal ran across the dirt road above the garden, he saw the man in the suit stomp up Joe's stairs.

Sal scuttled up the porch stairs past the kitchen window and crept to the corner of the house to watch. He hoped Mike was in position on the other side of the house. They would not let anything happen to Joe.

Before the big guy knocked, the front door cracked open, but from Sal's position, he only saw the business end of a shotgun poke through the door. Joe wouldn't make the mistake of losing his tactical advantage on those guys, so he'd stay well hidden.

"What the hell do you want?" Joe asked through the partially open door.

The man attempted a pleasant smile. Something about it suggested it was foreign to his face. "My name is Major Donald—"

"I know who you are." Joe cut him off, still not showing himself. "How in the hell did you get in here?"

"One of your ranch hands was gracious enough to allow me entrance."

Joe looked across the ranch yard at the barn. Then back at the guy. "I'm sorry he did because I want you gone—now!"

"You told Sophia I should speak to you personally about purchasing your ranch."

Joe shook his head. "She misunderstood. I only wished to see you face-to-face, so I could turn you down in person. This ranch is not for sale and never will be."

Major Donald clenched his hands into fists, his eyes bugged. "You're being unreasonable, Mr. Mack. I have another hundred thousand to offer for your ranch, a hell of a lot more money than the place is worth."

"Why?" Joe asked.

"Why? Why what?"

"Why do you want my ranch?"

The major rotated his big body around to gaze out over the ranch compound and out through the buildings to the surrounding grassland. "It's lovely here. I want to retire and … raise cattle." The last part sounded like the jerk forced the words through his gritted teeth.

Joe straightened to his full height, opened the door. He kept the shotgun leveled at the major's chest. "I'm telling you again, this ranch is not for sale."

"I'm telling you you're making a big mistake, right boys?" he asked the goons behind him.

They didn't say anything, just stood there smacking their hands together like they were dying for a fight. Sal's trigger finger itched.

"I see you brought some muscle. Are you going to beat me up if I don't sell? Don't you recall what I did to your companion who's sitting in a jail cell right now?"

"Now, Mr. Mack," the major crooned. "We'd never resort to such heavy-handed tactics. We're all reasonable men here. I'd like to own this ranch, and you need to sell it to me and become a wealthy man. You could retire and travel the world. There's no need to waste your life doing this hard, manual labor. Relax and enjoy life."

Sal could almost hear Joe grind his teeth. As it was, the long barrel of the shotgun moved up slightly to point at the major's head.

"Me and my shotgun are tired of this conversation. It's going nowhere. Time for you to leave my property and don't ever come back."

The major took a step back as his goons reached inside their suit jackets. Guns.

Sal cocked his rifle and stepped out from where he'd been hiding. At the same time, Mike did the same on his end of the porch.

"It's time you were leaving." Sal pulled the trigger. Gravel sputtered up on the legs of the black dude's suit pants. He moved his hand away from his jacket, held both up.

A shot rang out again. This time though, it came from the garage and hit the ground in front of the other goon. Papa stood there between the two dogs holding his rifle. "Señor Joe asked you to leave. Vamoose or I tell dogs to attack."

"There's going to be trouble over this, Mack," Major Donald shouted. "If you don't sell out, I'll run you out."

"You've already tried," Joe yelled back.

"You haven't seen my best." The major flipped around and stormed down the steps. He opened the driver's side door of the Jeep. "You watch yourself, Mack. I will have this land."

Joe raised the shotgun, aimed. The two goons piled into the Jeep, and Major Donald squealed away, tires spitting gravel.

Slowly, Sal felt his heartbeat return to normal.

Later that afternoon and Joe left for town, Sal sat with Mike on the farmhouse porch in the shade. "Do you think they'll be back, or try to sneak onto the farm?" Sal asked.

Mike glanced off toward the road. "How can they get inside? Robbie set up the gate-opener to stop people."

"This is the government we're talking about here. Did you see the size of those bastards?" Sal rubbed the back of his neck.

"Yeah, I did. Monsters." Mike took a deep breath. "I gotta finish up with what supplements I have left. Joe's picking up some more, so I can complete the almond grove."

Sal glanced at his brother. They weren't all that demonstrative in their outward show of affection for one another, but he felt something was about to happen, maybe tear his family apart. "Be careful. Keep your rifle with you at all times."

Mike grinned. "I'll take my Colt .38 with me. It'll make me feel like we lived in the days when Wyatt Earp shot Billy the Kid."

Sal chuckled. "Wyatt Earp shot it out with the Clantons, and Pat Garret shot Billy the Kid down in New Mexico. You don't have your cowboy history straight."

"Not something I majored in at college." Mike laughed. "I promise to be careful, big brother. I love you, too."

Sal squirmed. "Back at you."

Sal led a new horse in the corral on a lunge line, putting it thought its paces with the lunge whip. The horse jogged in a circle around him when the black Jeep returned and stopped by the barn. He hoped whoever was inside the car this time hadn't seen him. He didn't want trouble, but he'd end it.

He slipped through the corral and skirted around the backside of the stables to get the rifle by the door. By the time he picked up the weapon, the two massive men who accompanied Major Donald were snooping around the outside of the barn, only Major Donald wasn't with them. They must have doubled back after losing the major somewhere. Papa was in the barn. Sal's stomach dropped.

Sal was about to leave the stables, confront the men, and chase them off again, when Papa walked out of the barn, his rifle held stiffly along his leg. "What do you want?" He said to the two men caught snooping.

"*Buenos días. ¿Cómo estás?*" the black goon said in a pleasant voice but badly accented Spanish.

"*Ah, más o menos,*" Papa said his body tight.

Still speaking Gringo Spanish, the man said to Papa, "I'm Agent Ports and this" —he pointed to his companion— "is Agent Locke. Where is Mr. Mack? Is he here?"

"He has gone to town," Papa said back to them in Spanish.

"When do you expect him?"

Papa didn't answer.

"When will he be back, *hombre*?"

"I do not know, *señor*." Papa scowled. "What do you want?"

One of the men walked through the open barn door and disappeared inside. The barn had once held the horses with a hayloft above the stables until Joe built more modern stables where Sal was hiding. What could the goon be looking for in there?

The black man continued in Spanish. "We are looking for something you might have noticed out of place here on the ranch."

"Like what?" Papa asked.

"Have you noticed anything odd or out of place, something that doesn't belong here?"

"Just the two of you."

"Very funny. You don't mind if we have a little look around, do you? We're missing some … equipment.

Papa lifted the gun. "You are not welcome here. Come back when Señor Joe is here."

Ports lifted his hands. "That's not very friendly."

"I am not friendly."

"Like it or not, we're going to look around, and you need to convince your boss to sell the ranch to Major Donald."

"If government, where official papers? Señor Joe will never sell the ranch."

Ports took a couple of steps toward Papa. Sal cocked his rifle. "He has something that belongs to Major Donald, and we want it back."

"I don't know anything about that," Papa shouted. "Get off this ranch."

Ports took another step toward Papa just as the other man crept up behind him.

"Papa look out!" Sal shouted.

Faster than Sal thought possible for a man of that size, Ports whipped around and yanked a revolver out from under his suit coat, pointed, and fired.

The bullet hit Sal in the left side of his gut.

The force flung him smacking into the side of the barn. Dynamite exploded in his stomach. His legs gave out, and he slid down the wall. *I'm a dead man.*

Papa yelled, "*Bastardos.*" He charged Ports, fired the rifle, but the shot went wide of the man's head.

Pain, like nothing Sal could have imagined jack-hammered through his side. Had his stomach been hit, or his kidneys? Did he have broken ribs puncturing his lungs? What about his intestines or his spine? Would he ever walk again? What about his wife and children? He'd heard of excruciating pain before but never felt it.

In agony, he watched as Ports reached for Papa and twisted the rifle out of his hands and tossed it toward the barn door. Locke gripped Papa's arms behind his back and Ports slammed his huge fist into Papa's gut.

Papa doubled over, a heavy groan escaping his lips. Locke hauled him upright.

Sal opened his mouth to shout, but no sound came out. He was powerless to help Papa. Tears leaked from his eyes as he watched the goon continue to bury his fists in Papa's stomach, then again on his chin. Everything seemed to happen in slow motion.

Sal's body released a significant amount of adrenaline, and he felt his life draining out with the blood seeping through his fingers. Tingling waves surged through his body. Every breath was like a knife turning in his gut. *I'm going to pass out. No. I have to stay conscious for Papa.*

Sal fought the waves of nausea as blood splattered from Papa's mouth when the bastard punched him.

"Stop," Sal gasped in a whisper.

His strength waned fast. He had to act. With agonizing effort, Sal lifted the rifle, fought the trembling in his hands long enough to aim. It was impossible. His warm blood soaked his shirt adding to the pool of blood between his legs. He nearly passed out. So much blood. Had the bullet hit an artery?

Still, he managed to lift the gun, and with his last bit of strength, fired.

The bullet hit the ground next to Ports.

Ports whirled around, shock written on his face. *He thought he'd killed me.*

The goon pulled the gun out of his jacket again and aimed.

Sal prepared to die. I love you, sweetheart, kids, Papa, Mamá, Mike, and Lee.

However, when the shot rang out, the gun flew from Ports' hand landing near Papa's rifle and Sal heard the growl of dogs. Port's hollered. Mike had shot Ports, clipping part of his hand.

The farm began to spin and blur. Out of the haze, Mike ran forward holding his rifle and the dogs raced toward Papa.

Locke turned and fired his gun at Mike. But he ducked behind the pig house, the shot missing wide.

Papa whistled for the dogs, stumbled, and ran into the barn.

"That son-of-a-bitch shot me," Ports yelled.

Mike shot again from the backside of the pig house. This time he hit Locke's upper arm. The gun flew out of Locke's hand.

Sal's vision darkened. *Help me!* No words escaped his lips.

Before he slipped into darkness, he heard the crack of Papa's bullwhip, saw Locke grip his ear with his uninjured hand and fall on his knees.

"What the hell?" Locke howled like a banshee.

Spike held him put, snarling like a wolf.

Encouraged, Sal saw Papa lurch from the barn, one arm around his stomach, the bullwhip in the other. Ports took off running for their Jeep, Shep on his heels.

"Get off this land." The whip cracked, and Locke howled. "And don't come back." He whistled. "Kill, boys."

As the darkness overtook Sal, he heard swearing, feet pounding the dirt in retreat, and the start of an engine.

Then the world went black.

CHAPTER THIRTY-THREE

Revenge is a Dish Best Served Steaming Hot

April 21, 1998—Tuesday

T**HE TEENAGERS WORKING** at the feed store helped Joe load all his supplies into the back of his rig. He picked up a new bandana to replace the one Sal had loaned him during the fire incident and bought a new horse blanket as a gift for Sal.

He shut the tailgate with a slam and ambled toward the cab, in no hurry to get back to the ranch. The close call with the fire and the confrontation with Major Donald had left him shaken. It could've been so much worse.

He climbed into the cab and turned on the radio. Elvis Presley was singing, "Can't Help Falling in Love."

Directly, he was transported back to his and Cindy's wedding day.

During their reception, they had snuggled each other close and swirled to their favorite songs. A rented dance floor had been set up in the middle of the ranch compound for the occasion. Twinkling lights hung all around giving the outdoors a feeling of being bathed in starlight. Most of the town people came to celebrate their happiness. The robust scents of barbecued beef half and the delicious sides of corn on the cob, baked beans, and homemade rolls scented the night breezes. Joe floated that night as he held his wife—his bride.

Cindy laid her head on his shoulder. "What a wonderful day. I'm so happy I could soar up into the heavens."

"You wouldn't leave me so soon after our wedding, would ya?" he asked.

She laughed, the sound expanding his heart to near bursting. She had such a free laugh, unencumbered by life's harshness. Cindy never saw a day where she didn't laugh or find joy. She became his joy.

"I'm so glad I convinced you we needed to date," she said with a saucy grin.

He chuckled. "I don't feel so old anymore. I feel like a young bull in spring."

She raised one shapely eyebrow. "Do you now? We'll have to take care of that."

They swayed to Elvis' words, and she kissed him again.

He sang along with Elvis and told Cindy, "You complete me, sweetheart."

Cindy's eyes clouded over, her smile faded away. "We need to go home right now, Joe."

He chuckled. "We are home."

"No," she cried. "You need to go home to the ranch right now. Something terrible has happened."

Joe glanced around again. The lights and the tables and the people were all gone—fading into nothingness. Only Cindy stood before him, blood stains blossoming on her pure white dress like blooming red roses. "What's happening to you?" He swore and attempted to stop the flow of blood on Cindy's dress, but she backed away.

"Go home, Joe. Now." Then she was gone.

Joe gazed down at his hands, the vision of blood on them fading.

He shook his head, dizzy from the step back into the past and Cindy's insistence he return to the ranch. Another premonition?

The engine of the old truck turned over, and he sped out of town. He prayed that nothing had happened to Sam. As far as he knew, she was out at a ranch tending sick cattle.

About five miles outside of town, Joe heard the distinctive whir of helicopter blades through his open driver's window. He glanced up and saw a hospital helicopter heading in the same direction. Holy hell. What's happened?

The gate of Sunrise Ranch hung off its hinges at an odd angle, the mechanism Robbie set up broken. Dammit. Major Donald must have come back. Those men who accompanied the major appeared to be brutal killers, and they wouldn't hesitate to murder his people in cold blood.

His blood froze in his veins. Pushing the truck as fast as he dared on the rough road, he prayed again, hard and fast. "Please Father, keep Sam and my people safe."

The ranch yard was chaotic.

Before Joe could exit the truck, Mike ran over to meet him. "What the hell's going on?" Joe asked.

Mike gripped Joe's arm and pulled him toward the middle of the chaos. "Those two goons who came earlier today" —Mike panted hard— "with Major Donald. They returned and searched the compound. Sal and Papa fought with them. They shot Sal in the stomach and beat up Papa. But Papa got in a good lick with his bullwhip. Took off one of the goon's ears." Though Mike's voice held pride, his face paled.

The helicopter Joe had seen landed on the widest spot in the yard. Paramedics quickly loaded Sal onto a stretcher and were working feverishly over him. Joe's gut clenched.

Ricardo, bandage around his head, was hunched over, gripping his stomach. He moved to the open door of the helicopter. Lettie, next to him wept silently. Sal's wife stood back, her warm tan face deathly gray, her whole body trembled. Sal's four children gathered around her, and clung to her and sobbing. Mike's wife and three kids stood behind Lettie, clutching their mother.

Joe rushed over to Ricardo, laid his hand on his shoulder. Ricardo winced. "What's happened here?" Joe asked.

Ricardo turned a bruised and battered face toward Joe.

Joe gasped, lightly holding Ricardo's chin in his hand. "Those bastards did this?"

"Sí." Ricardo, one front tooth missing, blood smeared around his mouth, and one eye black and blue, said, "I am sorry we could not stop them."

"Not as sorry as they will be when I get hold of them." Joe smacked a fist into his palm. He filled the air with curse words. "Why would they do this?"

He knew why. It was his fault his people were getting shot at, beat up, run off the road, and had rocks sent tumbling down from canyon walls to kill them. He'd never meant to involve them in his personal war with the SRM and Major Donald. He should give back the plane and maybe all this would stop. However, at this point, it was a matter of principle for Major Donald—he wouldn't let Joe and his loved ones off the hook that easily.

The paramedics halted half-way in the chopper with Sal's stretcher. "Joe," Sal sputtered in a weak voice, waving a hand feebly.

"Yeah?" Joe leaned over him. Bright red blood stained his clothing, and around his mouth. Had they needed to revive him?

Heat rose in Joe's body. He touched Sal's shoulder, leaned close. "What is it, my friend?"

Sal was hooked up to needles and bottles, his face pasty and his breath shallow. "Don't let them take the ranch from you."

"Look, Sal—" How could he tell his brave ranch hand the ranch wasn't worth their lives?

"I mean it…" Sal coughed, his face twisted in agony. His voice was barely a whisper. "I would do anything to defend you and your home."

"Sir, we have to go now," one of the paramedics said. "It's imperative we get Sal to the hospital in Sacramento pronto."

Joe nodded.

The two paramedics finished loading the stretcher into the helicopter. One turned to Ricardo. "You need to fly with us."

Ricardo shook his bandaged head. "I will drive with my wife. You take Sal's wife. We bring the children."

The paramedic helped Sal's weeping wife into the back. "Okay. Let's roll." The kids ran to their grandparents and clung to them. The paramedic signaled to the chopper pilot. As soon as the door was shut and locked, it lifted up in the air flinging dirt in all directions.

Joe shut his eyes and covered his mouth. When the air settled, he opened his eyes. Ricardo was leaning heavily on Lettie.

Mike ran to them, supported his father over to the ranch rig, settling him inside the back seat of the dual cab.

Joe jogged behind them, fury building up in his chest like a volcano ready to blow. Those bastards would pay for this.

Mike aided Lettie into the backseat, so she could hold onto Ricardo. Two of Sal's kids jumped in the front, and his oldest son climbed into the bed of the truck. Before Mike hopped into the driver's seat, Joe stopped him with a hand on his arm. "When your father and Sal can travel, I want you to take all your families and return to Mexico."

Mike shook his head. "He won't leave you alone."

"I don't give a damn what he wants. Your family must be safe. I'll stay and fight this out to the end."

Mike's brows drew together as he frowned. "You're going to sell, aren't you?"

Joe didn't answer. Was he? Would it come to that?

"Don't do it." Mike covered Joe's hand on his arm. "This will pass. These thugs aren't legitimate government agents."

Joe glanced into Mike's eyes, surprise raising his eyebrows. "You think?"

"You need to contact someone in the real government like the FBI and ask about these guys. I'll bet my orchards they're on the opposite side of the government, something like contracted assassins."

Mike might be right, but that didn't stop them from coming to take him out, and along with him, his friends. What if they went after Sam next?

"Take care of your dad, and we'll talk."

Mike shook his head. "I'm not leaving."

Joe scowled at him but released his arm. He glanced at the barn to see Shep and Spike sitting there nervously watching the situation. "Stay. Guard," he said to the dogs. They jumped up and ran to the perimeter of the buildings to do their duty. Joe trusted his life to his dogs.

He needed to get to town.

Before heading to Ruby's, Joe called Sam's cell phone. No answer. He left a message for her to stay at her vet clinic until he came. He stopped at the Shadow Pines Clinic, where he figured the two goons who attacked Ricardo and shot Sal might have gone to attend to their injuries.

The doctor told him he patched up a couple of hulking brutes and after they left, he called Sheriff Warner. He thought they might have gone to drink at Ruby's.

Perfect.

Ruby's steakhouse was crowded. Unusual for a Tuesday evening. The black Jeep wasn't hard to spot out front. The passenger side door was bashed in and bore streaks of blue paint embedded in the crunched metal—the same blue of Sam's big Suburban. He'd make sure those bastards wouldn't be chewing steak for a long time. Nobody hurt his friends.

Joe drove his old Ford over to Ruby and Bill's, angled it behind the black Jeep until he blocked it in. Let them try and leave before we have a little chat.

He pulled his cell phone from his pocket, punched Ruby's number. She answered on the third ring.

"Ruby's," she shouted, her smoke-roughened voice extra raspy tonight.

"Ruby. Joe Mack."

"Hey, darling—"

"Don't say my name, Ruby. I'm looking for two big men, might be sporting some bandages. Do you see them?"

"Yeah, two gorillas in the corner. Wary eyes. Leering at my gals and making lewd comments."

"They beat Ricardo to a pulp and shot Sal."

Ruby swore. "Should I have Bill kill them?"

"Yeah, but I'd like the pleasure of doing it myself." Joe waved a hand at someone he knew passing by in a green Chevy rig. "Let me know when they head outside, would you, darling?"

"Sure thing, hot stuff. Say, Sam's here too."

Dammit. "Can you keep Sam in there?"

"I'm on it." She disconnected.

What was Sam doing there? Why hadn't she called him to say she was eating dinner out?

He didn't have to wait long for Ruby's call giving him a head's up.

Joe stretched his arms. His gunshot wounded shoulder complained. His leg muscles were still sore from fighting the forest fire. He wasn't a kid in Vietnam anymore. However, he knew how to fight dirty and he didn't need a gun to do so.

He climbed into the bed of the truck, hunkered down. Better to take the advantage and attack from above.

The two goons stumbled out of the front door. One had his hand in a sterile bandage, and the other, his upper arm and ear.

Bandaged Ear staggered to the passenger's door. The driver, not in much better shape, stared at Joe's truck.

"Hey," he slurred glancing up at Joe. "Move the piece of crap out of the way. I can't get my Jeep out."

Joe stood, towering over the goons and pointed at Bandaged Ear. "Hurt your ear?"

"Yeah. What of it?" Bandaged Ear said, leaning heavily on the Jeep and reeking of alcohol. "Move your truck."

"Which one of you is Ports?" Joe asked.

"I am," the driver said. "Why do ya want to know?"

Joe stared at Bandaged Ear. "So, you're Locke?"

Locke turned his head, so he could hear Joe with his unbandaged ear. "You're that rancher dude, Mack, aren't you?"

"Yes. My name's Joe Mack. You've trespassed on my ranch, roughed-up my foreman, and shot his son. You're going to jail for a long time."

"The hell we are." Locke sneered and reached into his bloodied jacket.

Joe gripped the side of the truck and vaulted feet first into Locke's mocking face, catching him on the nose, and breaking it with a substantial whack.

Locke slapped into the side of the vehicle, covered his nose with his free hand, blood spurting between his fingers. "You son-of-a-bitch." He mopped at his nose with his shirttail.

"Hey," Ports said, standing next to the driver's door. He uttered some other ripe words and stumbled around the hood from the effects of the alcohol he'd consumed. "You can't do that."

242

"The hell I can't." Joe shoved Locke again.

Locke lunged at Joe off balance, but Joe grabbed Locke's unbandaged hand and snapped it back at the wrist. Locke's shriek vibrated off the wall of the restaurant. He then cuffed Locke's bandaged ear.

With a cry of agony, Locke went down in a heap, wailing and cursing.

Ports wobbled over to the passenger side and looked down at his companion. He swayed. "What the hell did you do?"

When Ports reached inside his jacket for his gun, Joe stepped over Locke and shoved Ports hard up against the Jeep. He swung low to the gut.

Ports let out a bellow to wake the dead.

With a hard-hitting combination, Joe punched Ports' face repeatedly. Blood gushed from the guy's nose and a cut near his eye.

Ports swung limply at Joe with his free hand.

Ducking, Joe grabbed Port's uninjured arm, yanked until his shoulder popped.

Ports groaned.

Swinging back with his leg, Joe kicked the guy squarely in the knee. Bellowing out a tormented scream, Ports dropped beside his companion clutching his knee with his bandaged hand.

Sirens wailed in the distance. People gathered along the sidewalk outside of Ruby's. Someone must have called the sheriff. Warner or one of his deputies would be here soon.

Joe stood over the two goons breathing hard. "You tell your boss, my ranch is not for sale and to stay away from me and my family, or you'll be in for more of the same."

He picked up their pistols, emptied them of their clips, and tossed them in a trash can round back of Ruby's.

Joe turned and walked around the corner of the restaurant and saloon and strolled inside to have dinner with his wife.

Ruby met him at the check-in podium. "Are you all right?"

"My knuckles are a little raw, and my shoulder and leg hurts, but otherwise, I'm fine." He took a breath to calm his nerves. "You got a soda for me and some Band-Aids?"

She pointed to a door at the back of the bar. "You bet your sweet ass, darling. Right, this way."

CHAPTER THIRTY-FOUR
A New Ranch Hand

May 1, 1998—Friday

FBI **SPECIAL AGENT** Ana Penn grabbed her single carry-on bag and trailed after the passengers exiting the Airbus and into the San Francisco International Airport. She'd flown direct from New Orleans after she helped wrap up the sex-trafficking case. Liberating those malnourished, abused women held as sex slaves filled Ana with joy and amped up her sense of purpose. She loved working for the FBI. Working the lead on the last case had been the opportunity for the advancement she craved.

Stepping onto the escalator heading down, she recalled what her handler, Jim Ports, had told her on the phone about her new assignment—to stop an old rancher with Mexican drug connections. This guy was one mean bastard living near Auburn. He'd stolen government technology. He'd then threatened to rat out Jim to his drug cartel friends, lying to them that Jim and someone called Major Donald were developing drug-fighting technology.

Ana would take down the rancher quickly, and she would be the bait since he was a widower. She hoped he wasn't too old to flirt.

Her deep cover identity had come in a flash. Needing help pulling off this operation, she had to squelch her apprehension and called her ex-husband, Reed, asking him to stop by a thrift store for her and pick up some things. She needed to get through seeing him after two years. The last time hadn't been all that joyful as they faced each other in divorce court.

Ana still loved Reed, but with her assigned to the Washington, D.C. office and him assigned to San Francisco, where his parents lived, there was no way they could maintain their dual-coast relationship. She hated seeing betrayal in his dark eyes. Yes. She needed advancement, D.C. offered her that. He'd

245

been upset she put her career before him. Well, the reverse was also something she couldn't handle. He had not wanted to leave San Francisco for her.

Reed Jin-ho Penn, leaning casually against a pole, peered at her. His dark eyes lit up. However, they quickly faded to no-nonsense. Her heart dropped. She hoped for some of the happiness they'd shared during five years of marriage to show on his face. Unfortunately, he was cold and professional when she stopped in front of him.

"Did you have a good flight?" He bent forward and placed a small peck on her cheek.

"Fine," she said. Reed still had the power to turn her inside out. Could she turn her head and meet his lips? A lock of his straight black hair dropped over his forehead. Her fingers vibrated with the need to smooth it into place.

"You're looking awfully skinny. Did you have to lose weight for your last assignment?"

"Yeah."

He nodded. "Car's at the curb." He picked up her grungy duffle bag and pointed out one of the large automatic doors. "This all your luggage?"

"Yes."

They walked through the doors and toward a huge black SUV. "I picked up the supplies you asked me to get. I'm confused, though."

"Thanks."

"Ofukuro and Chichi send their love."

"Lovely."

He opened the passenger door, and she slid inside, hugging the door. After skirting the hood and watching for close-driving traffic, he climbed into the driver side. He sighed. "Are you going to say more than one word at a time to me? After all, we lasted nearly five years."

She couldn't look at him without the desire to kiss him—really kiss him and a whole lot more. "It's for the best."

"Whose? Yours or mine?"

She winced. "Mine."

Without another word, he started the SUV and squealed away from the curb. Ana felt like a slug. She had made this meeting of ex-lovers rough on both of them.

Two and a half hours and a deathly silent drive later, Reed pulled the big vehicle to the side of the road. "Are you sure you're going to walk the rest of the way to Shadow Pines? It's about two miles."

"I need to walk, clear my head."

"Ana." He looked so forlorn.

She held up her hand. "We can't get into it right now. I appreciate all you've done for me—"

He cut her off with a wave of his hand. "You know I'd do anything for you, cookie."

She flinched. Reed had always called her cookie because she was obsessed with chocolate-chip cookies. It was the only thing she could cook. "We had to have different things."

"We could have worked it out," he said.

"I don't have time right now to discuss this. I need to get to town, meet with my contact and begin my next case." She gazed off to the east along the lonely highway. "Thanks for the clothing." She didn't look at him again, just slammed the SUV's door closed and strode up the side of the highway, thrilled that Reed might still want her. But how would that work?

On her walk to Shadow Pines, she admired the gorgeous countryside—thick pine trees, rolling hills, fertile green ranches, groves of fruit-heavy trees, and red, white-faced cattle. She chose to hide behind a pine tree that could have been about ten feet in circumference to change out of her FBI issued pants suit and shoes.

Reed had found her a pair of jeans and a hideous plaid cotton shirt. Perfect. He'd even managed to scare up some cowgirl boots in her size. In the old duffle bag, she found a couple of other shirts and more pants, all looking centuries old.

For good measure, she dropped to the forest floor and rolled around until she was covered with dirt, dead leaves, and forest muck, and brushed some of it off. She even pulled her dark hair out of her unflattering bun, letting it cascade over her shoulders. She rubbed some dirt into it. Lastly, she smeared some muck on her face. Truly homeless-looking and smelling now—like she'd slept in the trees on the forest floor.

The town of Shadow Pines was little more than two stop signs. The main street sported a couple of restaurants. Ana chose the Steakhouse. Maybe she could beg some food.

An older blonde lady at the check-in desk raised a thickly-penciled eyebrow when she shuffled inside. "Can I help you?" she asked.

"I was hoping for a nice cup of tea," Ana said in a small voice colored with her Virginia drawl. With all the weight she'd lost while playing the homeless woman in New Orleans, she easily looked gaunt and hungry.

"Come on in here, sweetie, we'll fix you up."

The woman, compassion in her eyes, took Ana's arm and glided her into the steakhouse, and tucked her into a back booth. "My name is Ruby Green, and this here's my establishment. When was the last time you ate something?"

Ana wouldn't grin. "Yesterday, I think."

"Where in the devil have you come from? Don't you have a car?"

"I had to get out of San Francisco. Too many weirdos on the streets. No. I don't have a car."

Ruby gasped. "You walked all the way here?"

"I hitched, mostly."

"Oh, my Sweet Lord, with all the maniacs on the road. Let me get you some roast beef, mashed potatoes, and country gravy. I'll bet you're famished."

Ruby left but came back a moment later with a basket filled with an assortment of bread. Ana's tummy rumbled on cue.

Ana waited, nibbled on a dark molasses bread. She didn't have long to wait for Joe Mack to arrive. Ports sent her a picture. Jim had informed her the perp, Joe Mack, made the innocent looking Shadow Pines, a HIDTA—high-intensity drug trafficking area. She hated cowardly, dirt-licking bastards like him who fed drugs to America's children. So close to Tahoe, she didn't have to wonder where Mack sold his goods. Despicable monster. She couldn't wait to take this drug kingpin down.

Ports also told her Mack sometimes took his evening meal at the steakhouse since his foreman or somebody on his ranch left, and he lost his cook. Didn't matter. He was here, and he was her target.

The drug boss, Joe Mack, greeted Ruby with a wink and tipping his cowboy hat. Since it was still early, and the crowd was small, Ana could hear their conversation.

"How's Ricardo and Sal?" Ruby asked after seating him across the room from Ana.

Mack's face paled, he took off his hat and fingered the rim. "Ricardo will recover with only a scar through his eyebrow and a couple of broken ribs. Sal was not so lucky. They had to operate, and he nearly died on the table. Thank God the bullet missed major organs."

"Oh, merciful heavens, no." Ruby clutched her arms around her middle. "Are they still in Sacramento?"

"Until Sal is ready to travel," Joe said. "They're staying with a friend of mine. He's got a big house near the hospital. Then they'll go to Mexico for a bit."

"I'm so sorry." Ruby glanced over at Ana.

Funny. Mack sounded like he actually cared for the people working his drug farm with him. Ana's attention diverted when the cute teenage girl delivered her roast beef plate. The heavenly aroma nearly made her pass out. Guess she was hungry. She dug in with vengeance.

Through the restaurant's archway, a woman with dark, straight hair entered and stopped by Mack's table. She wore scrubs like a nurse or doctor, but calf-high boots. She bent to kiss him. Ports hadn't mentioned a girlfriend.

"Hey, Ruby," the woman said and waved at the owner.

"Hey, Sam." Ruby lifted her chin in greeting and went back to pouring drinks.

The woman, Sam, sat beside Joe, holding his hand. "The resort had a mare that foaled this afternoon. Cute little bugger," Sam said. "Appaloosa colt. Healthy."

Mack smiled. "I'm glad you're safe."

Ruby came to their table, and they both ordered steaks and red wine.

Ana observed Mack and his woman, Sam, after the girl delivered her hot tea. She sipped it gingerly between copious amounts of fork-tender beef and creamy mashed potatoes. She even had corn on the cob. Yum.

"Don't you need some more hands to help on the ranch?" Ruby asked Joe when she brought over their wine bottle and glasses.

"Maybe," Mack said. "Who'd you have in mind?"

Ruby pointed in Ana's direction. Thank you, Ruby. Ruby leaned in close and said something to Joe Ana couldn't hear. Most likely how sad it was a homeless gal had walked all the way from San Francisco. And how sorry Ruby felt for her.

Ruby nodded at Ana and disappeared into the back.

Ana watched Joe rise from his chair and mosey in her direction. Bingo. You're mine, you dirty sucker.

Calm, no reaction.

"Do you mind if I sit?" he asked.

Ana glanced up, letting surprise color her dirty face. "Nah. Go ahead. I like company."

"What's your name and where you from?" he asked.

"Ana Penskie and I'm from all over. Lately from Frisco. Didn't like the mean streets."

"I'm Joe." He nodded. A man of few words. The drug-dealing ass.

"Nice to meet you, Joe." Ana held out her filthy hand. He shook it. She glanced out the window saw an old Ford truck. "That your truck? The venerable three hundred-cubic inches four-point nine-liter, straight six motor? Does it have coil springs? It's got that twin I-beam suspension, right? Love the turquoise and white paint. Custom?" She was proud of herself for remembering all of what her dad had taught her.

He tilted his head, studied her, a bemused smile on his lips. "Who taught you about cars?"

"My dad. He had a bunch of old junkers in various conditions of running, and I helped him fix them so he could get to work." The absolute truth.

Ruby emerged from the kitchen and strode over to Ana and Joe's table. "Mind if I join you two?" Ruby asked.

Ana pointed to the empty chair next to Mack. She gazed down at her plate, all her food was gone.

"Where you headed?" Ruby asked Ana.

"Maybe I'll head Tahoe way, see if there's work around the hotels, or maybe work with horses on a dude ranch, or something." That part was true. She loved horses.

Joe raised an eyebrow. "You've worked with horses?"

"Yep. Love 'em."

He exchanged a look with Ruby.

"Joe, don't you need some help on your ranch?" Ruby said.

Scowling at Ruby, Joe nodded. "What other types of work do you do?"

"Whatever there is, I can do it."

Mack grinned. "Ruby, keep this young lady's food coming until she's full."

Ruby waved at a serving girl to tell her to bring Ana another plate.

"Why are you being so nice to me?" Ana asked.

"You look hungry, and I'm right sure Ruby doesn't need you passing out when you leave here from a lack of nutrition."

Ruby stood. "I see your order's up, Joe."

Returning to the kitchen, Ruby came back out a moment later with Mack and his gal's slab of beef, still smoking, and smelling of a spicy barbecue rub. Ana licked her lips. When was the last time she had a huge hunk of meat like that?

Her second plate of roast beef arrived, and she dug in.

Mack returned to his table and his gal who was tossing Ana an awful evil eye. After he sat down, she whispered something to Mack. Had to be about her. Was she jealous?

When Mack and his gal finished their supper, he leaned in and kissed Sam. They whispered some more, Sam turned and glared at Ana again, but got up from the table and left the restaurant.

He returned to her table, nodded at the empty chair and sat. "Sorry about that.

"Girlfriend?" Ana asked.

251

Mack nodded. "You ever work on a ranch?" he asked. Ana nearly sighed. Her plan was coming together.

"Yep. I worked with a lot of animals. Chickens, hogs, sheep, some cattle, but mostly horses." So what if it had been her folks' place in Washington, D.C., the Virginia side and years ago. She could remember the hard work. "You a ranch hand?"

Ruby, who'd returned to join their conversation, interrupted with a laugh. "Sort of." She poked at Mack. He glared at her. She ignored him. "In the beginning," she said, "Joe was a ranch hand, but he worked his way up to becoming the boss. Didn't hurt any that he married the boss's daughter. Got the whole gosh-darn outfit left to him."

Ana blinked. That sounded normal, not like a drug-dealing sociopath who stole property from the U.S. government and sold mind-blowing, killer drugs to innocent kids.

"My ranch, Sunrise Ranch, is about fifteen miles out of town on the road east. If you can get there, ranch work starts at five a.m." He threw some bills down on the table, nodded at Ana and ambled out of the restaurant.

Ruby gathered up Ana's plate and utensils. "That there's a good job offer. Joe is honest and won't mess with you. However, he will work your tail off."

"Thanks," Ana said, confused by the "honest" comment. Didn't these folks in town know about their resident drug-smuggling, S.O.B.?

It didn't matter if they were blind. Ana was sent here to take Joe down.

CHAPTER THIRTY-FIVE
"Say No To Drugs"

May 2, 1998—Saturday

T**HE ALARM SOUNDED LIKE A BOMB** going off next to Joe's head. He hadn't slept well. Sam yelled at him for hiring a woman ranch hand, and they had words before bed. Joe didn't care if she was a woman or not. He needed bodies to do the work around the ranch with Ricardo and Sal gone, especially someone who could work with horses. He'd find out today if Ana Penskie was true to her word.

Four o'clock came way too early. Where was Sam? Her side of the bed was cold to the touch. Mumbling to himself, he struggled to sit up and swung his legs over the edge of the bed.

There would be no breakfast burritos this morning, no machaca con huevos, no chorizo chilaquiles, huevos rancheros, or warm home-made tortillas. Lettie wasn't here to fix them for him. She wouldn't be here to grind his favorite coffee, served blistering hot, and smelling of roasted sweet Arabica beans from Brazil. If he wanted anything to eat, he'd have to fix it himself.

He trudged to the east-facing windows and twisted open the blinds, then nearly jumped out of his skin. Sitting on the porch railing was the homeless woman he'd met at Ruby's yesterday. Ana.

Slipping his arms through his shirt and tugging on the Levi's he'd worn yesterday, he strode into the living room. Sam wasn't in the living room or the kitchen. She must have taken off early.

He yanked open the front door and found Ana standing on the porch. With a come-ahead motion of his hand, he signaled for her to come inside. "You're up awful early."

"Had to get started early," she said as she moved past him into the living room.

"How did you get here? Ruby drop you off?"

He motioned her to the couch. He took his comfortable leather chair.

"Nah," she said and sat. "I walked."

"From Ruby's?"

Ana glanced down at her hands twisting on the handle of her dirty duffle bag. "Wasn't that far. I walked further from Frisco."

He rubbed a hand down his face. He needed a shave. Must look as homeless as she did. "Let me shower and dress, and I can show you around, tell you what you'll be doing."

"Sure."

"There's coffee in one of the cupboards in the kitchen. Go on and get a pot going. I could use some too."

"Thanks." She grinned.

Nervous as a barn cat, she set her duffle on the floorboards by the coffee table and made her way into the kitchen. Joe watched her for a moment wondering if he could trust her with Cindy's belongings. He shrugged. She'd gotten herself out here from town without help. He'd give her the benefit of the doubt.

Joe stepped from the shower sometime later. The deep roasted scent of his favorite beans hit him with full force. Ana found the good stuff. Did he also smell eggs and bacon? Dressing quickly, he hurried into the kitchen.

Ana stood at the stove, spatula in hand, wonderful aromas rising from the cast-iron skillet on the burner. She'd set the table with two place-settings, juice, flapjacks, and bacon. Joe's mouth watered. Lettie very seldom made him pancakes. Sam only made healthy stuff. Where had she gone? There was no note on the wall message board. Had she been that upset about Ana to leave before he got up?

"I hope it's okay I went ahead and cooked some breakfast." Ana's face reddened.

He waved his hand. "Yeah. It's fine." More than fine. He was famished. "You're a cook, then?"

"Dad said my chore was breakfast. Got to be the only thing I could cook, well, that and chocolate-chip cookies." She looked mighty proud of herself. He liked seeing her confident instead of cowering.

"Since you're familiar with horses, I'd like you to keep the stables clean by mucking out the stalls, spreading around new straw, and keeping them fed and watered." Did she wince? He went on. "I'd like for you to exercise the horses in the corral, keep them limber."

He stuffed some buttered and syruped flapjacks into his mouth savoring the incredible flavor. "What did you put in the flapjacks to make them so delicious?"

"Sweet cream butter, vanilla, and almond extract." She beamed. "I'm glad you like them. I used my mother's recipe."

He didn't want to know anything personal about this woman. He had a feeling she wouldn't be staying. There was something professional about her, the way she carried herself and her speech, although she spoke with a heavy Southern drawl. "Your mother still around?"

She wouldn't turn and look at him. He could tell he'd hit a nerve. "She left my dad and me for another man when I was six."

"Damn shame." Sounded like his ma. Too good for a poor dirt farmer from Texas. She took off for the bright lights and phony promises of New York City with their neighbor. After that, his old man turned abusive. Joe joined the military when he was seventeen to get away from his old man fast. He wondered if his pa was still alive.

Ana lifted the skillet and walked to the table. Heaping steaming scrambled eggs onto his plate, she said, "Where am I gonna bunk?"

He scooped up a spoonful of eggs, jammed them into his mouth. Sighed. "There's a little casita out by the garden under a grove of large scrub oaks and pine trees. It's a small two-bedroom guesthouse." It was the house built by Elmer for Olina before they remodeled their cabin. Bert and Frances had lived there until they took possession of the farmhouse. He and Cindy had lived in it as their first house together. "It's nothing fancy, but it will serve your needs."

She loaded up her plate with eggs and put the pan in the sink. Turning, she smiled at Joe. "I can't thank you enough for helping me out. I was … just a little desperate at Ruby's."

He could see that, but something else as well. "Don't thank me yet. By tonight, you'll be cursing me."

After breakfast, and while it was still about an hour until dawn, Joe grabbed the keys to the casita and had Ana follow him. "It might be dusty and in need of a good cleaning. I think Lettie, my housekeeper, or one of her daughters tries to keep up with it, but they have their own homes to look after."

"Not a problem. I lived just about anywhere."

He'd just bet she had.

Joe had loved living the first few months of his marriage in this single-story casita, two bedrooms, kitchenette with a small island complete with two barstools. The tiny living room had an old suede loveseat, matching chair, and bright floor lamp. In the corner, stood an old model nineteen-inch TV on a rickety stand.

A rock fireplace he and Bert built faced the front door. The bedrooms only had enough space to walk around queen-sized beds and dressers. At least the place had a full bathroom and small walk-in closet with a small laundry room.

Ana scrutinized each room as if she were buying the place. Guess that's what women did when considering a place to live.

"It's nice."

Joe didn't know why he felt relief. Maybe she'd stay for a bit—if she proved to be useful. At least she could cook.

Ana sat on the bed, bounced a couple of time. "Good mattress."

Joe turned away and marched back into the living room as bitter tears stung. The bed in this room had been his and Cindy's marriage bed. They'd attempted for months to conceive a child, but nothing took. The burn of bitterness scorched his gut, and he sniffed back tears.

"You okay?" Ana asked.

"Swell." He sucked up his feelings, turned to face her. "We need to discuss some rules. One. You will stay out of the main house unless I invite you inside. Two. My dogs are not pets. They won't hurt you. They have jobs to do on the ranch, and they will attack if they feel you're a threat to them or me." Joe took a breath, looked her in the eye. She kept a stony expression. "Three. If I allow you to drive the ranch rig, you will not leave the ranch with it. And four. I will not tolerate drinking, smoking, and absolutely no drugs allowed."

Ana blinked, and her mouth hung open for a split second. How dare he say "no drugs?"

"Will that be a problem, Ana?"

Ana shook her head. "No problem."

"Good. I will pay you the same ranch wages as the other ranch hands you'll meet sometime today. Right now, they're out on the range protecting my cattle." He jammed his hands into his pockets. "Mike Sanchez is the person in charge of my farming. You'll be expected to help him out whenever he needs you. We go to town every few days. You may ride along with me or Mike, my stand-in foreman."

"Stand-in?"

"His … father was my foreman until some thugs snuck onto the ranch, beat him severely and shot his other son, nearly killing him."

She gasped. "No. Are you having a dispute with a neighbor or something?"

"No." That was all she needed to know. "Anyway, he and his wife, son, and his family, went to Mexico to recover." He spun toward the open front door. "I'll let you settle in, but meet me in the stables in an hour to learn the horses."

Ana couldn't help but wonder about Joe Mack. He was a curious bird. He didn't seem anything like the picture Jim Ports painted of him. His rule about "no drugs" really threw her as odd coming from a maniacal drug dealer. She hated being confused with a case.

The little casita was quaint, 1930s old, but updated and well maintained. Minimal dust covered the surfaces, and it looked as though someone cleaned regularly, just not for a few days.

Ana ran water in the sink and found a glass in the cupboard. Clear water ran cold. She took a long drink. As far as case assignments went, this was pretty sweet.

Deciding she could use a shower, she strolled into the small bathroom, stripped off her forest-muddied clothing and turned the shower tap on hot. Personal sized bottles of shampoo, conditioner, and body lotion sat in a tiled indentation in the shower wall. Lavender. She loved lavender. After sudsing off the road dirt and from only catching a few Z's out in the night air before her fifteen-mile hike, the hot water felt like heaven on her sore muscles.

Dressing in another clean pair of holey jeans and a faded plaid cotton shirt, she found a clean pair of socks. Perhaps with her first paycheck, she could get some new clothes.

The sun peeked over a sizeable snow-covered mountain when she left the cozy little casita. It had been a long morning since she'd begun walking to the ranch about eleven-thirty last night. Today was her chance to search Mack's property for his stash of drugs. Ports told her to look for something out of place. If she stopped Mack, it would be a real coup for her.

Mack's stables were a typical shelter for horses. Several watched her as she entered the warm area, their dark eyes curious. How had she forgotten about the foul, pungent smell of fresh horse manure? She fought wrinkling her nose and acted like the reek was natural for her.

Mack led a tall buckskin from one of the stalls—gorgeous horse, obviously well cared for and loved. He spoke softly to the horse, patted his chest and long nose. The horse nudged Joe's shoulder. He laughed. Mack's carefree laughter struck her as odd.

He walked the horse out a double door at the west end of the stables and removed his bridle, slapping him on the rump. The horse tossed his head in glee and galloped into the large corral with a variety of horses already in the grassy pasture.

Joe had a swagger when he walked toward her. He wasn't as old as Ports told her, maybe in his late forties. Sort of ambled a little John Wayne'ish. He was a cowboy for sure. How could this man be such a monster?

"That was my horse, Checkers."

She laughed. "Great name."

"This horse here." He pointed to an ancient Palomino mare lying in her stall. Ana's heart broke for the old gal. "Take special care of Ivy."

"Of course. How old is she?"

"She's twenty-five."

Ana gasped and covered her mouth. "That's incredible."

Joe walked past the other stalls indicating specific care for each horse and what to feed them. After that, he showed her where to get and mix the food.

"A chart hangs on the wall, in case you forget," he said. "The stall cleaning supplies are in a room next to the tack." He moved over to a row of farm tools hanging from a tool rack. "The manure gets scraped into a pile just outside the door, then we'll haul it over to the garden for spreading or composting. Mike's got his way of doing things.

"We'll leave for town at four p.m. to make the feed and general stores for supplies. When we go to town, we usually eat supper at Ruby's." He looked down at the stable floor, shuffled his feet. "You ever go to church?"

Weird question. "When I was a kid."

"We go to church around here. In town, we'll see about getting you a Sunday dress for services tomorrow morning."

That was sweet of Mack. Why would he do that? "Okay."

He moseyed out of the stables after that. A man of few words.

She needed to call Ports and find out more about the mysterious, Joe Mack. Had Ports made a mistake? If not, Joe Mack was a terribly proficient liar.

What the hell was going on with Mack?

CHAPTER THIRTY-SIX
Saturday Night Out on the Town

May 2, 1998—Saturday

ANA HAD ONLY ONE CLEAN blouse and a clean pair of Levi's left in her duffle bag to wear to town. She wondered if eating at Ruby's on a Saturday evening would require better clothing than she had. Luckily, next to the little walk-in closet was a laundry room with an old washer and dryer. Jackpot. That meant she'd have to wash every day. Didn't matter. As long as she could move the case along, she didn't care.

The casita had a working telephone. Ana called her handler, Jim Ports.

"Bout time you checked in." Ports growled in her ear. "I figured the bastard murdered you or something."

"I need more intel on Mack. Things aren't adding up."

"You're on a need-to-know basis, and you don't need to know anything more than what I already told ya. We … Major Donald needs that spy plane back, and he needs it last week. That's your assignment. Nothing else."

Ana cocked her head, although Ports couldn't see her. "I thought I was to find the drugs and Mack's connection to a cartel from Mexico. And when do I get to meet this shadowy figure, Major Donald?"

"Don't worry about it. Just do your job." He hung up.

Something smelled like the manure in Joe's stables. Why the big ambiguous brush off? Ports always dealt straight with her on past assignments.

Joe wore a fancy western shirt with a turquoise bolo tie, cleaned and pressed Wrangler dress pants. He had on a new Stetson covering most of his freshly washed hair. Had he dressed up for her? Ana felt homeless and insignificant next to him all duded out like he was.

Riding to town with him gave her enough time to learn more about the baffling rancher.

"So, what's your story?" Joe asked her as they bumped down the ranch road toward the highway.

"I was married for five years. But the wife thing didn't work for me." That was the God's honest truth. But she couldn't blame all of it on Reed. She hadn't been available for him.

"Your dad still around?"

"He died a while back." She'd been undercover in Guatemala. "What about you? When did you come to Shadow Pines?"

"I've lived on Sunrise Ranch for a long time." Joe chuckled. "Before they built the bunkhouse in the barn, I lived in the tool shed, slept on a cot. I began as a ranch hand working the cattle." He smiled but gazed straight ahead as if viewing his life on the ranch in his head. "I married my wife, Cindy Johnsen in '75. Her pa owned the ranch. He'd inherited it from his father. When they both died, Cindy inherited the ranch."

Ana had to know about his wife. "What happened to your wife?" She held her breath thinking it might be the gal from last night.

The late afternoon sun gleamed off the river down the mountain side. Ana shielded her eyes and wished she had her FBI-issued sunglasses. She wondered if Mack would answer her.

He heaved a large sigh. "Cindy died of breast cancer in 1995."

"I'm so sorry." It sounded so trite. "I saw some brightly colored casitas on the ranch beside the one where I'm staying. Do others besides Mike and his family live in them?"

"Ricardo, my foreman lives in one. His son, who was shot, lives in another. Like I told you, they'll be in Mexico for a while."

Joe wouldn't say anymore, and she wondered who would have come on the ranch to beat up his foreman and shoot the foreman's son. Did Ports have anything to do with that? Is that why they called her in—because the beating and shooting hadn't forced Mack to give up the spy plane?

At the general store, she found a selection of pretty cotton dresses. One was a sleeveless button-front, long-waisted floral with a swingy skirt. Unfortunately, her usual size eight hung loosely on her body. Had she lost that much weight? She found a size five and slipped it on. Perfect fit. Well, what about that?

Joe found her and held up a long-sleeved flannel work-shirt in red and blue plaid, along with a new pair of jeans. Amazed that he knew her size, she blushed.

"Cindy was about your size and weight. You can get a couple of sets. You can pay me back when you get paid."

Loud country music blared out of Ruby's Steakhouse and Saloon when they drove up. People were streaming inside. If Ana had to guess, she suspected most of the citizens of the fair Shadow Pines were eating out or dancing here tonight. Even though there was a line of people waiting at the bar and in the entryway, when Ruby saw her and Joe, she waved them forward.

"Sam is already here," Ruby said to Joe and winked.

Joe's cheeks flamed. The color looked good on him. He cleaned up damned nice, too. He took off his cowboy hat. He was attractive, tough, and fair-minded. Ana better be careful. She was on a job.

Ruby motioned one of her young waitresses over and whispered something into her ear. The girl smiled at Mack and said, "I'll take you to your table, sir."

Joe looked back at Ana for a second. "I'll see you later." And walked away.

What the hell? Wasn't he eating with her?

He approached a table in the corner where, Sam, the woman with the long black hair sat. Her warm tanned skin glowed, and she had a dazzling smile. When Joe stopped in front of her, she gripped him hard and planted a big kiss on his lips. So, this must be a girlfriend, at the very least.

Stumped, Ana didn't know what to do. Ruby grabbed her arm. "Joe has a date with our wonderful town veterinarian, Dr. Samantha Stone. I think it might be leading somewhere, if you know what I mean."

"Oh. Okay." She did know what it meant—complications.

"Come sit by me, and I'll order you a steak."

Ruby led Ana to a tiny round table on the crowded and noisy saloon side. Raucous and twangy country music blared from a western band on a raised dais in the corner. People danced a country two-step on a square parquet floor. More people crowded the bar. It was a total pickup scene, just like in Washington D.C., only the pickup artists there were married senators and congressman.

"Can I get you a drink?" Ruby asked.

"Scotch. Rocks," Ana said out of habit and blushed. That sounded more sophisticated than a homeless woman ought to sound.

Ruby lifted an eyebrow but ordered with a waitress from the bar. She returned and sat. "So, how you gettin' along with Joe?"

"He worked me hard today as you said." She yawned to prove how tired she was. "But I like the little casita I'm staying in. Mack … Joe doesn't talk much."

"Did Joe tell you about his wife?"

"Not really. He just said she died of cancer."

Ruby leaned her elbows on the table, rested her chin in her hands. "Wow, what a love story that was. Joe worked for Cindy's pa for about ten years while Cindy was growing up and then went away to college. After graduation, Joe had a special gift for her, something she'd always desired. He and Ricardo found a wild Palomino, cutest little spindly thing you'd ever seen. She named it Ivy."

Ana perked up. "I clean her stall and care for her. Joe walks her around the corral."

"He's picky about that horse. Ivy is the only living thing he has left of Cindy."

"I'm sorry," Ana said. "Didn't they have kids?"

Ruby's expression darkened. "They tried. Those two were made for each other, but it wasn't in the stars for them to have children, I guess. They sort of adopted a latch-key kid from here in Shadow Pines. Brilliant kid. A computer geek."

Ruby heaved a huge sigh but went on. "When Cindy became so ill she couldn't help around the ranch anymore, Joe sat with her. He had such hopes she would recover, and he wanted to give her his hope. He knew how important it was to hope for a miracle."

She glanced down at her hand on the tabletop. "Sometimes we overlook the fact that our loved ones who are dying are going to leave us behind, and they're hurting inside for us, as we fight hard to hang on to them. Joe fought hard. He's never gotten past the day Cindy died. His house still looks the same as the day she died." She folded and unfolded a napkin. "Except for the hospital bed and all."

The waitress brought Ana's Scotch, and she downed it in one hot gulp. She didn't want to feel compassion for this man who'd taken in a stranger and let her stay in his dead wife's house. She was supposed to be an emotional brick wall during a case. No getting involved with the suspect.

Was Ana getting in way too deep?

Samantha couldn't stop touching Joe during their dinner of medium-rare ribeyes and corn-on-the-cob. She opted for steamed broccoli while Joe had a fully-loaded baked potato and a chopped salad. They sat close. She kept her hand on his thigh, occasionally brushing at his hair that needed a trim.

He turned serious eyes on her. "Why did you leave so early this morning? I was worried."

She nearly said he had company and didn't need her around. But that would be petty. "I had lots of paperwork to finish up at the office. I required the quiet of the morning to work." Liar. She had been upset when he'd offered a job to that tramp ... that woman as a new ranch hand. Bull. Under all that dirt and muck, the woman was gorgeous, and she was making a play for Sam's husband. She almost took Joe's shotgun and ran the woman off before leaving this morning.

"You okay?" Joe asked.

"Fine." Sam hadn't meant to sound snippy, but she still didn't trust that woman.

"Are you jealous of Ana?" Joe asked laughter in his voice.

She swatted at him but missed. "Yes, if you must know."

He laughed and laid down his fork and steak knife. "Is that why you deserted our bed before four a.m.?"

She frowned. "I was upset with you."

"I'm sorry." His expression turned reflective. "She means nothing to me. You're the only woman I want by my side, angel."

"I'm not accustomed to this whole" —she motioned between the two of them— "this man/wife thing. Give me a little while."

Joe reached out, took her hands. "I love you, Samantha Mack. You never have to doubt that. I'm totally and completely devoted to you." He stroked the back of her hand resting on the tabletop. "That's why I wish you'd stay in town for a while. It's dangerous at the ranch."

Samantha nearly choked on her steak. "What? Why?"

"You're my wife, and I want you protected." He closed his eyes, blew out a breath. "Those creeps could come back any minute now with something else planned."

"You say you love me." Anger crawled up her neck. "We've discussed this before. I'm not leaving you. That's why you need my gun ... and me." She wiggled her eyebrows up and down.

With a grin only for her, he leaned across the table. "You don't know how much I need you in my life, and in my bed."

Her face blazed. "Have you heard what happened to the two guys who beat up Ricardo and shot Sal?" She changed the subject.

Joe released her hands, picked up his fork, and shoved in a bite. He chewed, frowned. "Seems they have friends in really high places. They made bail after the doc patched them up."

Samantha flipped a lock of her long hair behind her shoulder. "I'm sorry, dear. Will they be put on trial?"

He shrugged. "Who knows?"

"Have you heard from Ricardo and Lettie? Have they taken Sal to Mexico yet?"

"Not since their last call on Sunday. I'm assuming they're still in Sacramento. It might be a few days before Sal's ready to travel."

"I can't believe all this trouble that's happened to you." Sam held up a bit of broccoli and examined it. "I want to help you."

He gazed at her—really looked. So deep, Samantha figured he could see into her soul. Eventually, he smiled. "You are one in a million, aren't you, my beautiful angel? I love you."

Her heart, which she didn't know had paused when he gazed into her eyes, galloped hard. "I love you, Joe," she whispered.

"Well, ain't this cozy?"

Samantha glanced up at the man approaching their table. Sheriff Warner. Hellfire.

"What do you want, Warner?" Joe asked in a not-nice tone of voice.

"I came to tell you I had to bust loose those two … gentlemen you had words with the other night."

An angry glare marred Joe's handsome face. "We already heard."

The sheriff took the empty chair at their table, flipped it around, and sat backward on it. "Look, I tried to get the judge to set bail at one million because of the shooting and altercation, but he took into consideration what you'd done to them and let them go for less. I think someone way up the food chain got to the judge." Warner's forehead puckered. "I'm sorry I lost the people who hurt Ricardo and Sal."

The sheriff said he was sorry?

Joe took a hard look at Cody. A muscle in his jaw convulsed. "I know you did your best, Warner. I'm up against something that's hurtling out of control."

"What the hell did you do to these people?"

"Their goal is to enlarge SRM Facility's property, and my place stands in their way, especially after I told them I wouldn't sell."

"Dammit, Mack. You sure know how to stir in the manure."

"They've been quiet since the attack, but I'm still leery."

Cody jerked his head toward the saloon. "I heard you picked up a new ranch hand. She's a looker." He wolf-whistled.

Joe's tanned cheeks reddened.

Samantha narrowed her eyes at Cody.

"Ruby took in a homeless person. I just happened along when she told the gal I needed help on the ranch," Joe said.

"That's all. The woman's a drifter." Joe glanced at Sam. "Probably won't stay a month, if that."

Cody's eyes twinkled with mischief. "So what's her story?"

"Her name is Ana Penskie, she's homeless and hungry, much the same as I was after Vietnam when I just happened to take this highway. I felt sorry for her."

Samantha shook off his hand and leaned back in the chair. "She is pretty."

"Come on, Sam, no one could compare to you."

Crossing her arms over her chest, she scowled at Joe. "Well, she better not."

Joe chuckled. "She looked like she'd rolled in dirt out in the forest when I first saw her."

"And now?" Sam glanced at the table where Ana chatted with Ruby. "She looks right fetchin' in her new cotton dress."

Cody held up his hands. "Count me out of this lover's spat. I'm going to have supper with my wife." He got up and strolled over to the table where his wife, Beverly, sat.

It was good to see the lout taking his wife out for an evening away from home. Now back to her ... man. "And now that she's cleaned up?" Samantha asked.

"Sam." Joe drew her name out with a mixture of exasperation, impatience, and love. "Why do you think I asked you to marry me? I love you and couldn't live without you. I don't want anyone else."

She didn't like feeling the jealous fool. "I'm sorry."

Patience returned to his voice. "I'm sorry about Ana. She's quiet, efficient, and keeps to herself."

She eyed him warily but grinned. "That's okay. But she's still pretty. I better not see those baby blues wandering."

Joe took her hand, placed it over his heart. "As God is my witness, Sam, angel of mine, you're the only one."

CHAPTER THIRTY-SEVEN

Calling in the Big Guns

May 8, 1998—Friday

P**AUL BASUA DROVE** the last bit of the dirt road leading into SRM Facilities in his rented SUV. The sheriff impounded the car he left up on the north side of the mesa and Major Donald hadn't got it out of hock yet. He loathed returning to work on the SRM spy plane project.

During the past week, he had flown to Texas to speak to the aerospace engineering team who helped construct the little drones, and personally picked up a new camera and the other missing parts to get the second AIDA up and running. While there, he took a holiday and seriously considered not returning. However, his dad and mum told him to stop talking rubbish and get back to finish his responsibilities.

Bollocks. This whole deal with Major Donald was dodgy. Paul knew he was in over his head.

The sergeant at the guard shack waved him through. Holy hell, he missed his home in London.

Before taking the lift down to the lab dungeon, he secured a dolly to transport the weighty wing still in its box and the other equipment. He feared seeing Major Donald once more. That man would make Paul's life a living hell.

He rode the lift down, pleased with himself for recovering the missing wing and other parts. He could have the drone up in the air by tomorrow afternoon, then he hoped things around the lab would be hunky-dory. Perhaps he should stop the lift, return to the surface, and send down the equipment before disappearing.

Paul wanted out.

Unfortunately, he knew Major Donald wouldn't stop until he'd found the silver mine and killed Mr. Joe Mack. Did he have the same plans for him? This situation was one bloody-hell of a mess.

Major Charles Donald was on a call to Italy when he heard that screw-up, Basua, stroll into the lab like he was mincing down Piccadilly Park lane. At least he pushed a huge box into the lab ahead of him which better be the missing wing.

Finally, someone picked up on the other end of the line. "Yo, what do you want? I told you I wasn't coming."

"How's your mom?" he asked.

Butch Henry—his go-to sniper from the Gulf War, and Charles' security chief from their days in the jungles of Brazil—sighed. "We buried her a week ago."

Charles could care less. "I need you to come to California, now. I have a special job for you and you alone."

"When?"

"Pronto."

"Target?"

"Rancher who runs a cattle spread, and anyone else who stands in our way. He stole government property and I want it back."

"Gimme a week. I have't tie up loose ends around here. Secure the villa and estate."

"No longer. I need this son-of-a-bitch planted six feet under."

Butch laughed. "You never change." He hung up.

Charles smashed the receiver back in its holder. He needed Butch a month ago when he'd first spoken to him by phone. It was insubordination for him not to report for duty when called.

Basua approached looking like a whipped dog. Maybe Butch should have a talk with him out in the woods, tie up another loose end. "Did you get the correct parts?" Charles asked the doctor.

"Yes, Major. The company was pleased to construct a new wing and just barely got in the new camera. I'll have the new spy drone up in the air by the afternoon tomorrow."

269

Charles cracked his knuckles. "You'd better. If this last plan doesn't work, I'm letting my specialist clean up this mess."

"Hasn't a closer ground search of the mountain turned up the plane or the silver mine?" Paul shifted from foot-to-foot. "And what about the silver operation on this side?"

"They've covered every inch of that side of the mountain. No sign of either. How can you hide a silver mine and a tiny plane?"

Charles stood, too angry to sit, and paced. He should have eaten this morning, his gut churned. "I wish we'd never discovered the silver. We'll blow this end before we leave, but the jet aviation company needs their silver and is paying top dollar for it. I have to have another source of the pure stuff."

He swore and watched Basua wince. Lightweight. "The whole point of this Peter Pan Project was to get the spy plane operational and us back to our work in South America." Mostly the cartel in Brazil under-the-table funded his projects. He loved working both sides of illegal. "How did I get caught up in a mining operation?"

Basua gripped his limp hands together. He was a loose end.

"Don't look so worried, doctor. My men will clean this mess up." Or he'd do it himself.

May 12, 1998—Tuesday—**Too Quiet on the Ranch**

Joe rode Checkers out to the pastureland early this morning to check on the cattle. The three young ranch hands he'd hired to keep the herd safe and move around to fresh grass were doing their jobs well. They kept their rifles handy at all times and he'd told them to keep their eyes on the sky and the mountains. He didn't know where the next attack would come from.

So far, no more spy planes. Having the one he shot out of the sky even this close to the ranch made his gut grind with anxiety. If only SRM would look around on their side of the mountain. He couldn't imagine what they were waiting for. He hoped and prayed they wouldn't find his mine. He'd never get rid of them then. However, there had been no more attempts to burn him out, buy him out, or shoot him out since Ana arrived.

So why was suspicion sizzling under his skin?

The calves were growing, getting fat off their mothers' milk and eating grasses growing from a couple of nourishing rainfalls. As he stroked the horse's silky side, he couldn't keep his mind off Sam. Damn, he loved her. Part of him feared he would forget his love for Cindy. It still astonished him that he could open his heart and feel a deep love for both women. Knowing his love for Sam was totally different from how he'd loved and cared for Cindy helped.

Seeing her jealous over Ana had warmed his heart. He'd bet his bottom dollar that in a fight, Sam would probably take Ana.

Joe rode through the cool morning, letting Checkers have his head until they reached the compound. He dismounted and for a moment, waited for Sal Sanchez to come take Checkers to rub him down and feed him. The memory of Sal's pinched face, the sight of all that blood, had Joe's chest tightening to the point of not being able to pull in a breath.

Joe would have to attend to his horse himself. He pulled the hoof pick and brush out of his back pocket and tapped Checkers' leg. The horse lifted its leg and allowed Joe to scrape its hoof clean of rocks and debris. When he finished, he rubbed Checkers down, gave him a bucket of oats. Checkers followed Joe to his stall where Joe filled his water trough and feed bin.

He paused to watch his horse munch on the oats, leaning against the stall gate. Ana had proved to be a hard-worker, keeping the stables clean and fresh smelling. She was up before him most days feeding the animals and gathering eggs. All of this before she came inside his house to cook breakfast.

In the afternoon, she exercised the horses and helped Mike in the groves. The mandarin trees had set their fruit from the April blossoms already, and it looked like a bumper crop. The almond trees had begun to transform their blooms into a fully developed almonds in their hulls. They, too, were plentiful. Mike knew his stuff. Joe expected a bounteous harvest, enough money to perhaps replace his 1958 tractor and keep Robbie in school, even graduate school, if he so desired.

Joe took an apple out of the bin and held it out to Checkers. He gobbled off Joe's open palm.

"He loves you, you know."

Joe flipped around, startled at Ana's voice.

"He's a good friend." Joe stroked Checkers' long nose. He nickered softly and bent his head again to munch on his allotment of oats.

"All of your animals adore you." She gestured toward the open stable door where Shep and Spike sat on their haunches at attention. "Do you ever allow them to enjoy themselves?"

He laughed. "They're relaxed right now."

"If you say so." She chuckled.

With Sam home with him, Ana didn't come into the house except for breakfast. He hadn't invited her in at other times. He and Sam were still on their honeymoon, and he liked his privacy with her. Ana cooking breakfast for him was a bonus.

Sam, a decaf coffee and harvest grain bread sort of woman, was up at three and gone by four. She usually left the ranch before he got out of bed. With endless rounds to make, like the ranches up in the hills surrounding Shadow Pines and some on the west side of Tahoe, she stayed swamped. Later, she worked in the animal hospital in town with her assistant. At night, she returned to him.

"You gonna marry Sam?" Ana asked when he locked Checkers' stall gate.

None of your business, and we're already married. "Maybe."

"She's nice."

He nodded. "She is."

"Is she like your wife?"

Joe froze, a stone stuck in his gut. "No."

He whistled for the dogs and clomped out of the stables, striding across the open area to his house. Ana had no right to ask him such questions.

Opening the door, he motioned the dogs inside. They didn't come inside often. Their spot was the large rug in front of the fireplace. They sat gazing at him for permission. "At ease." They hunkered down.

He was agitated and upset. Something still didn't fit right about Ana Penskie. He knew she wasn't telling him her whole story no matter how many times he'd asked about her past. He didn't like it.

He trudged through the living room and the kitchen and stopped in front of his locked office door. He considered his options. He hated thinking Ana might be messing with him, that she wasn't a homeless waif at all, but someone with a more sinister agenda.

Unlocking the deadbolt, he entered his dark office. Only the flashing of lights on a control panel and the split screen of the computer monitor were on. Joe yanked out his chair and sat. He wasn't sure he wanted to know if Ana was jerking around with him, not telling him the truth.

He keyed her name into the search bar on the goofy-sounding browser. A N A   P E N S K I E and hit ENTER. His old modem whined and screeched.

Robbie purchased him a new computer. It was fast, but his internet service was slow as molasses. After a few moments and a fruitless search, he decided to call the Geek.

Robbie answered on the third ring. "Hey, Yo Mr. Joe. How's it going?"

"Joe." Always cheered by his boy, Joe smiled. "Could be better."

"Yeah, Joe. I heard about Sal and Ricardo. Oh, man, that's brutal. They catch the guys?"

"Yes. But the judge set them free."

"Wow, man. Are you okay? How's Sam?"

"We're fine for now, but that's why I called." Joe roughed-up his hair. "Can you find any information on your fancy computer about a gal named Ana Penskie? If that's her name."

"Who's she?" Robbie asked.

"She's a new hand I hired for the ranch, but I got a feeling she might not be on the up and up."

"Uncool, Joe. Here, give me a minute."

Joe could hear Robbie speaking to someone in the background. A female. Most likely Jessica. Joe shook his head. Sam would bust a gut if she knew they might be living together.

"That's a tough one," Robbie said coming back on the line. "You got any other info?"

"She said she was from Virginia."

Silence.

After a couple of minutes, Robbie shouted, "Bingo. Got her. Some hick newspaper had a tiny write up about an Ana Penskie when she was in college. I'll read it." He cleared his throat.

"Georgetown debate Decathlon-winning, Ana Penskie and Reed Jin-Ho, her fellow debate team member, captured the National Debate Tournament championship for Georgetown University at the formal debate competition hosted by Emory University April 3, 1985."

Silence again.

"What the hell?" Joe rubbed his stiff neck.

"Does that make sense, Mr. Joe?" Robbie asked, concern in his voice.

How the hell did this Ana Penskie—Georgetown debate champion—get to San Francisco and become homeless, and just happen to make her way to Shadow Pines and his ranch?

This situation smelled as rotten as week-old manure.

"Thanks for your help, Geek. I owe you one."

"Nah. You'll never owe me."

"Have Jessica call her mother." Joe chuckled.

He heard a female gasp on the other end of the line.

"Anything else?" Robbie asked.

"Nope. Thanks." Joe hung up.

What did Ana want with him? Was he the reason she was here?

Joe keyed up the split screen of his cameras on the ranch. Ana must not know about his hidden cameras. He watched for a moment as she cleaned up the stables and put away her tools. Dusting off her hands, she headed out and closed the door.

He switched to the ranch compound camera.

Ana, stood outside the stables, eyeing the large barn. The only time she went in was to replenish the oats and grains for the horses. She glanced toward the house and the casitas then slunk along the wall of the barn and opened the door. What was she up to?

Switching to the barn camera, he saw her eye the upper loft. However, she began to walk the lower level of the barn looking through the huge grain sacks and loose feed bins as if searching for something. The Guernseys Joe kept exclusively for milking mooed at her. She patted them on their rumps. She apparently didn't find what she was looking for and climbed the ladder to the old hayloft where he had stored the clean straw for the stalls. She searched everywhere, poking under the bales and gazing up into the rafters.

What was she looking for?

Appearing disappointed, Ana climbed down the ladder and went into the barn office. She flipped on the light and rummaged through his papers on the desk and then through the file cabinet. Dammit. If he were a betting man, like crazy old Elmer, he'd bet she was snooping for someone. Maybe even a *major* someone.

Damn.

What was he going to do about her? Should he talk to Sam? That would mean telling her about the spy plane he took down and hid from the government. He was sure he'd broken a lot of laws and could do time. But he had every right to defend his property. He had a silver mine to protect as well. And he would defend it all even if it killed him.

But first, he needed to know about Ms. Ana Penskie.

After eating a cold turkey and Swiss sandwich and drinking down a fresh glass of milk, Joe went looking for Ana. He found her in the stables just before quitting time. He'd climbed up into the hayloft to toss down a couple of bales of hay for the horses. Ana walked in and stroked Checkers' nose. He nickered at her, and she laughed. Joe shuffled around making noise so she would know he was there.

She moved back a few steps, so she could gaze at him. "Say, I'm sorry about butting into your business."

"Water under the bridge," Joe said.

"I'm sorry anyway. I had no right to pry." She went to fill the horses' water troughs.

Joe shoved another bale of hay close to the edge of the loft. Time for a test. When he heard her step out into the aisle, he pushed. The bale went over the edge of the loft with a whoosh.

"Look out below." He craned his neck over the edge. Ana sprang out of the way like a rabbit, doing a professional acrobatic roll. She shot to her feet. She'd clearly had special training. "I'm so sorry. I didn't know how close the edge was." He shrugged.

She dusted off her jeans, glanced up. "That's okay. Could've happened to anyone."

"You're pretty quick. That's quite a move."

Ana's face pinked, she glanced at the hay-strewn cement floor. "I did a stint in a small circus in San Antone for a stretch."

Joe didn't believe her. "You must've been a highlight in their show."

"I did okay."

"How about some target practice?" he asked and climbed down the ladder. "I'm going jackrabbit hunting tomorrow and wondered if you'd like to come along."

"You shoot rabbits?" Her big brown eyes opened wide.

"They're destructive and dig holes my cattle stumble into and break their legs. Would you rather I shoot a steer?"

Her eyebrows puckered. "No. Of course not. It's just that … Bugs Bunny."

He chuckled. "They make great stew." Lettie made delicious rabbit stew. He could freeze the meat for when she returned.

"I'll grab a couple of rifles," he said, "and meet you out behind the barn."

She followed him, dragging her feet like a little child.

"Ready?" He pointed to a couple of fluttering straw scarecrows hung from posts set up to use as targets.

"Coming at you." He tossed her a rifle to catch her off guard. Snapping to attention, she caught the Remington in both hands as if she'd always handled loaded weapons of death before. "Let's see if you know how to use a rifle."

She smirked at him, the light of challenge flashing in her eyes. Oh, yes. Ana would rise to the occasion.

She dropped down on her knees, rested her left elbow on a bale of hay to steady the rifle, and emptied her fifteen long rounds into the head of a scarecrow, ripping it to shreds.

Joe would have sworn she hit the scarecrow in the eye each time in the same spot. No doubt in his mind, this woman was lethal. "Some fancy shooting."

She smiled up at him. "Daddy hunted rabbits as well, not that I liked it."

No chance in hell she only shot rabbits. Who was this woman with poise and elegance, who couldn't hide her college-educated speech or her quick moves?

He aimed to find out.

CHAPTER THIRTY-EIGHT

Will the Real Ana Please Stand Up?

May 14, 1998—Thursday

"I HAVE GOT TO ATTEND the conference in Sacramento. Are you sure you can't come with me?" Sam asked Joe as she tossed a sweater into her small suitcase. Joe had just walked into the bedroom after his morning cup of energy.

He worried the back of his neck with his hand. "We've been over this, Sam. I can't just up and leave the ranch with only Mike in charge, especially if someone tries something again." Although he suspected Ana was the next "something" to hit because of her snooping and was now employing the soft approach to get to him. "Besides, what would I do at a veterinarian's conference?"

She stopped packing, fisted her hands on her slender hips. "You might learn something about your animals. And we could celebrate our almost one-month anniversary."

He stepped closer and drew her into his arms, kissed her long and hard. When he pulled back, her eyes fluttered open, a dazed look in them. "We'll celebrate when you get home. I'll miss you," he said.

"Maybe I'll change my mind and stay home." Sam grinned and kissed him again. "Hmm," she said and stepped back.

Joe would plan a return visit to South Lake Tahoe, stay with Sam in a beachfront cottage. His heartbeat sped up just thinking about it.

He chuckled. "Go. Have a good time. Just don't get involved with any of those handsome vets from Sacramento."

"I've made my bed." She wagged her eyebrows. "And it's with you."

After Sam finished packing, Joe walked her to her SUV and made sure she had her cell phone and a full tank of gas. "Be careful driving down the river. I don't want to hear you've had another demolition derby on the road."

Sam leaned on the open window of the car. He moved toward her and they kissed. "You save those lips for me."

He laughed. "Be safe."

After watching the blue SUV until it disappeared around a bend of trees, Joe dropped into one of Cindy's Adirondack chairs. He felt at loose ends without Sam there. She had become the center of his life.

Robbie's cell phone rang in Joe's pocket. He removed it and examined the screen expecting to see Robbie's number. Instead, it was a Sacramento number. The government assayers?

He snapped it open. "This is Mack."

"Mr. Johnsen, this is Marshall of the Department of Mines and Geology. I have some excellent news for you."

Joe's hand trembled on the phone. "I'm all ears."

"We ran the atomic absorption test and mass spectroscopy scan. There's no doubt about it. You've got eighteen-carat gold there."

He swallowed.

"Mr. Johnsen. Are you still there?"

"I'm here. How much is that?"

"There wasn't much in the sample, only slightly less than a troy pound, about thirty-five hundred dollars."

Joe felt numb. "You're kidding."

"At the Department of Mines and Geology, we don't kid about gold, son." Marshall had teasing in his voice.

"Do you pay that for the gold or do I take it somewhere else?"

"We would be happy to pay you for the gold. It's fairly pure, but you may decide to call around at different brokers and see what their going rate is." He took a deep breath. "Are you sure you don't want to tell us where you discovered such a find? We could help you mine it and refine it."

Yeah, at an enormous price and tear up his mountain. Not gonna happen.

"Say, I'm curious about the silver content," Joe said to distract Marshall.

"Ah, yes, the silver. Today, silver fineness rates at or near 92.5% pure silver, with about 7.5% copper, and other metals in the mix. Yours was extremely pure, about .999 fine silver." He took a breath. "Unfortunately, silver prices have plummeted since 1980, going down from $20.63 a troy ounce to $5.10. Your sample netted about 6.5 troy ounces for only $33.15, I'm afraid."

"That's disappointing," Joe said. What a shock for Major Donald, needing a lot of silver for his mercenary purposes. "Thank you for calling."

"It's my pleasure. I assume you'll be in touch."

Joe stood, too antsy to sit. "Yes. I'll be in touch."

Well, hot dog and hallelujah. Enough money for a new stud bull, or another trip to Tahoe with Sam. He could hire some extra hands, some with gun-handling experience.

Before that, he still had Ana to worry about. When would she strike? What special surprise did she have planned? Well, he had something designed for her first.

Joe heard the rumbling of the Geek's old Mercury long before he saw it turn on the same curve Sam had taken not ten minutes before. Perhaps they'd passed on the ranch road. Had Sam accepted the Geek and her daughter being in love yet?

He walked down the porch steps and leaned into the window after Robbie killed the engine of his car. "How you doing?"

"Fine, Mr. Joe."

"Just Joe."

"Joe. I got what you needed, but not why?" He pointed to a couple of plastic shopping bags.

"Let's just say we're going hunting."

May 16, 1998—Saturday

After a two-day hunting and fishing trip into the mountains with Robbie, Joe felt like a new man. He couldn't wait to get back to the ranch and find out if he'd caught the real big one. Robbie left as soon as they returned, to see Jessica. Joe told him that when school let out, they both needed to stay at the ranch for their protection. Jessica needed to be with her mother.

Right now, he had some fish and big game to fry.

He'd left his office door unlocked on purpose, and he never locked up the house. Thinking he might have a backstabbing, S.O.B. spy on his hands didn't exactly thrill him.

Mashing his teeth together, he tramped into his office and booted up his computer. The four cameras around the ranch appeared on his monitor. All looked quiet. Then he saw the top of Ana's dark head in the corner of one.

He ran the tape machine backward a bit. Sure enough, Ana was searching around Ricardo and Sal's casitas, snooping in their small flower gardens, and in their sheds. What the hell was she looking for now? If Major Donald sent her, perhaps she was looking for the little spy plane. She wouldn't find it here.

He re-wound the video machine from the new house camera Robbie picked up this last run. Around five a.m. this morning, Ana waltzed into the house as if she owned the place. She searched the living room, apparently decided it wasn't productive, and then headed for his office.

He switched to receiver broadcaster and watched Ana explore his office. Ana had booted up his computer and waited. The little snoop. What a dope he was to be suckered in by a pretty face. She was no homeless woman. The whole thing was an act— a set up to win his heart before dumping him and keeping his ranch? Or before killing him? Thankfully, Sam was with him during the night.

Time to go on the offensive.

D-Day on the Home Front

Joe found Ana in the stables rubbing down old Ivy. The horse revived and preened under her gentle, soft touch and easy words.

"You're good with her." He leaned his arms on the stall gate.

"She's easy to care for." She stroked Ivy's long silky neck. "She's beloved."

"Say, when you finish, I have lunch set up on the porch. Ruby was kind enough to send out some steak sandwiches from Bella, some pie, and lemonade. Would you care to join me?"

"Where's Sam?" Ana continued to brush the underside of the older horse.

"Vet conference in Sacramento."

"So, when the cat's away, huh?" Her eyes twinkled with slyness.

Joe chuckled with an angry edge but didn't answer. He spun on his heel and stalked to the porch where he'd set up dinner. How dare she assume he would ask favors from her?

He stared at the food on the table. Nice spread for a last meal. He walked through the house to the kitchen and poured the icy lemonade. He added a special present for Ana.

"This looks lovely and smells better." Ana sat at the card table Joe set up on the porch.

Joe sat opposite her, placed the lemonade in front of her. "I figured it would be fun to eat outside this afternoon. I enjoy this time of day. I've finished my morning chores, and it's time to ride the horses."

Ana clinked her glass against his. "Cheers," she said and took a long drink of her lemonade, dabbed at her lips. "You ever think about selling your ranch, traveling around the world?"

Clever girl. "Never. My wife's father gave me this ranch and made me swear never to sell it."

She batted her eyes. "Good for you."

"How do you like your work on the ranch?" Joe asked.

Ana took a bite of her sandwich, chewed. "It's hard work, but I enjoy it all right."

"No regrets you didn't keep walking up the road to Tahoe?"

"None."

I'll bet. "You have any family living?"

"I think…" She paused to stifle a yawn. "I think my dad has a sister back east somewhere." She blinked like she couldn't keep her eyes open.

"Are you getting acquainted with the ranch, the ranch hands, and learning what you needed to find out?"

"Wait. What?" She took a bite and chewed slowly, but yawned again. "I'm awfully tired all of a sudden." When she finished another big yawn, shock blanketed her expression. "What have you done to me? Did you slip me chloral hydrate?"

"I gave you plenty of room to prove your loyalty to me, but you broke my trust. Did you find what they sent you here to look for?" Joe slammed his fist on the table making everything jump, including Ana. "I told you to stay out of my house, yet there you were while Robbie and I were in the canyons. You searched through my personal and business files, checked out my computer. Luckily, the Geek encrypted my files."

Her eyelids fluttered. She fought to keep them open. "You spied on me?"

"A man can't be too careful."

"But … but w-where d-do yooou hide your d-drugs?" she garbled her question. It wouldn't be long now.

"Drugs? What the hell are you talking about?"

"Major said … had drugs … you ran … for cartel…." Ana shuttered

"Major? Major Donald?"

"Yeeees."

He swore intensely. "Call Major Donald and get him out here. You're finished working for me on the ranch. It's time to report your findings."

He took off his hat and pulled his hand through his hair. "Drugs. I have no idea what you're saying. I'm a rancher. Raising cattle and minding my own business. Where's your cell phone?"

She lifted her hand, attempted to curl her fingers into a fist. "I-I oought to shooot yoou."

"I'm sure you'll get your chance unless you don't prove of worth to your people. Give me your phone."

When she didn't, he jumped out of his chair and searched her pockets.

"Whhhhy?" Ana garbled her question, attempted to grab at him.

"I don't like spies."

Joe scrolled through the most recent calls and texts. "Jim. Is this your contact?"

She fought answering, but the drug had a bit of truth serum, like sodium pentothal thiopental in it.

"Yeees. But so is m-my hus … band, Reed P-Penn. I need h-him."

He dialed and held it to her ear. "You tell Jim he needs to extract you. Now."

Her eyelids drooped, her head teetered. "C-can't … talk."

Joe slapped her face. "Wake up enough to talk to him." He heard a voice on the other end of the line. He covered the speaker with his finger. "You talk to him, or I'll kill you both."

She nodded. "J-Jim …. I-I need to come … in. Yeees, usual spot off the old logging road." The phone fell from her fingers as her head hit the table with a thud.

Joe dumped Ana's lemonade on the flower bushes and wrangled Ana to the floor of the porch. He bound her feet and wrists with zip ties. Joe didn't know how long she'd be under and if she'd come out of the drug like a tiger. And … what did she mean about finding drugs on his property and him involved with a drug cartel? Crazy stuff. Unless … Major Donald had filled her head with filthy lies about him to get her cooperation.

He jogged around the house and into her little casita. Did she have a wallet or a driver's license?

Rifling through her meager possessions, he found a false bottom sewn into her duffle bag. Jackpot. She had several drivers' licenses. One read Annika, Stripper Extraordinaire. He flipped through some more. She wasn't Penskie at all. Finally, one read: Ana Chase, 10410 Stratford Ave., Fairfax, Virginia. Damn. How many other lies had she told him? He also found her Glock.

Angry enough to use her for target practice, Joe needed to get her to the pick-up point. The place Ana met her handler was in the southernmost part of his ranch on an old logging road. SRM must not have figured he wouldn't have eyes on that part of his property. But Robbie hid a camera up in a tree covering all that area.

He gathered her clothing, even the dress, Levi's, and shirts he'd bought for her at the general store and stuffed them all into her duffle. Time to take out the trash.

Still unconscious, he carried Ana to the back of his rig and tossed her in. Then her duffle. He had to hurry, or he'd miss her contact.

The drive to the spot hidden in the tall pines took only five minutes. Joe overthought things on the drive there. Her people would not be happy with her, primarily since she hadn't found what she'd been sent to find, nor had she convinced him to sell. He'd told her what holding onto the ranch meant to him and Sam. He hated getting conned by someone.

Didn't matter. Joe needed Ana now.

He pulled her out of the rig and propped her up against a large tree trunk like she was sick. He cut the zip ties and leaned her head back against the tree before hiding the truck out of sight.

Not long after, the black Jeep rumbled up the old logging road.

Ports, the man Joe thrashed in front of Ruby's, parked and got out of the vehicle. "Ana. You all right?"

He knelt in front of her and shook her. When Ana didn't respond, he slapped her, hard.

She sputtered. "I'm so sick."

"What happened? Did that bastard find out about you?"

While Ports questioned Ana, trying to make sense of her slurred words, Joe crept under the Jeep and placed a bug under it. Thanks, Geek. He could track it now and see where Ports took Ana. Then he'd call Sheriff Warner.

CHAPTER THIRTY-NINE
Agent Penn Comes in Out of the Cold

ANA COULDN'T SEE. Her vision wavered in and out of total blackness. Her head felt like someone stuffed it with oozing mud. She was so sleepy, and her mouth and tongue felt like she'd chewed on sand. Where was she, and why had someone just slapped her?

"Wake up Ana," Jim Ports said. "Tell me what happened."

"What?" His voice swam around with the mud in her brain.

Ports slapped her again, making her head ring with pain. "Are you compromised? Did Mack find out who you are and what you were doing?"

She leaned forward, cradled her head in her hands. Her body convulsed with the effects of the chloral hydrate, if that's the drug Mack used. Deep cut marks on her aching wrists and ankles told her he'd bound her after knocking her out. "I'm sick, can't you see that? I think I fell off a horse and had to crawl over here. I must have landed on my shoulder."

Joe must have thrown her in the back of his truck when he transported her. She couldn't tell Ports she'd blown her cover and Joe had found out and left her here for him to find. Perhaps Joe knew she'd get punished for failing to perform her duty. "I just need to come in for a few days … until I recover."

Ports' face twisted into a mask of fury. "Why didn't you tell Mack you'd been thrown, stay on the ranch, and let him take care of you? You could have been pumping him for info."

Darkness threatened to take her under again. She had to fight it off. "I searched everywhere while he was gone, even dug into Joe's computer files. I couldn't find any reference to drugs or see huge amounts of money in his bank accounts."

Ports' face wobbled in front of her. "Did you find the plane?"

Plane? What plane? "If he does have it, it's well hidden, or not on the ranch compound." The mud in her head was beginning to decrease. "I didn't go into the mountains, though."

Ports uttered some creative oaths. "Let's get you in the car."

He had to yank on her arm to pull her to her feet because she couldn't stand on her own. What drug had Joe given her?

After Ports dumped her on the passenger seat, he ran around the Jeep and climbed in, just as his cell rang. She laid her head on the headrest and closed her eyes.

"Yo. Yeah, Major Donald. I have her ... what?"

Ana could only imagine what Major Donald's reaction would be. She heard him shouting foul language.

"No. Ana didn't find the plane in the compound." He paused to listen. "Said she fell off a horse and injured herself."

Another longer pause. What was Major Donald saying?

"Yeah, I'll take care of it. Sure." Ports hung up.

Ana's heart pummeled the back of her ribs. She opened her eyes, faced Ports. "Are you taking me to see the Major?" she asked.

"Soon. Let's get you fixed up first."

"I don't need fixing up. I demand you take me to see the major. Now."

Ports' gaze was cold and flinty. She knew what "take care of it" meant. This lovely country provided many well-hidden spots to dump a body that would not be found. "Okay, okay." He started the car.

"Go to the left instead of back toward the highway. I know a quicker way to get to SRM." She was lying but needed to buy some time. "I can draw out a map for you through the trees, in case I pass out again. It's tricky." Holding her breath, she asked, "You got a pen and paper?"

"Yeah. In my briefcase. Back seat."

Still groggy, but functioning, Ana leaned into the back seat and opened Ports' briefcase. She found a ballpoint pen and a yellow tablet. "This will work. Just turn left and follow the old logging trail."

As he turned the SUV, Ana struck. Buried the pen deep in his neck. Blood squirted on her hand as he yelled. "You're dead, Penn. Dead." Then his eyes rolled back in his head, and he slumped over the wheel.

287

Ana hauled him back, his head lolling against the seat. She yanked on his pant leg to lift his foot off the gas and managed to get her left foot on the brake. When the Jeep stopped, she opened the door, rolled off the seat, and nearly collapsed in the forest dirt. She had to call on all her strength to stand up. She clung to the vehicle and stumbled around the hood, opened the driver's door and shoved Ports into the passenger seat.

She shook her head to clear out the rest of the mud, spun the vehicle around and headed for the highway. She'd dump Ports closer to town, so he could get medical attention since she hadn't hit a major artery. She had to get away from here and think. Major Donald wanted her dead for screwing up. This bogus case wasn't what she signed up for. Something smelled rotten, and it wasn't the rancher, Joe Mack.

Joe followed the black Jeep up the logging trail. It weaved and pitched then came to an abrupt stop. Ana staggered out of the passenger side, closed the door, and stumbled around to the driver's side. She must have taken care of her handler.

Shoving the limp black man over into the passenger seat, she jumped in to drive. How could she drive while still under the effects of the drug he'd given her?

Ana turned the Jeep and headed back toward him. He needed to get out of sight quickly and backed into a grove of tall cedars. She barely missed seeing him as she sped past. That was close.

The big man slumped in the passenger seat. She must have incapacitated him somehow. Maybe even killed him. However, if they were both from the same branch of the spy business, why would she hurt her handler?

Joe had more questions than answers as he followed her.

A few feet from the small Shadow Pines Medical Clinic, Ana stopped.

Joe pulled his rig off the road and killed his lights to watch. She ran around to the passenger side and yanked open the door. Gripping Ports, a much bigger man under his arms, she hauled him out and maneuvered him over to the sidewalk. After getting back in, she laid on the horn until the nurse walked out of the clinic and noticed the man on the ground. Ana hit the gas and barreled through town.

Joe drove past the nurse who'd called to the doctor. They were examining the guy on the sidewalk when he drove past. How was Ports involved with Ana? Had she been called in as an expert in undercover tactics? She'd been good at pumping him for information, making herself attractive enough he'd let down his guard.

For a moment, Joe considered following her with the tracking device. Maybe this was just a diversionary tactic, and even now Major Donald and his other thugs were on the ranch. No. He didn't have time to follow another agent. He had the device on the Jeep, he could find her anytime.

He turned his rig around and headed back to the ranch.

The drive to Lodi took Ana about an hour and a half. She drove to the bus station first, where she and her ex-husband had kept extra clothing, credit cards, money, and various passports under various names. She had a duplicate locker key she could use.

She abandoned the Jeep in a grocery store parking lot and walked to a cheap motel not far away. She found a burger and fries at the local hamburger joint.

Still half loopy from the knock-out drug Joe Mack fed her, she stumbled into her room and stepped into a much needed, revitalizing shower. She hated herself for allowing Ports and this Major Donald to trick her into spying on Joe.

After her shower, she dressed in her extra clothes, a blue cotton blouse, and jeans. With the new burner cell, she called Reed.

"Ana? Are you all right?" he asked when he answered.

"Not completely. Can I meet you somewhere tomorrow?"

"Is your current assignment over?"

"It's a long story. One I'd rather not discuss on the phone."

"You've never called me during an assignment, you must be desperate."

"I'm in a lot of trouble." She fought the panic in her voice. "What time can we meet?"

He paused, most likely looking up his calendar. "How about you meet me for lunch at our favorite place on the wharf, say one p.m.?"

"Perfect. I'll see you there."

"Do you have money and a car?" Reed asked.

"I went to our bus terminal locker and got a ticket."

He was quiet for a moment. Did he remember their locker? "See you tomorrow." Then he hung up.

May 17, 1998—Sunday

The bus ride from Lodi to San Francisco took about two hours. Traffic across the Oakland Bay Bridge was tight. The bus driver maneuvered the big vehicle through the noontime traffic and stopped at The Embarcadero, close to the casual restaurant, Pier 23. Ana grabbed her duffle bag and strolled into their favorite seafood spot. She was early, so she ordered her favorite, a Giesen Sauvignon Blanc, and waited.

Nothing seemed to have changed here in the past two years she'd been on the East Coast. Tourists still dominated the restaurant with their kids and cameras and savored the sights and sounds of the Bay area. Ana had to admit she missed living in San Francisco. She missed Reed.

Her handsome, strait-laced Korean ex-husband rushed in right after her drink was delivered. Reed's face was pleasant but concerned. "Ana. It's good to see you." Then he looked closer and frowned." You look like you were dragged behind a horse."

"Thanks." She laughed. "Not far off. I was drugged."

"Oh, my gosh. By whom?

"My assignment. I blew my cover."

He laid his warm, gentle hand over hers which fiddled with the stem of the wine glass. "How do you know your cover was blown?"

"He set up cameras all over his ranch, even in his office. He spied on me."

He uttered an oath in Korean. "That bites."

The waitress came over to the table then. "What can I get for you?"

Reed turned to Ana. "The usual?"

"Of course."

He smiled at the young lady. "The lady will have the tuna poke and I'll have the raw oysters and blackened salmon. To drink, I'll have a hard apple cider."

"Got it," the young girl said, flipped around and hurried away.

"You remembered." Ana felt her face heat.

His hand tightened on hers. "I remember everything about you, darling. All day, every day. You're never far from my heart."

"Reed...." She couldn't do this. Not now.

"Do you ever think about me, Ana?" Did his lips part a touch in anticipation?

Could she tell him all she thought about was him while lying alone in her small apartment in Virginia? Their food arrived, sparing her from having to answer right away. She dug in like she hadn't eaten in a week.

After they finished eating, she glanced around to make sure no one was within hearing distance. "I'm in a lot of trouble."

"What sort of trouble?"

"I can't talk about it here. Can we go back to your apartment and discuss it?"

For a moment, he looked like he would object, but nodded, the thick black lock of hair falling across his forehead again. The desire to push it back in place overwhelmed her. She wasn't here to repair their relationship. She needed his help. That's all.

"You remember where our apartment is, don't you?" he asked and rose from his chair. Turning his back on her, he walked to the counter and paid for their food. She didn't want to feel she owed him something but sucked it up.

The apartment she'd shared with Reed was a ten-minute drive in his sedan from the Embarcadero. When he opened the door, she found nothing changed from what they'd bought as a married couple. Knowing he'd kept the things they'd purchased together warmed her heart. He also didn't dust much.

Reed made his way to the corner of the living room and sat at a desk. He booted up his laptop—special issue computer. "All the bells and whistles 1998 and the government could provide for me," he said. "Tell me who you were working for."

"Can you get into the computers for SRM Facilities out of Shadow Pines, California?"

He glanced up, wiggled his eyebrows. "I have my ways, Natasha." It was a game they played while living together. He was Boris Badenov, of the old *Bullwinkle and Rocky* kids' TV program from the 60s, and she had been his wife and accomplice, Natasha Fatale. They'd had fun for five years, then it wasn't fun when she wanted D.C., and he hadn't.

"See if you can find anything on a Major Charles Donald and a project called Peter Pan."

He pressed some buttons. She walked behind him, leaned over his shoulder.

He inhaled. "If you're going to stand that close, I won't be able to work."

Against her better judgment, Ana placed her hands on his shoulders and bent her head and caressed his neck with her lips. His reaction was swift and everything she desired. They barely made it to the large leather sofa.

Hours later after the sun had dipped in the west creating its golden and orange palette of dazzling colors across the east wall of their—yes, their—apartment, Ana redressed and met Reed at his computer.

"I still love you, darling." He held her hand in his. Reed wore only trousers and a goofy smile.

"I know," she whispered. "I can't stop loving you either."

"We could make this work, you know."

"Let's discuss it after I've finished this assignment." Ana hoped he wouldn't think she was brushing him off. "I need your help, and the life of one stubborn rancher depends upon it."

Reed stiffened, dropped her hand, but continued to work the keys of his computer.

"Here it is. The Peter Pan Project is a spy plane, or drone project featuring a smaller than normal airplane with which to spy on drug operations in the jungles of Brazil and Columbia." He pointed to the screen. "It appears your Major Donald is the security hired by a Senator and someone in the C.I.A. to oversee this project."

"Can you look him up in the C.I.A. database?"

Reed worked his magic. "Bingo. Discharged for misconduct in 1980. There's something about him playing the black market while he was supposed to be on duty in the Sinai in September as part of 'Operation Bright Star.' He played footsies with a colonel's wife and stole some gold from the Egyptians. He had quite a racket going until his colonel found out about the affair. Booted him out of the Army, but they never found all the gold he stole.

"Looks like he did some time, but was released. The person or group gaining his release is redacted. This report suggests he went into private security work with Greystone out of Louisiana."

Ana frowned. "I can't believe he's private security for a government project."

"He's not military, that's for sure." Reed smoothed down the hair she'd finger-roughened. Messy looked good on him.

She eased herself onto Reed's lap and curled her fingers in his hair again. "He's lost that spy plane and is beyond furious. He thinks rancher Joe Mack, my assignment, stole it."

"You were sent in to retrieve the plane?"

"My FBI contact, an associate of Major Donald's, Jim Ports, told me the rancher headed a Mexican drug cartel drop-off for Central and Northern California. What a crock."

Reed kissed her, lingering on her lips as though savoring a good white wine. "I've found some interesting reading from the *Shadow Pines Gazette*, the little town's newspaper." He kissed her again, a quick, sweet peck, gazed at the computer screen, reaching around her to type. "Says here they had some excitement when a man was found snooping around Joe Mack's ranch and attempted to kill his adopted son and his girlfriend."

Ana straightened up, pointed at the screen. "That's Joe. The kid is Robbie, and his girlfriend is Jessica."

He flipped to another section of the article. "Who's Dr. Basua?"

Ana pointed at the screen. "Says here in the Peter Pan Project report, Basua's the lead scientist and designer of the mini-spy plane, with a military contract company in Texas footing the bill."

"You're good at this research." She smiled at him.

Reed nibbled on her neck and waggled his eyebrows. "I'm good at a lot of things."

Ana felt her face heat and her stomach twirl.

He gazed at the screen again. "There's another photo of a couple of goons Joe Mack beat up outside a saloon in town. Not nice-looking goons."

She jammed her finger at the screen. "That's Ports, my handler. Hell, I'm not sure if he's legit FBI."

"According to this article, he and his companion, Hale Locke, were bailed out of jail after beating up Joe's foreman and shooting the foreman's son. Damn. Why aren't they still in jail for attempted murder?"

"Major Donald has a long reach." Ana removed Reed's hands from the keyboard and typed something. "While you were still asleep, I looked up Joe Mack. He served in Vietnam as part of the military advisor's task force and fought on the front lines after the Gulf of Tonkin incident. In 1965, Joe mustered out after an eight-year career in the Army. He was awarded the Purple Heart." How could she have believed this kind man would run drugs?

"Do you think he stole the plane and has hidden it somewhere on his ranch?" Reed asked. "Is that why Major Donald is harassing him?"

"I didn't find the plane anywhere on the ranch compound. I didn't look in the mountains where there are any number of caves to hide a thing that size. I think Joe's just a man protecting his ranch, from whom and why he doesn't know."

Ana eased off Reed's lap and paced. "They searched for the plane, then sent the doctor to try and take out someone close to

Joe. Ports told me Major Donald tried to buy the ranch. Joe is honor-bound to keep his ranch because of a promise he made to his dying wife and her father. When those things didn't work, they sent those goons to beat up Ricardo, his foreman, and shoot his son."

She fisted her hands. "What the hell am I still doing here, Reed? We have real enemies out there, and it's not Joe Mack. I have to go back and help him."

"Major Donald and his companions have backed themselves into a corner, and now they don't know what to do." Reed stood. "That's why they sought you out. You're the Chameleon, ever able to blend into your surroundings for your assignment." He rubbed his chin. "Ana, they're going to do a full court press on the ranch."

"I know, and I have to get back there to warn him." She paced to the windows overlooking San Francisco, sighed.

"What is this rancher to you? You could get killed."

She moved to him, Reed opened his arms and held her. "He's my friend, even after what I did to him. He doesn't deserve what's happening. My job is to cull out the bad guys in our country, not terrorize the working folk."

"I can't come with you. I'm needed in Los Angeles tomorrow early," Reed said flatly and kissed the top of her head.

"I know. I wish you could."

He rubbed his hands up and down her arms. "Will you keep in touch, keep me informed as to what else you find out, and call me if you need me?"

She nodded and kissed him hard on the lips.

Against her better judgment, she thought about the FBI office in Kansas. "I love you. But I need to save Joe Mack and his ranch."

CHAPTER FORTY
A Warrant for the Arrest of Joe Mack

May 18, 1998—Monday

MAJOR **DONALD PACED** the SRM Facilities lab, fists convulsing with rage. One of his men had screwed up … again. He fought the desire to plug his old Army buddy, Ports, through the heart. Nobody screwed up on his watch—nobody. Hawke cleaned his nails with the point of a shiny new Bowie knife over in the corner. Coward. Ports sat hunched over in a chair. "How did this cattle rancher fool you and your 'Chameleon,' Ports? You told me she was the best."

"That double-crossing bitch will be found and punished," Ports' sputtered around his neck bandage. "I got five stitches to close the hole in my neck from that, that…" he said an uglier word. "The country doctor in Shadow Pines had been curious about how I got the hole. I couldn't tell him, or he would've called the sheriff. I can't go back to prison."

"I believe it might be better for you in prison than jerking me around," Charles shouted. "This was supposed to be slick and clean. Your 'Chameleon' was our ace, find the plane and finish her mission."

"When I see her again." Ports slammed the table sending a glass shattering to the lab floor. "I'll kill her with my bare hands."

"You'll get your chance. I gotta regroup and figure out my next move." Charles scratched his chin. "The hills and canyons have been searched."

Hawke spoke up. "We haven't been able to find the damn plane, even with the new one up in the air."

After this morning's flight across the mountains swooping into all the hidden valleys and canyons on Mack's side, Basua had disappeared. Charles hoped he would come back. But the scared rabbit didn't find his company agreeable right now. They had until the end of May to produce both planes in working order for shipment to Brazil. His ass was on the line, and that made it Basua's problem, too.

"It's all coming to a head. I'm running into Shadow Pines and looking up the incompetent sheriff to put pressure on him to charge Mack with stealing government property and arrest him. We'll see who's going to prison."

He glanced at Ports. His face had gone a little pale, even for a dark-skinned man. "You'd just better hope the 'Chameleon' won't come back to tell Mack what she knows."

An hour later, Charles marched into the Shadow Pines Sheriff's Office and slammed his hand down on the front counter. The round-faced woman at the desk jumped.

"Can I help you?" she asked but cowered away from him.

"I want the sheriff to charge Joe Mack with stealing government property and to get a warrant issued for his arrest."

"Why? What's he done?"

"That is none of your business, lady." He pounded the counter with his fists.

The black deputy sitting in the corner stood up and made his way toward the counter. "Perhaps I could be of assistance, sir."

"Why? You haven't been doing your job up till now." Charles scowled.

The deputy's hand automatically moved to his sidearm. *Go ahead, deputy, reach for it.* The Magnum .357 nestled under Charles' arm was anxious to be yanked out and fired. "Where's the sheriff?"

"I'm right here. What do you want?" Warner's scowl riddled holes in him.

Charles could've blown a crater a foot wide in the sheriff's chest leaving him standing there gaping at him. "I'm here to demand you arrest Joe Mack."

Warner reached his side of the counter, leaned close, and growled, "What has he done to you?"

"Joe Mack has stolen secret government property and hidden it on his ranch. When my ... associate went there to retrieve it without causing a problem, Mack convinced you to arrest him for trespassing and attempted murder."

Charles held his hand up when the sheriff opened his mouth to object. "When another one of my associates went there to ask for the property back, Mack tortured him, nearly pulled his arms and legs off of his body. And to cap it, I went there personally to ask politely to purchase the ranch from him, but Mack pulled a shotgun on me and my comrades who'd come with me."

"However, when your *comrades* returned to force Mr. Mack to sell the place" —Warner shook his head, his voice rising— "they beat up his foreman and shot the foreman's son nearly to death. I know the details."

Charles wanted to chew this hick-town sheriff up and spit him out. "Mack attacked them without cause when they just went there to search for our property." He snarled. "Then Mack followed them into town and beat the crap out of them for no reason."

"Oh, I saw a reason, and I arrested them for aggravated assault and attempted murder. Only the intervention of someone from the government got them released. They're still supposed to show up for their arraignment in a few weeks," Warner said.

His associates would be long gone by then, and Mack would be six feet under. "Mack or one of his farm hands stabbed one of my men in the neck."

"The doctor told me about that. He was the one who shot Salvador Sanchez." The sheriff chuckled. "Where's the proof Mack stabbed Ports in the neck?"

Charles leaned over the counter, got in the sheriff's face. "Look, you backward hayseed, if you don't arrest Mack, I'll talk to my superiors and see about getting your ass removed as County Sheriff, and you'll never work in law enforcement in this state again. Do I make myself clear?" He watched the sheriff's face pale.

He straightened up, eyeing Warner. "Now do your job, Sheriff. I want that menace behind bars."

Warner swallowed—his Adam's apple bobbing. "Deputy Sayer take down this gentlemen's information, then we'll get an arrest warrant from the judge." The sheriff walked back into his office and slammed his door.

Charles smiled. Retribution was delicious.

*May 18, 1998—Monday, late—***Ana Comes Back**

Ana took a room for the night at the Mountain Shadows Hotel across the highway from Ruby's. She needed to relax and prepare. When Major Donald hit Sunrise Ranch, he'd hit it hard, and with no mercy. Joe was alone with only Miguel Sanchez as an extra gun and three kids who rode with the herd. It wouldn't be enough firepower to protect Joe. And what if Sam, her daughter, Jessica, or Robbie were there? She couldn't protect all of them.

First light Monday morning, she'd be at Joe's front door whether he welcomed her or not. He had to listen to her plan to keep him, his friends, and the ranch safe. She hoped she could at least convince Sam she meant Joe no harm. If she had believed Ports, she might have killed him at any time during her two-week stay.

*May 19, 1998—***Tuesday Morning**

Before Ana returned to Joe's ranch in the hopes he'd listen to her and not shoot her on sight, she stopped in at the Sheriff's Office. A deputy told her he'd walked down the road to eat at Ruby's.

Getting her office in D.C. to sign off on this new assignment without backup had been rough. They couldn't believe Ports tricked her, and that he was doubling up as an FBI agent and mercenary.

She found Sheriff Warner sitting at a table eating a steak salad, chatting to a young waitress who cracked her bubblegum when she spoke.

"Sheriff Warner, can I speak to you?" Ana asked, her professional face in place.

He looked her up and down before pushing out a chair with his foot. "My pleasure, ma'am. Why don't you join me?"

"I'm here on official government business."

The young girl frowned but whipped out her ordering pad. "What can I get you, ma'am?"

"Iced tea, please." Ana sat.

Warner asked, eyes dancing. "What branch?"

"FBI." She held out her badge.

He glanced at it, nodded. "Fancy suit." He gave her black pantsuit a cursory glance. "Pretty conspicuous."

"Joe Mack is in trouble."

He snorted. "You got that right. Bigwig from SRM came over earlier, demanded I arrest Mack. I'm going to serve the arrest warrant … sometime soon."

Ana relaxed her shoulders. "I suppose you know this 'bigwig' is not acting on the government's behalf, but his own."

"I figured." Warner took a bit of steak and lettuce.

"Sheriff, I believe they mean to kill Joe and take over his property. I've been sent here to stop it."

"You and what army?" He drank his soda, his gaze fixed on her face.

Ana smiled. She found Sheriff Warner more than a little handsome—in a devilish Latin way—intoxicating black eyes and just a little salt in his black hair. The scruff on his jaw made him appear dangerous. She trusted him right off.

"I'm capable of handling Major Donald and his heavies." Ana sat up straighter.

"Do you have a phaser under your jacket I don't know about, maybe a couple of photon torpedoes in your car?" He chuckled.

"No, Sheriff, I'm not from Starfleet, I'm only FBI." She inclined toward him. "Major Donald doesn't know that. He believes I work undercover as a double agent."

Warner took a long pull of soda. "How can I help you?"

May 20, 1998—Wednesday, **Have Fun Stormin' the Castle, —** *Mad Max from* The Princess Bride, *(Ana's favorite romantic movie)*

At four thirty a.m., Ana drove her rental car to the gate of Sunrise Ranch and stopped. She pushed the button.

"What the hell are you doing here?" Joe shouted through the intercom.

"Good morning to you, too, Joe," Ana said. "I need to talk to you."

"The hell you do. How come your handler didn't kill you?"

She winced. "He tried."

Joe said some volatile words. "I never want to see you on my property again. Do I make myself clear? Now get going."

"I know you're upset with me, but I need to explain something—"

"Who is it, Joe? Who are you yelling at?" Ana heard Sam in the background. After that, raised voices.

After a few minutes and a lot of arguing peppered with harsh words, there was silence. Ana hadn't meant to cause problems between Joe and his girlfriend.

"I'm sorry about Joe," Sam said, and the box squawked. The large wrought iron gate swung open.

Yay for Sam. At least she maybe had one friend on the ranch.

Ana drove around the last stand of tall pines before Joe's ranch house came into view. Joe stood on the porch, shotgun in his hands, feet spread wide apart. His shirt unbuttoned like he'd just thrown it on. He'd left the top button of his jeans unfastened, and his feet bare. The dogs stood like sentinels at his side. Spike bared his teeth.

Sam walked out of the house wrapped in a fluffy bathrobe, her feet bare as well.

Something was afoot. Ana couldn't fight her smile. "Well, Joe, you old dog. Good for you, Sam," she said to herself.

Ana stopped the vehicle, killed the engine. Keeping her hands above her head, she rounded the open driver's door and took slow, cautious steps to the porch stairs. Her gaze never left Joe's face. His fingers twitched on the trigger of the gun.

"I ought to kill you where you stand," he ground out.

"That would be a shame, Joe, because I'm an FBI agent and you'd have worse than Major Donald down on your neck in about a half-minute."

Sam reached Joe, threaded her arm through his. "Really? How exciting for you." She leaned up and kissed Joe's scruffy cheek. "Give her a chance."

"I don't want her here. She's a spy for Major Donald."

"He and my handler, Jim Ports, were working in collusion and lied to me," Ana said.

Sam leaned close to him. "See, Joe, dear, I told you there had to be some reasonable explanation."

He thrust the business end of the gun at Ana, aimed at her heart. "Why did you come on my property to deceive me?"

"Can I put my hands down?" Ana smiled, hoping to appear positive, but the dogs snarled at her. "And can you call off the dogs?"

"Keep them where I can see them." Joe didn't lower the gun. "Shep, Spike, at ease." The dogs relaxed. Shep's tongue lolled out. He'd always liked her. Spike looked ready for lunch with her as the entrée.

"Can I talk to you? Please?" She didn't mean to beg.

"Come on, Joe." Sam tugged on his arm. "Let the lady explain herself."

His frowning scowl could peel skin, but he lifted his chin in a semi-nod, jerking the barrel of the rifle toward the house.

Ana jogged up the stairs, keeping her hands out in front of her.

Sam led the way inside and motioned for Ana to have a seat on the l-shaped leather sofa. The thing was curl-up comfortable. She sat on the edge, her back ramrod straight. The coming fight wasn't going to be easy. However, at least she had Sam on her side.

Joe stood by the fireplace, never said a word. Ana explained about Ports and how they'd worked together on other cases. She didn't know Major Donald, or what he did. She'd only been told Joe operated a drug distribution point for a Mexican drug cartel.

When she finished speaking, silence greeted her. Ana hadn't meant to scare them, just let them know they had to defend themselves, or Joe had to give them back what he'd taken.

Sam stood by Joe's side, wrapped her arms around her body. Joe looked like someone with a life or death decision to make. He didn't speak.

After a long silence, Joe asked, "Why should I trust you now?" His face was an angry mask. "You work for Major Donald."

"You're right, I did. But I don't now. They fed me incorrect intel about you and your situation. I contacted my ... friend in San Francisco and he did some research on SRM and Major Donald." Ana took a breath, gripped her hands in her lap. "Seems his men are ex-military and former C.I.A. as well. They're mercenaries who now work for private security firms for the U.S and anywhere else in the world."

Joe gripped the rifle until his fingers turned white. "Why would they keep scouring my property day after day, scattering and killing my beef cattle?"

"I'm so sorry. I have no idea." Ana's fingernails pressed into her palms. She didn't know what Major Donald or Ports were doing.

"What were they looking for in the canyons up by Sunrise?"

"I don't know. Jim told me they'd built and were testing a reconnaissance plane to spy on drug cartels in the Central and South American jungles. They told me it was missing."

Joe glanced at Sam as though he didn't want to tell Ana what had happened. Sam smiled and nodded.

He stared at Ana, his nostrils flaring, chin jutting out. "They spent weeks flying over the ranch and the mountains on my side like they were mapping out the whole area from Sunrise Mountain peak to my compound."

Ana shook her head and shrugged.

"Maliciously, they swooped into the middle of my herd, scattering them, and killed a new mama cow and her calf."

"I'm so sorry, Joe." Ana twisted her hands.

Sam took the rifle from his hands and laid it on the table. "It was after that when Dr. Basua, an associate of Major Donald's, tried to kill my daughter and Robbie."

Stomach roiling with anger, Ana swore.

Joe's scowl said he still didn't trust her. "After that, the attacks on the ranch increased. On our Easter celebration, a fire started up on Flat Ridge. Later, I caught one man snooping around, and tied him to my two draft horses, Indian style."

Ana snorted and covered it with a tiny giggle. "I would love to have seen that."

"The big man himself came to see me after several failed attempts to purchase the ranch from me. The major brought two of the biggest S.O.B.s I'd ever seen as backup. The black guy, Ports was with him."

"I didn't know any of this."

"But when Ports and Locke came back and beat up Ricardo and shot his son, Sal, I'd had it and followed them into town and took them both down."

"I wondered why Ports' wrist was in a cast and he was hot to get you." She frowned. "And after all that, you had no idea why they were searching your property?" Although, from the shrewd expression on Joe's face, she'd bet her apartment in Virginia he knew what Major Donald was looking for and why. It didn't matter to her, only that mercenaries were harassing him, and it had to end.

"So." She leaned back against the sofa. At least it didn't look as though Joe would use the rifle on her just yet. "How'd you figure out I wasn't a homeless person looking for work?"

"I gave you a couple of tests."

Ana huffed. "Right. The hay bale in the barn and rabbit hunting test."

"Yep. I also searched your duffle bag, found some of your other names and addresses."

"You nearly got me killed." Ana folded her arms. "Major Donald told my handler to take care of me. Luckily, I took care of him first."

"You killed him?" Sam's dark eyes widened.

"No. I dumped Ports off in Shadow Pines at the doctor's office."

"I should get dressed and go to work," Sam said after another long pause.

"I don't think that's a good idea," Joe said. "They could pick you off at your office, on the road to and from, or when you're at clients' homes."

Sam gripped her hands in front of her. "I can't live my life afraid of what might happen. I have to do my job. People depend on me to take care of their animals. The Harris' mare is about to foal. I can't just sit here waiting to be picked off should I go out our door."

Joe held Sam by her elbows. "It might be better if you stayed in town, keep Jessica and Robbie there, too."

"Don't tell us what to do, dear." Sam stroked his beard-roughened jaw. "We're in it for the long haul."

"Damned stubborn woman."

"That's right. I'm your damned stubborn woman."

He grinned and tapped her chin. "Don't I know it? Take my .38. It'll fit in your doctor's bag."

She smiled and kissed him solidly on the lips—didn't matter that Ana was sitting less than five feet from them—face blazing.

They all jolted when a horn sounded outside. Joe grabbed his rifle and strode to the front door. Sam tightened her bathrobe belt and dug the .38 out of the coffee table drawer. "You never know when you'll need a gun." She grinned.

Ana pulled her Glock out of her shoulder holster. "Nope. You never do."

"What the heck is goin' on?" A sleepy-eyed Robbie Meyers asked as he and a mussed-up young lady—Ana could only assume was Jessica Stone—faltered out of the hallway leading to the two back bedrooms. Ana gaped in surprise to see the young couple in the house where Sam had stayed the night with Joe.

When she, Sam, Robbie, and Jessica reached the porch, Joe was throwing his arms around a frail-looking Mexican man. Must be the infamous Ricardo, Joe spoke so glowingly about.

Joe clapped him on the back. "Welcome home, amigo."

An attractive Hispanic woman came around the front of the truck and embraced Sam. "Who is this?" She pointed to Ana.

"A friend who's come to help," Sam said.

"Oh, Holy Mary Mother of God." The woman crossed herself and moved to Ana squeezing her in a bear hug. "Welcome to the ranch. I'm Lettie. I trust Mr. Mack hasn't been starving to death?"

"No. I—" Ana stuttered.

A very handsome Hispanic man inched his way out of the back of the dual cab passenger door and sort of fell into Joe's arms. Joe held him for a moment in a warm embrace. "Sal, you son of a gun. How are you?"

"Fine, Joe. Getting stronger all the time." His gaze fixed upon Ana. "Who's that?"

"A friend."

Ana ran her finger around the inside of her collar. That black-eyed stare could unnerve and tempt a nun.

After patting Sal, Joe released him to a woman, probably Sal's wife, and walked over to Lettie and gave her a hard hug. "Man, have I missed your cooking."

"Hey," Sam protested. "I'm insulted."

"Yeah, me, too." Ana laughed, but sobered. "I hate to break up this loving, happy family greeting scene, but Major Donald or his goons could be closing in on the ranch right now, and you'd never know until a sharpshooter picks one or all of you off." Ana shuddered. She couldn't lose any of them. "You'd better get inside and find cover. Don't leave your dwellings without a gun or someone with a gun with you."

They all quieted and stared at her.

"Who is this woman?" Sal asked after his wife helped him hobble to the steps.

"FBI Agent Ana Penn," Joe said, frowning at her like he didn't quite trust her. "She's here to help take down the major. We'd better listen to her."

CHAPTER FORTY-ONE
The Darkness Begins

May 21, 1998—Thursday

"**Y**OU CAN'T DO THIS, MAJOR.** It's bloody uncivilized." Dr. Paul Basua wiped sweat from his brow after working over his precious spy plane. Hawke bastardized it with a dumb bomb, an unguided explosive projectile. He had conceived the bomb to be attached to the plane and then released by a radio frequency command. Killing wasn't right. They could kill some people or some of the animals on the ranch. It was cold-blooded murder.

Major Donald stalked over to Paul, gripped him by the lapels of his lab coat, jerked him to his feet. "Look, you Indian pansy, you'll do as you're told, or you'll find yourself taking a ride on a plane and dropped from a great height with no parachute."

Paul trembled, his fingers numb as he strained to pry the major's fingers off his coat. "I do not care, this is murder."

Major Donald back handed him, knocking him into the counter. He slid down to the floor, clutching the side of his head.

"Major," Hawke roared. "Watch it. That's live C-4 I'm strapping to this toy plane."

"Basua, help Hawke get that bomb attached. I don't care how you do it." The major stomped around the lab, cursing and shouting. Most of his words were unintelligible, rantings of an unhinged mind.

Paul struggled to his feet. He picked up the screwdriver he had just set down on the counter. His hand shook as he worked in a screw to attach the bomb's harness on the plane's top.

"Hold it still, will ya, Doc?" Hawke hollered from the underside of the plane. "I can't secure the bomb with you jerking it around."

Paul had not signed up for this. He never imagined the once agreeable Major Donald was a psychopath in a suit. What kind of

307

monster was he to keep calling himself a major when the military drummed him out of the service?

He killed innocent people. Paul never hurt anyone, nor would he steal silver from the government, or take out Mr. Mack. How had things turned into such an untenable situation? He should tell Major Donald to bugger off, flee the facility for good.

Major Donald stopped pacing, glanced at the men in the lab. Paul looked at them, too. All of them criminals, thugs, and gangsters, like being in a *Godfather* movie. He waited for the severed horse's head, or someone's head, to roll.

"Basua, you're gonna drop the bomb on Mack's house at precisely five a.m. tomorrow morning. Butch will shoot from his hiding spot. Hawke will fire from the opposing area, so we create a good crossfire area in the ranch compound. Meanwhile, me, Ports, and Locke will be taking down the main gate fence and attacking from the road into the ranch. We'll catch them completely off guard and kill them all. No one will come to their rescue, especially not 'Sheriff Andy Taylor,' from Mayberry. No one."

The major's eyes burned with insanity and fury. "No one stands between me and what I want." He marched to the door leading out to the elevator still mumbling about "no one."

May 22, 1998—**BLACK FRIDAY**

Butch Henry never missed his target, not even in combat situations. This wasn't combat, but a simple pop-and-drop—a total moonshot.

At 0345, Butch parked his rented SUV below Flat Ridge and lifted the tailgate. He needed to assemble his Remington M24A2 sniper rifle. This model had a detachable five-round magazine. He'd modified the gun himself, re-barreling the weapon so it could take the silencer. Let them try and determine his position after he constructed his ground nest in the tree line. It would be like dropping flies off the window screen.

He located the barely used cow trail through the trees and headed for the ranch compound. Major Donald promised the fireworks would begin precisely at 0500. He still had a good hour to reach ground zero and set up. If the bomb sent everyone in the house scurrying outside, he could pick off most targets before the major and his associates even got to the compound. It would all be over in a few seconds. Then he could lay back in his nest and savor the thrill of the kill.

At 0410, he reached what he'd already searched out, a perfect clearing between two huge pine trees. A good hide needed excellent concealment for cover and observation.

The ground was fertile with pine needles soft enough for his nest and great to pile up for elevation for the bipod. He dug in two hundred yards from the porch of the house.

Time to run through the steps he'd have to take from the instant he saw Mack appear through the front door. He considered the rise and fall of the grassy range, the gentle morning breeze blowing, and prepared himself for a likely one-shot kill. Butch adjusted his scope right twenty-eight clicks for windage, and six clicks down for elevation. He'd put his first shot dead-center of Mack's forehead.

He'd shoot on empty lungs, thinking "squeeze, squeeze, squeeze, squeeze more air out" as he slowly applied pressure on the trigger until the surprise break. If he couldn't get the shot off in three to five seconds, he had to resume breathing. Not breathing for long-range shots was imperative. He had to adjust his body's normal rhythms, slow things down. Visual acuity faded with declining oxygen, but shooting on the verge of passing out was another thrill.

Ana couldn't sleep. She listened as the clock out in the tiny kitchen ticked off the seconds. In her bones, she knew Major Donald was planning his attack for this morning. It would be too tempting a situation to pass on. With Ricardo's family home at the ranch, the major could do some severe damage. She should have asked for reinforcements. Technically, Reed was her handler on this, but she was here and in mortal danger. Could she call and ask him to come?

At three fifty-five, she rolled from her soft, warm bed and dressed. This time in all black—sweater, jeans, and tennis shoes. She needed to be quick and invisible. She twisted her dark brown hair into a ponytail and smeared black face paste to hide her lightly tanned skin. Strapping on her shoulder holster, she loaded her Glock 19 and stuffed her Smith & Wesson .9mm in the back of her jeans. Lastly, she strapped on her leg holster under her jeans and slid home her .38 Special. For extra firepower, she grabbed the Winchester .30-30 rifle Joe lent her in case of a long-distance firefight.

Ana fought the trembling. Not from fear, never from fear. The anticipation of taking out the bad guys was a thrill she couldn't duplicate. She opened the front door and listened.

Nothing but the lowing of cattle the hands had brought into the ranch compound and the other night sounds of creatures in the grasses and trees. Nothing man-made. That worried her.

A light popped on in the house. Damn them. They needed to keep all the lights off.

Crouching, Ana scurried down her steps and running a crisscross pattern, covered the open ground between her casita, through the vegetable garden, and onto the ranch house porch. She jimmied open the locked side kitchen door and walked inside to yell.

"What the hell?" Joe said as he turned away from the coffeemaker and saw someone dressed head-to-toe in black entered through the mudroom. Instinct had him reaching for a large knife from the butcher block.

"Joe, turn out the light, dammit." Ana crouched below the window level. "Do you want them to see you and take you out in your kitchen?"

Joe flipped off the kitchen light, plunging the room into darkness. He felt his way back to the counter and pushed the coffee maker button for brew. "Do you think they're out there this morning?"

"I'd bet my life on it." She gazed out the kitchen window that faced her casita and the lane toward Ricardo's family's homes. All were dark. "I should have warned you last night they might try a sneak attack before dawn."

Joe moved away from the window. "I guess I should break out the arsenal."

"Wake the others, and we'll meet in your office," Ana said. "It has the least number of windows."

He crouched-walked to the hallway leading to the bedrooms. Joe felt fear seeping into every cell of his body. He had to protect what was his.

Sheriff Cody Warner didn't know what woke him at four this morning. But it was as if someone had spoken to him, "get to the Sunrise Ranch and fast." He glanced at his sleeping wife, her face relaxed in sleep. She was a beautiful woman. Why had he ignored that for so long? She'd greeted him in the bedroom last night wearing a short silky thing and a big smile. Now he wore the big smile.

Dressing quickly and quietly, he moved to his SUV and jumped in. He radioed Deputy Vargas and told him to meet him at Mack's ranch. Also, he called Deputy Sayer and got him out of bed. He knew in his bones Major Donald would be taking the law into his own hands today and that Joe had women and children on the ranch.

Cody drove the fifteen miles to the ranch cut-off in a coffee-deprived haze. When he turned off onto the dirt road to the ranch gate, his headlights swept the broken gate and the busted camera. Dammit. He was too late.

Near Joe Mack's ranch house, Major Charles Donald let the Jeep coast to a quiet stop. He glanced at Ports, Locke, and Hawke. "That bastard Basua better drop one of those bombs precisely at five, or I'll nail his Indian hide to the wall." Charles got out and crouched down, dew wetting his camo pants.

Ports, Locke, and Hawke exited the vehicle, shutting doors quietly.

"Ports, circle the corral and come at the house from between that and the stables," Charles said. Ports nodded, the white bandage covering the hole in his dark neck glowing like a freakin' warning sign.

"Couldn't you have put a darker bandage on that hole?" Charles shook his head.

"It's white so you won't shoot me in the back." Ports hunkered down and maneuvered his way east through some of the cattle, attempting not to make them moo. The white on his neck made him look like one of the black steers with a white spot.

Charles turned toward Hawke. The man disturbed him on so many levels. "Circle east through the forested area, find Butch, and then the two of you approach from the east."

Hawke nodded but didn't move.

Charles made a motion with his finger and said to Locke, "You circle north of the house through the cattle, but be careful, they spook awful easy. Come at the house from the north through the vegetable garden."

Locke nodded and took off in a running crouch.

Hawke aimed his Glock at Charles. "This deal sucks. I should send you to the farm right now, so you don't double-cross us."

"I swear. You'll get your cut. I'll take care of you."

"I'll do the same if you skip out on us." Hawke jogged over to the tree line and disappeared.

Before Charles could take his position on the bedroom side of the house, he heard the engine of a car heading toward him. "Dammit."

Through the darkness, he saw the sheriff's vehicle. He'd have to take him out before he reached Mack. Oh, well. What's one more body?

The sheriff pulled alongside the Jeep and turned his car off. Charles hid behind Warner's vehicle. When the sheriff climbed out of the driver's side, he prepared to pounce.

From under the sheriff's Bronco, Charles watched until the sheriff finished searching all around the Jeep and headed toward him. He listened for each crunch of a footstep on the dewy dried grass. When the sheriff drew close enough, Charles flipped around his Glock and stood, catching Warner off-guard. Charles hit him square on the back of the head, knocking him out cold. The sheriff collapsed to the dirt. He should have shot him but didn't want to warn the house.

With the sheriff out for a while, Charles made for the side of the house. "Time to go nite-nite, Mack." He glanced up into the still dark morning sky. "You'd better hit your target, Basua, or it's the end for you, too."

Joe stood inside his small office. Sam, Robbie, Jessica, and Ana crowded in there as well as the two dogs. The dogs had always slept with Robbie since they were puppies. Jessica and Sam looked like they were going to cry. Joe held Sam against him, stroked her long hair gentle like he was calming a wild horse. Robbie held onto Jessica, looking equally as frightened.

"You need to get dressed," Joe told them. They nodded. "My rifles are in here, and there's plenty of ammunition. I want you to stay in the house until Ana, and I search the yard."

"Do you think they're here now?" Jessica's voice quivered.

"I do." Ana placed a calming hand on Jessica's shoulder. "It's best if you stay inside until we can determine their plan, most likely to surround the house, so keep a sharp lookout."

"I've called Ricardo and his boys." Joe glanced at the computer monitor. "He and Mike will hide behind the pig house and chicken coops. Sal is too injured to help, but he'll have a rifle to protect his and Mike's family. Lettie and her daughters-in-law have rifles, too."

"Gosh, it sounds like we're preparing for the Alamo." Robbie's voice quivered as well.

"Not the Alamo," Ana said, her black-painted face grinning. "We're prepared and sheltered. "I've called Sheriff Warner and left him a message to get here A.S.A.P."

"A message?" Sam's eyes went a bit wild. Joe stroked her back in soothing circles. She clung tight to him.

"Okay, family, it's time to take these bastards down and protect our ranch." Joe sounded more courageous than he felt. He worried his new love, her daughter, or Robbie might get hurt in all this crap he'd caused. Was it time to raise his hands along with a white flag and give in? He couldn't bear losing Sam now he had her in his home, in his heart. He couldn't lose any of his friends, Ricardo's family, or even Ana.

She'd come back to help when she could have abandoned them to their fate. He should show Major Donald where his piece of crap plane was and bid them farewell. But he knew the major wouldn't back down now. Joe had pushed him too far.

When everyone was dressed and outfitted with rifles and ammo, he whistled for the dogs. They came running and halted before him. "Sit." They plopped down, tongues lolling. "It's time to guard and take down," he said. "Go."

Joe stepped quickly to the front door, yanked it open. He stood off to the side as the dogs ran past him, quietly slipping into the darkness. They made it to the chickens' yard when Joe dropped into a crouch to watch them run through the yard.

The first bullet missed his head by half an inch, splintering the wood of the door jamb. He jerked but made the mistake of reaching for the door to shut it when the second bullet hit him below his right collarbone—the bullet hole burning through his shoulder furious and intense. Light-headed, he fell inside the doorway. Sam screamed. Another shot pinged inside the living room, taking out a vase of flowers.

Ana rushed to one of the windows, broke it for a small hole to fire. She shot again and in the general area of the trees eastward. "Get him inside."

Sam rushed to Joe and tugging on his good arm, pulled him into the house and slammed the door.

He'd been shot.

How stupid he'd been to not let the dogs out the kitchen door. He cursed himself for his stupidity, at the same time an enormous explosion rocked the house. "What the hell was that?"

CHAPTER FORTY-TWO
Caught in the Crosshairs

BUTCH UTTERED SEVERAL black oaths. He'd missed his target—twice. He'd only nicked Mack in the shoulder. Totally unacceptable, worthy of a court-martial. Major Donald would string him up.

Breathing hard and hands trembling, he fought to catch his breath. He had to make the next shots count. If he couldn't get to Mack, he'd take out his woman, or Ports' asset, Ana, who screwed with them.

He hugged the gun to his chest. Calm. Calm. Calm. He adjusted for the wind—again, adjusted for elevation—again. Butch breathed deep and blew out, out, out. Thrill. Remember the thrill.

He aimed. Steady. Steady. Steady.

What was that sound? A click of nails on the ground? Panting?

Just one shot. Now. Shoot.

Again, his wide shot sent splinters flying as he only nipped wood. The next thing he heard was a snarl. He turned, glanced up into black eyes, saw brown and gold fur. A wolf or bear? No, a dog?

Oh, hell. I'm a dead man!

The animal attacked, sinking its fangs into Butch's arm in a vise-like grip. Pain. Blood. So much blood. Get the animal off me. He shook his arm, the pain unbearable. A growl from the other side of his nest drew his attention. Another animal—black as midnight. Two wild dogs? "Good doggie."

Blackie lunged, shoved him into his nest, and snapped its powerful jaws too close to Butch's throat. With maximum effort, he pushed his forearm against the black dog's heaving chest. He couldn't have his throat ripped out by this wild animal.

The first dog continued to gnaw on his arm. The pain intense and wicked, he nearly passed out.

315

Blackie lunged again, missed his throat, but tore a chunk out of Butch's jaw and lip. His scream pierced the morning air like a tortured animal. His knife, he needed his knife. If he could reach it with one arm.

When Blackie retreated, Butch reached for his boot, drawing out his knife. He swung at the brown dog, jaws fastened on his arm. He missed, but the dog let go and backed off, growling. He kicked out at the pair, knife in hand.

Swiping at the iron-scented blood oozing from his face and arm, he licked his hand. He'd always liked the taste of his blood.

"What are you waiting for?" He taunted the animals. Both growled but didn't leap. He had enough time to reach for the handgun lying on the side of his nest.

The brown and gray dog jumped. Butch fired. The dog's body flinched, but flew across him, landing in a whimpering heap. Blackie ran to its companion, sniffed, then turned on him, a feral glaze in its dark eyes.

"Come on, let's finish this." Butch waved the gun and knife in the air.

Blackie attacked, ripped the gun from his hand and went for the knife.

Samantha's hands shook as she pressed the rolled-up towel as tight to Joe's wound as she dared. The bullet missed the artery, thank goodness.

"W-hat was that explosion?" Joe hissed through gritted teeth.

"I don't know."

Ana returned with a first-aid kit. "How is he?"

Joe struggled to talk. "Don't talk about me like I'm not here and bleeding to death on my hardwood floor."

Samantha shushed him. "Apparently, he's okay. Now lay still and let me look at you." She glanced up at Ana. "Luckily, the bullet entered just a centimeter below his clavicle, a direct through and through of his subclavius muscle since there's an exit hole. It missed his upper rib by another fraction of an inch," she said, her human medical training kicking in.

"I found a flashlight." Ana pushed the button, shined it at Joe so Sam could see the wound better.

Joe pointed at Ana, hands shaking. "What was that explosion? Is anyone hurt?"

"I don't know," Ana said. "I'll see."

Keeping below the window level, she crept out of the darkened family room.

Samantha took a deep breath and blew it out. Another few inches closer, she would not be holding down a living Joe.

She cleaned Joe's wound with a bottle of water Robbie brought her. Then disinfected the area with a bottle of alcohol until he swore and nearly passed out. Dressing the wound carefully on both sides, she was pretty sure the bleeding had stopped.

Joe did black out. Samantha rocked him in her arms, praying they'd survive this day.

"That sure was some explosion. I wonder what happened." Robbie sat with Jessica on the floor of the living room, holding hands and rifles.

Samantha nodded to them. "I don't know. Ana went to find out. I think you two need to get back in the bedrooms, cover the west side of the house and keep watch."

They nodded and crawled away. Samantha worried for her daughter, but they needed to help.

On her hands and knees, Ana returned to Samantha and Joe. "Looks like someone was a little anxious. They blew up your vegetable garden. Carrot shrapnel everywhere." She chuckled. "Fortunately, their bomb took out one of their henchmen. I don't know his name, but I believe he's dead."

"Which one?" Joe's face paled.

"I don't know anyone other than Ports," Ana said.

"Why would they blow up the garden?" Samantha asked.

Ana rubbed her arms. "I think they meant to hit the house."

"Oh, hellfire." Samantha felt the blood drain from her face. "We should move Joe behind the leather sofa to protect him."

"N-no," he mumbled. "Need to ... get ... to the truck."

"You're not going anywhere." Samantha held him against her.

"They might send the plane with another bomb." Joe's voice faded in and out. "They might not miss again."

Mike and Papa, hunkered down between casitas, guns ready. They'd seen the bomb hit the garden from their vantage point and a man fly into the air and land near the squash. He didn't move again.

Mike heard whimpering behind him. He turned. Shep hobbled toward the garage.

"Papa, Shep's been shot," Mike said. He gripped Papa's shoulder, turned him toward the east pasture. "Look."

Ricardo gazed where Mike pointed. Limping, Shep made it as far as the grassy area behind the chicken coop before he whimpered and collapsed.

"We have to get to him," Papa said.

"We can't go out in the open until the sniper is neutralized." If he could only get to that bastard firing from the tree line, he'd kill him.

The sky was on the verge of lighting with the dawn. Mike noticed a black blur racing across the open grassland toward them. When Spike drew closer, his muzzle appeared covered with blood. Had he been shot, too? "Come Spike. Come."

The dog ran to him, almost knocked him over in his haste. He looked up at Mike and then at Ricardo as if begging them to help. Mike ran his hands over the dog. "No injuries."

"I no hear more shots," Papa said.

"I'm going to go with Spike and see if that guy's still alive. Stay here. Protect the houses." He patted the dog's head "Come Spike. Find the bad guy."

The dog leaped into a run with Mike running all out to keep up.

"Stupid son-of-a-bit— Basua." Charles uttered some more colorful words. "Idiot." Basua missed the house with the bomb. Locke hadn't moved since the bomb hit. He was pretty sure

Locke bought it. Had Basua done that on purpose? "Wait till I get back to SRM, Doctor. Your number's up."

Charles couldn't locate Ports in all the confusion, and he wasn't answering his commlink. And the shots from Butch had ceased.

He'd been right to send Hawke into the forest to locate Butch. Something must've happened to that psychopath sharpshooting assassin. They should be charging in from the east now. This sneak attack hadn't taken anyone by surprise.

Mike could barely keep up with Spike. The black dog covered the dew-dampened grassland like a ghost. About two hundred yards from the compound, Spike tore off through the trees to the south of Joe's property. Had the sniper set up there?

He didn't wait long to find out. The smell of death hit Mike. The rusted iron stench was heavy here. He crossed himself, kissed his thumb. Holy Mother of God. What lay before him had once been a man. Spike stood before the kill, his tongue lolling like he was saying, "Look at what Shep and I did."

Mike couldn't help the man now. He had to get back to Shep and see if the dog survived.

Sheriff Cody Warner came to with an anvil pounding in his head and blurred vision. What had happened to him? He was lying in bed next to his loving wife and then … and then? He'd had a feeling he needed to get to Joe Mack's place. Someone clobbered him from behind—bushwhacked. Now he was lying in the wet grass, possibly bleeding from a gash on his head, and had no idea what was going on.

He reached for his cell phone, dialed Mack's cell phone.

A woman answered on the third ring. "Hello?"

"Who is this?" Cody asked.

"FBI Agent Ana Penn."

"Where's Mack?"

Ana sighed. "He's been shot."

"Damn. Is he alive?"

"Yes. We need help."

"I've been … held up myself. I wonder where my deputies are."

"We're all in the house. I think two have circled the barn and stables. The major is somewhere to the west side of the house by the cattle. The goon on the north side was eliminated, but we have a sniper up in the trees."

"Dammit." Cody got up to his knees, head on fire, vision floating in and out of focus. "I'll get there as fast as I can. Do you think Mack can make it to a truck so we could get the hell out of here?"

"I'll see if he's up to it. He's lost a lot of blood."

"I'll be there in a minute," Cody said. "And … tell Mack I have a warrant for his arrest."

Ana chuckled. "Good luck serving it." She hung up.

Tender arms held him. Cindy? "No, my love," Cindy said to Joe. "I'm not going to come here anymore. You have Sam to care for you now. Remember, I'll always love you." She tenderly kissed his cheek and faded away.

"Cindy. No. Don't leave me."

"I'm here, Joe. Just me," Sam said.

"Sam." Joe's eyes fluttered open. "My Sam—my brave Indian angel."

She kissed him softly. Another shot rang out and smashed into one of Cindy's favorite lamps shattering it.

Ana returned fire. "I think Ports is in the stables."

Joe felt strength returning to his legs. He had to get them out of the house. "We need to get to the truck and get out of here."

"Sheriff Warner just called," Ana said. "He'll be here in a minute."

"The cavalry's here." Sam half-grinned. "Ana, Joe needs a sling."

"There are sheets in the master bedroom. Second drawer," Joe said. "I'll be ready to run when Warner gets here."

Ana crab-walked through the hallway door of the bedroom. Nice place. Again, with the western theme, turquoise colors. She crept to the chest-of-drawers. Most of the sheets were turquoise, but she found a white top sheet and ripped a long strip from it.

A shot rang out, hitting the wood of the chest an inch above her head. Dropping to the floor, she belly-crawled to the broken sliding glass door. She poked the rifle through the crack, sighted the loft door, and waited. "Come on, you jackass. Show yourself."

The barrel of Ports' rifle punched out the open door.

"Just a few more inches," she said.

He stepped in the doorway for a second. Ana fired. Wood splintered at his head level. A shout of pain rippled through the air.

"Got him." Ana hurried into one of the back bedrooms, the one where Jessica crouched, looking out the window. "You okay?"

"Fine." She didn't look okay. She kept twisting her long black hair, nervous as a cat.

Ana patted her shoulder. "You're doing okay."

"Is that man" —she pointed toward the garden— "is he dead?"

"Yes."

"This is unreal." Jessica's eyes were dilated.

Ana glanced out the window. The morning was blossoming bright and colorful. Red streaks danced across the grassy field beyond the back porch. Something moved between the legs of a big cow. Major Donald.

"Jessica, do you think you could hit the ground in front of that big bull over there?" Ana pointed to a large black bull with his head in the grass.

Jessica knelt up and peeked over the window sill. "I think so."

"Don't hit the bull. Joe'd kill us."

Jessica grinned. "He would."

"I'm going to shoot at the bull on this side. See if I can't get the cattle to run over our friend, Major Donald."

Jessica giggled nervously. "That would be fun to watch."

"Okay. Aim carefully. On three."

On her count of three, she and Jessica shot. The bull bellowed and took off running. A hop-skipping Major Donald danced around the stampeding cattle until he was in plain sight. Ana sighted his heart and squeezed off another shot, she only managed to hit his shoulder. He spun around, then took off running. Her next shot might have clipped him in the butt. She continued to fire, only hitting the ground behind him. Damn. He ran around the side of the house and out of her vantage point.

"Keep your eyes open and let me know if he comes back." Ana patted Jessica's shoulder.

Jessica nodded, her hair bouncing forward. "Okay. And thanks. That was exciting."

Ana said nothing. She was a trained killer, but anytime she didn't have to kill was a good day.

CHAPTER FORTY-THREE
Shootout at Sunrise Corral

JOE, SOMEWHAT REVIVED** after Cindy's brief ghostly visit, shook off his lightheadedness and fought to regain his feet. He wobbled just getting to his knees. Where was his rifle? The gun lay on the floor where he dropped it after being shot. He slowly moved to the front windows. This crap had to stop and now.

"You can't do this, Joe." Sam's dark eyes shimmered with fear. "You're seriously hurt and have lost a lot of blood."

"Look, angel, it's the only way out of here." Joe opened the Winchester .30-30, checked for shells. "We're easy targets in this house. That first bomb could have taken us out."

Sam wiped a tear away. "You'd be the same running out in the open."

A noise drew Joe's attention back to the kitchen.

"Look what I found crawling around outside." Ana, hunched over, crept back toward him and Sam. Sheriff Warner crawled into the family room behind her.

Joe growled at Warner. "About time you got here."

"Can I use your cell phone?" Warner asked Joe.

"Why?"

"I need to warn my deputies they're walking into an ambush. Perhaps they should circle around and come in from Flat Ridge."

Joe handed Warner his phone, standing without hanging onto anything. Doing that much took all his energy.

Ana took her position in front of one of the windows. She'd opened it instead of busting the glass.

Warner spoke to one of his deputies, telling him to call in reinforcements from Auburn. He handed the phone back to Joe. "You got more rifles?"

"On the table." He pointed to the coffee table lined with rifles and ammunition. Warner grabbed the Winchester .30-30 and some shells, loaded it, and pocketed the rest.

Shots continued to ring out from the stable door. Joe had to get to his truck. About one hundred feet of open territory and at least three gunmen, if not four, between the house and the garage. They were surrounded.

"Ana, Warner, I'm gonna need some cover so I can make a dash for the garage and get the truck." Joe loaded his pockets with shotgun shells.

"That's impossible." Sam shook her head. "It's suicide. We don't know where this Major Donald is, and what about another bomb?"

Ana spoke up. "Actually, Major Donald is probably around the north side of the house. I shot him, and he ran around there."

Joe glared at Ana. "But you didn't kill him?"

She shrugged. "Anyone can have an off day."

He shook his head. "What we do know is if we stay in the house and they drop another bomb, they'll kill all of us. I don't have time to argue with you, Sam."

She drew her bottom lip between her teeth, tears glazed her eyes, but said nothing.

"Wait," Ana said. "Look."

Joe and Warner scooted up to the windows. Beyond the garage in the grassy meadow, Mike was carrying Shep. Joe saw blood dripping from the dog's paw. "Shep's been hurt."

"Mike's bringing him to the house." Sam's voice vibrated with fear. "How can we warn him to stay back, and get to the truck instead?"

"I've got this." Ana moved away from the window and scampered out of the family room before anyone could stop her.

"Wait, Ana," Sam cried. "It's too dangerous."

"She's trained for this, my angel." Joe gripped Sam's shoulder to comfort her. "Take her place by the window and cover me."

A tear ran down Sam's cheek. She swiped angrily at it and reached for the rifle she'd laid down while she'd attended to him. He could kiss her for her bravery.

"Look." Sam pointed. "There she goes."

They peeked out the front windows. Ana streaked like a shot across the dirt lane between the ranch house, Ricardo's casita, and the chicken coop. She was good. A bullet hit the dirt at her feet. She rolled, came up to her knees, and fired at the stables, smashing off a piece of the barn door. Damned good shot, too.

"When she brings Mike and Shep back, I'll have the truck ready for us all to jump into." Joe touched Sam's cheek, brushing away another tear. "We're going to be all right, but we have to work together."

"Jessica, Robbie. Shoot at anything that moves within your field of vision, okay?" Joe hollered, the effort nearly knocked him flat.

They both shouted back in the affirmative.

"When you hear the truck, come running. We'll only get one shot at this."

Warner smiled at Joe's pun but nodded.

Joe sucked in a deep breath, blew it out. "I'm going out the same way Ana did. Cover me."

"You be careful." Sam gripped a handful of his shirt and hauled him close for one last kiss.

A bullet broke the front window and whizzed past where Joe's head would have been.

Ana hid behind the pig house and gagged at the pungent odor. She glanced toward the east and into the rising sun. Mike was struggling to carry the big German shepherd. A shot rang through the clear air and struck Mike's arm, flinging him and the dog around. Both went down, the dog whimpered in pain. Mike grunted.

She studied the spot by the barn where the rifle fired from and got off a couple of shots. That'll keep him down for a minute.

"Are you all right, Mike?" she called to him.

The tall grass hid him and the dog. "I'm okay. Just nicked my arm. I don't think I can carry the dog and shoot."

"I'm coming. Hold on."

With Joe and Cody keeping Ports pinned down in the stables, Ana shot in the direction of Mike's shooter and took off running. Behind her, someone scrambled around the vehicles parked in the garage where Joe's dual cab ranch rig was parked.

She had to get Shep and Mike and help them back to the truck. Halfway there, she dropped and rolled, coming to rest on her belly. She scanned the forest to the east and south of her position, searching for movement, a sign, anything. Nothing.

Mike called to her. "Shep and Spike took out the sniper, but there's another man loose in the woods behind the barn. And then the guy in the stables."

For a moment, a ray of the new day's sunshine bounded off a metal object at the edge of the barn. Ana aimed and fired. Wood splinters flew into the air, and someone groaned in pain. "Gotcha."

She rose to her feet, running to where Shep and Mike lay. "Can you make it? You weren't shot in the leg, were you?"

"No." Mike's face twisted in pain when she checked his shoulder wound.

"I think you'll live." Ana tried to smile.

He grinned. "Thanks, Doc."

"Here, take my rifle. Keep shooting toward the edge of the barn. I know I got him, but I don't know how bad." Mike took the rifle and loaded in some shells she'd handed him.

Ana knelt and gently slid her arms under the whimpering dog. With great effort, she struggled to lift him against her chest.

"He's heavy," Mike said.

"No kidding," she huffed. "Cover me and run."

A shot rang out and hit the dirt in front of Ricardo's feet. He raised his rifle and shot at the shadow in the stable's hayloft. Inside, the horses would be loco. He had to get to the stalls. Raising his rifle, he shot again, chipping wood off the upper stable door frame, and ran across the yard.

The horses stamped wildly around in their confined stalls, nickering, and whinnying in fear. Ricardo placed his gun against the boards of the stall and opened the first gate. "There now, boy. *Calmarse, calmarse.*" He stroked the horse's long neck and led him by his harness to the outside door. With a click of the lock, he sent the horse galloping out into the open corral. Better outside.

He did the same with the other horses, even his horse, Chaco, and Checkers, Joe's horse. But what about Ivy? He soothed the old horse with even strokes and soft words. "*Calmarse, calmarse.*" She might be better off inside. No sense giving the old gal a heart attack.

"Come out of that stall, old man."

Ricardo's heart pounded. He glanced up to see the black man who'd shot Sal and beat him up. The man held his own rifle on him.

¡Estúpido, estúpido!

Sal Sanchez watched what was happening from the small family room of Papa's casita, anger building like thunderclouds in his aching chest. Mamá, his wife and kids, and Mike's family were in the back bedroom with the children all huddled beneath a mattress. His gunshot belly burned watching his friends take bullets, and unable to help. For all he knew, his friends and family could be laying around the ranch compound bleeding or dying.

"I gotta help, Mamá," he said to her when she laid a hand on his shoulder.

She looked pained. "Give me a rifle."

He loaded a rifle and handed it to her. "I have to find Mike and Papa, bring them home."

"Yes." She bowed her head to hide her weeping.

"Will you cover me?"

"Yes, *mi hijo*, be careful."

He kissed her age-spotted cheek and cautiously opened the door. No one was watching the row of little casitas. He slipped between the chicken and pig house, and back around the side of the open garage. Joe started his rig and was backing out when a bullet pinged the back fender.

Sal glanced toward the source of the shot and saw the big black man who'd shot him. He walked out of the stables with a handgun to Papa's head, his other massive arm still in a cast around Papa's throat.

Sal's gut injury turned hard and cold. He crouched behind the old stake-bed truck of Elmer's. All he needed was one clean shot.

"Everybody stop shooting, or I'll kill the old man," Ports shouted. "Put down your guns and come out of the house." He motioned with his gun. "You too, Mack. Get out of the truck."

Hearing the whimpering dog, Sal glanced eastward, raising his hand to shield his eyes from the rising sun. The FBI agent, Ana, clutched Shep to her chest and was struggling to reach the safety of the garage. Mike followed, his usually tanned face pale. His hand clutched his bloodied shirt. Had he been shot?

Joe stopped the truck in front of the ranch house but didn't throw out his weapon. "Don't do anything stupid, Ports," Joe hollered at him. "We've got a lot of guns trained on your head."

"I'll kill you all." Ports moved his gun from Papa's head and fired in Ana's direction. She halted as the bullet kicked up grass in front of her feet. Mike held his weapon at his side out of sight.

Sal couldn't handle the fury.

The noise of a small engine filled the morning sky. Another spy plane—Papa's demon silver plane. "Son of a—"

Sunrays bounced off the plane still some distance from the compound. However, the noise was enough of a distraction for Ports' gaze to stray to the sky.

Resting the rifle on the hood of the old truck, Sal aimed carefully. An inch too low and he'd shoot Papa in the head. Too high, he'd miss Ports.

He held his breath, softly and slowly squeezed the trigger.

Ports' head jerked back when Sal's bullet hit him right between his eyes. He opened those brutal, evil eyes wide in shock, then rolled them back in his head. With his finger still on the trigger, Ports managed to squeeze off a wild shot, then the gun dropped to the ground.

Papa rushed to Mike, clutched him around the waist and helped him run to where Sal stood still shaking from the shot. Together they hurried back to Papa's casita and safety.

He'd killed that jackal. Sal never felt more justified.

Ana raced for Joe's truck idling by the front porch steps. A bullet coming from the side of the barn dented the truck's fender. Hawke? She laid Shep gently down on the truck bed, slid him over, and climbed in. "I've got Shep."

Sheriff Warner opened the front door of the house, got off a couple of rifle shots at the barn. Jessica and Robbie ran out, shooting in two directions. They opened the back door of the truck cab and scrambled in.

Sam was next. A bullet zipped through the air and notched a porch post above her head. She screamed but raced down the stairs.

Ana pulled her Glock from her shoulder holster and fired in the direction of the barn. "Hurry," she said to Sam. "Jump in the back with Shep."

Sam nodded and climbed into the bed, lying down next to the dog. She stroked and comforted him as he whined.

From between the garage and the chicken coop, a furry black dart streaked. It vaulted into the bed of the truck, tail wagging. Spike.

"Warner. Now," Ana shouted. She turned and glanced in the direction of Ricardo's home. Mike, still holding his rifle, crouched down and jogged across the lane until he reached the truck. Ana helped him in and made him lay down. No one else came from the casitas.

Ana shouted, "Go, go, go," at Warner. "We have to go now."

He rushed from the doorway just as a rifle shot rang out. The bullet hit Warner in the upper thigh, spinning him around, and flinging him to the porch floor.

"I'm hit," he hollered.

Ana pounded on the sliding window of the cab. "Pull the truck forward, Joe. We have to get Warner."

The truck inched forward, everyone inside ducking for cover. Ana jumped out of the back and reached Warner, gripping his arm to pull him to his feet. He howled in pain.

"I can't walk." He moaned.

"You can and you will." Another bullet hit a post near her head. "Move. Now."

She struggled under his weight, his arm around her shoulders, her arm around his waist, as he hobbled to the truck. Robbie opened the back door. Ana helped Cody climb onto the running board and into the back seat where he collapsed with a groan against Robbie and Jessica. "See you at Sam's office." She slammed the back door and hurtled over the side of the truck bed.

As they roared around the corner of the house, a man dressed all in black except for a brightly colored scarf waving in the breeze, stepped from the barn and fired. His shot dinged the tailgate of the truck.

Ana fired her Glock at him catching him in the arm, but he didn't lower his gun. Even with blood dripping, he raised his hand to fire.

She raised her gun and tapped him two times in the forehead, one mid chest. Hawke crumbled to the ground. Was that the last of Donald's hired guns? Gosh, she hoped so.

Major Donald, now standing on the south porch rifle in hand, fired. He hit the fender of Joe's truck. Ana turned and shot in his direction. Porch wood splintered. He gripped the side of his head.

Sirens split the morning air. The major and his thugs—no matter how many—would think twice about staying on the ranch with the added law enforcement closing in fast.

Ana relaxed against the inside of the truck bed. Her new friends had been injured, but they were alive.

Something silver in the sky was illuminated by the sunbeams. A small plane—the spy plane. Holy crap. It headed for the house. She should tell Joe to stop, but she couldn't. To go back would jeopardize all their lives.

Something dropped from the plane when it neared the house. The bomb.

The explosion rocked the truck and sent a fireball of flames and a thick plume of black smoke boiling into the air. Joe's beautiful ranch house—gone.

Dear God, they'd come so close to being killed.

Ana needed to call Reed.

CHAPTER FORTY-FOUR
Tying Up Loose Ends

GROGGY FROM THE SHOT Sam gave him to stitch up his shoulder, Joe faded in an out of consciousness. The bed beneath him was uncomfortable—an animal exam table. His shoulder blazed like someone had branded him clean through. Sam and her assistant ran around in the back of her vet's office. Jessica was helping, too. It was much easier to stay in the dim state of floating than to wake up. Waking up meant facing what had happened to his family and friends, remembering the destruction of his home.

Slipping back into unconsciousness, the nightmare he hadn't had for three months swamped him.

The day of September 1996 had been hot and miserable. Joe had purchased a wall air conditioner for their master bedroom to keep Cindy comfortable. He had it on low even though the temperature outside had soared past one hundred degrees. He sat on the side of his and Cindy's bed holding her ice-cold hand.

"Joe, you're going to be okay." Dark purple smudges made Cindy's once clear, unmarked skin look bruised and battered. Her bright blue eyes were dull against the shrunken gray skin of her face.

"Why would you say that? I'm not going to be okay." He yanked his hand through his hair. "I don't understand. They just found this ... cancer a few months ago."

"Darling, there's no explanation for why cancer strikes, it just does." A coughing fit hit her and nearly doubled her over. He wiped the blood from the side of her mouth when she settled down.

"What am I going to do? How can I fix this?"

She gripped his hand to the point of pain. "There's nothing you can do to fix this. Just do what you have always done—work hard, take care of the ranch, and love me." She coughed, but only

331

once. "Joe, darling, I am so proud of you. How lucky I am to have been your wife."

She was silent for a moment, and Joe leaned in to make sure she was still … awake.

Her eyes fluttered open. "Do you remember the summer when I came home after graduating from college? I never imagined you'd fall in love with me, and you'd be my husband by fall."

Joe kissed the papery-thin skin of her cheek. "I'd been in love with you for a long time, but I knew your father would've skinned me alive if I'd ever acted on it."

She chuckled, but her body seized up, pain twisting her sweet face into a mask of anguish. "Oh, Joe. It hurts!"

Grief was like a dull, empty gnawing at his heart. "What can I do, sweetheart?"

"Hold me, darling, just hold me." He drew her gaunt frame into his arms and fought to be gentle. Cindy sighed "That's better."

"Hey," he said. "I have an idea. Tomorrow morning let's take a picnic to the Flat Ridge and watch the sunrise like we used to do."

"I'd like that." Cindy closed her eyes, her head drooped against his shoulder.

"Sweetheart, you have to hold on. I can't lose you." Tears scalded his throat, burned in his eyes. "We'll get through this, with all the faith and strength we have. Don't give up, please don't give up. Oh, dear God, don't take her from me."

Cindy opened her eyes once more, but her gaze was far away as if she saw something beyond his shoulder. "I love you."

"I know." He choked on the words.

"I wouldn't leave you if I didn't have to, right?"

"Oh, God." He placed a finger on her lips. "Don't talk."

"I have to say this. I don't have much time."

Joe rocked her closer. "Don't say that."

"We've had a good life. I'm just sorry I didn't leave you a child to love." She paused. "Take care of Robbie," she sputtered "He loves you..." her voice trailed off.

"Cindy? Sweetheart?" Joe didn't mean to hold her so tight. He held her away from him for a moment. Still breathing— barely.

"Joe?"

"Yes?"

"Remember that I love you. But it's time to give all your love to Sam and take care of my ranch." She coughed, glancing up toward the corner of their bedroom, her eyes open wide. "I'm coming Father and Mother. Howdy Grandpa and Grandma. Oh, the light is so beautifully bright...."

She closed her eyes once more, and her slender, emaciated body relaxed in death.

Joe had continued to hold her and rock her, his tears had soaked her sunny blonde hair.

Someone called his name, "Joe. Joe. Wake up now." They touched his uninjured arm jerking him out of his dream.

"Sam?" He opened his eyes. The face of a dark-eyed, raven-haired angel appeared above him.

"Yes. I'm here, my dear one. I'll always be here for you."

"My beautiful angel." Joe gripped her hands in his. He said goodbye to Cindy. No more regrets. He could move on. "How's Shep?"

She sat on the edge of his bed. "He'll pull through. The bullet hole in the shoulder didn't hit anything vital, thank God. Spike is keeping him company."

"How's Mike?"

"The bullet ate a chunk of skin out of his upper arm. He'll be in a lot of pain and won't be able to work the fields and orchards for a while, but he'll recover."

"Warner?"

"Had to dig one out of his thigh, the same leg he injured in high school football."

Joe chuckled. "He forgot to serve me with the warrant."

She laughed, the sound like choirs singing in heaven. He'd found his home and Sam was his next adventure. Taking that quick trip to Tahoe was the best idea he'd had in three years.

"Will you marry me, Sam?"

Her mouth shot open, and her dark eyebrows disappeared under her black bangs. "I already did. Don't you think our trip to Tahoe was legal?"

He squeezed her hands. "I'd like us to get re-married in front of all our friends—in the church this time—by Pastor English."

Her dazzling smile warmed him clean down to his toes. "Yes. I'll marry you in church—just to make it official for our friends."

Major Donald ran through the trees east of Mack's place. The undergrowth tore at his camo pants as he darted around trees and bushes. The county sheriffs from Auburn were all over the place like ants at a picnic. It wouldn't be long before they caught him. He had a general idea where Butch had set up his sniper nest.

It was the smell and the low circling of a single turkey vulture that alerted him to the whereabouts of his former friend and brother-in-arms. He located Butch's mangled body lying in a sniper's nest with his assault rifle. Damn hard to look at him, worse yet to fumble around in the guy's bloody pants pocket for the keys to his vehicle. But Charles had to get back to SRM and rip Dr. Basua apart—joint and limb. He'd missed the bomb-drop twice allowing Mack and his friends to escape.

He didn't want the sheriffs to make the connection between him and Butch, so he stole his wallet and his cell phone. Might as well take the gun, too.

Ana, the witch, had shot him. Thankfully, her bullet missed. Unfortunately, it shattered the porch post sending splinters piercing the side of his face. Blood still ran from his wounds down his cheek and neck and dribbled into the collar of his shirt. He must look a sight. Didn't matter. That son-of-a-bitch, Mack, would know he couldn't mess with Major Donald. The spy drone planes and the silver mines were his, and no one messed with him or his possessions.

Butch had parked his SUV below Flat Ridge. Charles tossed the guns in the back seat and climbed behind the wheel. He flipped down the visor and stared into the mirror. The open splinter wounds on his right cheek would need stitches. It'd give him character, and he could claim another war-time battle won. Didn't care if Hawke bought it, he was scary anyway. Ports and Locke got whacked. Not his fault. At least he didn't have to pay them for their services mostly rendered.

He pulled the SUV out onto the highway leading around the cliffs and toward SRM. Looking up, he noticed some cave openings. Why hadn't he seen those before? Could that be where Mack hid the first spy drone? He'd have to check after he buried that betrayer, Basua.

The over-zealous sergeant was on guard duty at the shack today. Charles hoped he could hide his face from scrutiny.

"Good morning, Major." The young sergeant saluted. "You all right?" He moved closer, but Charles turned his head away.

"I'm fine, and I'm in a hurry. Open the gate."

"Sure thing, Major."

Charles floored the SUV and sped through the Facility. Basua's rented Land Rover wasn't in the main parking lot. Could the big lump have swung around and parked near the freight elevator? Was he trying to get away with the other spy drone? Charles would kill him for his betrayal and theft.

Sure enough, Basua had parked his SUV near the elevator. The lowered backseat held the body of the drone. The passenger seat held boxes of files and lab equipment.

"That British scum." he swore, and parked Butch's vehicle out of sight. He'd catch Basua when he came up. It would be tango down for Basua.

The large doors opened on the elevator as Charles crouched near the front bumper of Basua's vehicle. Fury swirled in his gut like hot lava. His sore hands curled into fists. No one betrayed Major Charles Donald. No one.

A whistling Basua carried the wings off the drone and gently placed them next to the plane's body. He was stealing Charles' baby.

Charles crept along the driver's side of the SUV, ready to pounce like a wolf. When Basua turned away from the liftgate, he jumped, catching Basua on the side of the head with a fist. The big British Indian went down in the dirt of the parking lot with a holler of pain.

Basua gripped his head in his hand. "What the bloody hell…." Dark eyes opened wide with fear. "Major Donald?"

Charles' chest heaved with hatred. "No one double-crosses me."

"What are you talking about?" Basua sat up, but Charles kicked him in the side. He groaned in pain and writhed in the dirt. "Stop, Major. I can explain."

"Explain this." Charles reached down and gripped Basua by his lapels, yanking him to his feet. He backhanded Basua across the face, snapping his head to the side. Spittle sprayed out of his mouth, mingled with blood.

Charles pulled back his fist, prepared to jab Basua in the face when he heard scuffling behind him.

"Stop Major, or I'll shoot."

Charles peered over his shoulder and found the sergeant pointing his M16 at him. He released Basua, who collapsed in a heap, and raised his hands. When he turned around, he saw the black deputy from Shadow Pines also holding his service handgun on him, and a Korean man dressed like FBI, with a piece of paper clutched in his hand.

He swore with enthusiasm as his face throbbed.

He had a feeling he would not be going back to the freedom of the jungles of Brazil anytime soon. That wouldn't stop him from getting what he wanted. "I'll get you all," Major Donald cursed. "See you in hell."

CHAPTER FORTY-FIVE
Friends and Loved Ones

May 24, 1998—Sunday

HIS ARM IMMOBILIZED in a proper sling, Joe stood in the dirt staring at the remains of his still smoldering home. The dining room, kitchen, and living room were a blackened hulk of charred wood. The north porch was gone. The roof over half of the house weakened by fire, collapsed under the weight of the water from the fire department.

Ana sidled next to him. "It could be worse."

"Yeah, we could have been in there." Joe rubbed his sore neck.

Sam stepped up beside them, linked her arm through his good one. "Only a few minor repairs and it will be good as new."

Ana and Joe glared at her.

"You are optimistic, aren't you?" Ana said.

"Bert's last words to me were 'take care of my Cindy and the ranch, you've earned them.' Look at it now," Joe said, defeat in his voice. "I couldn't save Cindy and practically destroyed his home. Bert'd turn over in his grave."

Sam scowled at Joe. "You know better than that. I'm appalled you'd even suggest you might have let Bert down. You had no control over either incident." She jogged up the porch steps and gazed in through the burned-out window of the dining room. "Hellfire. Cindy's beautiful table is toast, and about three-quarters of the house. We'll have to rebuild."

Her eyes sparkled when she spun around to face Ana and Joe. The weight of the burned-out ranch house, his wounded ranch hands, the cattle, the horses, his struggle with the government over that stupid plane—it all seemed unreal, like he was looking at someone else's life. "I don't know if I can rebuild."

"I have an idea where to begin." Ana walked up the stairs and turned to gaze at Joe. "You have to start somewhere." She bent to pick up some broken glass from one of the front windows, set the pieces on the windowsill. "I have some time off coming. Actually, I have a lot of time off coming. I would love to stay for a while. I have a big empty apartment in Washington, D.C. I need to sell." She stepped over the charred front door and picked up a picture frame. The picture was intact. Cindy, Joe's first wife. "My dad was in the military, and we traveled all over the world. But your little casita is the most comfortable place I've stayed in a long time, and the chores made me feel important like I was a big part of something special." She blushed. "Well, besides my work in the FBI."

She handed the painting to Joe who clutched it to his chest.

"I hated deceiving you." She grinned, hopeful. "So, what do you say? I'll stay. Sam's here. Robbie and Jess will be around. We'll rebuild. Make it better than ever."

Joe opened his mouth to say it was no use, but Sam squeezed his bad arm gently.

"Sounds like a plan," he muttered around the pain.

After checking on the horses and giving an upset Checkers an extra apple and oats, Joe walked with Ana and Sam and headed back to the house. Before they reached the porch, the honking of a horn coming down the ranch road sounded.

"It's Robbie and his Geek mobile." Joe laughed. "Gonna be a great summer. Riding herd, fishing, and hunting up Sunrise way."

Robbie stopped his car in front of the house and helped Jessica out. He grinned. "Hey, Joe, Sam, Ana."

Joe nodded. Sam didn't exactly smile. She still wasn't used to her Jessica being with Robbie.

Robbie poked Joe. "Looks like a lot of work to do. When do we get started?"

"I—" he grunted but was interrupted by a car honk.

A late model gold Cadillac turned the last corner before the house. Ruby, and Bill Green, and Bella, from the Steakhouse and Saloon. They parked next to Robbie.

Bill hollered. "Ruby figured you might be hungry as we tear this place down and help you rebuild." He reached into the back seat and pulled out a huge tinfoil container. "Steaks all around."

Joe's mouth watered as the smell of grilled ribeyes hit him. He

grabbed Sam by the hand, tugged her toward the car.

Not far behind the Cadillac, a brown station wagon driven by Pastor English headed in and parked. In his car were men from town came with shovels, hammers, axes, and power tools.

"What the—"

Sam pulled him down for a kiss. "Your friends have rallied around you."

After the Pastor's station wagon came other vehicles, farmers were pulling trailers with tractors, a bobcat, and a forklift.

The general store owner drove up in his bobtail truck filled with lumber, plumbing supplies, and roofing material. Plumbers, electricians, and contractors' trucks pulled in and parked. It looked like everyone from town, the old, young, and in between, came, and they brought food, too.

Joe's jaw hit the dirt. These good people—his neighbors were coming to help him.

Pastor English approached him, smiling hugely. "You and Cindy and Sam have done so much for this town, your friends are paying you back. There's a lot of work to be done, and you'll need some help to get back on your feet. Your friends are surrounding you now, just like you've always done for them." He shook Joe's hand and went to help set up the food.

Happy tears pricked the backs of his eyes. God does work in mysterious ways. *Thank you, sweetheart.* But there was no reply. She was home now with her folks.

Ana made a beeline for the last vehicle to pull in—a plain black sedan. The man who stepped out was anything but plain. He rushed to Ana and scooped her up in his arms, spinning her around and plastering her face with kisses.

"Must be Ana's Reed." Sam giggled.

"Her what?" Joe frowned.

"Her ex-husband."

"Doesn't look ex to me." Joe grinned. "Anyway, I guess there's gonna be an old-fashioned barn ... make that ... house raising tonight."

He put his arm around Sam's waist and spun her in some fancy dance steps. He twirled her out, reeled her back in, and dipped her. "I'm so happy."

She laughed. "So am I. We are blessed."

May 31, 1998—*Sunday*—**A New Life**

Joe was surprised by how quickly the scorched remains of the once comfortable home had been torn down, the debris removed, and some of his belongings salvaged. A new home had been framed and new roof put on. Somehow, the rooms were much larger than when Cindy's father remodeled the old ranch house Elmer built.

Sam told him she had a new design in mind for the house. Looked like another bedroom had been added, and another bathroom, as well as an open kitchen-dining room-family room. Was she expecting long-term company? Some family he didn't know about coming to stay.

So many friends had worked hard each day for him and Sam, some working into the night after they worked a full-time job. Sam returned to her veterinarian work and delivered two new colts and a whole slew of piglets. She was happy, lively, singing all the time. Totally out of character for the serious Doctor Samantha Stone ... make that Mrs. Joseph Mack.

Joe removed some of Cindy's treasures and wrapped them carefully to be stored away in his cellar. Even her hand-carved cedar chest filled with baby clothes he'd moved down the stairs with Robbie's help. He'd have them for Robbie when he and Jessica needed them. He could hope for grandchildren, couldn't he?

Some of the neighboring ranchers had helped his ranch hands gather the herd, settle them back in the green pastures at the foot of Sunrise Mountain for the summer. Being kids, his ranch hands had taken off to the mountain to hide when the shooting started. Just as well. Joe didn't want them to get involved in his trouble or get hurt.

He told Sam about the gold and silver mine of Elmer's he'd found. Eventually, he'd put her and Robbie's name on the claim at the Placer County Courthouse in Auburn. Get it all legal. He promised her a real honeymoon at their favorite spot in Tahoe. He couldn't wait for that. Time to move on from the past.

Wednesday morning early, Joe and Robbie took the horses and mules, Harry Truman, and Dwight Eisenhower, up to Flat Ridge to the bear cave where he'd hidden the spy plane. They hauled it down to the ranch. Ana's ex-husband, Reed Penn, took charge of it and turned it over to the FBI.

Joe was glad to be rid of the thing that caused so much trouble. What a terrible secret he'd kept hidden up near Sunrise Mountain. He could have gotten his friends and his wife killed.

Reed moved in with Ana in the casita next to the garden she helped restore and replant. Might be a late growing season, but at least they'd have fresh vegetables by fall. Reed and Ana acted like newlyweds. Joe didn't know when they'd go back to their FBI careers.

He did know they'd become his and Sam's good friends.

Today, on the barbecue spit, he was roasting a side of beef for his hard-working friends. Sam and Jessica were busy with Lettie and her daughters-in-law baking beans and creating side dishes.

Mike, Sal, and Ricardo set up tables and chairs. Joe watched from the porch in Cindy's one remaining Adirondack chair. He was exhausted and so damn happy. He hadn't heard or seen Cindy since the last dream in Sam's office. But that didn't make him sad. She was home and at peace with her parents, and that's where she'd be until they met again.

Joe moved over to a lawn chair by the grills. Half a beef rotated slowly over the flames. He breathed deep, stomach rumbling. Looking up at the sound of a car, he saw Sheriff Warner drive in and park.

Warner stiffly got out of the SUV with the help of his wife, Beverly. She looked young and beautiful today—something she hadn't looked in quite a while. Using a cane, and Beverly's help, Warner hobbled over to where Joe sat. Beverly said hello to Joe and then scurried off to help the other women.

"Mind if I sit?" Warner gestured to a chair next to Joe.

"Free country."

"You've had some excitement out here of late."

"Yep." Joe grinned.

"Government thugs killed, you shot through the shoulder, Mike too, and me, well, shot in my bad leg. All over a toy plane that riled up your cattle."

"Yep."

"Major Donald will be spending a mighty long time in federal prison for the assault and attempted murder against you, other law enforcement officers, and the Indian doctor. Basua will answer some questions, but I don't think he was involved voluntarily."

"Ah-huh."

"From the recorded footage from your cameras, we found a lot of illegal activities going on here." Warner shook his head.

"Sure 'nough did."

Warner laughed. "It's ironic you hid the plane on the government's side of the mountain right under their noses."

Joe laughed. "Yep."

Warner faced Joe, seriousness in his gaze. "You miserable S.O.B. I'm glad you're all right."

Joe examined him. "Thanks, Sheriff. I'm glad you didn't bite the big one either."

"Well, hello, gentlemen of leisure," Sam said as she approached the pair of one-time enemies. "Can I talk to my man, Sheriff?"

"Sure 'nough, ma'am." Warner doffed his hat and hobbled off on his crutches to find his wife.

Joe and Sam walked hand-in-hand past the corral and out in the field where the cattle grazed.

"It's peaceful here." She linked her arm through his, resting her head against his shoulder. "I love your ranch. I'm glad things have settled down and have gotten back to normal."

He stopped walking, pulled her close. "I won't be completely ecstatic until we've said 'I do' under the pines at the Shadow Mountain Christian Church. When?"

She giggled. "How about two weeks from today."

Joe leaned down, caressed her lips with his, savoring the sweet smell of peppermint. "Mmmm, our friends will enjoy seeing us get hitched."

"I've got something to tell you," Sam said with a wink.

"Is it about some new critter you brought into the world?"

She glanced shyly away. "Not exactly a critter."

There was a long pause before she lifted her beautiful eyes to his.

"What is it, my angel?" He nuzzled her neck, inhaling her.

She gripped his face, smiled, and kissed him. "You're going to be a father."

The Adventure Continues

With love and gratitude to my readers!

Me and my dog Roy, thank you for reading my western mystery *The Secret of Sunrise Mountain*. I am so pleased you took a chance on a new author and read my story. I hope it was everything you've wanted in a western mystery fraught with danger and love.

If you enjoyed reading about Joe, Cindy, Sam, Robbie, and Jessica, and found something that made you laugh or cry, and if you feel the book deserves a 4- or 5-Star rating, I hope you'll leave a review where books are sold. *Reviews for an author are like standing ovations to an onstage performer—only sweeter because they last longer.*

If you would like to comment about the book, or find out when my next book launches, please visit my website, JRM-Productions: http://jrm-productions.com/. Please sign up for my newsletter or follow my blog and receive life-changing and humorous articles. I often have giveaways and prizes for my faithful readers. Come by and see what's happening. Any of my friends can comment on my blog, and you are my friends.

I'm always eager to hear if something I said makes a difference in someone's life. Please feel free to contact me at my **email:** jrmproductionsco@gmail.com.

About the Author and Storyteller

John Richard Marsh (O'Brien)

 John loves to tell stories and has been a storyteller all his life. He desires to share them with his friends and fans. His background is not typical for an author. He has had careers in manufacturing, sales, commercial construction, mortgage brokering, and now as an author.

He has enjoyed being married to his wife for thirty-seven years and she still likes him. They have four children, four grandchildren, and two great-grand-children. "I have been given a blessed life," John says.

He and his production company, JRM Productions have a motto: We share compelling stories! Join us for an adventure! As you know if you've just finished *The Secret of Sunrise Mountain,* John can tell a marvelous mystery.

John is the author of three books: *The Book of John, The Secret of Sunrise Mountain,* and *Sunrise Ranch—The Search for Home.* The last two are epic historical western mysteries following the lives of one family through four generations as they traverse the American Continent settling in Placer County, California, with all the tragedies and hardships that accompany tough ranch life.

You can find him at: http://jrm-productions.com/

Facebook: https://www.facebook.com/john.obrien.3726

John is a member of the Ventura County Writers Club, https://venturacountywriters.com/, and enjoys working with other authors as they "Encourage the Craft" of writing.

Other Books by John Richard Marsh
Dangerous Journey to Sunrise Ranch

Book 1: Sunrise Mountain Western Suspense Series

In the tradition of Craig Johnson's "Longmire" mysteries comes a new epic saga.

1906—Elmer Johnsen's dream is to chug across America aboard the smoke-belching locomotives of the G.N.R.R. And though Elmer and his best friend have spectacular adventures, danger stalks them at every turn.

Elmer finds his passion in the striking blue eyes of a bold and sassy Norwegian girl, Olina, and the raw, untamed beauty of the ranchland of Placer County, California. But ranch life is not idyllic for Elmer and Olina when someone wants their ranch and will stop at nothing to possess it ... and Olina.

Surviving earthquakes, cattle rustlers, drought, the Depression, and a World War, are nothing compared to the prejudice of someone filled with bitter hatred who's threatening to destroy Elmer and his family.

Coming: Spring of 2020

Murder on Sunrise Ranch
Book 2: Sunrise Mountain Western Suspense Series

In the tradition of Craig Johnson's "Longmire" mysteries comes a new epic saga.

A riveting epic western historical mystery about a panicked rancher, Bert Johnsen's, quest to investigate and free himself from a false murder charge.

Coming: Winter 2020

The Secret of Sunrise Mountain (this novel)

Book 3: Sunrise Mountain Western Suspense Series

In the tradition of Craig Johnsen's Longmire mysteries comes a new epic series.

1998—someone or something is stampeding widower rancher Joe Mack's cattle threatening his livelihood and killing precious cows and calves.

The local sheriff won't help. He relishes punishing Joe for "ruining" his life, so Joe is forced to take matters into his own hands.

When his friends are beaten up and shot, his new gal nearly killed, Joe finds himself in the middle of a war with mercenaries with the deadly possibility of losing everyone and everything he holds dear dangling over his head.

Saving Sunrise Ranch

Book 4: Sunrise Mountain Western Suspense Series

In the tradition Craig Johnsen's Longmire mysteries comes a new epic series.

An unforgettable story about a discouraged rancher's son, Jake Mack, and his hesitant girlfriend, Olivia Warner's struggle to confront their desire and save the ranch from failure.

Coming: Fall of 2019

Sign up for John's book announcements on his website: http://jrm-productions.com/